PENGUIN BOOKS

The Wake

Praise f

'Striking, funny, terrifying. I admi

'Stunningly good. Captures the la
colourist's touch. His ear for Norfo

'A powerful new voice. Funny, flavoursome. Page brilliantly evokes
Norfolk's bleakness, the harsh round of the seasons' *Independent*

'With mesmerizing attention to detail . . . *Salt* will transport
and transfix' *Good Housekeeping*

'Unforgettable' *Guardian*

'Remarkably haunting, an atmosphere you can taste on the tongue'
Time Out

The Wake

JEREMY PAGE

PENGUIN BOOKS

PENGUIN BOOKS

Published by the Penguin Group
Penguin Books Ltd, 80 Strand, London WC2R ORL, England
Penguin Group (USA) Inc., 375 Hudson Street, New York, New York 10014, USA
Penguin Group (Canada), 90 Eglinton Avenue East, Suite 700, Toronto, Ontario, Canada M4P 2Y3
(a division of Pearson Penguin Canada Inc.)
Penguin Ireland, 25 St Stephen's Green, Dublin 2, Ireland
(a division of Penguin Books Ltd)
Penguin Group (Australia), 250 Camberwell Road, Camberwell, Victoria 3124, Australia
(a division of Pearson Australia Group Pty Ltd)
Penguin Books India Pvt Ltd, 11 Community Centre, Panchsheel Park, New Delhi – 110 017, India
Penguin Group (NZ), 67 Apollo Drive, Rosedale, North Shore 0632, New Zealand
(a division of Pearson New Zealand Ltd)
Penguin Books (South Africa) (Pty) Ltd, 24 Sturdee Avenue, Rosebank, Johannesburg 2196, South Africa

Penguin Books Ltd, Registered Offices: 80 Strand, London WC2R ORL, England

www.penguin.com

First published 2009
1

Copyright © Jeremy Page, 2009
All rights reserved

The moral right of the author has been asserted

Set in 11/13 pt Monotype Dante
Typeset by Rowland Phototypesetting Ltd, Bury St Edmunds, Suffolk
Printed in England by Clays Ltd, St Ives plc

ISBN: 978-0-141-02772-2

www.greenpenguin.co.uk

Penguin Books is committed to a sustainable future
for our business, our readers and our planet.
The book in your hands is made from paper
certified by the Forest Stewardship Council.

For Liz and Barley

I

Within each horseradish leaf, where it unwinds from the stem, there's a small bead of rainwater. He sees one there, shining brilliantly in the morning sun, as if it's been placed, a jewel, pure and dazzling. It's perfect. This will be lovely he thinks, leading his daughter towards the plant, her hand so small and cool in his own, both of them crouching over the leaves till their shadows merge. Briefly, the sunshine becomes extinguished from the drop of water, he repositions himself, and it sparks back to life. He imagines a direct unbending shaft of light, taut and without substance, stretching between the sun and its own captured sparkle, a miniature sun in itself, caught in some bend of the refraction.

She is captivated. Surprises like this, especially beautiful ones, always bring a brightness in her, too. She's four years old, and already there is a sense of such conspiracy between them, father and daughter, such gorgeous intimacy. They share the fascination of pausing to look at things they discover, in detail, her waiting for him to explain what they see. It's a familiar routine. And he knows even then, that he will want to hold on to this moment for the rest of his life, like the leaf holds its soft capture of that beautiful jewel, to be with her, in that wide sunny field in East Anglia, crouching by the horseradish plants.

From his position in the grass he has a low-angled view of his wife, Judy, sitting on a fallen branch about twenty feet away. She's wearing dark glasses, and is bent over a small open book on her lap. He knows what she's reading – a collection of poems, it's for inspiration, for some lyrics she's working on, and she likes to make notes in the margins. She has the pencil poised, and every so often he thinks he can hear her humming the tune. So typical of her, really, surrounded by such a perfect morning, to enter into her own private world, so readily. He smiles at her, at the thought of her, smiles at the way her knees are drawn together and the way both ankles bend awkwardly beneath them, giving her a childish look. She's pretty, he thinks.

His daughter leans as soft as a reed against him as she looks down at the water droplet. She's wearing one of her favourite dresses, and it smells of washing powder and warm cotton and just a hint, even in the field, of her bedroom's mix of books and toys. It's lilac, or had once been brighter than that but has faded, and is cut in an old-fashioned style which makes her more doll-like than usual, with a wide band round the waist which she tends to stroke in a comforting gesture. Around the hem at the bottom of the dress is an unusual trim of farm animals in a printed design, running after each other. They'd made up stories about these animals before, how the goose seems to chase the dog, and how the pig is seen chewing a flower. He looks at this design, stretched across her knees as she crouches in the grass, and he knows she's itching to reach out and touch the bead of rainwater. She'll probably knock it off the leaf, so he whispers *Freya, watch this*, as he holds the plant gently, from underneath, bending it gradually so the droplet begins to stretch and tremble. The leaf has prominent raised veins running across its surface in a root pattern, and the water adheres stickily to one of them, then begins to slide along the vein's length, rolling, leaving absolutely no mark of wetness behind it, constantly gathering into its own flattened egg shape. The little sun in there dances and sparkles with new brilliance, and he can see how the shine from it has added an extra point of light on to the surface of the leaf.

'Is it a raindrop?' she asks.

'No – not really.'

'Daddy, is it a piece of the sun?'

He smiles. 'That's lovely,' he whispers. 'A sun-drop.' He coaxes the water further along the leaf. 'Look, it's like mercury,' he says, marvelling at it.

'What's mercury?' she asks, carefully. Her voice is slow and deliberate and made a little husky by a child's effort of whispering.

'It's a metal, but it's liquid – I mean it's wet like water.'

'Oh,' she says. He smiles at that, at the apparent nonsense adults sometimes say.

He encourages the droplet towards the tip of the leaf. 'Look,' he says, 'look into the drop – can you see your reflection?'

Freya peers closer. He smells the malty scent of her breath which is always there when he is this close, whatever the time of day or night. She sucks in her lower lip for concentration, and he watches the corners of her mouth bending up in a little smile. A few tiny hairs there, above her upper lip. Keep it still Daddy, she says, and he tries to do so, but even the touch of his hands below the leaf, even his heartbeat in a far off part of his chest is enough to make the droplet tremble.

'See the sun in there?' he whispers. 'The whole world's in there if you look close enough.'

'Can I touch it?' she says. He nods, then waits while she reaches out, deliberately choosing a finger, then deciding on a different one, before she touches the water. Both of them see how it sticks instantly to her skin, making a small curving bridge between itself and her, before it separates into a pinhead of water on the tip of her finger, just below the nail. She holds her hand up to inspect the new, smaller droplet.

'Is that like mercury?' she asks.

'Yes,' he replies, thinking, No, it's not like mercury at all – which is so grey and flat and without reflection, a dead and poisonous thing.

She pretends to lick it off her finger and begins to giggle. He laughs too, a child's happiness so infectious. But her laughter deepens, becomes something else, not just amusement, but a reaction now, the kind of laugh she has when she watches a cartoon on TV.

'What is it? What's so funny, Freya?' he asks, still smiling.

'It's silly,' she says. 'That pony's being silly.'

He looks at her eyes, how she's angled her eyebrows into an expression which is half amusement, and half worry – an expression of not quite grasping something, a complex expression she must have copied from somewhere. They try so many things out. And even there, even her being so young, there is a little worry-line above the nose on her forehead, like the tiniest of scratches.

'What pony?' he asks, amused.

'. . . it's doing a silly dance,' she says, the laughter breaking through her words once more and the worry-line vanishing.

Guy half-turns, still crouching. He sees not a pony but a horse, a stallion, half-way across the field, and for a moment he smiles too, because the stallion does indeed seem to be dancing. It's standing in a patch of bare earth where the rest of the pasture has worn away, and is rocking curiously back and forth in a restless motion, as if it's caught in something. He has the feeling the animal may be in some sort of trouble. Maybe it actually *is* caught – snagged on a loose wire or section of fencing.

'What do I do with it?' Freya asks, lifting her finger to inspect the drop of water.

'Whatever you like,' he says.

'I can't take it home, can I?'

He smiles. 'Freya, you're lovely. I'm afraid not.'

She pretends to put it in the open pocket on the front of her dress, patting the pocket for safekeeping effect, then suddenly lifts it again and peers into it – the droplet almost touching her eyelashes. 'Daddy, I can't see the pony in the raindrop.'

'No?' he says, imagining the horse suspended upside down in the lens of water and, when he looks beyond at the field, he's shocked to see the stallion is closer, much closer, as if it indeed has been magnified.

He sees then what he hopes Freya doesn't see. The stallion has a startled bloodshot eye, and is rocking to and fro in an agitated motion, with an edge of wildness that makes it look untrustworthy. His first unconscious movement is to put an arm round his daughter. He feels the thin bones of her shoulder and realizes he is already starting to stand. She seems a lot smaller then, lower to the ground, closer to the field than him.

'What's the matter?' Freya asks, her face angled up at him. He's never been able to mask his surprise.

'Nothing. Nothing's the matter,' he says. He glances at the stallion. He can't gauge it. It's a mottled grey with long unkempt black hair down the nape of the neck, and has a tail that's short and flicking as it stands, side-on to them, at the other edge of the marshy area. It watches him wide-eyed, with a look of madness. He sees a quiver develop in the muscle on its flank, rising quickly across its back.

'Judy,' he says, in an urgent whisper, *'Judy!'*

She deliberately finishes the line she's reading, then looks up at him, raising her hand to shield her eyes from the glaring sun. He looks at the two blank reflections of her sunglasses, and then sees a sudden and minute tightening of her mouth. The shock of it, seeing what he has only just seen himself. Involuntarily she too begins to stand and he puts out his arm to stop her, stop, movement is a thing to be cautious of. He looks at his fingers and he feels a tension he can almost grasp, in a widely emanating circle around them, centred on his hand as it holds the air still, holds on to nothing.

'I don't like that pony,' Freya says, standing like a little statue by his side. She sounds disappointed – her love of horses is usually so overwhelming. Stop the car, she'll say, every time they pass a horse field, clucking her cheek even as the car slows down, but here, she's silent.

Where is he, he thinks, taking in as many details as he can. The field's an open one, and rises all round them in the shape of a shallow dish. They're just about in the middle of it. In the middle, at the bottom, it amounts to the same, with a marshy stream running from left to right, dividing the field roughly in

7

two. The stallion's on the other side of the stream, perhaps fifty feet away, still strangely rocking and lifting a front hoof hesitantly off the ground, looking lonely and deranged. What else – a tree, yes, the ancient oak under which Judy's sitting, that was the thing they all headed for when they entered the field. It's close. He keeps an eye on the horse and gathers Freya to him, holds her hand which has suddenly gone compliant and cold in his own.

'Let's go to the tree,' he says, quietly, amazed at how calm his voice sounds. 'That oak tree.'

'All right,' she says. He's glad to hear her voice, that she's still talking, glad to hear her voice is as steady as his own.

They walk slowly to the tree, to Judy, who has now risen to her feet as if she's balancing something on her head, the book of poetry has fallen from her lap on to the soil. They approach her, across the marshy ground, which he notices for the first time is deeply rutted with the hoof marks of horses not in the field any more.

Beyond the stream the stallion does an abrupt theatrical stamp with one of its front hooves. Guy sees the ripple of the shock dart up the cartilage of the leg, so thin at the knee, but solid just above that, and rising into a slab of muscle which curves up to the shoulder like the side of a car. The stamp doesn't scare him, but it makes him angry, angry that this animal has hijacked the moment, that it might scare Freya more than it needs to, maybe even put her off horses. And with some relief he notices the stallion has continued to face them side-on, and appears reluctant to make any kind of movement whatsoever, apart from the repeated jerks of its head as if it's wrestling with invisible ropes.

'What's it doing?' Judy says, quietly.

Guy shakes his head slowly. 'I think it's just showing off,' he says, hopefully.

Judy has done a strange thing. She's stepped the other side of the log, as if it's a great barrier, and is holding out her hands for Freya to come towards her. Each hand stretches woodenly, pathetically, like she's sleepwalking.

He can tell Freya has become scared. She's gripping on to him and that might not be helpful, he thinks. He'll have to make all the decisions, he knows that, but she'll have to go along with them instinctively, without question.

He tells her not to worry. 'He's upset by something, that's all.' But as he's saying that he knows the only thing that is possibly upsetting the stallion is the sight of them. The three of them, in this field.

Judy takes hold of his arm, above the elbow, her fingers are sharp and tensed on his muscle. That's good, he thinks. It feels like an advantage of sorts, although he knows it's no such thing. She's strong – small, but with a mother's strength. With her other hand she has grabbed Freya, on her shoulder. It's like they're lashing themselves together.

'Where did it come from?' Judy whispers.

Guy doesn't know. It had been an empty field, like all the fields they'd walked through this morning. He'd been at the horseradish leaves, crouching, close to the ground. She'd been sitting on the fallen branch, reading. Sunglasses, he thinks, remembering how she had looked to him, so absorbed, both of them, and he notices she isn't wearing them any more. They are lying a few feet away, unfolded on the grass.

'It'll move off,' Judy says. 'It's probably just startled to see us here.' Guy says yes, more to Freya than Judy and, trying not to alarm them, looks about for anything that he might pick up to ward it off. But there are no sticks, no weighty logs, only this knobbled dead branch lopped from the oak – huge and twisted and a perfect reading spot for his wife and her book of poems, but not something you could lift. The oak itself is above them, with a wide span of heavy dark arms, but the closest of the branches is at least twice his height. He notices Judy also looking up at the tree, and even Freya, this small person between them, looking up for heavenly answer, reaching the same conclusion a few seconds behind her parents.

'We can't climb it,' he says, quickly looking for ways up the trunk, and seeing the countless bumps and calluses of the tree's life but no clear hold.

'You sure?' Judy says, feeling the necessity to voice all options. Nothing he can easily scale, let alone with Freya and Judy too. You can cling to an oak but you can't climb them, he thinks, and it would only make them more vulnerable to attempt it. He doesn't want to make a wrong decision.

'What shall we do if it doesn't go?' Judy asks, giving him a natural permission to act, to take the lead.

'Let's keep still,' he whispers, 'really still.'

Freya's frozen to the spot anyway, but he sees her nod obediently below him, and he hears her swallowing. He has a strange impression of himself, standing with the others in the centre of the field. He must look ridiculous, all angles and vulnerable and out of his depth.

'We're here,' he says, pathetically.

'Didn't you see it coming?' Judy says, unable to mask an accusation.

'No. No, I didn't. Did *you?*'

The stallion makes a deep snorting sound and half-turns so its eye is again completely side-on to them. He sees the bend in its body just behind the front legs, where the skin has rippled into long lines that run the height of its flank. The grey hair has mottled patches of dirty brownish-black hair. Its head is a squared-off anvil which starts to dip and swing as he looks at it – as if the effort of keeping it in the air is not easy.

'Perhaps it's ill,' he offers to his wife, worrying that that might be a worse scenario, and he hopes the horse might suddenly kneel down in the dirt. It would be a relieving sight, to see it keel over. He looks again at the stallion's head: it has a wide brow and a long nose with prominently raised veins running across it, and dark nostrils surrounded by wet purplish skin. He sees a thickly matted scar poking through the whorls of black hair on the top of its head, and a small mean ear which twitches at flies whether they're there or not.

'Here's what we're going to do,' he says, calmly. 'We're going to stand like this, perfectly still, till that thing moves off, OK?' Neither Judy nor Freya say anything. 'OK?' he repeats.

'Yes,' Judy says, formally.

'Right. Are you scared?' he asks Freya.

'No,' she whispers, lying.

'Neither am I.'

It's ridiculous, to be standing like this, like scalded children, while this animal makes a blustery show of strength. Or territory, who knows. Keep your sodding field, he thinks, glad to discover some anger, but knowing also the world has reduced effortlessly in a matter of minutes to a few simple truths, just this field, and around him the intricate details of things that are no use – the grass and twigs under the oak tree – the dried tops of last year's acorns, the patches of bare soil. A busy sense of nature which is indifferent and safe and nothing to do with him any more. Beyond that, the field itself, curving up a small rise towards a thin and distant hedgerow. It's not a large field, but they're a good three minutes run from any edge of it, slower if he's carrying Freya, and there could easily be boggy patches that might be disastrous. The field's like a desert, he thinks, an open space, exposed and dangerous, and the hedgerows around it are the borders to another country entirely – a country where he can make a thousand decisions and has all the time in the world to make them. He lets his thoughts run, hoping they might quarry a solution, then consciously he forces himself to think calmly, without panic. How did the horse get in here, he wonders, how did it just manage to appear like that on the small patch of dirt, and he has an unsettling vision of how it must have been, a few minutes ago, the stallion trotting noisily across the field, its hair shaking with the movement, while they'd been looking at the droplet of water, while Judy had been reading her poem. And while he's imagining this he spots a five-bar gate on the brow of the field which is clearly half-open and leaning as if it's come off its hinges. *The gate's open*, he mouths to himself.

'Daddy,' Freya says, a little too loudly, 'is it a pony or a horse?'
'It's a stallion.'

Perhaps there's a mare and foal beyond that gate, on the other side of the hedge – it's possible. Maybe the mare is afraid of them approaching the foal and the stallion is trying to warn them off? Who knows? It feels plausible, in a moment full of uncertainties. He doesn't even know how long they've been standing here. Probably just a minute or two. But Judy's reached her limit.

'Let's go,' she says.

'Judy,' he answers, 'it's going to move off, you know, it's going to get bored. We're doing nothing to bother it.'

But at that moment the horse seems to drop a shoulder and lurch forward, stumbling into movement in fast trotting steps, beginning a steady jog which runs alongside the brook and turns into a wide curve towards them. Judy pulls at his arm, fixing herself to him, and Freya twists behind them, hiding, almost tripping him up as he takes a step back. It's moving too quickly. His mind freezes, staring at the ridge of coarse hair, shaking with each step along its spine. At the random pattern of splattered mud across its back, at the heavy sense of muscle bending along its side, details, he's trying to take it in, trying to work it out, when suddenly it stops, as abruptly as it started, mistrust in its every move, on the edge of the marshy grass, its stilt-like hooves sinking, readjusting, making puncture holes in the ground that fill immediately with dirty water.

Judy swears, pulling him and Freya back as she does so, towards the oak tree.

'Let's get behind that trunk,' she says, practically, and he knows that's what they have to do and he has the unsettling image of the three of them, trying to skirt the big tree while that horse comes at them, and all three of them tripping up on each other and tripping up on those big roots he can see sticking out along the ground. It's full of its own perils.

'I'm not sure,' he says. He takes a quick look at her expression, gauging it, and sees how dark and intense her eyes have become, her face is as sharp as an axe head. She's not to be disagreed with. But just as they have started to move they all immediately stop, reacting on instinct to a new series of actions from the horse. A tossing and throwing of its head, its lips pulled back to reveal a dirty set of wide flat teeth. He sees strands of saliva falling from the mouth, the bumps of skin above, around the nostrils. Nostrils flaring in dark holes like the barrels of a gun, and he realizes he's seeing these things in more detail now, because the animal is closer, much closer.

Freya is twisting in his grip, doing the wrong thing, he looks at her shoes so clumsily placed in the soil, oddly turned. He imagines her running, how ineffective it would be, and he hopes the horse might tire or trip off to another edge of the field. Just a show of strength. Protecting its foal and family. A show of strength. And at that moment the stallion decides to come at them, dropping its shoulder like it did before but this time directed towards them, head on, in a stamping, bucking trot which shakes the horse as it gathers pace. It slews one way and for a second moves sideways at them, as if approaching a fence, its dark brittle hooves rising in uncertain steps – but still closing the distance, the horse snorting loudly and Guy sees its lips peeled back once more as it swings its head and neck from side to side. One crazed eye looks at him, then the other, afraid, but compelled to act. The head lowers in three sudden movements and he hears Freya scream and knows she's frozen. They all have. But with the scream he knows this is really happening – this is the beginning of a chain of events. They hear the hooves punching the wet mud and then the eerily hollow sound as it gallops across the dried earth under the tree, beneath the tree which until that point had been their tree, their protected patch of earth.

Guy does everything to avoid the mouth that lurches at him. He shouts a manic *wharr!* at it and the horse bridles, pulled up by phantom reins. For a moment he sees it impossibly tall, reared up, its onward momentum held at bay then, falling forward at him, scaring itself and rushing by in a skittish, terrified dash. The stallion has thundered past, close, a shuddering dark shape of hair and solid curves, in the middle of it he had seen part of the head, tossing violently as high as his own head, the white of the horse's eye stretching, blurred, into the carpeted hair of its cheek. He'd seen a filthy tobacco stain of wetness, around its eye socket. And then the glisten of saliva, a thin strand of it, looping through the empty air after the horse vanished, with a snake-like motion, twisting as it fell. Guy has been stamped on; his foot feels shattered, leaving a hot sensation in his shoe, and he smells the stallion's unmistakable odour, a dark musk of outside fear which holds his jacket like a grip, even now.

He looks for the others and cannot see them, the way things must wipe away after a hurricane and, instead, he sees a glimpse of the horse as it trots away, an oddly feminine gait to it, much less fast than he thought it had been. He stares at the ugly raised stump of its tail, so like a bend of old rope, and the dry waxy folds of its backside.

An awareness floods him, quite suddenly, an overwhelming sense of strength surrounding him and he knows his body is at its centre, capable, intact, and with an arm which feels entirely disembodied from himself he reaches out into the blue nothingness that engulfs him and he literally sweeps Freya up in one curving motion which has her suddenly held to his face. She stares deeply into his eyes, trying to find a father's answers. He stumbles, wounded but invigorated, to the tree, and tries to push Freya up into it while Judy shouts something from near to him, or not so near, he's not that sure, and the tree almost comically seems to grow higher out of his reach as if wanting to be no part of this and Judy is shouting a warning again and Guy turns this time to see the stallion, once more, circling faster now, building a new momentum, still throwing its head up at imaginary riders. Guy hears an ugly rasping *huh* noise across the field and he stares unbelievingly as the animal stumbles into a light-footed trot, coming at them. Judy must distract it, he thinks, she must wave at it and split its target so its run will miss them all. But she doesn't. The hooves begin to hit the ground faster, an accelerating rhythm of one after the other, then in unison, bucking the front part of the stallion higher in quick shaking jerks, as the head lowers, swinging from side to side, until he sees the length of hair stretching down its back.

The second charge has more purpose. Guy screams at the horse, finds himself taking a rash leap towards it, and for a second he is across the animal's neck, lifted up, moving across the ground – he sees the grass blur as his separation from the others increases. A glimpse of the horseradish leaf, then of his daughter standing as rigid as a small scarecrow, white with fear, whiter than he's ever seen her before.

He falls forward from the stallion and seems to be overrun, run over, slipping down the animal's front under its head and his cheek becomes smeared with a great wipe of wetness from hair or skin, and then the relief to be falling, to be separate from the horse at least, although he sees it in terrible closeness, even the swinging motion of its throat, brushing him off, and the hardness of the animal getting even harder and more solid as he falls beneath it. Soft marshy ground here and the stallion's front leg punches into the mud like a steel piston right by his face and Guy gets splattered by drops of soft wet mud and is then alone again.

The field has a kind of stunned silence to it as Guy lifts himself on to one elbow and sees the oak tree and Judy and Freya still standing a little way from it. Judy, wanting to run to her husband, holding herself back to be with Freya. Both of them look so relieved, so happy in this little instant, it's a sight which fills him with love, their care, their absolute loyalty. The others are safe. He must have been brave, leaping at the horse like that, and perhaps it balked as a result, at the last minute; the danger's over now. He looks at Judy, and surprisingly they smile at each other. It's a strange moment, but it's really there, a warm smile between them, no sense of panic or recrimination or anything other than sheer relief.

He lifts himself up, a little groggily, and limps towards them.

It's actually a surprisingly little distance to be together again, and he hugs them, he's winded and defeated but he was their best chance, and then he looks for the stallion, knowing he's now acting instinctively, without caution. He's declared himself – he's declared that their life came before his. It's given him a wonderful sense of rightness, to be thinking this way.

'It's OK now,' he says, and then he says, 'where is that thing?' and he sees it trotting in a wider circle, collecting itself, the bastard, getting its breath back.

'The horse is so strong,' he says, absurdly, to the others, and he looks at the animal as it shakes itself down again, as if shaking off the memory of the man who'd briefly hung on its neck.

The first attack, yes, that was terrible, but the second one, I won that, he thinks. It's been scared off. Learn your lesson, and as he looks at the horse now he wonders how long it had taken to better this animal. It hadn't been agile. When it came at them, it didn't even try to deviate from the run. There was no disguise to the direction. It was determined, but it was really just a blatant show of bullying aggression and force.

There was an element of sport too, to have faced this thing. The stallion's runs had been brief and had clearly taken their toll. It had seemed petrified, even as it ran at them. Disorientated. He sees it across the field, breathing too quickly, its snorts and whinnies almost overlapping themselves. He imagines its great lumbering heart jerking rapidly and beyond its limit, and he wants it to die.

'I think it's over now,' Judy says, calmly, bringing his attention back to being with them. She's holding him tenderly and he notices she has the book of poems back in her hand, she's picked it up, in itself that smallest of gestures must mean the danger has now passed. The stallion has proven its point, it can go back through the gate to be with its family, if there is one, it can receive their gratitude and adoration if that's all it needs. He sighs with relief, and crouches down to take a breath, and to make himself equal with Freya, to be on her side, her support and friend. Freya comes to him, so upset, so terribly small, her love for horses shattered, and he holds her, feels her warmth like it's the most precious substance the world can offer, which it clearly is. She whispers to him in a dry voice that she wants to go home now, can they go home now, and he smiles and says yes, let's go. And as he holds her and nestles into her neck he hears Judy's dead calm voice whisper *Oh no, oh dear God no* and Guy doesn't even look, he just pushes Freya away, pushes her to get behind that tree, that great solid tree, Freya can run round that trunk all day – the horse is too frightened to keep this up for long, and Guy has his daughter safe behind that commanding oak, at least, when the stallion begins to face him a third time. When he turns to confront it he discovers he now has a stump of wood in his fist, it's not a branch but it's heavy. The block of wood has been by their feet all along, but only now he's realized it's in fact a pretty good weapon. He can use it like a brick to club the horse on the jaw. Maybe break a tooth, or he can try and jam the corner of the log into the eye. He's capable of anything. He's seen this animal up close, knows where the patches of skin might be softer. He's earned an understanding of this danger, and a right to be cruel.

Guy has made this fight his own now, and the stallion knows it too, preparing itself, its head swinging in small movements from left to right. Perhaps a horse cannot see absolutely straight ahead, he thinks, abstractly. He knows that whatever happens at the end of this run the horse will lose interest, will stand panting in the pasture with total indifference and he and Judy and Freya will be able to walk calmly back to the gate as if nothing happened. He'll be able to brush the mud from his jeans, wipe the sweat from his palms and internalize the fear as his own, protect them, make light of what's happened. He sees its eye and flash of hair across the head, the spot just high of the mouth he will dig the log into. Guy braces himself for the arrival of the force as the animal canters at him, knowing instinctively that the tiny colourful disturbance at the edge of his vision is wrong, a wrong thing, his daughter, abandoning the tree in a reckless dash. She's stumbling in little trippy steps across the grass in what seems to be a crazy intersection towards the stallion. Guy hears a simultaneous panicked shout from Judy and he knows this next second, this next momentous second, could become the worst moment of his life, the worst moment any man would ever have to witness, and he's struck rigid with the sudden overwhelming effort of keeping the impossible from happening, the effort of keeping these things apart.

II

The North Sea

Position: 52° 01'.5N 1° 47'.5E

Just savour this feeling, he thinks. Hold on to it. He can hear the crying of seabirds, perhaps hundreds of them, echoing across the water, but he can't spot where they are. He imagines the sound coming from terns or gulls, with slim greased white throats and softer greyer wings. The colours of sea and cloud.

His boat is fifteen miles offshore, but the North Sea is strange today: it's completely calm. From where he's standing, the water sparkles quietly up at him with a thousand pinpricks of light, each one from a miniature sun scattered in a line across the sea. In every direction it stretches as a single glassy object, without any swell or current, to a horizon which is a pure line, like a child's drawn it, the simple curve of the earth. And the air is so fresh and so perfectly still, filled with its own sea light, it's as if it could be bottled and brought back to the land – where it would sit on a shelf, shining.

Guy has been standing on the deck of the *Flood* since dawn, watching the water, occasionally looking for basking sharks through his binoculars. He hadn't expected this. September can be a stirring month.

Just in front of the boat he notices something floating. It looks like some glorious beetle on its back, with a shell wide open. But it's not. It's a bird. He watches, amazed, wondering whether it's alive or dead – these things always have the appearance of being in both states. Then it moves, trying to lift its head from the water, with a feeble paddling motion of its wings.

Guy runs to unclip the gaff and he plunges the metal tip into the water cruelly short. The bird has a tiny beak which sticks above the surface like a twig. Hold on, he says, to the bird, wait for me, he adds, meaning don't die, not now, not now when you're so close to being saved, don't die in front of me. And by hanging down from the sea rail, off the side, he's able to touch it, just, and he sees how impossibly wet and dark the bird looks, how absolutely close to death it is, yet as the gaff nudges it, it still tries to escape, making a single oar stroke with its wings which plunges its head, briefly, underwater.

After five minutes he has brought the bird to the side of the boat, where he can reach down to gather it in his hand. Its body feels weightless, like a palmful of wet leaves, like nothing could live in it any more, and he sees that it's a finch, a greenfinch, driven offshore by some sudden gust, or by the shadow of some magpie or crow. Had it been trying to reach his boat, with its last effort, or had they drifted together in coincidence? And as he holds it a simple truth strikes him: you remember the things you save; you cannot forget the things you lose.

The *Flood* is a ninety-foot Dutch coastal barge, built in the Voorhaven yard in Scheveningen in 1926, and till the seventies it freighted cod-liver oil between the three Hs of the North Sea: Hamburg, Harwich and Hoek van Holland. At least, that's what he was told when he bought it. The boat's main feature is the wheelhouse, which sits higher than anything else on the deck, with glass windows on all four sides and a ship's wheel in its centre as tall as a man's chest. The wheelhouse is spartan, always bathed in the white ozone of the sea, with a swivel chair bolted to the floor and bench seats behind, wooden mullions, a door either side giving access to the deck and an ornamental ship's bell which Guy had engraved with the word *Flood*.

Originally the barge would have been a male space, solitary and smoky, the way men tend to make things, probably messy too. What was once the cargo hold stretches in a low flat shape in front of the wheelhouse, painted white. The hold is now mostly a saloon. It has too many chairs. Despite all the time

Guy's lived on the barge, he's never managed to lessen their number.

It's been his home for nearly five years, moored to a stretch of quay on an empty part of the Blackwater estuary, in Essex. The only buildings there are a few isolated houses, some fishermen's sheds, and the Tide Mill Arms. The *Flood*'s one of several houseboats, some are more wrecked than others, and the whole anchorage has the oily scent of a shipyard, mid-repair, a place where boats have been scuppered and salvaged, wrecked and neglected. There, the *Flood* sinks into the mud twice a day, and the rest of the time it floats, soaking up the brackish water into its hull like a sugar cube. The estuary feels like the sea and looks like a river, and is neither, it's both inlet and outlet, flooded and drained, it's always a contradiction. That's his home. Empty, strange, big-skyed.

Right. Where are you? he says, unfolding his maritime map on the floor of the wheelhouse and running his hand over the nonsensical tree rings of the seabed depths below him. IMRAY Passage Chart C25, the Southern North Sea, it reads, full of underwater cables, pipelines, explosives dumping grounds and wrecks. There are rippled contours of sand and gravel banks, England continued, hills and sloping meadows down there. He can just about work out where he is – although the nearest feature is appropriately vague, a depth mark of eighteen metres. Not much to look at, his spot on the world. He gazes at the coast of East Anglia on the map, with the muddy mouths of its estuaries, like mythical eels sniffing the ocean, and its complicated filigrees of saltmarsh and creeks, swelling with water twice a day and somehow, implausibly, holding the North Sea back.

The maritime map's not particularly interested in his own stretch of quay, other than recording its depth as an anchorage, but has made more effort to record the tricky deep-water channel that snakes out to open water. *Channel is Variable* is the warning there, and he'd felt it last night, practically bumping his way between the mud and sand and gravel till he'd rounded the final navigation buoy at the mouth, which had seemed the end of a journey whereas in fact it was the start. The start of the sea. The flat-drained river water had given way to a subtle ocean roll, the thick chug-chug of the engine had risen and fallen in line with the swells, and the breeze itself had seemed to promise a new emptiness, a blank slate.

He'd arrived in this place, if it can be called a place, just before midnight. He'd cut the throttle, lifted the inspection hatch in the corner of the wheelhouse and climbed down the steep metal ladder into the engine compartment, and by torchlight he'd held his hand above the manifold, feeling its heat, shining the bead of light on the gasket seals and then the piston heads. After that he'd rinsed his shirt in the sink, then hung the shirt on a peg in front of the wheelhouse. All that time he'd tried to ignore the sheer quietness, the sheer absence of this place, since his engine noise had gone. He'd played the upright piano in the saloon, loudly, he'd made an omelette, he'd drunk a bottle of wine, and surprisingly, he'd slept. And just before dawn he'd woken, listening to all those crying gulls, to find the North Sea vanished into this eerie calm.

He places a kipper in a shallow pan to poach, then makes a paste of anchovies, a drop of Tabasco, a spoonful of cream and some horseradish. He grinds this with a pestle, then tastes it. Lemon required, which he squeezes. The smell of the fish rises from the pan – under the glaze of the water he can see its skin becoming a dark honey colour.

He checks the greenfinch, which he'd put in a box on the worktop. It's sitting in the corner, collapsed and waterlogged, with its beak laid out on the cardboard.

When the kipper is lifted out on to a plate, he sits a knob of butter on top, and watches it gradually slide down one side. His mouth waters. And then he thinks of a surprising addition – he suddenly fancies it – several raw onions which he cuts in quarters and quickly blanches in the fish pan. He's never had raw onion for breakfast before, but he's at sea, so what the hell.

He crunches into one of the onions after sliding it into the anchovy paste. It's sharp, then sweet, and surprisingly juicy. The paste is dry and dark and curiously smoky. Urged on, he starts to pull apart the fish, working along the crease of the spine, exposing the hair-like bones and pulling them softly through the flesh, a job he's always loved doing. Hurry hurry leads to worry, that's a thing his mother used to say, doing the same thing when he was a child. Pray to St Blaise, she'd also say, so you won't get a fish bone. The kipper gives up its meat in precise oily sections, leaving a skeleton like the ones drawn in cartoons, the one a cat finds in a metal dustbin, and a case of skin which Guy rolls to one side of the plate like a surgeon, with the flat of his knife.

After he's finished, he looks at his plate. It seems suddenly poignant. What was it they found on the *Mary Celeste*? A half-eaten meal and a broken rail?

He removes all his clothes, folds them neatly on deck, and climbs down the stepladder into the sea. He winces with the cold as his feet touch the water – it's not summer out here any more. He takes another step down and touches the bottom rung, below which there is nothing. Clinging like that, to the sheer metal side of the barge, the *Flood* seems enormous, its skin an animal hide of blotches and dents and paint and over-paint.

Looking down he sees his foreshortened body disappearing into the green water, the pale bend of his long legs, his mammalian feet spaced wide apart on the bottom rung. This is it, he says, sinking himself in till his nose is level with the surface. The sea ripples around him and then he hears the cries of sea gulls – this time sounding like a warning as he swims, away from the boat, one arm following the other, his head down, a breath after every four strokes, one minute, two, ten minutes, more, perhaps for half-an-hour. Maybe more. His arms grow heavy and the joints in his legs begin to ache. He becomes warm, then he goes cold, then he gets warm again, knowing this decision is a foolish thing to undertake and missing a voice of someone else telling him just what he can and cannot do. It's hard to give up on authority, especially where there is none.

When he finally stops swimming he turns on his back and floats, staring up at the sky. It's a deep empty blue, and it seems so high he has a moment of vertigo – suspended as he is in this taut line of nothingness, no above, no below. The water laps cold in his ears. His skin is numb.

It's the first time he dares to look back in the direction of the *Flood*. He sees it, but it's frighteningly far away, like a sketch of a boat, clog-shaped but without detail, and his first thought is to panic – this is just too far, just too stupid a thing to do. He wasn't prepared for this, not yet.

The panic fills him, naturally, before he controls it. No, this is what he wants. This is part of the whole process, to find these moments, to be in a place where there is nothing, to be drawn to emptiness, to stare at the naked sea with an unflinching eye.

And gradually he adjusts. He thinks about the water which is lifting him, funereal, to the cloudless sky. He can hear fragments of the sea: tiny drips and lapping sounds. He sees things he hadn't at first noticed: a soaring bird moving in circles at least a mile up, each circle completed it glides further away, to do another ring. Eking out some terrible hold on life up there.

Floating this far away from the *Flood*, he feels disembodied, both of them in some kind of weird orbit, both adrift. It gives him clarity. Clarity to view his last few years like a frayed rope, each strand of it working itself loose from the thing it had once been, each strand still with the curled shape of the life it was once part of. Now unsupported, weakened, unravelling.

Searching for the *Flood* again he notices it's turned. Will it drift further and faster than him, because it is so large, or is their distance a constant thing? He doesn't know but he senses, instinctively, that he is wanting to return. But instead he forces himself to swim the opposite way, further from the barge and, within seconds, he knows it's wrong – *Don't* – he hears, he actually hears it, a soft quiet word spoken in his ear and he stops, quickly, struggling to raise his head from the water to hear it again. There is nothing. But then a growing presence, close by, the belief that something is floating next to him, a solidity in the water, a tiny shape that gives him comfort. He smiles, not daring to reach out or turn towards it. *Hi*, he whispers, *we're a long way from home, aren't we?* And he hears no answer. He reaches out with a hand, feeling with his fingers the cold water, and briefly he experiences the merest of touches, lighter than the brush of seaweed, like he's felt a child's dress in the water.

Reaching for the ladder, he thinks he might not have the strength to climb back on board, and again he has a sense of vertigo, below such a high blue sky which seems impossibly distant up there, without cloud or vapour of any kind. Just the stark vertical wall of his barge, with its relentless geometry and ancient steel skin to stop him falling.

He nearly hadn't made it. Swimming back, his arms had been heavier, and the boat hadn't seemed to grow any closer. It had played games with the distances, as if someone was pulling it across the sea with a magnet. The exhaustion had crept up on him, played tricks with his mind, made him think that there was something he feared, a few strokes behind him, nearly at his feet, reaching out for him. He knew what it had been. It had been the thought of giving up. Keeping that behind him – that's what had kept him going.

He stumbles on cold numb feet across the deck into the wheelhouse, then down into the saloon, where he wraps himself in towels. His fingers are blue and wrinkled like a drowned man's. In the bathroom mirror he notices how the sea has given his expression a startled, frightened look. His eyes are wide and glistening along the lids as if he's been crying, and his stubble seems to have grown, in the hours that he's been out there – each hair has become the point of a mini thorn in his skin.

He looks at himself in the mirror like he's a stranger. He's not unattractive, he's never been fat, but he's a little unkempt. His hair is dark brown and naturally curly and getting a bit too long and prone to looking windswept. He's never been able to do anything other than let it grow. Let the others be neat. He wears glasses, not at this moment, but he can see the marks they've left over time across the bridge of his nose. He's had the same pair for years – with thick horn-rimmed frames. Without his glasses he looks shocked, as if he's just been slapped, he must be so used to them. His eyes seem calm today, but so often they tend to be emotional, a little too ready to give his feelings away, he's always been told that. He tries a smile, then a grin which looks ridiculous.

'Well done,' he congratulates himself. 'You made it back.'

After night falls, he stands at the ship's wheel, looking into the blackness of the North Sea which, for a moment, appears like a hole, without depth or end. Before he came out here, he had thought the sea was all about sunlight, but it's not, it's about darkness. It presses towards him, large as a desert.

He notes the barometer and battery levels, checks for leaks from the pipes, then opens the rear hatch and climbs down into his cabin. Guy already feels a great deal of time has passed since he came out of it this morning. The air has a trapped quality, left over from last night. His bunk is shadowed and messy and next to it is the desk where he sat up late last night, on a creaking chair, writing in the diary under the piercing light of an anglepoise. He sees the open book now, with his neat handwriting going across the pages, and is a little wary of approaching. The final few sentences on the page look overwhelmed by the whiteness of the paper that follows them. Writing calmed him last night, but what can save you at night can destroy your day. That's something he needs to remember.

Guy knows this is the time he must make up a new entry in the diary. By now it's unavoidable. He feels the familiar mix of emotions: the fear of the empty pages, where they will lead tonight, the excitement that, for a time, he will be able to lose himself in a dream of his own creation.

He's written every evening for the last five years, since his life changed irrevocably. And thinking this way, he's able to begin, knowing he can no longer imagine his days passing without doing it.

Guy stands behind the art deco hotel in the soft warm night air of Florida. The pool he looks at is out of this world. It has the appearance of an iceberg – lit from within, with water pouring round its edges in a smooth silky curve. Further off, palm trees and bougainvillea stand in the shadows, and small curved columns of water leap surprisingly from concealed nozzles set in the lawn. Somewhere beyond the grounds, beyond the palm trees, is the Atlantic Ocean – he's felt its breath in cool shallow waves that come in bands across the night air.

He's mesmerized by the pool, can hardly take his eyes from it, but sensing an approach he looks up to see Judy walking towards him on the other side. He'd sensed the familiarity of her walk before he'd seen her. For a moment it looks as if she might be rising up through the pool itself, magically, without breaking its surface. A lady of the lake, miraculously dry, holding two cocktails in her hands. His Judy, small and birdlike, with dark hair brought to one side of her neck and gathered in a low tie. A bag hanging diagonally across her chest. She comes to him and passes one of the drinks, a margarita, with beads of cold water on the outside of the glass.

'I can't believe we're here,' he says. 'Are we here?'

'We made it,' she says, dreamily, and it does feel like a dream, to be standing there at all, after such a long journey from England, with the rush of images from the last twelve hours being held back by the slightest of pressures. The sheer exhaustion has made him relax, made him at ease with being here, by the luxurious pool in a night which is so fragrant and alien to him.

'Well, to us,' she says, simply, raising her cocktail for a toast. They clink glasses, and he takes a sip of the ice-cold liquid, feeling the crusty edge of the salt on his lip. 'Here's to travel,' she adds, grandly, always one for finding a hint of the melodramatic. 'Being here, right now, I think we could just set out and drive all night, don't you? Drive as far as we can, having cheap coffee at roadside diners, till the sun comes up.'

He's taken by the thought. They're abroad, they have the right to leave themselves behind, back home. They could be anything here.

'I'd like that,' he says. Her eyes have darkened with tiredness. They shine at him mysteriously. She's beguiling to him, even after these years, there's so much to learn about her, still. 'You look nice,' he says, captivated by Judy in this Floridian warmth, how utterly familiar she is, yet also changed, subtly, by the travel. Her edges are softer.

Later, he and Judy travel up to their floor in the soothing motion of the elevator, and he imagines the thick heavy cable pulling them up through the building into a darkness he can't see. A distant whirr of a turning wheel at the top of the shaft, covered in axle grease, and at some point, the ghostly pass of the counter-weight. These things, just inches beyond him. The smell of electricity and heated rubber in the elevator, and in the hallway it opens out into – the smell of all hotels: dry, carpeted, layered with the scent of polish and warm light bulbs.

They walk along the corridor on a deep carpet which is patterned with wavy blue bands – a child's drawing of the sea – that seems to stretch further than the building is wide. Judy sways with the drink and with her own tiredness, and he can feel her pressing against his arm and the heat in her bare shoulder which she always has when she's been up too long. A kind of warm flush which precedes sleep. When they reach their door, she leans against the jamb, patiently, while he finds the key, looking up at him with a shy smile which gives him a surprised thrill.

'Hurry up, lover,' she whispers. She closes her eyes and yawns, and as he unlocks the door for her she curls round the frame, disappearing into the darkness of the room.

'I don't even know what day it is,' she says, wearily, from the shadows. 'It's good though, isn't it? It's good to be here.'

'Yeah,' he says. 'I'm excited.'

'Me too.'

'We're on the edge of things. It feels like there are going to be good things whichever way we turn.'

It settles them to talk like this, to exchange bland statements, to know they're in agreement. She kicks off her shoes and walks flat-footed towards the en suite, humming a quiet song under her breath. He recognizes the tune as *Tidal Joe*. It's been years since he heard that one from her – she doesn't sing those seashanty tunes so much now, they're too breezy for her. As she's aged, her singing has changed in a way he hasn't quite understood. Her voice has sought new things, has flattened towards minor keys he never used to associate with her. So it's good to hear her humming, here, one of the old ones. It's always a good sign.

While Judy prepares herself for bed in the en suite, he sits in an easy chair by the window. Only then does he feel the inevitable flood of images and sensations from the long day. Of how cold it had been standing outside their house at four this morning, the engine of the taxi running, a thick plume of exhaust emerging, and when they'd sat in the car, the heater on too high, the smell of a man's car. Then the tired, resigned feeling in the airport, the inevitability of being processed, followed by the loud ozone drone of the plane, the sheer noise and light of it. The excitement of seeing America for the first time – low and sunny and below them a line of cars' windscreens glinting like a vein of mica in the earth – and the hit it had given, like a coffee, which had quickly tipped into weariness.

Glowing beneath his balcony is the brilliant blue oblong of the hotel pool, illuminated by expensive submerged lighting. Totally still now, its surface looks waxy and false – he can see how the tiles on the bottom have an unusual and constant magnification. It's beautiful. It seems full of an expectant calm, a silent composure that appears motionless and unreal. A warm scent of palm and tamarisk and bougainvillea is in the air, mixed with the corporate smell of the hotel: soap and carpets, and a smell of wet concrete paths below him, where the terracing has been washed down. Then suddenly, while he's looking, the pool's lights go out. It shudders, vanishing into a slippery blackness and, surprisingly, the lights are instantly replaced by a new single illumination: a moon, perfectly reflected on the surface.

Guy smiles, the moon is always a joyous sight. Always. Then he draws the curtain and listens to Judy's switching on and off of the taps, the sounds of her bottles and tubes being opened and placed down on the shelf, the fast brush of her teeth, the soft plastic tap of her moisturizer lid being put on the sink. It all has the same pace and sound of being back home. She carries it with her, unknowingly, wherever she is. Women are so busy, he thinks, and their busyness is like a fond tune to be listened to over and over again.

He sits in the chair and watches the harsh light of the bathroom cast out in a strange shape across the bedroom floor – they both feel the bedroom should be dark before they go to bed – then he reaches for his Hildebrand's road map of America. It gives him an oddly tingling stir, just to look at it, to see the long snaking roads of the interstates running up through Florida like a body's circulatory system, near the edges, rooting out into thinner veins and capillaries that end in nowhere. He senses the sheer size of it, the countless miles of rolling cinema from here to the Pacific Ocean, thousands of miles away. Can they really drive that far? It seems daunting. He imagines the mishaps, the wrong turns, the tiredness and the exhilarations, all at points on the map without markings for him yet. Florida, Georgia, Alabama, Tennessee, and that's only half way. Then he sees where they are, right now, a tiny dot amid the grey crosshatched shading of Miami Beach, and it makes his morale fall a little, it's so tiny, his place on the earth.

He closes the atlas. It doesn't really matter where you are, he thinks, the world's just a series of backdrops.

When he stands he notices Judy's lying in the bed already, her head turned away from him on the pillow.

He goes to the other side of the room, to the camp-bed the staff have brought in. He bends down and pulls the covers up round the girl who is asleep there, pushing a strand of hair away from her forehead.

She's nearly ten, and her face is filling out a little, it's losing the softness of childhood already. He likes to look at her, sleeping, he likes to catch glimpses of dreams as they flicker across her face. Her lips, right now, a small jut to them as if she's about to speak, a fold of her skin above her nose where she's pulled her eyebrows together in concentration. A busy sleeper, he thinks, he feels he knows most about her in this state, where her thoughts are so close to the surface.

He kisses her on the cheek and smells the warm toasty smell of her skin.

'Night, Freya,' he whispers.

Night, Freya, Guy repeats, quietly, in the soundless cabin of his old barge. He looks at the sheets of paper now covered with his familiar handwriting. Filling in the diary has calmed him, given him a sense of depth and time he didn't have before, a sense of possibilities and choices. He closes the book lovingly, stretches, a little click in his shoulder, then gets into bed, and switches off the lamp.

Position: Run aground on Cork Sand. 51° 54′N 1° 20′E (approx five miles offshore). 5:50am

As the sun rises Guy's standing on a sandbank with a coil of rope in his arms. His boat has run aground, sometime during the night. He looks up at the prow, as it sits high as a sluice gate in the wet sand, and he walks away from it, feeling worried and stupid and chastized, paying out the rope till the bank becomes dryer.

'You beached yourself,' he says to the *Flood*, as he hammers a metal stake into the ground, 'like a whale.'

Now, sitting on the sand, the foolishness of running aground is hard to shift. He stares at the *Flood* and at the rope as it tightens and slacks. A watched tide will never rise, he thinks, feeling watched himself – his predicament is so embarrassing. And to be on the sandbank – what a surreal place – it's land, but it's not – at the highest tides he suspects the water actually closes over it like a giant eyelid. It unnerves him, being on this bank. Its surface is flattened by the tides that overrun it, it's as solid a thing as any land, able to sink at any point, yet on all the maps across the centuries, Cork Sand, sometimes longer, sometimes more curved, but always there.

As he waits, he thinks about his diary. For five years he's written about Judy and Freya, even though neither are in his life any more. Every night, how they've grown as a family. It's such a regular part of his routine it's been more real, at times, than the life they all had, when they were together. Freya has become tall for her age, has few friends at school because she lacks that edge that makes girls popular, is interested in nature. Like him. Judy's changed too. In his fictionalized version of her she's become a little famous, oddly; after singing in a local folk and festival circuit for years without being noticed, she's beginning to receive letters and emails and phone calls, and now they've flown to America to go to Nashville of all places, to record some backing vocals for a movie soundtrack. All a bit far-fetched, now he's thinking about it.

So it had felt good, last night, to write about himself and Judy, arriving in Miami. He remembers how he'd described the moon magically appearing to float on the pool in Miami Beach. A nice moment, he thinks. Moments like that, they're unforgettable. It had been a balmy night in Florida, and he felt its balm now, on the sandbank, like a remembered dream which gave you hope and company for hours to come. It's a wonderful thing to write. You can reclaim the things you lost.

The advancing tide reaches the stake he hammered in. He unties the rope then goes to the boat, wading into the water by the prow. This will be tricky, he thinks, moving gingerly along the side until the depth falls away disconcertingly into a deep channel, forcing him to swim to the boarding ladder. There are currents and bars and deep holes where the fish crawl into; the entire geography of this place feels dangerous.

He puts the prop into reverse and gradually brings up the speed. The *Flood* groans, injured, slides awkwardly to one side, then all the movement stops. He hears the engine straining against something thick and unyielding. He cuts it. Behind the boat the sea has the churned-up honey colour of fresh sand.

After re-starting the engine he unclips the inflatable and drags it on to the bank, making sure he's tied it to the front of the *Flood*. He digs under the thick shadow of the prow, forming a sticky pool around the front of the boat. Several times his foot or arm sinks into this fresh quagmire and he thinks he could be sucked into it, deep under the crushing weight of the *Flood*, which might just slide over him.

At the point where he has exhausted himself, at the point

where his efforts to shift a sixty-ton boat from a bank of sand is most futile, the *Flood* glides away from him, as if he's just launched it from the yard, into the open channel. He yells for joy – for the sheer achievement of it, and collapses backwards on to the inflatable arms of the dinghy. The line attaching it to the *Flood* snakes across the sand, then he feels a lurch as the boat pulls the dinghy off the bank, with him on it, into the sea.

When he's in deeper water, with Cork Sand just a thin membrane of solidity a few hundred yards behind him, Guy lowers the outboard, starts the engine, and comes aside the *Flood*'s ladder. After a few seconds he's in control again, in the wheelhouse, totally exhilarated. He did it. He bloody well did it.

That's when he sees the fishing trawler, a few hundred yards off, steering in a wide curve towards him. *Oh Christ*, Guy says, knowing the only reason it would be heading his way is they think he might be in some kind of distress.

It stops, some distance away, and he sees some men come out on deck to face him. Guy waves at them, then decides it might be best to cross over to it in the inflatable, in case he needs to explain himself.

The trawler's called the *Indomitable*. As Guy approaches it on the dinghy he smells its stink of engine oil and fish oil and wet metal, and he sees its hull is deeply pitted and stained with rust the colour of dried blood. Two men lean over the side to greet him, amused. Both are heavy-lined with short hair and thick necks. They could be brothers. Guy's helped up a rope ladder and pulled over the side by his armpits and put down on the wet old wood of the deck.

'Not there,' one of them says. 'There.' He points along the planking. Guy moves away from some coils of cable, chain and loose D-shackles. The working deck is littered with bright nylon ropes, netting, links of metal, winch handles and plastic buckets and crates. 'Mind the cables,' the man says, then moves off to look down an open hatch.

'Ah, that's a nice boat. You got a nice boat,' the other man says. 'I'm Karl – is it a coaster?'

'Yeah, Dutch.'

'Dutch,' he says. 'That's good.'

'Used to cargo cod-liver oil. I was told that.'

'Yeah?' the man says, not particularly interested. A sound of machinery turning in the hold has taken his attention. 'That's a lot of cod livers.'

Guy laughs, politely. 'I'm Guy,' he says.

'Yeah. Karl,' the man says again. 'Go on in. Mind the cables.'

Guy goes towards the wheelhouse which is much larger, much more robust, more steel than his own. This boat's built for anything the sea can throw at it. The dents, the roughness, the sheer welded plating of its structure unnerves him – he's out of his depth here. Each rivet and join has a stain of rust like the trawler has wept with pain. This boat has been smashed about by a sea he hasn't yet witnessed, and the *Flood*, in comparison, it's like a pleasure boat.

'You in trouble?' the skipper says, greeting him with a cold heavy handshake.

'Not really,' Guy answers. 'This morning . . .'

'. . . that's OK, we saw what you was up to,' the man says, turning to his instruments. The pilot's seat is surrounded by readings and gauges, of computer print-outs and flat screens for sonar and shoal finders.

'We had us a busy night. How old's your boat?'

'1926.'

'Crossing to Holland?'

'No.'

'Could do, today, good all the way to the Hoek,' the skipper rubs his beard hard, bangs on the window and points at something on deck. One of the others acknowledges him and kicks a brush away from being on top of a hatch. 'Not going to Holland then?'

'No,' Guy answers.

'Don't go too far then, sir,' the skipper says bluntly, looking straight at him for the first time with small blue matter-of-fact eyes.

'Right then,' the skipper says, 'one minute.' He leaves the wheelhouse by the opposite door and shouts something at the slower of the two men. Again Guy hears a grinding noise coming from the hold.

The wheelhouse is a formidable male space. It is metal and salty and there are wires and switches and knives and ropes. The only decorative touches are some banners hanging from the roof and a notice-board covered in postcards. Ijmuiden, Dieppe, Whitby, others, further afield, some naked girls lying on a Caribbean beach, their breasts covered in oil and sand grains, another beach, another two naked girls, this time bending over. *Beach Bums*, the logo reads, pleasantly. There's a picture of the skipper with a dead pike lying across his arms, like a roll of carpet – it seems like the man fishes when he's not fishing. And a picture of a Norwegian fjord which catches Guy's eye. He recognizes the photo as Aurlandsfjord – a place where he had been once, with Judy. Even though the postcard's wrinkled with damp, he's amazed to make out the small *hytte* where he stayed, that winter night, and the local bar where they'd had a disappointing and overpriced meal.

'Look,' the skipper says, reappearing in the doorway, 'we're about to have us a fry, so why don't you join, yeah?' He looks at Guy questioningly.

'Ain't nothing special,' he adds.

They sit crammed round a curved Formica table that's bolted to the floor on a single aluminium leg, sharing two plastic benches. A fourth man has joined them in the galley – a dark scrawny man named Alexie who doesn't speak much English. He hasn't looked at Guy once. The skipper's in a high mood, he's passed round bottles of cheap French beer and is generally taking the piss out of the deckhand who's not Karl or Alexie. Steve, his name is.

'So Steve comes in, he's carrying this inflatable armchair he's found in a skip right, like one of them you get in a posh swimming pool, with one o' them things on it . . .'

'. . . drinks holder,' Steve mutters.

'Yeah, OK, drinks holder, and he puts it down there, right in that corner, like there's room for it in here. It don't even work! The bloody thing's got this puncture which he fixes 'stead of doing the rig, anyway, he fixes it and then he spends – bloody hell, how long did we have it – he spends a week sitting on it each night like some rock star.'

'We reckon he had piles,' Karl says.

'Right! Piles!' the skipper bellows out. 'I'd forgotten that. He sits on this thing, with his piles, it's purple too – *purple* – I gotta hand it to you you took one *hell* of a lot of stick, din't ya? You and that blow-up friend of yours.'

'I didn't have piles,' Steve says, readily falling into the role of the bullied.

'So you have said, my friend, on so many occasions,' the skipper chimes back, stroking his chin for comic effect. He has two tobacco streaks of ginger in an otherwise grey beard, which grows high up on his cheeks almost to his eyes.

'What happened to it?' Guy asks.

'Tell him, Skip,' Karl says, his eyes glinting darkly.

'Feck me, this is funny,' the skipper says – he almost cannot speak. 'You gotta know Steve here ain't that bright, are you, Steve, ain't no one said you're bright, have they? Well, we got this calm day like we had yes'dee and we said to him, "Reckon that thing'll float with you on it?" Like who's gonna fall for an obvious prank like that?'

'Steve did,' Alexie says, in a thick foreign accent.

'Right, he did. He climb down the ladder with this blow-up armchair on his back an' he just sit in it, in his boxers, on the sea – well it nearly sink but it does work, right. Then we only go an' start the feckin motor don't we . . . !'

'. . . and we're all waving at him off of the side,' Karl says.

'Yeah, yeah,' Steve manages.

'. . . and you're this – ah bloody hell –' the skipper gasps, 'this little armchair in the sea. This little *purple* dot!'

The size of these men, round the small table, in the cramped galley, it's oppressive. Through a small oblong window the North Sea gently bows – Guy can hear the water slap against some deep metal flank of the trawler – it feels like he's left his freedom elsewhere. Occasionally he sees glimpses of the *Flood*, un-piloted, another world away. He can't really remember leaving it, it seems so long ago, though it's only a couple of hours. The air in the galley is smoky with cigarettes and the fried fish which they'd eaten, simply, in battered strips. They'd had it with oven chips which the solemn Alexie had brought to the table with a pinny tied round his waist, though no one seemed to find that strange. Guy can see the head of the fish, cast to one side near a microwave, looking sadly back at him.

'So you ain't told us,' the skipper says to Guy, the remnants of his bullying tone still lingering, 'what you're doing out here?'

'Well, I live on the *Flood*, in the Blackwater estuary. I've come out to sea.'

'That's it?'

'For a while.'

'Ain't no playground, you know.'

'I know.'

'You get a forty-yard swell it'll roll that. You have a ship's bell?'

'Yes.'

'That's the sound you'll hear the moment it tips. Believe me you don't want to hear that bell. Taken ballast?'

'Some. Several hundred-weight of flint.'

'Don't look like it. She's sitting high.'

'And I have a piano,' Guy says.

'A piano! That's about as much use as his blow-up purple friend!'

'At least it's heavy,' Karl says, unexpectedly, 'I mean, it'd be like having extra ballast, right?' he says to Guy, afraid of the skipper.

'Whatever,' the skipper says. 'Mate of mine skippered one of them barges 'cross the sea – he don't like that flat bottom they've got so he floods the hold full of water for the ballast. Thing is, it's a calm hot day and he gets thinking about all that water in the hold so you know what he gone and did? He tied up the steering and had himself a swim – up and down the hold, doing lengths, right across the North Sea.' The skipper slaps the table, satisfied with his story. 'Fingers,' he says to Alexie, 'more beverage.'

New bottles are handed out. Guy's had three or four already, the galley feels like a theatre set to him, like he's a character in a scene, a dream of a scene where he doesn't know his lines.

'I'm drifting,' he hears himself saying, not really knowing whether he's talking about being on the *Flood*, or being in this strange smoke-filled galley, in a filthy trawler off the side of a North Sea sandbank. He thinks of the sandbank, low and lethal and sober out there. Others like it, waiting to rise out of the sea unexpectedly. Should he be more aware of them? How come they don't just get washed away, like everything else?

He's silenced the skipper with his abrupt change in mood.

'You drift away,' the skipper says, unconvincingly.

'I was just thinking,' Guy starts, unsure what's to follow, 'that I haven't thought about her, my daughter, for a couple of hours. That's strange for me.' The other men look back at him watchfully, their arms flat on the Formica table. 'I mean, out here, aren't we all without attachment? You know, no anchor? Aren't we all like him on his purple armchair?' A single teardrop falls surprisingly on to the table, landing in a perfect crown shape. It takes Guy a moment to realize where it's come from. He wipes both eyes with his sleeve. 'Yesterday, you know what I found, floating – I found a greenfinch, on the sea – it was drowning in front of me and I was the only person in the world to see that.'

41

He looks up at Steve. 'How did you feel out there – sitting in that thing on the sea?'

Steve feels obliged to answer. 'I don't know,' he says quietly.

'Je-sus Christ!' the skipper says. 'What's up with you, man?' he says to Guy, not meanly, but without understanding what's going on. 'You shunt be out here,' he says.

But Guy meets him head on. 'You're wrong. This is exactly where I should be.'

The meal is over soon after that. Guy asks to leave and the men slide off the bench to allow him to get out. He's embarrassed for being emotional, but despite what's happened he notices himself standing more upright, less cowed than he had been when he arrived on the trawler. He's been honest. He's not intimidated. Some of this must have conveyed itself, because all four men come out on deck to see him off, and the skipper gives him a quarter bottle of Danish *Gammel Dansk* liquor. He warns Guy it tastes like ear-wax.

'You take care,' the skipper says, because he has to voice something and the others aren't up to it, but at the boat's side it's the man called Alexie who unexpectedly reaches out to take his arm. It's not to steady him – it's to hold on to him. The other men are looking down into the forward hatch at this point, and Guy looks at Alexie's thick-skinned hand clasping his forearm, while the man reaches into a pocket of his jacket. He pulls out a tattered photo. It's of a dark-haired girl, about sixteen, sitting at a bus stop. The anonymous boxy shapes of a European city suburb fill the background. The girl is very overweight, with a round smiling face and deep dimples in her cheeks.

'Is daughter,' Alexie says, quietly.

Guy examines the picture, at its moment of captured happiness and the plump daughter that has emerged from this scrawny man. She's holding a bag tightly to her thigh and has a sequinned purse in her other hand.

'Where is this?' Guy asks, pointing to the city behind her.

'Gone,' the man says, inexplicably. He points to a scar on his chin and shakes his head.

Guy looks on as Alexie folds the photo back into his pocket. Alexie glances back at Guy and nods, once.

'Are you dead?' he asks, gently, nudging the greenfinch with his finger. It flaps a wing in fright, then lies still again.

'Right,' Guy says.

It hasn't moved all day. It lies unbalanced in the corner of the box, wings awkward, beak slightly parted. A grey film of skin covers its eye like a cataract.

A few minutes ago he'd heard the trawler's engine start. He'd watched it move off down the line of the bank, leaving behind a thick cloud of diesel smoke, its gantry lit up like a Christmas tree and a pool of bright floodlight on its deck. He's struck by how late it is, and how suddenly dark the North Sea is growing around him. It's deeply unsettling, the speed nightfall arrives offshore.

Guy looks at the postcard he managed to steal from the trawler's notice-board, which he's pinned behind the wheel – the tiny picture of Aurlandsfjord and its oppressively brooding mountain in the distance. The *hytte* they'd stayed in had been warm, built without fuss, with a Scandinavian sense of resilience and self-belief which had put them at ease. They'd slept in bunk beds and, through a precise square window in the door, Guy had watched the top of the nameless mountain on the other side of the fjord – its broad far-away back, impossibly high, smooth and glistening with snow in the moonlight. Its Arctic glimpse had frightened him a little. How remote it had looked, framed by the window as if it was a picture, but out there, so close.

He remembers how the following morning had felt so crisp and still, and how the boots he had left outside the night before had been covered in a hoar frost so thick it seemed they'd turned into crystal. Even the laces, like long bright spiky pipe-cleaners. There was more frost growing along the log joins of the cabin – increasing in depth almost while he looked at it, making tiny cracking noises, and a row of icicles hanging from the porch, pure and smooth and with a drop of water at each tip.

He'd run his fingers along the rail of the balcony, the frost scooping up so fluffily it seemed to have no substance at all, and when Judy had come out they'd stood under the icicles and let the drips fall into their mouths, like a couple of kids. The water had splashed cold and messily on their lips, forcing them to blink, and it had tasted of wood.

They'd been giddy that morning, not because of the excitement of travel, or because of the curious wooden cabin, but because during the night they'd reached a decision: that they'd start trying for a baby. It was a decision they'd made in hushed whispers, even though there was no one else on the hillside, both of them crammed into the lower bunk bed.

'Should we start now?' Judy had asked, her eyes glinting in the dark.

'How do you mean?'

'With the business of procreation. The messy stuff.'

'I don't know.'

'Neither do I.'

Around them the cabin had sighed and creaked in the cold mountain air. Guy had shivered, totally in awe of Judy's willingness to change, to carry a life, to embark upon such a journey with such simple poise.

'Should we wait? I mean – let it settle with us?' he'd said.

'Maybe,' she'd whispered, sliding her hand delicately across his belly.

'Maybe not,' he'd said.

The next morning, Judy had kissed him – refreshed by their momentous decision and filled with a certainty they could now face anything. Her lips had been as cold as the ice.

'Some people actually live here,' Judy had said with renewed wonder, looking out at the dark huddled hamlet of buildings next to the fjord. 'It's unbelievable to think this is what they call home. How do they do it?' Wood smoke was rising, mixing with a freezing mist around the houses. On the other side of the fjord the mountain rose like a terrifying trackless tower of granite. It was incredibly bleak.

'They drink,' Guy had said.

He steps out of the wheelhouse and climbs on to its roof into a complete and overwhelming silence. The air feels gritty and confused – warm bands of it pass by, wedged apart by cooler layers. Small waves roll forward, each wave just a smudge now, vanishing into an obscuring twilight.

The sea smells strong. It reminds him of a song Judy had written: about the smell of the coast, drifting across the water while she'd stood by the rail of a night-time ferry. She'd composed it after crossing the North Sea from Hoek van Holland back to Harwich. Not so far, in fact, from this place. She'd been on deck even though it was a freezing night, stood there wearing a chunky Aran jumper while she faced the wind. Below her was the cold vertical drop of the boat's side, which had seemed an absolute in a sea full of dark coiling movement. The water had been black and undefined. It had both frightened and exhilarated her. She had marvelled at how the boat slapped the backs of the waves and scarred them white, making a surging scattering sound. That's where she'd been when suddenly she'd smelled cows and pasture, an unmistakable warm scent of farmland, carried by the wind. It had come and gone like a phantom, a thing without connection to any reality, then gradually she'd begun to see the low dark coast of East Anglia, or rather, had realized there was a long unfilled patch of the sea where no stars were shining. This empty blankness could only have been land. Then she'd seen lights – thin strings of lights along a road, a dusting of streetlamps around a harbour, and as the boat had veered, inexplicably the lights had vanished, wiped away by an unseen part of the coastline which must be passing before them.

All this she'd put in her song, a beautiful song about being on the fringes, smelling the land like a cherished memory. He remembers it now, imagining the homely smell of East Anglia on the cold sea air as if he's back there and, briefly, he experiences the muddy scent of heathland, the green fragrance of woods and gorse, of cows in their sheds, their sweat and breath mingling with the sweet straw and mixing now with the cold damp breath of the North Sea itself, so far away, not so far away, him and Judy in their moments of wonder and awe, partially fictional, separated.

He knows he must write his diary.

Dusk has fallen too rapidly. Some of the cars out there have been caught out too – he can see their headlights being switched on miles away in the distance. It gives the road a new sense of length and absolute flatness which is amazing. Already, on their first interstate, to be driving into one of America's infinite vistas, he's a lucky man.

On either side of the road is a simple verge, a long chain-link fence which dips and lifts as the car speeds by. Beyond the fence on both sides are dark channels of water, with heavy clumps of sawgrass floating in heaps, moving and rising in soft swells which makes him think there's a life to that water he can't quite fathom. For as far as he can see the Everglades are utterly, relentlessly flat, without light or any sign of life, and it stinks of a musty green vegetation.

How deep is that water? How far down do you have to go before reaching something more solid? He wonders. It's as dark as a sea out there. The Everglades have the texture and look of iron filings, stretching to the horizon. He thinks he can see hundreds of birds there, rising in a thermal plume at the edge of the world, but it's probably a trick of the light.

Judy's been quiet. She's been looking through the window and has angled her head to rest on the glass. Guy knows the mood well – that little tilt of the head, as if she's letting her thoughts drain – it's her dreaming time, when she begins to let go.

Freya's in the back, listening to her headphones. The music player's a fairly new gift, for her ninth birthday, and Guy's already regretting the little bubble of silence it puts his daughter into. He was surprised at the speed with which she took it up, her willingness to listen to it for hours on end. A step towards independence, a privacy which he remembers so well, a fascination with himself too, when he was her age.

Both his women, in their individual spheres of thought. It suits him. He pretends he's alone in the car – that he's crossing America with his own set of glorious possibilities. An impression begins to take form, of meals he might eat, lonely women he might look at along the counter of a diner, encounters, that's what it amounts to. Encounters and reinvention, it makes him almost giddy, and he looks at the passing swamp with a renewed sense of liberation – a desire to stop the car and wade out there, feel the sawgrass and the unmentionable things that lurk in the water that would be oddly warm and tropical.

The tin–tin–ta–ta of a slow beat is all he can hear from Freya's stereo.

'What are you listening to?' he says.

Freya doesn't answer. Or doesn't hear. Each time she puts the headphones in, taking a step into her own world, he follows her with this question, reaching out to her as if to say don't go too far, please, not too far.

'Freya,' he says, looking at her in the rear-view mirror.

'Some of Mum's stuff,' she says, casually.

'Who is it, honey?' Judy says.

'Alison Krauss,' Freya replies. Judy nods appreciatively with a little pursing of her mouth – it's a gesture which annoys Guy, in fact, has always annoyed him. It's an affectation and she doesn't have to do that here, but still she does.

Guy pushes down the pedal, imperceptibly, and begins a

slow acceleration to seventy-five, imagining a valve opening somewhere in front of them, a release of fuel deep down in the dark metal innards of this strange car, unknown to his passengers. It makes him complicit with the machine. It makes him feel good. He eases back on the pedal and looks out across the swamp. The glow of his dashboard lights reflects on his window, but beyond that, there's only darkness. What lives out there, he thinks, what horrid bodies slip by each other in that ink? Immediately he pictures the alligators, sliding past one another in the black night, their bodies even blacker, log-like, segmented, unblinking. He hates the way their legs jut out, their four-fingered feet so un-relaxed, like the taxidermist's already stuffed them.

'Don't drive so fast,' Judy says.

'I wasn't,' he says, guiltily.

She looks at him and grins. 'We don't want to go off the road here,' she says.

He smiles. 'I was just thinking that myself,' he says. 'I'm not keen on meeting the gators.'

'It's great, isn't it?' she says, 'all this nothingness. It's like someone's just rubbed the world away.'

She's speaking quietly – it's just the two of them, because Freya's still listening to the stereo. It's like they used to be before she was born. Alone in a car travelling through the night, sharing a private moment. Both of them are enjoying this now.

'Are you tired?' she asks.

'I think I could drive all night if we had to. And we might have to,' he adds, lightly.

'I love it, Guy, I just love it,' she says, girlishly. She still has that lovely inflection in her voice, that illusive crystal quality which makes you want to hear more. When she sings with that in her voice, she's amazing.

'I was just thinking,' she says, 'when we're in Nashville, you should spend some quality time with Freya. Get to know her.'

'I do know her.'

'You know what I mean. I'll be busy and I don't want you two getting frustrated.'

'We won't.'

'Get her kitted out like a pageant queen.'

'OK.'

'And you need to buy yourself a Stetson.'

He feels calm in this pocket of his family – the three of them, cocooned, surrounded by miles of water and dark swampy death. But he's rattled by her mention of Nashville – not that he can put his finger on why that should be. He senses the malign unknowing shape of it like an interruption, a thing which is gathering form, an awareness that life has its surprises plotted out already. And we rush towards them, regardless.

'Want to stop?' he says. He's seen a gas station lit up like an island in this dark sea, and is already slowing the car down.

He pulls off the road into the station and when he cuts the engine there's an immediate silence followed by a flood of insect noise, a wide humming that fills the air above them. It's a hot night and the cement of the forecourt has a baked dry smell, the smell of foreign airports, and the lights strung under the canopy have a sick blue glow to them.

Freya gets out, stretching, pulling the earphones from her ears.

'You tired, Dad?' she says.

'Not really,' he replies. She looks out towards the endless swamp.

'God, what a place,' she says, then heads towards the shop. She's already as tall as her mother, and has a thickness to her legs Judy's never had, a gift from him, his size, coming out in her. Maybe she'll be one of those women who are just too big for men to deal with, too strong. But maybe not. There's a clumsiness to her which is endearing, after all, and she's always had a friendly expression, it will get her places.

Judy gets out of the car too, and gives him a small kiss on his neck. *'Mon brave,'* she says, 'where the hell have you brought us?'

The shop is poor and wooden and there are too many things

in it. Above the counter is an old painted sign of an egret or heron taking wing, draughted with great care once, and written above that a slogan saying *Welcome to the Sovereign Miccosukee Seminole Nation*. He'd seen a similar sign along the road about half-an-hour before, but it's news to Judy and Freya. He sees them look at the sign, then look at the man behind the counter. He's small and dark featured, with a thin face and a wide dry mouth, and is looking their way. It's not clear if he's sitting down or standing up. Behind him is a rack of Indian crafts, basket weaves, beads, dream catchers from various Indian nations, but it's the pile of alligator feet that attracts Guy. In a large basket near the counter, there must be a hundred of them, dried, polished and heavily scaled, with twisting claws like the hands of an Egyptian mummy. It gives the place an eerie voodoo look, and the entire shop has a fungus smell which might be coming from them.

Freya has seen the alligator feet. She picks one up and has a close look at it, turning it round in her own hand like a devil's handshake.

'Good luck,' the man says, 'that is if you like a gamble.' The man has long hair swept back over a pair of thin sloping shoulders. His head seems too big for his body, as if something's eating him from within. 'You like gamblin', miss?'

'Sometimes,' Freya says, warily. Her voice sounds wholesome and polite and out of place.

'I used to,' the man says, 'used to a whole lot.'

'Do you want it?' Judy says. Freya's unsure, being corralled by adults into making a decision. 'I'll get it for you.'

'There are CDs here,' Guy says. Judy looks to where he's pointing and sees a rack selling Indian chants, sacred songs and dances.

'They ain't nothin',' the man says.

But Judy's interested. A collector of music. She picks up a CD with an Indian woman on it, sitting cross-legged on rush-matting.

'Lady,' the man says, 'don't buy it.'

Suddenly there's a single laugh and they all notice a second man, his head face down on the counter behind a nut dispenser, a cigarette burning from a hand which hangs nearly touching the floor. 'Leave 'em be, Glynn,' the second man says, and laughs again, though he doesn't lift his face. Guy sees an odd angle of the man's cheek, hot and sweaty and covered in insect bites.

The man behind the counter smiles, revealing a shiny set of false teeth, possibly the whitest thing in the shop.

'You want coffee?' he says to Guy.

Guy takes the coffee outside and stands for a while by the chain-link fence that borders the swamp. Through its diamond pattern of wire the darkness is absolute. A bird is sitting through there, by the side of a dark channel of water.

Some large and impossibly leggy insect flies near him, attracted to the acidic lights of the gas station, and he moves instinctively back to the car. Inside, it smells of the journey they've been having, their breath, the warmth of the seats. This car is his friend already. Men love their children and dogs and a little less they love their wives, but they always have a special thing for their cars.

He sits there, drinking his coffee. If he gets the chance, he's going to talk to Judy tonight about his suspicions. Maybe suspicions is too hard a word, and too alarming, but there have been changes in Judy, changes lately that need to be mentioned. He doesn't want to get to Nashville so completely unprepared.

Through the windscreen he spots the insect again, as it spirals awkwardly up towards the lights. It looks like a clump of hair you might pull from a shower trap. Near the roof it touches a wire grill built into the light's casing and bursts into fire.

He sees the others coming out of the gas station. He feels his life returning, the blood and marrow of it, the comfort of family.

The girls get back in the car and Freya shows him the gator foot she now owns.

'Freaksville!' she says, making Judy laugh. 'Drive, Dad.'

He pulls out of the station, all of them in good spirits, in the same car, in the same seats, but a little closer to one another now.

Judy reaches for the radio, tunes in to a selection of local stations, before settling on something which turns out to be Seminole Nation radio. It's full of gaming adverts for the casino, then more adverts for airboat trips.

She switches it off. 'Want a song?' she says.

'Yoo-betcha,' Freya says, enthusiastically.

Judy undoes her belt and half turns in her seat:

'Before you were born, Freya – in fact, before this man was in my life too, I had a boyfriend in Amsterdam. I used to get the coach to Harwich and cross the North Sea on a ferry – waste of time that was, as it turns out. But I did it a lot – he'd never come to England, never did in fact.

'But the best thing was coming back, for me, on that ferry. It was a night crossing and I used to stand up on deck, whatever the weather, crossing the sea and waiting for the moment I smelled the shore. I used to smell it before I saw it. So this is the song I wrote, about standing on the deck of a ferry, crossing the North Sea from the Hook of Holland to Harwich, one night. This is how it starts:

On a windy quayside, in a warm rain
The smell of cigarettes and leather
Never
Leaving him.

He has the look of a man
In another man's jacket,
He's frayed at the edges.
Never
Leaving him.

53

He has the smile of a man
Who leans on the railings.
Looks down at the rain on the water
Ought to be
Leaving him.'

Guy leans back in his chair, humming Judy's tune. The cabin is silent. It's late, and his shoulders and back ache with the writing. Night-time ferries, even now, crossing the seas in a blowing gale, lonely figures standing on deck by the ship's rail. Right now.

He never did know much about Judy's ex-boyfriends, other than there were quite a lot of them. The Amsterdam boyfriend – Allan his name was – he used to surface from time to time, but Guy didn't learn much about him. She had no pictures. He has some ideas of how it must have been, Judy so young her skin was thinner, bluish-white below the eyes, a creamy shine at the top of her cheeks, her hair shorter, sitting in a suede jacket smoking roll-ups in his flat in the Grachtengordel. Good sex probably, plenty of it, it would have taken a lot to go through that sea crossing so often. He wonders whatever happened to him? What happens to those ex-boyfriends, those impossibly cool guys living in loft spaces, with their leather jackets and their pockets filled with the right brand of cigarettes? Maybe Judy, or the girlfriend who replaced Judy, or the girlfriend who replaced that girlfriend, maybe they all told him to grow up, and now he has, encouraged to do so by all those rejections. Maybe he's boring and middle-aged now. Maybe he fell in a canal. The point being, Judy had been Allan's, Judy became his, Judy is someone else's now. It's clear. We borrow.

Suddenly the *Flood* is rocked, violently, and as Guy bolts up the ladder to the wheelhouse the boat is rocked again, throwing him against the side of the hatch. Immediately he knows what has happened. A ship has passed, nearby. Too close. Through the windows he can see the wide streak of its wake in a pale scar across the sea.

Going on deck, he realizes the *Flood* has drifted into the shipping lanes off Harwich and Felixstowe, where the heavy cargo ships have to snake in a single deepwater cut between the sandbanks. He can see freighters and container vessels and ferries, illuminated with their own constellations of lights, their superstructures bathed in cold white fluorescence, sliding magically across the dark.

From the line of marker buoys he can tell the *Flood* is at a dangerous point near the mouth of the deep channel. He goes in to start the engine, but at the wheel he suddenly does a strange thing – impulsively, he switches the cabin lights off. Following that, he extinguishes the red and green navigation lights on the bow and wheelhouse roof. The *Flood* vanishes.

He puts his coat on and climbs on to the wheelhouse roof. Parts of the coast can be seen, quite close: the sodium-lit glow of the Harwich docks, appearing like an orange chemical fog underneath the high pylons; the fragile glimmer of a seaside town, its promenade stretched either side of it in a single string of streetlamps, as if the town's suspended on a cable and the top of a church in its centre, its flint castellation and copper-work spire floating above a tower which seems to have been rubbed away.

Guy listens, aware that he's at the limit – the absolute limit – of where the noises of the land can reach. These are the furthest sounds that England transmits – a low growl of machinery from the docks, in uncertain waves, and a distant car-alarm, quietly unanswered.

But a third noise rises nearby – the sound of a ship's engine, churning the sea like it's ploughing soil. He feels its reverberation before he sees the ship itself, a vast cargo-container vessel turning through sixty degrees a couple of miles away and, although its hull and sides are completely blank, the superstructure is brilliantly lit. Along its deck he can see containers, each one the size of a lorry, stacked five high and eight deep in smudged pools of multicoloured light, at this distance they're like a pile of a child's wooden bricks.

New angles of the ship reveal as it continues to turn and he begins to hear odd discords, clanking sounds, the groans of steel settling and shifting as they come up through the sea underneath the barge.

Guy watches, mesmerized, as the ship completes its turn, establishing it within the notch of water between the navigation markers that will bring it to the *Flood*. It comes straight towards him, darkly menacing, the bow and sides as high as a cliff, blind with its sheer bulk, unstoppable. *It's unstoppable*, Guy says out loud, and another word occurs to him: inevitable. He knows its meaning now, and piece by piece the superstructure and deck of the ship begin to disappear as the huge bull-nosed bow rises in perspective in front of it, a giant anvil it seems, lifting out of the sea like a Greek colossus to club him down.

This is his moment, Guy knows, and he reaches out into the thick nothingness between him and the giant ship and he asks for her, he asks whether she's here with him, with him now. *You are, aren't you*, he says, and his voice sounds like two voices – one, so full of acceptance, the other, so afraid. *Oh no*, he says, *oh God not now*. And then he grabs the top of the wheelhouse, bracing pathetically, as the cliff edges of the container ship overhang, bear down, then slide enormously alongside the *Flood* in an impenetrable solid shadow. Above – way above – the single illumination of the ship's name, painted on the bow, wide and glowing wings spread like an angel, and he thinks he hears a shout, an alarm coming from someone on deck, a man at watch who is seeing the unseeable.

The *Flood* is tipped to the side by the bow wave and the cargo ship seems to bend in the sky, leaning away briefly, then returning as a huge steel wall. He hears something fall and smash from the saloon table, he wonders about the greenfinch, sliding from one side of the box to the other, and he smells the passing ship – its ocean stink of diesel and grease as the engine noise grows and finally roars by and the sea bursts into a beautiful cascade of rising foam. It's like a firework sizzling all around, a simple celebration it seems, in that instant, of his survival. And gradually it recedes – the sound, the danger, even the sea itself, till all that's left are the last soothing bubbles of the ship's wake.

Position: Moored. 52° 01'.15N 1° 21'.36E.
Anchorage off the Rushcutter's Arms,
in the River Deben estuary

Soon after daybreak, as soon as it had been safe to steer, Guy had brought the *Flood* into the River Deben estuary. The low coast had reached out to sea in the shape of two embracing arms, welcoming him back, it had seemed, to calmer water. Water that smelled of water, rather than the sea. He hadn't slept much, and had been glad to see the familiar river landscape of woods, fields and damp brick houses. An estuary, like his own, but not his own.

He'd been to the Deben before, though not by boat, so he had had to steer carefully through the wide stretches of the estuary where the channels and gravel banks unbraided in long ribbons, the river becoming undone by the sea. But although it was new to him, he had an overwhelming sense of recognition – the glass-flat water of the high tide bringing him in, stiffened by the breeze along the deeper channel, the thick mats of saltmarsh in complicated blocks on either side. It had the texture and deep rich smell of his own estuary, forty miles to the south, but where his estuary curved along the quayside of the Tide Mill anchorage, here it had narrowed and, where there is the long strand of the oak wood at his own mooring, here was the Rushcutter's Arms, the pub where he came ten years ago, with Judy and the other members of their band, Fergus on the fiddle and Cindy at the drums and Phil on guitar. There, that spot on the slope of the pub car park, where they unloaded the gear, Phil in some ludicrous cowboy shirt the rest of the band hadn't sanctioned.

'Do you think Phil's gonna piss about all day?' Judy had said, as they watched him unzipping his guitar case in the car park and pretending to shoot the gulls with it, machine-gun style.

'Probably,' Guy had replied, 'he's good at it,' and on seeing Judy's surprisingly genuine concern he added, 'He'll be fine, once his nerves are gone. He plays the guitar well and that's what he's here to do. Play.' She needed this kind of assurance, every so often.

They'd only known Phil a few weeks – he worked in a music shop near Fergus's work, and had only just agreed to join the band after impressing Fergus with his guitar skills one lunch time. Judy had thought he was a prat and didn't want him in the group. She thought he didn't really share their country-folk taste and was probably in it for reasons she hadn't figured out yet. That's ironic, considering how it would all turn out.

'Have you seen his shirt?' she'd said.

'Yes. I've seen the shirt.'

They'd looked at the others through the windscreen: at Fergus holding his fiddle case, standing huge and bearded and slightly bow-legged on the gravel, rubbing his stomach when he laughed, with one of his shapeless cable-knit jumpers on, and Cindy, his wife, as thin as a reed, with long sensitive fingers and eyes the colour of browned apples.

'What are we doing here?' Judy had said, mischievously. 'I don't think we belong in a band.'

'Just what I was thinking,' Guy had replied.

'I'm just a bank manager's daughter,' she had said.

'Well – that's as good a reason as any for joining a band.'

He'd smiled at her, before looking up at the pub sign – a picture of a brawny man gathering reeds by the water, a long curving scythe across his arm, and Guy looks at the same sign now, over the estuary, moored at last.

Without the sound of the engine, the relieving silence rises up through the boat, the gentle swell of the estuary, the cubes of empty space in his wheelhouse, his cabin, the saloon.

'*One two three four,*' Judy whispers into the mic, alarmingly close now, from the stereo speakers in the wheelhouse. He's playing the rehearsal CD his band recorded, ten years ago, as practice for their gig here at the Rushcutter's. He hasn't heard Judy's voice for a long time. It's so lovely. So lovely to be coming to him from *before*, before anything bad happened to them. He hears innocence in it. She's bringing the band into one spirit, and then he listens to himself playing the piano, kicking off the jaunty intro to *Tidal Joe*. Within three bars Fergus has joined in on the fiddle, helping the piano with a messy rhythm before Cindy starts playing a muffled beat on the snare and Phil does a looping bass line on the guitar. It sounds really fresh to Guy, now, as he listens to it, waiting for Judy's voice to come in once again. He hears an oyster-catcher, caught on the CD, calling from one of the creeks with an off-tempo *pic-pic-pic*, just before Judy sings *The boat smells of diesel and pots full of crab*, a cheeky male inflection in her voice, evoking a sea-shanty, then she softens into the song proper, slowing the whole band down with a lilting rhythm that occasionally catches them out.

It's so evocative. They made that CD on a sunny autumn day. Fergus had set a huge jug of coffee on the trestle table at the back of the garage next to a fruit bowl filled with greengages, picked from his own tree. Fergus had been in a great mood. Picking fruit did that to him. He liked to provide.

Fergus and Cindy had only just moved into the house – a former warden's cottage on an island in the Blackwater estuary. To get to it you had to wait for low tide, before driving across a length of stone and seaweed causeway which was simply known as the Hard. It was an enchanting place. As you crossed the causeway, with the slick flat mud on either side, you saw the island from the seabed's perspective – rising from the estuary, girdled with a dirty high tide mark, and capped with a green mass of trees and hedges.

It was a great sight to see Fergus wrapping himself round the fiddle, as if he might accidentally snap it in two, with strings fraying as the bow sawed the notes, a far-away grin on his face and a gimlet tooth glimpsed between his lips. Cindy would stare at him, amused, both of them wearing similar clothes as if they were brother and sister dressed by the same mother.

Fergus and Cindy, Guy and Judy, the two couples of the band – Phil must have felt isolated having just agreed to join them, Guy considers, remembering how nervous Phil always seemed, stringing and restringing his guitar, smoking too much, reluctant to take his jacket off, ever. The key makes a shift in the song and the sound of Phil's guitar lifts to the front. That was good, Guy thinks, how Phil naturally brought the plucking forward, creating his own space in the melody. Yeah, Phil was a good guitarist, Guy thinks reluctantly, shame he was such a fool in so many other ways.

'That's nice,' Fergus says on the recording at the end of the track, not out of ego, but because the music always affected him. 'Yeah,' Phil adds, in his East Anglian whine.

Guy lets it play, thinking something might reveal itself across the years. There's a lot of silence and some things are said he can't make out. The sound of a band between tracks is a peculiarly expectant space – isolated notes, the twists and squeaks of tuning pegs – it's music unmade, unmachined. Cindy tries a few beats of the rhythm again, and Phil does an abrupt and fast riff on the E string, then starts to tune it even though it's already in tune, turning it down a quarter of a tone, turning it up again, settling where it was. He wants to drop tune it already, the clown. Guy remembers how Phil loved to pluck the string then pull back the headstock to bend the note. Do that too often and you can snap a guitar. A show-off. Guy can hear someone pouring out coffee and he thinks it might be himself, now standing at the back of the garage, and he remembers distinctly how he'd eaten one of those greengages and watched how Judy was sitting, on a Lloyd Loom chair by the microphone, in a dark bomber jacket, with her legs crossed once at the knee and then at the ankle too.

'You OK, honey?' he hears himself saying on the recording. It's followed by silence but he imagines Judy smiling warmly at him. Yes, a warmth, that's what he remembers, ten years ago when things were sunny, with the sunlight pouring in, the hot sweet coffee, the effortless way the music enveloped them all, bringing them together.

The second track is slower, more folky. It's one of Fergus's arrangements from a traditional tune, with a plaintive fiddle and, for this track, no piano. Again Judy sings – she was less trained back then, her voice occasionally mimics the singers she admires, especially the breathing, but already she has that behind-the-beat laid-back delivery, a semi-quaver, no, not even that, something that even a musician might miss, but the tiniest pause that gave her so much more dimension of feeling – yes, that was something she was born with, that was the elusive quality that made her voice so special.

Guy skips a few tracks and listens to more of the recording from later on that morning. They're doing a cover of *Rainy Night in Georgia*, which only gets half-way through before the song breaks down, but in that fragment of it he's touched by Judy's lovely voice. It feels odd to drop in on this moment in time, with such voyeuristic detail. She sings about shaking the rain from her sweater – Guy's favourite line from the song – just before the band stops playing. He skips forward. Another break between songs. This time he hears Phil, he thinks, actually eating from a bag of crisps, even though there was that glorious bowl of greengages, and Cindy had been up since six just so she could put together a moussaka for their lunch. And Guy's surprised to hear the remains of an argument in the recording. Phil and he have already had a bit of a spat – guitarists are such fidgeters, they should be made to sit like you have to at a piano, it would stop them causing a nuisance, improve their concentration. Phil's been messing around, spoiling things even before he tried to spoil, and although the rest of the band didn't care or were being polite because Phil was new, Guy had decided to tell him to keep still for a while. Guy backs up the CD, trying to hear the moment, but can't find it. But now he's left wondering about that altercation – it's a bit of a discovery – that even before Phil was anything other than the band's guitarist, Guy had known trouble would one day come from him. And Judy had said nothing to back Guy up.

Guy realizes someone on a neighbouring yacht is trying to catch his attention. She has a sheet of paper in her hand on which she's written a message. Through his binoculars he sees it's a woman in her forties, wearing a colourful sarong, looking at him with a mixed expression of relief and apology. Sweeping her hair back from her face she smiles and points at her message. It's a mobile phone number. Guy lingers for a second, unsure what she wants, trying to gauge whether she's in trouble or not – she seems quite relaxed really, but she points to the number again and mouths *Would you call me?* in an exaggerated manner.

Finding his mobile and switching it on, he keys in her number. There's a brief delay before he sees her raise her own phone, then a sudden immediacy of her voice in his ear.

'Hi, you were miles away,' she says. 'Am I disturbing you?'

He feels the need to explain. 'I was listening to music.'

'Oh, OK. Well, sorry,' she says. 'You have a lovely boat.' She has the slight trace of an accent. Possibly something Scandinavian.

'Thanks.'

'Is it old?'

'It's a Dutch coaster – pretty old.' Is this all she wants? 'It used to carry cod livers, or cod-liver oil, at least that's what I was once told.' It's odd to have this exchange, so suddenly but at a distance, with someone he's not met, and it's strangely rude to keep looking at her through the binoculars – as if he has some kind of advantage. He wants to tell her that he likes her sarong, that its colourful print of birds of paradise belongs to another palate entirely than the rest of the estuary's mud greens and browns.

'I was wondering,' she says, 'whether you might be going to the quay – it's just my daughter's there, on our dinghy, and it doesn't look like she's coming back soon. We had an argument.' A thought occurs to her, 'In fact, can you see her?'

'What does she look like?'

'She's tall, not quite as tall as me, with brown hair, lots of it, in curls – she's pretty.'

He looks at the few people milling about on the quay and car park and in the terraced garden in front of the pub. 'Ah, the fountain's still there,' he says, seeing an ornamental bricolage fountain of a whale, made of broken ceramic pieces found in the estuary.

'The what?' the woman says.

'Oh nothing – just a fountain I remember. I came here once before.'

'But Rhona is not there?'

'I don't think so.'

Looking back at her, he sees the woman has half-turned away from his gaze. She's leaning against the transom and is absentmindedly playing with a knotted key-ring, twisting it round her fingers. The phone's still held to her ear, but it's as if she's forgotten about it now. He waits, looking at her in more detail, how her dark hair seems to have a red henna tinge growing out in it, pinned back by a simple tie, exposing her cheek and neck. Can a face be sad, he wonders, thinking that her face – yes, it looks sad. The line of her jaw perhaps, a little thin for her age – maybe she's an anxious person.

'I'm Marta,' she says, quietly.

'Guy,' he replies, then he watches her chin lift as she turns towards him, and smiles. Caught, watching her, he waves back, too enthusiastically, and immediately offers to take her to the quay on the *Flood*'s dinghy. She accepts, and hangs up.

'Well,' Guy says. 'That was strange.'

Coming alongside the sailing boat on the inflatable, he reaches up to grab one of the thin aluminium rails. Marta appears above him, tall but foreshortened by this perspective. She looks at Guy, glances away, then returns her gaze more strongly. He's struck by how pale her eyes are. When she smiles he sees a broad row of strong teeth, and a single canine at the side, quirkily angled.

'I'm so sorry,' she says. 'She's always doing this. It's her unreliable age.'

Guy imagines the daughter from Marta's description of curls. A head filled with crazy direction. He wants to tell her he knows what it's like – to have a rebellious daughter – but he can't. She wasn't.

'Yes,' he says, simply.

Marta begins to climb down on to the dinghy. He guides her plimsoll on to the rubber arm of the inflatable then reaches up to hold her hand. It's a tricky manoeuvre. Her hand is dry, her fingers are strong in his. He sees a cross-stitch of blue capillaries at the back of her knee.

She sits at the bow, too close to the edge, facing him. 'I'm ready,' she says.

'Good,' Guy replies, bringing the revs up. 'Holding on?'

She nods. 'Did you arrive this morning – I didn't see?'

'Yeah, on the tide.' Again, he hears a faint trace of an accent which is not quite English. A clipping of the vowels and a lilting intonation, inside the words, that must be Scandinavian.

She looks at the *Flood* past his shoulder. 'Where from?'

Guy's struck by her steady gaze, her eyes are such a pale blue and one – the right one – watches him a little more inquisitively than the other. Maybe it's the angle of the sunlight catching the iris. But it gives her a mixed expression.

He decides to tell the truth. Or close to it. 'I've been out at sea for the last couple of nights – making the most of the good weather,' expecting it to be the start of a general boat talk of tides and conditions. But she doesn't fall in with it.

She seems suddenly thoughtful. 'Yeah, the sea,' she says, quietly.

As they approach the cement slipway she gathers the rope in her hands and sits, eager and helpful while he drops the revs and tilts the outboard. He imagines how they might look, the two of them, just another man and his wife coming in to shore – the dinghy's assertion of intimacy and familiarity is disconcerting and comforting in equal measure. It had been lonely out on the North Sea, he has to remember that. It was intense, and this, in comparison, feels calm. Calming.

Marta scrambles out of the inflatable's bending shape and manages to plunge a foot straight in the water. Uncomplaining, she merely looks down, as if very used to that kind of thing, and begins to drag the boat forward. Guy gazes at the water as it shallows to an inch, then less than an inch, where it finally becomes clear and transparent rather than the usual mud grey of the estuary. The edge of the sea, in such a fragile meeting as this, always reminds him of childhood. Squatting with a crab line and plastic bucket. A fascination between the two elements of water and shore that never passes.

He ties up the boat while Marta watches, and they walk up the slipway, walking close to each other – the inflatable's bubble of proximity still with them. Ten years earlier he had stood on the same patch of quay with Judy. It had been late at night, after the gig at the Rushcutter's, and Judy had just done an impulsive thing – she'd walked up to the pub's ornamental fountain, where the water sprang out from the bricolage whale's spout hole, and had put her face into it. She'd drenched herself, cooling down after singing for an hour-and-a-half and, when she'd come out of the water, she'd looked drained, ironically, with her dark hair flat to her head and eyes that looked big and emotional and starry.

'I could do that again,' she had said.

'You'll catch something.'

'It felt really good on stage, didn't it? Didn't you feel good?'

'Oh I don't know, it took me a while . . .'

'. . . yeah, yeah. But we did all right, as a band, didn't we? Especially the second half – I really forgot what I was doing, I just felt carried, you know?'

She'd kissed him, and looked earnestly in his eyes, still a hint

66

of the performer in her, the woman he'd just been watching by the mic. 'What I think we should do, Guy, is travel across America, you know, go to Nashville and Memphis and the Mississippi Delta. We'd *love* it, wouldn't we, with all that music in every state. Country, bluegrass, moun'ain moozic, *the blues . . .*'

She had a lovely enthusiasm about her back then.

'Promise me we'll go, Guy, sometime.'

'Across the States?'

'Listening to the music.'

'OK, I promise.'

For the entirety of their gig he'd felt the presence of the pub's bar, with three men leaning against it, somehow in opposition to him. Men, with their pints, representing something hardly tolerant of what he was, a man playing piano – it had reminded him of going to music lessons as a child, with a virginal-looking satchel – it had always felt vaguely shameful. Plus the looks they'd given Judy while she'd sung. He knew all too well that to pass the time they'd indulged in their own fantasies about her, enjoying the open opportunity to gaze at her in detail. That at times all three of them would have undressed her denim skirt, imagined her dirtily, bent her this way and that to suit themselves. It's what men do.

They had gone to the slipway, further from the noise of the pub, where the sober business of the estuary at night had charmed them – the curl of water lapping the bottom of the cement slope, the popping of mud below him, the passing of a small red navigation light half-way across the water.

'I'm going to get us a boat,' he'd said, promising her a sunlit future of his own, imagining something with a cabin, with Formica tables and quirky cupboard spaces, with a musty interior and a salt-washed exterior. The smell of Calor gas and fried eggs. In fact, not so dissimilar to what he had now, his barge, yet this was ten years ago, before Judy and he decided to have a child, before buying the *Flood*, before the sea came back to his days with its relentless advance of waves and tides, its absence of paths. All this to come, all to go, as if the estuary's cycle of water and flow could usher in and then remove all the things they had been, all the things he'd now become.

Guy leans against a low brick wall while Marta crosses the shore to the *Falls of Lora*'s dinghy. Her back has a soft curve to it, a shape of caring, and when she stands by the little boat she leans on to one leg, indecisive. He watches her hand rock the thin gunwale of the boat, and her plimsoll sinking slowly in the mud. She's thoughtful.

He finds the young woman he thinks must be Rhona in a small open-air swimming pool, set among the bushes behind the pub's garden. She's doing lengths down the centre, swimming breaststroke, with her head underwater. Each time she ends a stroke a mass of light-brown hair wafts in forward momentum around her head, before being swept out straight behind her once more – it has the hypnotic motion of a jellyfish. There are leaves floating, the water smells of old pipes, and Guy watches her, her pale limbs as they ripple under the surface, listening to the quiet gasps of air she takes every three strokes, each time sounding a little shocked.

Midway across the pool she suddenly stops and lies motionless, face down underwater. He sees her hair gather in a cloud around her head. He studies her in detail, looking at how her back rises along the surface of the pool while her arms and legs hang down. She's entirely still, not breathing, not moving. Transfixed, he begins to count under his breath, and at twenty she still hasn't moved. It's alarming. Everything becomes still, the trees round the pool, the sounds of the quayside behind him – it all fades away. Finally, he takes a panicked step forward and that's the moment she kicks forward, taking a huge breath and swimming once more.

At a turn, she breaks her stroke and glides, on her back, to one side. She turns her glassy face to him and smiles, a little cruelly, delivers a breathless 'Enjoying the view, are we?' before casually diving into the deep water with a glistening, blithe curve of belly and legs.

Ah shit, he thinks, stung by her accusation. He shuts his eyes – is he so used to his own company that he can only stumble into rudeness at every turn? Even though he had been, enjoying the view, that is.

When he opens his eyes he sees her, at the far end, holding the side, now with her mother leaning down above her.

'You can't be mean to our new friend,' Marta says, as much to Guy as to her daughter.

Rhona glances at him, assessing his connection to her mother, but offering no apology.

Marta laughs out loud, a bright girlish laugh, and ducks her daughter's head under with her foot. 'Stupid girl!' she says.

As he slides the inflatable back to the water he senses Marta coming towards him.

'So sorry for my rude daughter,' she says. 'It takes her a while to warm up.'

'It's OK. Actually, I'm sorry too, I think I *was* staring.'

'Well, she's pretty,' Marta replies automatically.

'I didn't mean that. I meant her swimming. I thought she was in trouble.'

Marta reacts like she hasn't heard. 'She's – she's deciding whether she can bear another night on the boat. Had enough of it, or of me, or both.'

'Right,' Guy replies, a little wary of Marta's confessional tone.

'You learn a lot about someone, being cooped up with them. Even your own daughter.' Marta laughs – again that girlish ring to her voice. 'Truth is, I'm no sailor. Howard's the sailor. My husband.'

Guy thinks he should get back to the *Flood* now. Its empty cubes of silent cabins feel a lot less complicated in comparison.

'Don't worry,' Marta says, brightly, 'I'm going to have a day of it,' she adds, affectionately. 'You must get back to your music.'

He takes the opportunity, and begins to slide the grey rubber inflatable into the water.

'But you'll come to the *Lora* for dinner tonight, won't you? We'll cook for you. What do you think?' She gives him a broad smile, again looking at him with a direct, simple appeal. He's caught off-guard.

'OK – yes, of course.'

She laughs. For some reason neither of them are making the effort to move away. 'So I should let you go now!' she says, cheekily.

'All right. I'll go now,' Guy says, deliberately staying. He's intrigued by this woman's mix of confidence and vulnerability that seem to exist in the same glance. And the unnervingly innocent look of her eyes. Her daughter's eyes are much quicker and darker.

Marta leans to one side, like she had done by the dinghy, and whispers to Guy, 'You know what she's doing now?'

'Who – Rhona?'

'She's watching us. Don't look.'

'Where?'

'She does it,' she says, almost proudly. 'She's a nosey girl.'

'Am I acting suspiciously?'

'She's going to quiz me about you.'

'Really? Well, stick to the truth and we'll be OK,' he says, wondering why he's flirting, and glimpsing Rhona on a bench under the Rushcutter's Arms sign, wrapped in a towel. Her hair hangs limply on one side of her head. She turns away and he looks at the youthful span of her collarbone, spread below her neck like the wings of a bird. Then she looks back, raising her eyebrows in a questioning gesture.

Marta is looking beyond him, out into the estuary. He sees strands of grey hair like stiff fuse wire where the dye has grown out. 'The thing is,' she begins, sadly, 'I hate being on that damned boat too. She's right. I hate everything it's ever meant.'

*

As Guy motors back to the *Flood* he watches Marta calmly walking towards her daughter. Marta is tall, and there's a hint of a stoop in her shoulders which suggests an apology of sorts, for being so. He didn't ask her about her accent. Danish or Norwegian, he thinks. She must be in her mid-to-late forties, and the daughter, she can't be more than twenty-two. Rhona's hair is already beginning to spring with curls, as it dries, and the mother's hair might once have been like that too, but is now cut straighter and shorter. Expression reigned in. They have a similarity of posture too, the way they sit at the garden table – they both push a shoulder forward – that kind of detail has a lot of charm. He wonders if they're conscious of it. He sees them looking and he raises a hand, not quite a wave, but something close to it, a gesture he's not fully understanding himself – it feels like a handshake, and he smiles, falsely, because he's suddenly feeling alone.

The truth is he's always felt on the edges of other people's lives. Even when he was a child he'd felt this way. He remembers being six, possibly seven, having to wait in his father's BMW each morning, looking at the strange details of its dashboard, at the controls he didn't know the purpose of, waiting for his dad to emerge from their small pebble-dashed house. The front door would be open, although Guy could only see shadows inside, as his dad collected the last few items of his luggage. Guy would sit in the car, with his school uniform on, ignored.

The time would be getting late, when suddenly his dad would walk briskly out of the house with a disarmingly apologetic smile on his face, crunching the gravel in his good conker-coloured shoes and his shirt only tucked in on one side, putting his suitcase of clothes next to his salesman's stock-bags of cameras and films in the boot, then slamming the boot and getting into the car and even while he was sitting down, he would already be taking a cigarette from a packet and pressing in the dashboard lighter. Guy's mum hadn't even known her husband smoked, and Guy would just sit there, in total awe of his dad's brazenness, in awe of his dad's ability to change identity at the flick of a switch. To light up, take a first deep puff, even while the car was still on the drive.

Guy's dad would take another deep inhalation of the smoke, then wink at his son. Our secret, he would say, grinning as he turned the ignition.

The appearance of that concealed cigarette, the glow of the lighter's coils touching the dry papery end, the indulgent inhalation, the wink – these turned out to be the first times in Guy's life when he'd known his family might not be quite as it seemed. Adults had their own lives and deceit could rise like genies from the end of those cigarettes.

Until then, Guy imagines his childhood passing in a hazy sunlit calm, tinted with the bronze and faded blues of old Instamatic photos. Damp plastic anoraks, polyester trousers, quiet country walks, apricot halves from the tin. Overwhelmingly, a sense of certainty. But the cigarette lighter, the knowing wink, it had undercut all that. 'Our little secret,' said without fail, every day.

His father had been a travelling salesman, selling cameras and photographic goods in the era when they were still relatively glamorous. He kept his Nikons, Canons, Pentaxes and medium format cameras in the boot, alongside a suitcase packed with several expensive shirts and a couple of suits. A navy blue suit, with braiding-edged large lapels, that's one Guy remembers his dad in.

Although Guy's not seen him for thirty years, he remembers his dad was small, with a quick energy that kept him slim, and he'd had an unusual name – Conrad. You can't have a name like that in an East Anglian market town, not without attracting attention. He had an acrobat's sense of balance, even while he walked, and the hours on the road had given him a seasoned, semi-rugged look, often mistaken for worldly-wisdom by his clients, but not trusted by his wife's friends, who viewed him exotically. *Got a sparkle, ain't he,* by which they meant he had an eye for the ladies. But in Guy's memory, his father had had the air of a traveller, always, even while he dozed in his armchair after an exhausting day on the road, his fingers ever-so-slightly clenched, and his curly hair, long at the temples, tousled by the wind from his open car window, even in the stillness of the front room. His chair and his house, but never quite at home in either of them – because he preferred to be in other people's spaces rather than create one of his own. The BMW was a more natural fit. It had wheels.

Guy remembers how his dad would contemplate the ash as it grew along the cigarette and watch patterns of smoke rising from its tip, as if they might fleetingly reveal a secret. The seconds ticking, all the other children already hanging their coats on the pegs outside the classroom, no doubt. And there would be Guy, watching his father smoking, looking at his small spiky moustache which was cut thin, like Clark Gable's. Large sideburns, an inch lower than the rest of the men in the area, not a single grey hair in them. Conrad would pass his son a Yorkie bar to put in his satchel – despite chocolate being banned from school – and Guy would see that famous glint in his father's eye which always seemed to sell himself as someone who has seen things, lived a life, lived by instinct.

He'd wanted to be like his father right up to the day his mother packed those expensive clothes into several tea chests, put them on the drive, and sent them away, mysteriously, seemingly off to a great adventure themselves.

'You're my little man, now, Guy, my own little man. All right?' Guy's mother had said that day, her tears falling on the gravel so the stones appeared to have drips of polish on them.

Those are the moments that make us, Guy thinks. We're the culmination of those moments. We're the culmination of knots and fixes.

Without her husband, Guy's mother had quickly seemed boring. She was unsporty, a joiner of societies, with the East Anglian habit of gentle humour and a vague way of expressing herself. Too soft and mussy in the mornings, kept her nightgown on till lunch time, always the first to look tired in the evenings. She took her wedding photos off the mantelpiece and put them in a drawer, and Guy found them in there, removed from view, and saw that in all the photos his mother had had a surprised look – outside the church porch, at the reception, in the back seat of the car.

And to fill the space his father had left, Guy's mother bought a piano. Lessons followed, scales and chromatics, practice and practice, making Guy fill the house with new noise. 'You'll thank me one day,' she would say, mantra-like, and he supposes he does, now, even though he certainly didn't back then. It seemed she'd anchored him to the largest, most unmoveable piece of furniture in the house. There'd be no more running off.

Years of piano practice left no mark at all, had no place in his memory, but a performance he went to aged thirteen did, at Orford Church. He remembers how shadowed and magical the church had seemed, filled with an air of expectancy, with the stained-glass windows looking like the mysteriously opaque images in his father's slide boxes, before a light was shone through them, and the cast dressed in robes from Japanese Noh theatre, sitting patiently by the raised platform which served as a stage. Then the opening plainsong of Benjamin Britten's *Curlew River*, so monastic in sound, *Te lucis ante terminum*, and the cast walking dreamlike into their places. The drum, beat with a finger, sounding like rainfall, the strange dissonant chords.

He had seen his mother cry that night, in profile; single tears moving slowly down her cheek, illuminated in the soft light of the performance, each tear forming like wax welling from a candle, as the Madwoman's grief became evident on stage. Guy had listened to the music and realized, for the first time, music was all he ever wanted to do. There, in that church, the strange layers of Britten's sound, simply embellished by each new voice and instrument, pared down, textured, it had truly inspired him.

74

Music's filled his life ever since. He has it within reach, always, a necessary addiction, not in neatly ordered CD racks and book-shelves, but in piles scattered here and there, like snacks. A messy heap of scores and arrangements on top of the piano in the *Flood*'s saloon, open CDs on the table, scraps of treble clef notation on corners of the newspaper. He whistles. He hums. He goes over melodies, messing them up with quirky modulations. Without that concert he might never have discovered this language. Might never have viewed the five lines of the bass and treble clefs as endlessly stretching out like the lanes of a racetrack, in perfect and unquestionable parallel for all eternity. The E line will never rise to cross the G. These geometric washing lines on which music notes are hung – they never alter. It is certainty in a life that lost its certainty. Like that Middle C, alone on its little peg of a line below the treble clef, so important, but pushed out nonetheless. Ignored. He's always felt sorry for it, really.

Guy stands naked, examining his reflection in the full length mirror on the back of his wardrobe door. The same mirror the original Dutch bargeman may or may not have bothered to look at. A reflection isn't always necessary, especially at sea. Guy looks at how pale his belly is – it's a little podgy too – he tries to lift it, then breathes in and turns to the side. Mm, getting hairy on the shoulders, that's something he hasn't noticed before. But he looks strong, he's always had that.

He'd tried to sleep in the afternoon, but had been unable to. Maybe it was the turning of the tide that heralded his unease, a direction under the boat that swung the *Flood* on its mooring till it pointed downriver. An implied direction, to go out to sea again.

He puts on a white shirt and his thick-rimmed glasses, then has a shave. He looks at himself in the mirror again, and pushes his hair back behind the temples – he's getting quite grey there, not that he minds. But in the shirt he begins to feel too clean, too stiff, his skin has a gleaming look on the cheeks that will undo him all evening, he knows it, he won't relax. He's still haunted by crying in front of the trawler men. He can't trust himself in company. It was easier to be alone on the North Sea, he thinks, with its endless water and air and sandbanks. But was it? Really?

Position: The Falls of Lora. *7:10pm*

'You're early,' Marta says, leaning over the rail to take his rope. She too has changed for the evening. She's in a dark-green crocheted cardigan, with baggy sleeves. It looks like a complicated piece of clothing, and has been held together by a large brooch. Guy thinks both of them making such an effort to look good is in some way embarrassing.

'This boat has seen some sailing,' he says.

'My husband's other woman,' she replies. She guides him down the cockpit steps towards the cabin, adding, 'It's horribly small.'

It's an understatement. The saloon is amazingly cramped, part galley, part bunk area, with a fixed Formica table and curved walls that follow the yacht's shape, but it's the shelves that are most oppressive. On both sides there are books crammed into any space that will take them, held in place by batons that run across their spines. They narrow the saloon and give the air the subdued sound of a library. He sees the books before he sees Rhona, seated at the table in an emerald-green knitted top. More of her clothes spill out from a large saggy holdall pushed to one side, none of them folded, full of their own unwrapping, and through an open door beyond, he can see a tapering bunk area filled with duvets and rugs and more clothes on the floor.

Guy is very aware that he hardly knows them. It makes him over-keen to put them at their ease, so he sets off the evening telling them about coming here ten years earlier, how the pub still had that bricolage whale back then, and how he and four others had been in a country-folk band doing a gig.

He wonders afterwards why he didn't mention that one of the band was his wife.

Marta replies politely, 'Are you still a musician?' She doesn't look comfortable in her cardigan. She keeps having to adjust it.

'Oh no, I teach kids how to play the piano. That's how I afford the mooring fees. I mean, I don't get much, but I don't need much any more, just enough to get by. I've got about ten pupils who have lessons after school, but not in the summer holidays. I have a piano on board.'

'Right,' Rhona pitches in. 'We've been guessing what you do.'

'Really?'

'Mum thought you were on the run.'

'That's nice.'

'And not true, either,' says Marta.

'Sorry to disappoint you.' Guy's calming down rapidly.

'We hate this boat,' Rhona says, dramatically. She has a curious mouth, slightly unconventional in the way the top lip rises. Her teeth are strong and prominent. It's attractive.

Marta brings a large bowl of pasta to the table. 'We thought we could manage and bring these dusty books back without them getting wet – though really we haven't been doing much sailing – we've used the motor. Ro's here to watch me fail.'

'You're not failing,' Rhona says.

'Very kind. But I am.'

'We used the sail the other day.'

'With mixed results. Problem is, the motor makes it boring, and it gives us too much time. We're not into too much time at the moment, are we, love?'

Marta gives her daughter a slightly testing look. Rhona shrugs and gives a warm smile back.

'Where are the books going?'

'Eventually, in the attic. In Cambridge. We've motored all the way round from the Solent, and we're going to leave it here, aren't we?' Rhona nods. 'You live by yourself?' Marta asks.

'Yeah. All year round, and I spend most of it thinking I'm not up to it.' He tells them about his estuary – the Blackwater – and his own mooring slotted between the wrecks and the soon-to-be wrecks of the Tide Mill anchorage. He tells them about the gulls landing on the wooden roof above his cabin, falling like sacks of bones in winter when the sea's cold and the birds are full of anger and empty inside. How they wake him up. And the flocks of starlings that blow up into the cold air above the estuary, turning in strange patterns in the dusk before they settle in the trees. The patches of phosphorescence that drift by in the flow during the middle of the night, sparkling like glitter lost in the water, and the cormorants that fish from his bow, wings outstretched in the morning sun to dry their feathers. It all sounds more enjoyable than he'd intended.

'That's great,' Rhona says, enthusiastically. She's not all cool young woman, after all.

'Ro's a fan of houseboats. Viking blood.'

'Right – are you Norwegian?'

Marta seems to find that hilarious. She laughs loudly and puts her hand to her mouth, concealing that quirky tooth of hers.

'Icelandic,' she says.

'It's not *that* funny, Mum.'

'To a girl from Reykjavik, it's always funny. Sorry,' she says, 'it's just I don't think I have an accent. I came to England at eighteen to study archaeology – and instead I fell in love and never went back.'

'How long've you lived on the boat?' Rhona asks, half interrupting her mother.

'Five years. I suppose it's not all bad,' Guy says, forcing a brightness, 'the way the tide lifts your whole life up just to put it back down in the mud twice a day, that's wonderful, when you're asleep and you start to float – I really like that – it's like you drift away in every sense, from yourself.' Guy realizes he might be talking too much; living alone has made him an unpredictable guest. He needs to rein it in. 'And the pub on the quay's good – they do crispy whitebait and sweet scallops, and dark nutty ale.'

'See – you like it,' Rhona says, downing a glass of wine. Rhona's top has small metallic threads woven into it. Guy notices Marta looking concerned.

'But the spring tides are scary – they stretch the ropes. And I've had enough of chemical toilets.' He gets the desired smile from the others, both of them with a slight crinkle at the edges of their mouths – he hasn't noticed that similarity before. He's buoyed by them. The simple pleasure of making a woman smile, there's nothing like it.

'What made you live on a boat?' Rhona asks.

Guy hesitates – he doesn't want to ruin the evening like he did on the trawler. But it's hard. He can feel the space where Freya should be, even here, where there is no space. He decides to be vague, 'Various reasons.' He can tell Marta senses a subject he's hiding, but she lets it pass.

'Yesterday,' he jokes, 'I woke up and the barge was stuck on a sandbank.'

'Told you!' Ro says, looking at her mother as if it's confirmed one of their dreads. 'Where?'

'About ten miles offshore. But the odd thing was how relaxing it was. The sand was only this much higher than the tide, and it's really very strange, to be walking around in the middle of the North Sea like that.' He goes into the story at this point, making it an idiotic adventure, describing how the *Flood* dragged him and the inflatable off the bank at the end, aware too that he's not telling them so many other things, such as his swim into nowhere, how he looked up at the sky and felt the presence of his daughter by his side, or the impenetrable steel cliffs of the container ship passing inches away from him last night. It almost feels like they're spending the evening with a dead man, that they've invited a ghost. But he sees that they're amused, and they respond with similar tales of getting lost and dropping things accidentally over the side and confusing one mud-lined estuary for another.

He tells them that he'd love to see a basking shark. That every time he comes across the plumes of plankton floating in the water, he thinks this will be the moment, expecting that great shadow of a body to drift by his boat like in a dream. How, with the calm sea, he's been scanning the water for the tiny tip of the dorsal fin.

Marta listens, spellbound it seems. She offers a toast: 'To seeing a basking shark, then?'

They clink glasses. Marta adjusts her cardigan again. She's too thin for it, he thinks.

Marta takes his glass, politely, to offer him more. Guy looks at a framed photo of a terraced stone cottage on the opposite side of the cabin. It's called Whalebone Cottage. In the photo Marta's pulling the front door shut. Above her head is what appears to be a whale vertebrae, set into the wall.

'That's a nice picture,' he says.

'It's in Scotland – it's our secret bolthole – we've had it for years.'

'So why isn't your husband here, doing all the sailing?' Guy asks innocently. The two women say nothing.

Directing her gaze straight back at Guy, Marta says, 'He just can't.' She leaves it at that.

'Sorry,' he says.

But Marta smiles warmly. 'Don't be,' she says, 'it's lovely having you here, isn't it, Ro?'

'After a week of being cooped up with you – I'd say yes, very lovely. Very lovely indeed,' she repeats, glinting at Guy with a bright-eyed look which, although she's young, has clearly been many a man's ruin. She glows. Her expression glows, surrounded as it is by the helmeted wrap of her curls. 'It gets lonely on a boat,' she whispers, mimicking a film starlet. Guy's struck by a hotness at the look she gives him as she leans forward, her head tilted up, her mouth slightly parted. She's about to speak, but holds it back so he has to look at her lips. She could have anyone she wanted.

Rhona downs another glass of wine. That's three, or four even, since he arrived, Guy thinks.

'Let's give you more food,' Marta says, taking his plate with her long fingers, and breaking her daughter's moment. Rhona's fingers are shorter, they look lazy, and are tipped in dark-red nail varnish. Rhona smiles to herself and looks away while her mother clambers awkwardly round the mess by the table. Marta's conscious of her height in this boat. Her brooch is a large smooth pebble of amber, flecked inside like it might have seeds buried in it.

Guy looks across at the crowded shelves. Whoever this man is, he's made his home away from the others, in rows of books. God, men are maddening – they're surrounded by the love of women, like these two, and all they can think about is their own private getaways – their books and their garden sheds and themselves.

'Are those your sketches?' Guy asks Rhona, over the table.

'She's good, yes?' Marta comments proudly. 'Especially the charcoal ones.'

It gives Guy the excuse to study them – he's been intrigued since he sat down. Most of the drawings are of Marta, in various positions around the boat, and they reveal glimpses of a woman he's not yet seen: sitting at the end of the bed, massaging her toes with thumb and forefinger; lying on the bed, looking tired, her wedding rings taken off and put to the side on a fold-out table; gazing out to sea, shielding the sun's glare with her hand, in the same way Guy had first seen her do. And that's the moment he spots a sketch of himself and Marta, standing this morning on the slipway. It's been pinned to a shelf. 'Is that me?' he asks.

'Yes,' Marta replies, drawing her breath in as she says the word. In the sketch he's angling his head up towards Marta – he seems more eager than he remembered being.

'I'm flattered,' he says to Rhona, thinking she's studied him, his posture and expression, she's judged him already. And she's tacked it to the shelf deliberately within his sightline, knowing he'd be sitting opposite it this evening.

Next to it is a photo of a man. He's stocky, standing in

swimming trunks and goggles, on a craggy rock ledge which slopes into the sea. It looks like Scotland. So this is the man Howard, Guy thinks. The man who's not being talked about, although his presence is everywhere.

'Ro's just dropped out of art school,' Marta says, a little aggressively.

'I haven't decided yet.'

'But you have, haven't you?'

'Yes.'

Faced with a rising bluntness from her daughter, Marta acquiesces. 'It's just a waste, that's all, love.'

'Spoken like a mother.'

'Spoken like a friend,' Marta says. 'Remember, I made a few wrong decisions when I was your age, I do know what I'm talking about.'

'You mean having me?' Rhona says angrily.

'Of course not!' Marta's stung by the accusation. 'Of course not. I mean giving up.'

'Mum – you've never given up. Don't be so hard on yourself.'

'Ro. I don't want to lose you. That's all.'

'Yeah.'

'Did you hear me?'

'I don't know why you say these things. You're not going to lose me.'

'Ever?'

'Ever.'

'I just needed to hear it.'

'Don't upset yourself. Why d'you have to say these things?'

Marta's suddenly embarrassed this is taking place in front of Guy. 'It's a fault of mine,' she says, apologetically. 'And a fault of this boat, too – it brings out the worst in us.'

'. . . and the best,' Rhona says, expansively. Abruptly she stands and puts her arms round her mother, kissing her tenderly on the neck, their moods shifting quicker than Guy can follow. He looks at Rhona's arm round her mother's shoulder, a tableau of a grieving couple, somehow, a churchyard stance, by the grave.

And as they hold the hug, Guy gazes down Rhona's body, at the twist she's forced into by the table edge, giving it an erotic curve, accentuating her slightly raised thigh and the flatness of her childless waist.

Back on the *Flood* he's surprised by how chilly it feels. It's early September, the estuary had felt strangely warmed as he'd returned on the inflatable, a calm stream of black ink, but in his saloon it's as damp as a cellar. All it takes is a few hours of not being on board and these boats take on the true cold of the river. He scrunches newspaper into tight balls and places them in the cylinder of the wood burner, a seventy-year-old cast iron furnace that came with the boat. He drops in the kindling, then a couple of seasoned quarter-logs, before replacing the hotplate at the top. He sets the flue from *zacht* to *matig*, its medium setting, then allows more air in at the bottom as the firebricks will be damp.

It's the first fire he's had since spring, the ritual is comforting. When he lights it, always just with the one match, he pats the curious nameplate on the front for luck. *ETNA SUN 1028*, it reads, with a raised steel outline of two men carrying a molten ingot between them. This more than anything is his sign that autumn will arrive soon and, sitting in front of it, as the fire begins to roar, he watches its light flickering across the surfaces of the room, giving it an underwater shimmer of life and movement it doesn't ordinarily have. It seems to emphasize how alone he is on board. A big space with big shadows, full of an empty presence.

This is his home, he thinks. He's made it for himself and it's all that he is, really. There's the spot in the galley where he wedges the wooden grinder between the worksurfaces when he's making coffee; there are his cup-hooks, placed at his own arm-length from the sink; there is a shelf for his oil and salt which he can reach from the cooker. It fits him, this boat, after five

years. It's full of his measurements: his arm-sp
preferred routes from table to chair.

He thinks warmly about his last entry in the dia
he described across the Everglades – what a place. He
how he wrote about the sawgrass floating eerily on
in the dark bottomless swamp, and the glint of his da
lights reflected off the side window. Then the curious gas-stop
with its random collection of souvenirs and stranger collection
of people, how his family felt as they walked in – vulnerable, out
of their depth, but together. The strange insect which looked like
something pulled from the shower trap – these things appear
now as if he has seen them in a film. A film of his own life, but
not quite his own life – a life made complete by imagining just
how it might have been. If.

They pull into a motel forecourt off the interstate in northern
Florida. It's been a long day, too long, and they're arriving late.
Guy's face is burning from the sun they had in Everglades
City earlier that day. He has the redness many soft-skinned
Englishmen get, that makes him look unhealthy, just a little bit
too cooked. It had been his idea to go to Everglades City, for no
other reason than it looked an odd dead end on the map, his
map, the map which by now he's almost able to draw out himself.
And it turned out to be a strange place too, with an extensive
grid plan of roads cut into the mangroves waiting for a city which
never, in fact, arrived. They'd taken a boat cruise round the
islands, spotting the exotic pink of Roseate Spoonbills in the
distance, and watched desperate-looking racoons hopping among
the mangrove roots, their fur muddy and spiky. Freya had loved
the boat, she loves all boats, and had taken it upon herself to
spot the first manatee, not that they saw any. Judy had stood
with a scarf tied round her head to stop the wind, and had
produced a pair of large sunglasses Guy had never seen before.
Her lipstick had looked glass-bright in the sunshine, every inch
a star.

...is insistence, they'd eaten stonecrab claws out of the shell .: the local raw bar, all three of them grimly silent while they cracked the claws open, under a reed canopy that striped their bodies with its shadow. And a coconut had fallen from the top of a nearby palm tree, landing on the ground with a soft hollow thud. Picking it up after lunch, he'd almost expected it to be warm, it was so freshly delivered.

He doesn't want to wake Freya, so he tries to carry her, asleep, into the motel room. It's an awkward reach into the car, and Guy's surprised at how solidly heavy Freya is when he slides his arm beneath her legs. He pulls her to him and her head falls against his shoulder. She breathes loudly and her cheek is clammy, there's a smell about her which reminds him of the child she once was, so hot in the skin. That malty smell, the dusty smell of her hair. He carries her, like that, while Judy looks on, amused, till he lies her down on the cot bed. Guy steps aside for Judy to take the shoes and socks off, and pull a blanket over her, and while he waits he still feels his daughter's heaviness in his arms, a dead weight of flesh and compliance which makes him uneasy. He wants to wake her, to make sure she's really there.

Judy busies herself, unconcerned by the new surroundings, into the routine of getting her bottles and unctions into the bathroom. She doesn't seem to notice the interior of the motel room at all, but when she goes through to the bathroom, she whispers the room is nice. 'We've done a lot of driving today, haven't we?' she adds.

He feels it, in the slight whirr his thoughts are in, the need to unravel the sense of motion and concentration he's needed for the past few hours. It takes its toll, and he's disorientated.

The walls are covered with the trappings of a home – prints of river views, a sunset off Sanibel Island and, oddly, a picture of a Western Star American Eagle truck. The wallpaper has an orchid print on it, the bedspread has a tattered fringe which hangs down to the carpet. Imitations of a home, but not a home at all, it's a place which holds no one, leaves no mark, is just for the passing through, where people barely unload their suitcases, have brittle rows, or sleepless nights, crash out on the bed, lean back against the wall with the TV remote in their hands. He's impelled to do exactly that, too, to sit back and flick channels on the TV, get a glimpse, even there, of other people's worlds to soothe his own.

Judy takes a shower. Every so often he hears the water splashing on the tiled floor – she's messy when it comes to washing – and he hears her singing a few bars from a country song he recognizes. That's a calming sound, surely, he thinks, to hear your wife sing. But again he feels strangely unsettled. Those thoughts he's been having, about how temporary everything appears, they won't be silenced, and he has that same nagging worry, a persistent numbness of thought which won't let him through, a cushioning he can't get beyond.

He looks at his reflection in the TV's blank grey screen: slightly distorted, watched, captive, like a reflection you see in a well, you want to snatch it back from being lost in there. He presses the remote and the TV springs to life with a lot of colour and sound and it takes him a few seconds to get it mute. He watches it like that, with the camera slowly panning across the shining floor of a shopping mall, a female presenter smiling and fawning over a man in a tight suit. She touches his arm when he makes her laugh. They're being excessively polite, and a bit flirty. Other channels flick by, weather and sport, then sport again, graphics spinning and laying down images on each other, such a brightly lit place, America, on its TV.

Then a film, a western, it's strange to watch it here rather than back in England, where westerns have always belonged for him. It's lost its distance and as a result the film looks unreliable and false. But he continues watching, it's calming, it doesn't rush by. The pocket of dry desert light is settling, Utah, laid out in such grandeur, it's across America right now, at the end of a long road that begins right at their door. The horses stop walking, a little dust of brown and red sand settles around their hooves. A brim of a hat is pushed back, a decision made about which way to head in a country without paths.

'You all right, Guy?' Judy says from the other room, too loudly, drowned out by the shower.

He gets off the bed and walks slowly past Monument Valley, a god in a god's landscape. A step further and he's in the en suite, which is surprisingly bright and tiled from floor to ceiling. He stands by the sink and looks at his reflection – too red, he might ask her for some of that cocoa butter he knows she has. He quite likes the smell.

She's the other side of the shower curtain. He can see her pink body made grey by the plastic. The steam fills the air and it smells of iron and pipes.

'Fine,' he says. 'Little weary.'

She's switched the taps off and is bunching her hair to one side of her neck. He can see her wringing water out of it.

'You think Freya's having a good time?' he says.

'Course. You worry too much about her. You've always worried too much about her. She just needs some space, that's all.'

'You think she's all right?'

'Yes, I think she's all right.'

'You think we are?'

'Guy,' she says, then says nothing more.

She pulls the curtain to one side, making a loud shuttling noise with the metal rings. She stands there, flattened it seems, against the tiles behind her. Her skin is flushed and still dripping with the streams running off her, as if some of her life might be draining away in front of them.

She's unashamed to be naked, so brightly lit-up before him, it seems a challenge for some reason, even her breasts have a challenge to them, in this view, pointing at him with such unblinking expression. Dumb eyes staring at him, one just a little bigger than the other, like a half-a-wink that knows something he doesn't. It makes him smile.

'So should I get my own towel?' she asks, cheekily. He hands her a big towel which was hanging on a rail, and watches, a sense of disappointment, as she wraps it, almost twice round her body. She doesn't look thin, but she's small, it always surprises him when an ordinary object like a towel can be so big on her.

'Come here,' she says, quietly. He steps towards her and they share a ridiculous embrace, her standing in the bath, while he's on the wet floor, still in his shoes and clothes. The damp curls of her hair touch his cheek, and she whispers, 'You're a big, soft, stupid man,' in his ear, before nibbling his lobe.

When they kiss her mouth is wet and slippery as if she's just come out of a swimming pool, she hasn't even dried her face. It reminds him of the times they've spent, swimming, floating, in rivers, in lakes, in the sea. Good times. Her eyes are so wet it looks as if she's been crying, and it checks him, makes him worried that she's about to say something alarming. But instead she undoes his shirt, deliberately and slowly, pretending to be fascinated by each button, and automatically he reaches round her and feels the shape of her body through the rough dry bobbles of the towel. The dip at the base of her spine, so accentuated, never fattened or changed in all the years he's known her. The bones of her shoulder blades, so thin, like the bones of a bird. In places, there's so little to her, where can her lovely voice come from?

He pulls the towel off her and lifts her from the bath and the room seems incredibly small for him, for them, for the thing they're thinking of doing. Bright too, like a laboratory, but neither of them are bothered by that.

Aware of the lack of space they settle for the floor – like being in a small boat, they're seeking the most solid thing around. But the floor is cold and wet and it takes an effort to get over that. A series of inconveniences and obstacles, it appears, to stop them, sober them. But Judy is determined. She's already pulled most of his clothes off and is awkwardly climbing on top of him. Her skin is hot and it sticks to him, unpleasantly. Her hair is wringing wet and cold on his face, he wants to shut his eyes and brush it away, but both of them are also getting lost in their routine, the one which has evolved over so many years, the lack of shame, the sense of naughtiness, and never getting used to the intimacy, the sheer rudeness of it, between them, with no one else around. Which is not quite the case here, because they can both hear Freya's breathing from the bed in the other room, and it only seems to add to the occasion, makes them act younger, more rash, a couple of teenagers on the floor of a strange bathroom, where they shouldn't be, doing what they shouldn't be doing.

Guy looks up at his wife, at the crease of concentration between her brows, it's the same expression he's seen on her when she's behind the mic on stage, during a heartfelt part of the song, she's such a committed performer, always. He looks beyond her to the underside of the sink, sees a bodged repair there to the pipe work, imagines the last person to be in his position was the frustrated man who tried in vain to fix the faulty plug. An odd sense of company for him now. And he sees Judy looking down, relieved, beyond him, the weight in her face falling forward a little.

'I'm going to take another shower,' she whispers, holding back a giggle.

Later, after they've got ready for bed, Guy has an idea. It's about that coconut he put in the car. He steps out of the motel room and gets it from behind his seat. He sits on the step and whittles away at the green husk with a penknife, but can't get into the nut itself. Judy joins him, offering to help, finding a corkscrew from the room, but it's no use. They want to do this, they don't want to be beaten. Finally Guy squats and jams the nut down on the corner of the kerb, his body bent in the aspect of his primeval ancestors, till the nut splits satisfactorily. They drink the warm watery milk in the cool Florida air, cooler here than where they'd been, they've driven into a different climate.

When they go to sleep, Judy seems lost to him on such a huge mattress. Again he has the sense that he's entirely alone, with the TV's dark grey eye looking back at him from the foot of the bed.

He can't quite settle, still. He gets up and goes to the bathroom again, sees the pile of towels messily dumped on the floor where they left them, the scene of a crime, he thinks. He squats down and looks under the sink, bends the metal and eases it into the hook of the casing, the solution which has come to him which escaped the last man to try and fix the drain. He tries the plug plunger. Yes, all working. All restored. Now he can sleep.

He's up early, sifting flour, sugar and salt into a bowl, then preparing a second bowl with hand-hot milk and water, on to which he's sprinkled a palmful of dried yeast. The yeast sits on top of the liquid in a brown raft of dust, fermenting slowly into a froth which reminds him of the autumnal tides in the Blackwater estuary, when the sea drives in a dark vegetative foam against the river.

The meal on the *Lora* comes back to him in fragments. Marta's way of straightening the simple necklace she was wearing, how she crossed her long hands on her lap, as if not knowing what to do with them, her gestures of politeness and then the occasional sigh, followed by a direct, unflinching gaze. Inward and outward signals. And Rhona, on the surface easier to read. A tease. Spirited, with fewer angles, but ultimately more guarded than her mother. A heavy drinker, too. She'd been flirting, he was sure, but was also sure that he couldn't trust her.

By the time he adds the bicarbonate of soda and lets the mixed batter rise a second time, his mouth is watering. As a result, he's impatient with the griddle, not waiting till it's spit-hot, not greasing the biscuit cutters he tends to use, so the first couple of crumpets he pours are too dense and too brown when he turns them. Gull food. But the next ones are perfect. The batter is soft as he spoons it in, and the bubbles rise calmly, bursting across the top in a gentle honeycomb pattern till they set. He turns them and runs the flat of a knife across their burnt golden underside, such a punctureable skin, with its thin lip where the batter has seeped below the edge of the cutter.

He melts cold butter on to the hot crumpets and, when that vanishes, he adds more butter till discs of it cover the surface, softened, like snow on wet wood. Then he adds honey, plenty of it, rich and dark, a sugary slippery taste in his mouth, hot from the griddle, cold from the fridge, sour from the soda and sweet from the honey.

After finishing up the batter he wraps half-a-dozen of the crumpets in a bag and rows the inflatable over to the *Falls of Lora*. He writes *Thanks for last night* on the bag, and ties it to the aluminium cockpit rail, reaching up in a pirate's manner, thinking of them asleep, still, somewhere in the boat, Marta in her husband's cabin, on one side of the bunk even though the whole bed's hers, and Rhona, no doubt in a mess of bedclothes and hair and an arm hanging off the bench in the saloon. Sexy in her disarray.

Back on the *Flood* Guy makes a coffee, licks the cooled butter and honey off his breakfast plate and looks at his navigation map. The Deben estuary. One of Suffolk's tongueless mouths, flowing into the North Sea. Time to move. But instead he gets the other map out, the *Hildebrand's Travel Atlas of America*. As a rule, he doesn't write the diary during the day – but he wants to see them, right now, he wants a glimpse of what they're up to. It's the taste of these crumpets, he thinks, a sugar-kick, compelling him on, he wants to know where to, where is his family right now?

They have just crossed the state line into the north-east corner of Alabama. Somewhere below Chattanooga, driving fast on a back-road, as it dips and stretches like a glorious ribbon in the bright afternoon sunshine. Judy has her window down and her sunglasses on, and has been singing along to a bluegrass CD. It has a great rhythm, when the banjo kicks in, and Guy's been driving the car like it's part of the music, trying to get the engine in tempo. Even Freya's been joining in from the back, for once putting her music player to one side, sitting forward in the gap between the two front seats to be closer to them. It feels good, this sense of well-being, this motion and sunshine too, and an empty road. America is rolling by, under the wheels, their third state already, Florida, Georgia, and now the top corner of Alabama – A-la-ba-ma, he thinks, everywhere that's on the map round here is in the lyrics of a song.

Judy changes the track, puts the volume up, and announces in her best Dolly impression that *Thish here nexsht song's the Muleskinner Blues*. Yee haah! That high and low answering rif on the banjo as it starts, fast like the cog of a machine turning, turning, setting the tempo too fast it seems, too fast but it's an invitation, right there, to tap your foot, to go-get your guitar, to go along with it and after four bars or so you can do nothing *but* go along, the rest of the music kicking in – the session sound of the lead guitar doing something more ordinary, a little wayward in fact, a tall upright sound doing a humorous answering call, and then that extraordinary sound – a wolf-whistle followed by that real live whip crack – has Dolly *really* got a whip in her hand? – just the once, and a *whey-up-there* from Dolly like she's just loving that sound, laughing through it, chasing the music like it's the best sound on earth and, right there, you have to agree with her, she's in the best mood on the planet and you're totally with the rhythm and swept up by it. And she strikes into the song with the most extraordinary opening line, *Good moorrrrrrrrrr-nin', captain*, dragging the high note out for a full ten seconds – how does she do it? – before coming down to *Good morning to you, sir, heh, heh*, then a cheeky *yeah* while other whip cracks go off in the background, like fireworks. *Do you need another muleskinner?* she goes, and you drive on, drive along, loving every last note of it.

They pull off the road near a large sign saying DOUGHNUTS, under which there's a giant red arrow pointing to a much smaller shop. Such clear signage, in America, it seems to be written for the planes.

'Just how many doughnuts do you think I can eat?' he says, provocatively. Freya's up for it. 'I'll match you, Dad,' she says. 'My metabolism can take it better than yours.'

'You're on, and you're gonna lose.'

Freya's excited about the doughnuts, at the sheer indulgence of a business that only sells them and nothing more, she can't be delayed, and when they step into the shop they are hit by a hotly overwhelming smell of sugar.

'Twelve types,' Freya sums up, efficiently. They're in a great mood, bamboozling the assistant with their excitability, and their sheer Englishness, their strange accents which must sound like royalty out here. They order half the range, change the order, add and subtract various blends of blueberry and crème, then take four greasy bags outside to sit under an awning at a plastic set of table and chairs.

'Oh, these are great. I love the blueberry ones,' Freya says. 'Try the blueberry one.'

Judy smiles, thinly. She's going to go slow and let the others have the lion's share. 'Guy, do you think they'd do us some boiling water?'

'For tea?' he says. They carry tea bags with them, from England. Judy's always had proper standards when it comes to tea. 'I'll try,' he says, hopefully.

He goes back into the shop and asks for three cups of boiling water. It's one of those moments when America seems more than a mere ocean away. The assistant, who's young, with a perfect smile that can't have been the result of eating the doughnuts, just can't get why anyone would want boiling water. She is shown the tea bags, and finds that endearing. Real cute, she says, smiling and nodding and looking at the tea bags, before getting some hot water from the coffee percolator. It'll have to do, Guy thinks.

Through the window he looks at the dumbshow of Judy and Freya, eating the doughnuts. Freya's making an extra effort to keep things light. She's clearly not sure, without her father's presence out there to ensure a light-hearted majority, whether

her high-spirits will last, and is showing that instinct again, an awareness that something's not quite as it should be between them. And he wonders. Why should the mood be slipping like this? After all that great music and driving? What is surfacing? What has Freya picked up on that he needs to get up to speed with? He can't help thinking that this little framed tableau of eating the doughnuts might have the appearance of a last supper for them. A moment of sweetness which he will someday need to savour.

'Snap out of it,' he whispers to himself, taking the Styrofoam cups of not-quite-boiling water out to the others, the thin bleed of the tea bags promising an acceptable, if not perfect, cup.

'I had some problems,' he says. Freya looks relieved he's back.

'I'll go next time,' Judy says, kindly, but she has a look in her eye he doesn't quite get. Sometimes, at night, her eyes look darker than they are, and she has this quality about her now.

'How far to Nashville?' Judy asks.

'Three hours,' Guy replies, always the authority when it comes to distances.

'I should let Phil know,' Judy says. She reaches into her bag and gets out her mobile. 'There's a signal here.' Her doughnut is left half-eaten on the plate.

'Are you getting nervous, Mum?' Freya asks.

'What about?'

'The recording.'

'Not really,' Judy says, abstractly, as she texts a message.

'How many have you had?' Guy asks, lightly.

'Three, Dad, and I've got plenty of room.'

'Oh yeah?'

'I could eat the whole display counter,' Freya drawls in a gruff voice, putting on a cross-eyed look. It's one of her characters – Guy recognizes – the monster one, full of appetite. She has several characters.

Guy responds in the way his daughter wants, becoming the father-monster – the one with no morals at all. 'I'd eat the display

counter, the shop-girl, if she was dipped in sugar, I'd eat you too.'
Freya laughs.

'You've had enough,' Judy says, curtly.

And Freya's voice snaps. '*Get you!* I'm not a *kid*,' she says.

Judy gives her a withering look. 'Yes you are. You are a kid and you've had enough.'

'Judy,' Guy says, trying to intervene, trying to calm the hot-headedness between these women.

'And you've had enough too,' she says, not entirely joking.

'Well you don't eat enough!' Freya pipes up, rashly. 'You eat like a bird and you're way too skinny – all you do is drink coffee.'

Judy gets up, not willing to be lectured to. Oddly, she glares at Guy, as if it's all his fault, how easily her family starts to argue. He puts his hands up in surrender, and let's her make her own way off.

'She's a *nightmare*,' Freya huffs.

'She's not.'

'Except she is.'

'OK. You're right.'

'See.'

'Don't get wound up,' he says, watching Judy leaning against their hire car. It looks like she's just got a text back. He imagines Phil spending his days gazing at his mobile, waiting for the texts to appear. He sees Judy's expression darken and he knows there's trouble. Damn that Phil. 'Your mother's probably on edge about having to do the recording. Be easy on her,' he says, wondering why he always has to be the peacemaker.

'Why *do* I have to be the peacemaker?' he asks.

'You're dumb enough to take the job.'

'Is that right?'

'Yep. You were born dumb.'

'So were you. I remember.'

He looks at Freya as she licks the sugar off her fingers. She used to be a messy baby, when she ate, he remembers trying to feed her with a soft rubber spoon and how he used to open his own mouth every time he wanted her to eat. He sees glimpses of that baby in her face, even now.

He reaches across the table and gulps down Judy's half-eaten doughnut. He grins at his daughter. 'I win,' he says.

They walk back to the car. Judy's in a state. 'I can't believe it,' she starts, 'Phil's been trying to get through – he says the recording's rescheduled.'

'Meaning?' Guy says.

'We don't have to be there today. Tomorrow's better.'

Guy tries to hide his unexpected sense of relief. 'But it's still going ahead, isn't it?'

'Sure,' she says, sounding American, sounding like Phil actually, who always wanted to *be* American. 'So what do we do?'

For a moment Guy pictures his family in a new light, suddenly without anchor, in the middle of Alabama's nowhere, a family divided by various pulls – of him wanting to be with them, and Judy, her shoulders deflated, really wanting to be in front of a mic in Nashville. 'I'll look at the map,' he says.

He leans against the car, looking at their page on the *Hildebrand's Travel Atlas*, searching for clues in the cross-hatching of roads and rivers and mountains where they might be happy tonight. It's like a mysterious code he has to crack.

'I've got it,' he says, pointing out a state park in nearby Georgia. 'Amicalola. It has a waterfall. How about it?'

'Makes no odds to me,' Judy says, resigned.

'Freya?'

'Whatever.'

Guy finishes writing, missing his family and its petty squabbles. Usually the diary empties his mind, calms him, but not this time. He has the sense that his journey had once been quiet and personal but now has become something else. More complicated. Not of his choosing. You just can't keep a story pure for long – it's always heading for compromises and turns and you're the last person to see them coming.

Writing about those doughnuts has reminded Guy of an occasion from his childhood, where tensions had similarly lurked under a seemingly innocent moment.

'I want to show you something,' he remembers his father saying, as he led Guy out to the silver BMW. With a great flourish he had produced the keys to the car and opened up the boot, the holy of holies, the centre of his life. Guy was only six or seven, the boot seemed an impossibly big space, and it was full of dimpled aluminium flight cases and cardboard boxes with Japanese writing on them.

'Nikon, Canon, Pentax, Olympus,' his father said, like the words were names of gods, gesturing towards the boxes with a casual wave of his hand. 'Olympus OM–2. A marvel – you have there the first camera in the world with automatic exposure *through the lens*, both on the shutter and on the film's surface. Integrated auto-flash.' His father paused with salesman's pride. 'It's nice.' He eased open a small cardboard box with his fingernail. Inside, he pulled out a dark black lens. 'Smell that,' he said. 'What does it smell like?'

Guy sniffed the lens. 'Like a leather belt?'

His father took the lens and smelled it himself. 'Not quite. You know, to me it smells of glass and metal and oil – it's my favourite smell in the whole world.'

'Better than chocolate?'

'Much better. Women like chocolate. Men like glass and metal and oil.'

'I know.'

'I'm only joking,' his father said, with that legendary smile of his. 'Here's something special.'

At the back of the boot was a locked metal safe box. Guy had never known what was kept in there, but he saw on that day. Inside the box was a series of foam compartments, each holding a dark metal camera or lens. They looked like an assassin's rifle, broken down into bewildering parts. 'I'm going to teach you a foreign word today. *Hasselblad*. That, Guy, is a Hasselblad – it's worth more than the car.'

Guy stared on, mesmerized, totally in awe of his father's treasure. 'Is it yours?'

'I wish,' his father had said, laughing. With practised skill he assembled the camera, which didn't look like a camera at all – it looked like a part of an engine, square, with handles sticking out of its side, and smooth chrome edges. 'Hold it – and for Christ's sake don't drop it.'

Guy nervously held the camera, immediately thinking he really was going to drop it – it was so heavy. It tipped awkwardly in his hands, as if it wanted to get away from a child like him. 'Here,' his father said, nipping a button on the camera and like a jack-in-the-box the whole top of it flipped open as four sheets of metal sprang up on their edges.

'Wow,' Guy said, looking down on to a strange glass screen.

'Yes. Wow,' his father repeated, close in Guy's ear, while he turned the mysterious pattern of numbers on the lens. Gradually, parts of the garden lifted into focus on the grains of the glass, the garden, but magically reversed, with sunlight falling beautifully through the trees along the road. 'Through that,' his father said, 'is the best-looking world you'll ever see. Everything's like a movie on that screen. It's like there's a whole new type of sunshine in there. It's perfect. When the astronauts went to the moon, that's the camera they took with them, exactly like that model you've got in your hands.'

At that moment Guy had seen something move on the screen. It was his mother, coming out of the house. She seemed small and fragile and strangely lit. 'There's Mum,' he whispered, transfixed by the little image moving the wrong way round towards him. 'She looks like a film star,' he whispered. Then louder, Guy had called to his mother, 'You look like a film star, Mum!'

Guy's mother stopped on the path and pulled a strange expression, pretending to be famous, grinning in a way he'd never seen before, it almost looked like she was in pain.

'Dad – can I take a photo?' he asked, aware that his father had gone silent.

And his father had reached back for the camera. 'Have you any idea how expensive film for this is?' he said, looking humorous but sounding anything but.

Marta and Rhona visit the *Flood* in the late afternoon, just as Guy has been watching a tower of thunder clouds building up over the shore to the west, threatening a downpour.

'Looks like we'll get wet,' he says, helping them up the ladder. He feels both their hands in turn, Rhona's, quick and warm and twisting in his grip, and Marta's steadier and dryer, and holding him more securely.

They stand a little awkwardly on deck before Guy realizes it's his role to be host.

'Right, this way then,' he says, a little embarrassed, sliding open the door to the wheelhouse on its old brass rollers. The women walk in, impressed at the barge's sheer size, the heaviness of its bulwarks and fixtures, its unavoidable solidity.

'Like it,' Rhona says, climbing down the steep ladder from the wheelhouse into the saloon. When Guy follows them in there, he sees Rhona standing in the middle of the room on the red rug. Surrounded by the old dark timber planking she has the appearance of a dancer, in the studio, with Marta and Guy naturally forming the audience. He's shy in their company, after spending the day wondering whether he might have said too much at the meal last night, or said too little, or somehow disappointed them. It's easy to replay an evening, re-light it, re-cast it, till you get a new scene entirely.

Rhona's wearing a knitted black beret and is wearing a short grey kilt. She's on show here, it seems, and is at ease in the centre of a room and at the centre of attention – the barge's sheer size has excited her, whereas with Marta he can sense the boat's brought out a new politeness. Marta's in a nondescript jumper – but it's strange that both women are dressed in black and grey. When he went to their boat for dinner, they'd both chosen green.

'It has a lovely smell in here,' she says to him, quietly, 'of wood and oil.'

'What's with the maps of America?' Rhona asks, suddenly.

'Oh, they're nothing,' Guy says, 'just something I'm working on.'

Guy sees his working area of the saloon for what it is – covered with road maps of the southern states, travel guides and city plans and, at the same time that Rhona spies it, his open diary.

'What are you writing?'

'It's a – story, I guess.'

'Yeah?' Rhona closes the book, politely. 'Couldn't help noticing the word "doughnuts",' she says, cheekily.

'Stop playing your games, Ro,' Marta says, sharply.

'Ah – I'm teasing,' Rhona replies wearily, as Guy hears himself saying, 'It's nothing.'

'Well don't,' Marta says, keeping her harsh tone. But Rhona's already moved on, she's in an odd mood, pulling their attention to the piano at the end of the room.

'I had it bolted to the floor,' Guy explains, wondering if he's facing some kind of interview here. 'It was best there because of the weight.' He offers them drinks and Marta comes to stand by him at the galley, leaning against the worktop, looking shy and tired. Judy used to do that, he remembers, Judy loved to lean against a worktop and pour out her mind while Guy made tea or coffee around her. She wouldn't even move to give him space – it was one of their domestic routines – Judy on stage even in the kitchen, making him laugh with her deliberately cruel gossip about all she'd done that day while he smiled privately to himself. Secure. Half a couple. At least, that's how he looked back on it now.

'What did you do today?' he asks Marta.

'We had a walk, and a long discussion about the future.' She rolls her eyes, in mock exasperation. Her eyebrows remain raised, questioning. 'What's this?'

'A bird,' he says, 'have a look.' He lifts the flaps of the cardboard box so she can glimpse the greenfinch. 'I found it floating in the sea,' he says, 'about fifteen miles offshore.'

'It's alive?'

'Only just. Half-drowned really. But every time I try to let it go it looks more dead than before. I don't know what to do.'

'You must give it time.' She looks into the box thoughtfully. 'I'm glad you were there, to save it.'

'Me too,' he says. 'It's a greenfinch.'

'Mind if I play something?' Rhona asks, a little annoyed that she's being ignored.

'Go ahead,' he says, 'I didn't know you played.'

'I don't.'

Rhona begins to play the TV theme from *White Horses*. Marta smiles. 'I taught her this,' she says, a little reflectively. It's a sweet tune, and Rhona plays it with surprising concentration, her bottom lip slightly drawn in as she remembers the notes. Even the tiny breaks and halts – when she reaches and resets her hands seem to emphasize the poignancy of the song.

'I thought you'd forgotten this,' Marta whispers, more to herself than anyone, and Guy studies his two guests – a mother looking at a daughter, both of them remembering a tune they've learned together, a tune that no doubt bound them many years ago and still, years later, a thing they cherish. He remembers his own mother – how she used to sit on a stool on the far side of the room while he played the piano. How her expression was like a pleasant dream she was remembering. It used to annoy and bewilder him, but now he's thankful for her moments of reflection. He's discovered them for himself, and through it a new understanding of his mother. Women are less of a mystery to him than they once were.

If only he'd managed to tell his mother that. She had died when he had just turned twenty-one. She died the way she had lived, without fuss, from a bronchial pneumonia brought on after a Christmas cold. East Anglia's notorious winter dampness had claimed her, and even as Guy travelled up on the train from

London, having dropped out of music college in his second year, he had pictured himself in a dreary provincial funeral parlour, wrestling with the business of form-filling, wearing a suit he was uncomfortable in, every inch the man he must now become. But his mother's funeral had been surprising, because it had been full of people he'd never met. Women hugged him, chatty, able women who met life head-on, and in all of them he saw shades of his mother. Shades he'd never quite acknowledged in her. Of resourcefulness, of faith. After all that time he realized she'd been liked, and was popular. It was just one of the many surprises he'd had; like the discovery that his mother had once been an accomplished tennis player, that she'd sold paintings at local fairs, that she'd been a visitor to the sick for many years. Guy rapidly had to replace the image he'd had of her – the one where she accepted hardship with a kind of dreamy resignation – to this new expansive and generous woman. He hardly recognized her. And sometimes he thinks he learned more about her after she had died, than he ever did when she'd been alive.

'You'll make me cry, Rhona,' Marta says, listening to the piano.

He's never played the theme tune to *White Horses*, but he mentally pictures the notes now, as they step down the treble stave, while the bass rises up to catch them, a head coming to rest on a pillow, he lets the music affect him, he feels its romantic persuasion, and he begins to gaze at Rhona, at the tightness in her neck and shoulders but the casual way her legs are bent on the piano stool, one shin tucked round the leg of the stool with the foot angled to the side. Blackcherry nail varnish on his keys. Her back, a shallow S shape, the breaths she takes nervously, endearingly, when the little bar-shape of a rest appears in the tune.

'How am I doing, teacher?' Rhona says, slowly. It looks like the kilt's been customized to make it shorter.

'Fine, just fine,' he says, wanting to give it away, there and then, just how gorgeous she appears, how, in that brief moment, he wishes he was alone with her, that this glowing young woman had come by herself, playing piano, then leading him, in this subtle or not so subtle performance, towards the cabin behind the wheelhouse.

Just to think – three days ago he was swimming off into the North Sea, suspended on that perilously taut line of nothingness between water and sky. But here – here he's out of his depth. In this shallow estuary, a sea and a river pressed in by a soft land, now pressed further by this feeling of company. Companionship, attraction, it raises things he's lost, it makes him more lonely in fact, he wants them to leave and to leave himself.

But just then a new sound mixes in with the music. A clattering of rain falling on to the pitched roof-lights. They watch the storm from the wheelhouse. The leading edge of the clouds has brought a wild wind, sending the rain to hit like gravel against the windows and, across the water, the lead-grey estuary gets a pitted texture as if it's boiling from underneath. For a quarter of a mile on either side the shores are shadowed and immobile and a kind of steam seems to be rising from the banks.

All three of them look on in awe at the estuary as parts of it vanish in shadow and then begin to re-emerge, and at the darkness of the trees on shore, weathering it out. There's a flash of sheet lightning, just the once, illuminating the view. The impression it leaves is of a large flat expanse of water, the deck of his boat in the foreground, the masts of other dinghies, and the fringes of marsh, reed banks and trees, all, reduced momentarily to the colour of bone.

Guy looks at Marta and sees her in profile – a slight upturn to her nose, a lack of Englishness there, he thinks. She's looking at a fisherman sitting at the back of his cuddy, moored half-way across the water. Guy's noticed this fisherman before – he seems to have been in the same position since Guy arrived, dressed in his oilskins, staring at the tip of his rod.

When the storm subsides, they go out on deck, smelling the wet wood and the rising vegetable stink of the estuary and the smell of iron in the air. The rain drips from the scuppers in thin streams all round them. Across the water, people are emerging from where they've been sheltering, and Guy wonders briefly how he and the others must appear, at distance. He has the feeling that for the first time in five years, he is part of a little group that could loosely resemble a family. Marta, standing by his side, the place a wife would naturally fill, within his circle, tall, like him, a slow thoughtful way when she walks which is similar to his own. Maybe they feel it too, Guy wonders. He looks every inch a possible father, a possible husband, once again. Yet he seems curiously in the middle of these two women, their ages are ten-to-fifteen years either side of him, and someone on shore might have to consider this when putting together the family ties: is he a younger husband to one, or an older boyfriend to the other?

It's not what Guy had intended when he motored out of the Blackwater estuary four days ago, bumping his way between the sandbanks. He'd been heading out to sea, where waves might have risen to shake him, where you can really face the things you spent the rest of your life avoiding.

A muffled noise interrupts his train of thought. Next to him is Marta, sitting on the wet roof of the saloon, looking towards the *Lora*. He sees her in detail – the faint weave of crows-feet by the side of her eye, the lines of a laughter he hasn't really seen in her yet, and her lower eyelid, which is tender in shape, and wet. He realizes that small noise had come from her – it had been a cry, of sorts. There's a mark on her cheek where a tear has braved it out in this enormous view of wetness. To the side of her nose he can see the fleshless skin of worry. Her face looks like it may have thinned with age, her mouth was probably wider twenty years ago, had more expression, was better exercised. Maybe we have fewer expressions, each year, or just new ones that reveal less?

Another tear begins to form, filling the curve of her eye, and he wonders how he should console her. Should he put his arm round her? But she interrupts his thoughts.

'I'm all right,' she says, 'don't worry,' and she glances at him, raising her jaw in self-control. 'It's just that boat, that's all.'

'OK,' he says. It begins to rain again, softly.

She sits still for a while, her head angled as if she's seeing something dawn for the first time. It's such a powerfully preoccupied expression that he actually looks toward the *Lora* himself, as if there might be something he's missed.

'You should keep out of the rain,' he says, quietly. He thinks she might not have heard.

'Yes,' she says, 'I must keep out of the rain.' And with that she gets up and walks slowly to where her daughter is, at the front of the barge. He watches them. Sees Rhona touch her mother's cheek and then put an arm round her.

Guy sighs. He goes to the wheelhouse and sits in his pilot's chair. Captain of nothing, he thinks, sipping the iced tea he'd prepared, thinking the afternoon would stay sunny.

He closes his eyes and immediately pictures Freya. She's sitting on his lap in front of the piano, hitting the keys with both hands. She's three years old and the piano's in the corner of the living-room and there's a fire lit in the grate and there's a sound of rain in the garden outside. Dampness and smoke and cold keys and a hot fire, it's the essence of East Anglia, and Freya's whacking the piano so hard her fingers have a slapped look.

'Like this,' he says, holding her hands in his and pushing one finger at a time on to the keys. How her finger bends and slips on each note but he gets a tune, nonetheless, and Freya goes limp in his embrace while the tune emerges, his tune, but played by her. She angles her head, watching how it's made and he smells the woody smell of her hair and the warm cotton of her collar. Then she pulls her hands out of his and twists in his grip and looks at him, shyly, telling him off, mimicking a teacher as she says *I like your tune, Daddy, but my tune is better*, and the smile breaks out across her face – he sees the thin row of her milk teeth and the way the smile makes a single crease in her cheeks, and the tiny pink triangle of skin at the very corner of her eyes, he's sure he's never quite noticed that detail before.

Then Freya blurs as she whacks the piano keys once more,

knocking hell out of them and he laughs, really laughs. Judy comes into the room and she says *What a racket* and, although she's joking, Freya immediately calms down and the moment is gone. And then so is Judy, back to whatever chore she was doing, and Freya wants to watch the telly now. She climbs off his lap, saying *You need to practise more* to him, an echo of the moment they had, the moment that is now lost, and Guy looks out through the wintry window at his garden in the rain.

Guy becomes aware that Rhona has joined him in the wheelhouse. She's sitting on the padded bench by the sliding door.

'Mum's upset,' she says.

Guy turns to face her, wondering how long she's been watching him. She has her sketchbook open on her lap.

'She wanted me to say sorry to you,' she says. 'She'll be OK.'

Rhona sits next to him, and on impulse has a swig of his iced tea. She wipes her mouth with the back of her hand and sniffs loudly. She smells of damp hair and shampoo.

'She's very sensitive, isn't she,' he says.

'Very.'

He picks up her sketchbook. 'May I?'

'Go ahead.'

He looks through the pages. Suffolk churches and Martello towers, saltmarsh plants, staithe posts and wading birds, the occasional seal, drawn comically with big eyelashes, and more interesting, sketches of Marta, illuminating the boat-bound side to these two he knows so little about.

Then a final few sketches with a starkly different theme: Rhona naked, in frank self-portrait, in the saloon of the *Lora*. The first has her reclined, one arm trailing along the back of the bench seat while her left leg angles provocatively to one side. An indecent view, in detail, between her legs, and Guy feels challenged, not just by the open-eyed expression in the picture, but by Rhona there by his side, watching him watching her. He's aware of her mouth, drawn tight, close by.

'You did these today?' he says, calmly.

'This afternoon.'

'Very revealing,' he quips, looking at two more sketches, just of her breasts this time, darkly shaded around the nipples.

Rhona leans forward. 'I like those,' she says, cheekily. 'Do you?'

'You're quite a tease, aren't you?'

'My finest feature.'

He closes the book. 'I like the Suffolk churches,' he says, with a smile, not quite managing to shake the fantasy he'd had of her, while she played the piano, of taking her to his cabin.

Rhona reaches for a hipflask from her bag. 'You mind?' she says, in a slightly challenging tone. It's clearly a secret from her mother. She takes a long deep swig from it, and puts it back in her bag. 'Rum,' she says, popping a mint into her mouth to mask the smell.

'Are you married?' Rhona asks.

'Why d'you ask?'

She's being casual, but there's a hint of a natural flirtation too. 'Most men your age are hitched.'

'Just how old do you think I am?'

'You could look younger, if you cared more.'

'I'm separated,' he says, hating the word and its association with failure. Of damaged goods.

'It happens.'

'Yes. It does.'

'Any children?'

That's the question Guy dreads, in fact, has dreaded every time it's been asked in the last five years. Any children? Yes, but no. What can he say? How can he possibly answer this? That he has a father's heart, but that he isn't a father any more? Being a father is complicated, it can't be so easily undone. There's a reason there's no word for when you are a father no more.

'No. I don't,' he says, with a helpless sense of betrayal against Freya, whose presence he still feels hauntingly by his side. Rhona looks at him watchfully, she's picked up on something, but this time doesn't pursue it.

'I always pry,' she says, humorously, 'it's one of my things.'

'And what about you? Are you with anyone?'

She laughs. 'I'm with my mother, stupid.'

'You know what I mean.'

She smiles widely, revealing a clean white row of teeth. A beautiful barrier. She's very attractive. 'Thanks for the iced tea,' she says, before getting up and leaving the wheelhouse.

As she crosses the deck to her mother, Guy notices, ruefully, that he's checking her figure. The small grey kilt seems to reveal more than it hides, or at least promises that. She has smooth-skinned legs and thin ankles. Two half-moons of dryness on the backs of her heels – skin that would soften up over the winter. A lightness to her walk he's long since lost. Her back tapers gracefully. She probably knows it too. He sees the faint knuckles of her spine as she bends to climb the saloon roof, and between the shoulder blades, there's the smallest glisten of sweat. The hair is lovely, he thinks, the way those brown curls – coppery in this after-storm light – hang spring-like on her shoulders, making their own little patterns of shade across her back. Oh boy. He's decided: once that tide rises, he should go.

Position: Waiting for the tide.
At the desk. Late.

Georgia has surprised him, it's so wooded. As soon as the hills started it had reminded him of England, Northern England, with a smell of dampness and soil which felt comforting and old, like the smell of an overgrown garden. The air had cooled as they wound their way into the mountains, and the trees became thicker, taller, closer to the road, with rocky outcrops tumbling down to the verge.

After it went dark he couldn't see how high these hills were, couldn't see any of the landscape they drove through, in fact, just a winding road that seemed to go ever upwards, ever turning, a smooth surface as if newly poured through the mountains. And it had started to rain, heavily, making him put the wipers on full and take the corners more carefully. The rain thundered on the roof of the car and down the windscreen, washing away the super-sized Floridian insects that had met their death there, and the rain mixed with the busy rushing sound of passing streams and rivers, somewhere in the dark, in tight narrow valleys, running alongside the road.

Freya's sitting in the front while Judy sleeps in the back. She has the road map across her lap and, unlike her mother, she's able to pore over it without feeling sick. She gets that from him, and she also shares his love of maps – it's enough to know precisely where you are, if not exactly where you're going – he told her that. He can sense the woman she might be one day: supportive, friendly, never quite losing her humour. It's comforting to think she has such a good heart.

He's had *Rainy Night in Georgia* constantly going round in his head for the last few hours, he's sure he hasn't been humming it out loud, but somehow Freya's picked up on it too, she keeps half-singing it herself, while she looks at the map. Guy thinks of his favourite line from the song, about shaking the rain from your sweater, and remembers Judy singing that same line in Fergus's garage when the band were practising. Nice, really, that they were now in Georgia together, in the rain. Life had an elegance about it sometimes, of moments playing out you never thought would.

'This here's bear coun'ry,' Freya says, looking out into the nothingness beyond the road. 'We gonna make us a camp 'n' cook us some bean stew.' It's another of her characters – this one's based on Calamity Jane, Guy thinks, a gun-slinging force of nature. Freya saw the film last year.

Guy plays along. 'I ain't never seen me a bear.'

'Then you ain't half as man as me,' Freya says, then laughs at her own wit, and slightly hesitates as if working out just what she's said. 'I think,' she adds in her normal voice.

'Think we'll see one?' Guy asks.

'No,' she says. 'They don't really exist. They're just in fairy tales.' Then she adds, more seriously, 'Dad, thanks for everything.'

'That's kind of you to say.'

'Are you jealous of Mum?'

'Doing the recording?'

'Yeah.'

'I've had my share of it – over the years – she's sung to me more than anyone else. I've always loved her singing.'

'Right,' she says, wistfully enough for him to glance at her. It's a dangerous thing these women have: intuition. Sometimes they don't even know it themselves, can't access it when they want, but they look to the side and it's there, like a second watchful face. He wants to know more.

'How do you think she feels about it?' he asks, casually.

'She's scared, Dad.'

'Scared?' It's not a word he associates with Judy. 'In what way?'

'Of failing. I think it's made her really scared.'

'You're a good observer,' he says, encouragingly. 'Has she said this to you?'

'Sort of,' she says, with a hint of backtracking. She's trying not to be disloyal. 'I shouldn't – you know . . .' she says, trailing off.

'You're all right,' he says. 'You and I have always talked, haven't we, I mean as equals. It's important – and it's important for your mum to know we love her – we're there for her.'

It's too much. He's lost Freya, lost her openness and he feels stupid for pushing it. Rashly, he continues in the same vein, asking her how *she* is, *really*. He gets nothing, but is left with the sense that something's wrong – something's wrong with his family – the invisible threads that hold it in one piece.

The road keeps on curving upwards. Surely a crest must be reached, a watershed between those streams that end up in the Atlantic, and those going the other way, to the far off flatness of the Gulf of Mexico. All this rain falling, dividing at some point for very long and different journeys back to the ocean, the simplicity is beautiful.

They nearly pass the sign for the Amicalola Falls state park. It appears, like in a film, caught in the headlamps and streaked with rain, and then vanishes as the car turns. Guy slows and steers into the park, passing grimly wet signs for camping and picnic areas, forks and bends in the road leading to parts of the park he must avoid. It's quite complicated, and he doesn't want to make a mistake so late at night. They keep on driving higher, till they suddenly see the long lights of a building, far away through the night. It's appeared like an ocean liner, wrecked on the crest of a hill, with tall windows and rows of corridors in a landscape which is otherwise completely without light.

The building keeps disappearing into black empty patches of the night as the hills get in the way, then abruptly, without warning, they are turning into a manicured car park. The slowing of the car wakes Judy, instinctively.

'Heh. We here?' she says.

'Think so,' Guy replies. 'Freya's been brilliant with the map.'

'Yeah?' she says, unimpressed. She lifts herself on to one elbow to look through the window. 'Christ! Looks like the Overlook Hotel!'

It does. The hotel is vast, built of wood and glass in a lodge style, with an airy atrium and an empty reception desk. They take their bags in and stand there, feeling a little small and washed up by the weather and the lateness of the night. Across the lobby are collections of comfy chairs and suede sofas, and there's a drone of a floor polisher coming from a long way off.

Judy takes it upon herself to find some staff somewhere, and she does it with remarkable efficiency – every inch the bank manager's daughter – shepherding a tall greying man to the reception and making him find a room for them. He looks at them through glasses half-way down his nose, and smiles gently, apologizing for the dreadful weather. It doesn't bother Guy. He loved the smell of the mountain air as he crossed the car park, full of the scent of pin oak and hickory. They make air fresheners of this kind of thing.

His excitement continues as they walk the long corridors to their room, through a hotel which seems entirely devoid of life. No sound of TVs behind the doors, no sound, in fact, of anything. Their room is high up, and through the huge plate-glass window of their bedroom there is nothing but an emptiness, a black nothing across the hills and forest that he knows is outside.

A few minutes later, miraculously, there's a polite knock on the door, and a tray of burgers is brought in. Well done, Judy, you pulled that out of the hat.

They sit round a low coffee table and scoff the food in a noisy silence, punctuated by their too rapid swallowing and licking of fingers. Their elbows jostle one another for the pile of communal fries on a plate in the centre. Freya's very capable of matching him, fry for fry, that's a recent development. It's family at its most vulgar and without inhibition – the kind of thing he's watched on a natural history programme, like those miserable hyenas, dragging and tearing at some poor rotten thing, their heads emerging wild-eyed with excitement. He dips the bun in the sauce, eats the wet garnish, licks the salt and animal grease from his fingers. Nothing like being hungry, he thinks, nothing like it at all – eating late and knowing you deserve it, it's about the best thing life can deliver.

They go to sleep exhausted – he's much more settled than he had been at the motel, the night before. This truly feels like an arrival and, outside, a sense that there is something huge and empty and full of wonder, the state park, Georgia, America, a journey, it's tremendous.

As he falls asleep, he thinks of the black bears out there, hundreds of them probably, crouching and shuffling in the forest, looking at the lights of the hotel on the crest above them, their fur as wet as carwash rollers. Unlucky bastards.

He wakes in the morning to see Freya standing at the bedroom window, the curtain pulled to one side. The room is shadowy, but a bright clean light washes in from behind her, it feels like a flood of cold white water pouring into the still pond which has been their sleep. Freya notices him stirring, or had been waiting for him, because she whispers, 'Come on, Dad, come and look.' It's good that she wants him rather than her mother; even after all these years he seeks the affirmation that he has a special connection with her.

'You won't believe it,' she whispers.

At the window he's amazed to see a giant white void of cloud, moving fast, drifting in sharp coiling fogs around the hotel. Right below them a patch of grey grass leads out to bushes, but beyond that, where there should be one of the most impressive views of Georgia's northern mountains, the miles of ridge and forest, the carpet of verdant green, there is nothing. It's like they're in the sky, rising through the clouds.

'Wow,' he says.

'I've been up a whole hour,' Freya says, proudly. 'Sometimes you get these glimpses of a mountain up there,' she points, 'and over there,' already an expert guide, it seems. 'It's amazing.'

It's mountain light, he thinks, blinding and white and full of ozone – as if the light they're used to, back in England, has been stained by damp soil.

While they look, a brief fringe of trees along a ridge begins to emerge, impossibly high up. Distantly the trees look like a rim of eyelashes, the cloud swirling and resealing in such a way that the ridge disappears in a downward motion, the curve of an eyelid closing.

'Shame we can't see them properly,' she says.

'Yeah. Although sometimes imagining views can be better.'

He and Freya go down to breakfast before Judy. The restaurant's a large wooden room off the reception, again with plate-glass windows looking out into the mist and fog. An elderly waitress moves immediately toward them, a bowl of black coffee held in her hand like a bowling ball. 'Y'all have a good night?' she says, sweetly, and follows it up with a 'hmm, ah-ha' before they've answered. 'Y'all hungry?' she says, ''cause we can do something about that, ah-ha,' and begins to move off.

Freya thinks that's funny, and begins to imitate her the second the waitress is gone. Guy's glad Freya's so buoyant this morning. More and more his mood seems to be dictated by the enjoyment the others are having. That's family, he thinks, as he sees Judy walking dreamily towards them, miles away, getting closer.

He eats a huge breakfast of grits and biscuits, salted sausage, ham, cheese and juice. He has several cups of black coffee, enjoying making a spectacle of himself in front of his girls, neither of whom can truly compete with his appetite. Freya tries, repeatedly going off to the breakfast counter in that little bouncy clumsy walk of hers, a couple of hair bands tied round her wrist, as always, but she comes back with the things Guy's not interested in – the figs, yoghurts and grapes. He stretches to prunes, but here, faced with serving bells full of meat, biscuits and gravy, he's got bigger fish to fry.

Judy sits curved into her chair, leaning on one arm, sipping her black coffee. She's never been one for breakfast. To her, breakfast is black, bitter and liquid, while all the others make fools of themselves, and she's looking disapprovingly at Freya, stuffing her face, filling out her clothes, being on the cusp of the largeness her body might be capable of.

Guy's missing this. He can pack so much food away he likes to leave the table aching. He loves this feeling that things are going well, that he's had a good night's sleep, that he's reinvigorated and alive. This is what he's travelling for, being the man he can never really afford to be back at home, free of routines, let off the leash with his appetite. A walk, a swim, reading a book, lying on the bed, all is permissible.

'Thanks for doing all that driving,' Judy says. 'I was a total wash-out.'

'I loved it. Didn't we, Freya?'

The waitress fills Judy's cup again – Judy's her best customer.

'You two go and see the waterfall,' Judy says, 'I'm not bothered.'

'But that's crazy,' Guy begins, 'it's a couple of minutes walk from the hotel, to the top of the thing. I mean, that's why we came here.' He's not even convincing himself, let alone her. It's raining outside.

'Really,' she says, 'I'm not interested.'

She drinks her coffee and gives him an amused, quick look. She's waking up, and he suspects she's woken up with all the answers, all the right sense of knowing what to do, and he's just blundering his way forward, stuffing himself with cheap food, getting excited, being ridiculous. She's just a very cool person, after all, too composed and clever for the likes of him, and she knows it.

'Besides, I need to do some voice practice. I'll just go to the room and do it there.'

And make some calls, he thinks, feel a bit glamorous, rather than be with this family holiday with its dumb trips to waterfalls.

'Y'all finished?' the elderly waitress says, her face lined and kind and made up like a young woman, her job done, another family fed and filled.

When it comes down to it, even Freya doesn't bother to come to the waterfall. She decides to read in one of the comfy suede couches they'd seen in the reception, while Guy, committed to going outside, suspecting he too doesn't really want to see the damn waterfall, trudges down a cement path, getting soaked within the first couple of minutes, till he reaches a small insignificant stream running through the trees. The air's still dense with mist, and the rain is spitting out of it in fast stinging needle points, and everywhere there's an overwhelming rushing sound of water, and he realizes it's coming from the stream itself, as it tips casually over the wide lip of a flat rock, beginning its explosive transformation into the highest waterfall this side of the Mississippi. A small brown stream, suddenly so white, full of action and noise, crashing on the rocks as it falls, rising in veils of steam and mist, and the others, they're all missing it. Freya's on the comfy sofa with a magazine open on her lap, and Judy's upstairs making phone calls. They might as well be a thousand miles away – while he's out here on a slippery path of rocks, getting soaked, and he climbs down while the forest rises around on the steep cliffs like something magical and primeval, covered in vines and smelling so fresh and earthy, and it's so overwhelmingly *wet*, so overwhelmingly *alive*, all these black bears out here, somewhere, driven mad by the sound of water constantly rushing through the hills, watching him now from behind the trunks, and he feels very little, very little indeed.

Position: Anchorage in Deben estuary.
About midnight.

After all that writing, Guy still can't sleep. Instead he sits in the wheelhouse, with the lights off, looking out across the estuary. Although it's late, a curious glow seems to be shining off the water, as if it's made of a strangely metalled substance.

He sees something move on the *Falls of Lora*, and realizes someone is standing on deck. It's Rhona, standing alone, and even at this distance he can see she's very drunk. She's guiding herself across the top of the cabin, reaching for the cables and ties like she's climbing through some impenetrable thicket. Half-turning, swinging her way forward, hampered by the blanket she's wrapped herself up in and a bottle in one hand, until she's standing at the bow. Guy smiles. She's a troubled one, he thinks. All that beauty and dangerous glances, and still she's drinking herself through the nights.

He observes her, making out her slender figure beneath the blanket, as she takes a long emptying drink from the bottle. She looks down into the water and reaches for a cable behind her and as the boat tips gently with her weight he sees her drop the bottle off the side. It disappears without a splash, and as he watches her, standing so ghostly still above it, she seems to shrink, sliding strangely through her own blanket and suddenly vanishing too, into the water.

Guy can't believe what he's just seen, can't believe what is happening, it's too surreal, and even while he's flinging open the door of the wheelhouse he's already anticipating the mad leap he will make off the side of his boat, already experiencing that strange feeling of weightlessness followed by the sudden overwhelming flood of cold black water.

He runs the length of the boat and throws himself, barefoot, into the estuary. When he hits the water he is plunged below it and he feels one foot go into the soft silky mud before he surfaces, disorientated, smelling the salt and the mud and seeing the *Falls of Lora* from a different angle, further away than it had appeared in the wheelhouse. He feels the drag of his clothes as he swims as fast as he can, splashing too much and trying to call out and it seems to take an age for him to reach the other boat and he still hasn't seen Rhona.

He dives, and surfaces, and dives again and briefly, he feels something that isn't water. A dress, a part of a dress, he tugs it and reaches further and grabs something else, an arm or leg and he pulls her towards him – both of them breaking the surface now and she coughs loudly in his face and half chokes and she clings to his shoulder as he tries to bring her along the side of the yacht.

As they reach the stern he realizes he's able to stand on the riverbed, on some bank of stones down there, and as he looks up he sees Marta above him, drenched to the waist where she's been groping for them in the darkness. She's shouting and crying and trying to reach out to Rhona where, together, they can haul her up on to the step near the transom.

When at last they have her safe on the boat, Rhona starts to giggle and cough some more and she tries to push them both away. It's the first time she's spoken. 'I fell,' she says, 'I just fell off this stupid boat.'

And Marta laughs quickly, nervously, brushing her daughter's hair to one side and asking, 'Did you? Did you fall?' over and over again and she looks at Guy, searchingly, and in the look she gives him she is full of questions.

'She fell,' he manages to say. 'I was sitting in the wheelhouse – I saw her. I think she slipped.'

And Marta nods, wanting to believe it, totally, and wanting to show how much she has to thank Guy for.

Position: Same, anchorage in Deben
estuary. 9:30am

He wakes in the morning, suddenly, filled with the images of last night. How he'd jumped into the estuary, the dreamlike motion of his swimming stroke that didn't seem to bring him closer to their boat, the feel of Rhona's dress, underwater, and the softness of her leg when he managed to touch her. How, before she went in, she had stood at the bow, so much like a ghost, staring down into the water.

She had fallen. She had slipped. Had she? He can't be sure. Marta said she must have slipped. It has to be that way, it's something they need to believe. But he remembers the look that Marta gave him. The look was unequivocal. Regardless of what had actually happened: he had saved her.

He tries to sleep more, but it's no use. He's too full of a sense of worry, of a deep-rooted problem without shape or answer. It's risen during the night like a tide.

When he goes to the saloon he sees his work area – his desk covered in maps and city guides of America – of street plans pinned above it and, seeing it now in the same way as Marta and Rhona must have done when they came to visit, he sees the library madness of an obsessed man. On notepaper he writes various words, hoping to see some hidden clue where this new anxiety is coming from. He writes 'Judy', 'Freya', 'the *Flood*'. Familiar words with familiar shapes so overlaid with meaning they appear, in this instant, impenetrable. The J of Judy, still an optimistic letter to him, despite all that's passed. The y of Freya, still looping at speed below the line, still giddy – Freya's y, the one she could write haltingly, had always been capitalized, two

121

strikes of the pen – she'd never joined her letters up. He tries some other words: 'estuary', a mystery to him really, neither a likeable nor unlikeable word, curiously lacking flow. Then he tries something: 'Marta' and 'Rhona'. It feels strange. Marta's name is oddly comforting, he likes it, whereas Rhona's name seems full of unease. And then a final word, written small on the corner of the pad, but full of questions for him: 'Nashville'.

His diary is beginning to consume him, he knows that. It's an addiction, a hit he needs every day, but it makes him feel balanced – it makes him feel emancipated. For a time. And this morning, more than most, he needs it.

He reads the relevant pages of a city guide to Nashville, looks at a street plan, studying the grey intersections of roads and buildings, searching for his place.

Guy finds himself sitting in an easy chair surrounded by several other easy chairs, all of them empty. The one he's chosen is fabric, cream, and has a swing to it as well as a tilt which he's not keen on. Not a thing out of place in here, he thinks, looking around. A low glass table with music magazines on it in a fanned-out design, a drinks bar in the corner, all of the bottles arranged in height order, a wall covered with pressed records, gold and platinum, in silver aluminium frames. Could be any-where in the world, he thinks, it has the air of international well-oiled business, except there are also a row of hand-signed Stetsons on the wall, and a couple of guitars with plaques below them, one, a beautiful Gibson Dove, with the famous white bird inlaid across a deep red pick guard. Nashville, finally, this is like no other place in the world.

He's been sitting in this room for about an hour. He has a book to read, he has a drink to drink, but still the time is passing slowly. Freya's been smart, he thinks, she's gone with one of the PAs for a bit of sightseeing and shopping, is probably right now looking at CD racks as her mother likes to do. But not Guy. He decided to stick it out at the studio, claiming tiredness, but really it's to do with not wanting to miss anything. If there *is* anything, then he won't be missing it.

As a result, he's in this glorified waiting lounge, thick with comfort, feeling uncomfortable, left alone. Through an open doorway he can see a wide corridor leading to other parts of the complex. Studio A and Studio B, written above a drawing of a hand pointing that way. Occasionally a man walks by the door – he's tall with dark hair, dressed in pale jeans and a flowery shirt. He wears cowboy boots, and the boots look out of place on the thick pile carpet. He thinks the man's name is Bradley, but he can't remember. He was introduced, and immediately forgot.

Guy goes to the bar and pours another drink, downs half of it, then walks through to the control room for Studio C. A very fat man is sitting by the panel – both he and his mixing desk look way too big for the room. The man Bradley is in there too, his feet up on a low table, eating some sort of roll. He nods and smiles at Guy, and carries on eating. Guy finds his own stool near the back of the room, away from the desk and its smell of warm electricity.

Through the glass he sees Judy, his Judy, standing off-centre in the live room. Wires lead to her, to her mic and to her headphones, and briefly Guy thinks he's about to witness some kind of operation, that she's being plugged in and kept alive in that little sterile cell so they can extract her life. It's not so far from the truth. She has her hair tied back and is sipping a hot black coffee. A small twist to her back, he sees her slender arm and the lightness of touch with which she holds the microphone stand. There's a man in there too, with silver hair tied back in a ponytail, talking her through something – but it's entirely silent through the glass. Judy's nodding and doing that shy smile from the side of her mouth which is giving the man a sense of assurance. Seeing that smile, Guy feels a little star-struck by her, more so because she's so clearly at ease. His wife, under such scrutiny and glare and she's entirely relaxed – she gets much more wound up by the smallest things Guy does or doesn't do. It doesn't seem fair.

Bradley says a soft *heh* to the engineer at the mixing desk – who turns, stiffly, and smiles at Guy. 'Right, mister, she's doing real good,' he says, kindly and automatically, his mouth drawn wide. He's sweating, and has a handkerchief in his hand which he keeps dabbing at his temple. It's not that hot in there.

For Guy's sake the engineer brings up a slide and Judy's voice springs into the room on four speakers. '. . . Feel it lower on the first then wait for the cue, yes?' she says, her words given un-natural volume and intimacy, like a hot bedtime whisper, so loud in your ear, but said from another room. Her voice seems owned by someone else, added to, enriched, taken apart by this massive calm machine into its mysterous threads before being wound back together. This machine full of wire might break the code that makes her voice so special, present the series of lights and levels which gives away its secret. Guy would love to find out just what that is. Even after all these years, he'd like to sit at the desk and remove parts of her sound, bit by bit, until he discovered the qualities that affect him most.

That's when he sees Phil, sitting the wrong way round on a chair at the back of the live room, his guitar by his feet. He's resting his chin on his arms and is grinning wolfishly at Judy, listening to the silver-haired man and smiling like an imbecile. Phil, whom Guy's known since he joined the band, since the time he was a market town music shop assistant, and a prat. He used to sit at the back of that shop playing the guitar, bending the notes, sweep picking the chords into arpeggios to show off. Fond of a loud shirt and a waistcoat, too. For ten years he's been gazing at Judy, laughing slyly and cracking jokes and being in love with her. Dickweed, Guy mouths to himself, enjoying the childish satisfaction it gives.

Of course, Phil has seen Guy come in, he has an eye for such things, and he performs an elaborate waving gesture which makes everyone look up and see who Phil's seen, including Judy. Guy lifts his hand to say hi and sees a brief mix of expressions flit across her face, a touch of annoyance maybe, overridden with a warm professional smile.

'Hi, love,' she says, amplified to the room.

'OK,' the silver-haired man says, 'we're cool and I think it's time we tried that, are you good?'

He comes out of the live room and Phil comes too, beating him to the door and holding it open in a fussy way. They come into the control room, and Guy realizes he must have taken Phil's stool. Hard luck, he thinks, you'll just have to find your own space.

'Isn't it great!' Phil says, all excited, his eyes have a thin gleaming expression of delight and awe. 'Who'd have thought we'd be here one day, huh?' He's like a puppy, all bouncy, probably couldn't sit down even if Guy hadn't taken his stool. He's all angles and energy, in a new shirt too, and can't take his eyes off Judy through the glass. Careful, Guy thinks, times like this you'll give it all away, Phil.

The equipment plus the four men makes the room seem very small indeed. The producer and engineer share the desk, used to their own proximity, but Guy feels wedged in, at the back. At least Phil's in a worse position, forced to stand by a door which is constantly being used. Guy takes a glance and sees Phil has hitched his thumbs through the belt loops of his jeans, country style. He's bought a pair of cowboy boots, and Guy realizes the others in the room probably don't know what he knows – that Phil has an artificial leg below the right knee. If they had known that, he would have been offered a seat. No. Phil's covered all that up, and Guy wonders about how he got that cowboy boot on. Did he have to ease that weird plastic foot with its rigid toes into the leather? Did he put a sock on first?

The track begins and Judy starts to nod the rhythm. Entering the song, Guy thinks, such a professional. Here comes the lead guitar, picking an interesting melody, not quite settling, then lurching forward, promising something, then a fiddle, faster and scratchy, messing the air like a wind – that's great – and suddenly the sound is sucked out of the air as the engineer pulls a slide and he sees Judy form the note and there it is, split into forty-eight channels, then rebound, intensively, and pushed through the speakers to fill the room. He hears Judy beside him, behind him, and from both sides of the desk, everywhere, it seems, but from Judy herself.

A few bars later she stops singing – another voice is now on the track, the one Judy's doing the backing vocals for. It replays quietly and assuredly. Judy listens, her head bowed respectfully, her eyes firmly closed. She takes her cue and rejoins, alongside the other voice this time, giving the voice a hand, for a moment leading it, then backing away, giving a texture that's needed. Guy's exited, for a second he knows it's working, the harmony is perfect, but then something begins to emerge which doesn't quite fit, an edge to the voices defines and juts forward, rubbing the way it shouldn't – the tiniest of discords, but he knows it's there.

'Yeah,' Phil says, enthusiastically, the moment they stop recording.

The silver-haired man leans forward and speaks through his own mic to Judy: 'I really love it, I really do. We'll just need to try that once more, OK?'

Nashville, Guy says out loud to his empty boat, leaning back from his diary.

It's been a while since he wrote about Phil – having to write about him now is upsetting. He tries to cheer himself up by thinking about that artificial leg. The real Phil has both legs in place, but the one in the diary, the one Guy imagines, was given a ridiculous accident a couple of years back – the fool got his shin snagged in a shopping trolley, of all things, and after an almost *impossible* secondary infection of the wound, had had to have the lower part of his right leg removed. Very painful it was.

Though it had been immensely satisfying to cause that amount of discomfort and disability, Guy suspects the stunt he pulled has backfired. If anything, Phil has been made more charismatic because of that false limb. The way he hops about on it, with an air of injured pride which is sickening – he's turned it to his advantage, with rattish tenacity.

Suspecting all now, he's anxious to get straight back to America. What's going on now in Nashville? Is Freya trying on a Stetson, insecure as to how she looks in a hat when she sees her reflection? Is Judy taking a trip to a music store, flicking through the racks of CDs with that amazing speed of hers, like she's counting library cards?

It's no surprise to Guy that he hears someone tapping against the wheelhouse glass, or that when he looks up the ladder from the saloon he sees that it's Rhona. But although he's been expecting her all day, having her here in the boat, suddenly, unannounced, catches him off guard. After last night, he doesn't know how she'll be. She stands briefly at the top of the steps, then begins to climb down, her hand holding the rail carefully, not looking at him once.

'You writing your story?' she says, quietly.

'Not really.'

'You look busy. It looks busy in here. Mind if I sit?' she says, sitting down on one of the chairs, perching slightly, as if undecided. She tucks one foot behind the other and looks down, smiling. 'You sure I'm not disturbing you?'

'How are you?' he asks, calmly.

'Not so good,' she replies, still looking at her shoe. 'Stupid, I guess.'

'There's no need to say that.'

'No?' she says. She looks directly at him. She has a shadowed look of sleeplessness below her eyes, and her mouth seems thinner, as if drawn tight by choosing what to say. Perhaps she's had to talk about what happened all day. 'I think I swallowed a lot of the river last night.'

'Me too,' he replies.

'I guess I should thank you,' she says, simply. 'It's why I'm here.'

She looks at him, questioningly. 'But you didn't need to throw yourself in the water like that, you know,' she says, sounding braver, more offhand. 'I wasn't in trouble.'

'I didn't know.'

'Yeah. Suppose not.' Impulsively, she stands, as if sitting down made her uncomfortable. 'How come you saw me fall in?'

'I was up late – I was in the wheelhouse.'

'Watching me?'

He remembers how she had stood at the bow of the boat, wrapped in that blanket, looking so beautiful. 'There wasn't much else to look at.'

'I was drunk.'

'Yeah. You were.'

'You saw me slip?'

'Rhona,' he says, 'the first time I saw you, in that pool behind the pub, why did you do that thing in the water?'

'What thing?'

'Floating, with your head under. Pretending to be drowned – why did you do that?'

She shrugs dismissively, as if not remembering, but her posture looks guarded. 'I'm not some kind of head-case, if that's what you're saying.'

'No. I think I'm saying the opposite.'

She smiles at him, regaining her composure. 'I don't get you,' she says.

'So why did you do it?'

'Probably because you were watching. I don't know. Give you something to look at. Men like a bit of that, don't they?'

'Yes. They do, but you're still not answering.'

She shakes her head and walks over to the piano, breaking the moment. You only get so far with her, Guy thinks. She's young. Being honest probably still feels too revealing.

He remembers how his hand had touched her in the cold river water last night. How she'd instinctively put her arms round him, the act of someone who knows she's being saved.

Rhona plays the first few notes of the theme from *White Horses*, like she did yesterday. But the comparison she creates, between yesterday's confidant, coquettish visit, and today's more cagey one, makes her stop.

'I should go,' she says. 'I just wanted to say thanks.'

'Is your mother OK?'

'She's sleeping. Finally. God, she's been watching me like a hawk.'

'Only because she cares.'

'I know. But she's suffocating.'

He looks at Rhona, at this moment without any strength in her posture, as if she can't hold herself upright, a lack of conviction in anything she says. All those seductive looks, that easy sexiness – it's all gone.

'Thanks for coming over,' he says. 'But be with your mother today. She needs you. What she saw last night – it's something a parent shouldn't have to go through.'

Rhona frowns, about to react to his lecturing tone – before she stops herself. She realizes he's saying something from the heart here, and it's something she doesn't know about. She nods in acknowledgement, and comes to put her arms round him.

'You have an injured air about you, Guy,' she says.

'Do I?'

'Yeah. Same as Mum.'

They stand together, in an embrace which surprises both of them, and he feels one of her arms under his shoulder blades and the other one low down on his back, bringing him in towards her. He feels her adjusting herself, making herself comfortable, turning her face into his chest, like a child would do. He smells her hair and he wonders. He wonders about all the embraces he's missed, over the years. All the comfort he has to offer, going nowhere.

When she pulls away from him he sees her eyes are a little wet and her face seems younger, more vulnerable and uncomposed than he's seen it before. She kisses his cheek and leaves him, wordlessly, calmly, without looking back.

They're walking into downtown Nashville, on a wet pavement that reflects the neon from the bars they're passing. Judy's in a suede jacket and a skirt he hasn't seen before, a pale buff cotton one with patterning up the sides. She's shining, Guy thinks, she's absolutely loving this, with her hair dark and glossy and hurling the neon back off it in little bright curls of light. The air's cool, and he imagines Judy's skin is warm, glowing, full with life. Which isn't how he feels. He feels marginal.

Phil's with them. It's Phil, Judy, Freya and Guy, and Phil's walking a tiny bit faster than the rest of them. Guy's aware of Phil's pace like it's a little nag – a little tug among the group and he's not liking it. Judy's sailing on, oblivious, and Freya's being a bit dreamy. The things we have to keep an eye on, Guy thinks, it never stops.

'Heh, Guy?' Phil says, sounding a little American. 'It's going to take a while setting up – you could go take a walk or have a drink, I mean, it's not worth hanging around.' Guy gives Phil a look, tries to steady him with an expression which says I'm the calm one here, I'm the adult, but Phil's not interested. Phil's Tennessee spending spree has continued. Sometime in the afternoon he's bought himself a sunburst Nashville B-bender Tele – it must have cost the earth.

Guy resents being told what to do by Phil, but he knows the man's probably right. Freya will only get bored while they set up the stage.

'I'll take Freya off,' he says, making it his decision. Judy nods, and immediately gives Guy a quick kiss. 'There's music all along this row,' she says, as if she's lived here for years. Guy doesn't pick her up on it. He's made a pact with himself to be tolerant tonight.

Phil and Judy walk up the road to go into the club, while Guy leads Freya the other way, feeling himself cast in an uncle's role. Come on, he thinks to himself, you're projecting this. Keep a lid on it.

Soon he's enjoying being alone with Freya. She's had a good day – she's already been round these streets – and is pointing out the shops and clubs she was shown earlier. Record stores, boot and hat outlets, it's been an eye-opener for her. They peer into a shop and see hundreds of pale Stetsons hung along a wall – it looks not too dissimilar to a hunter's trophy wall, he imagines all those cowboys shot in the fields and their hats hung for display, and he thinks I'm here, I'm really here in Nashville. It's amazing.

At the river they sit alone, watching its swift black ink flowing in strong muscular sinews. It looks unearthly and wild and silent in the dark.

'How did you and Mum meet?' she asks.

He smiles. 'In a record shop. It's very corny. We both wanted the same CDs.'

'Really?'

'Well, they were half-price.'

She smiles to herself. 'Still, it's sweet.'

'Yeah. It was.'

Guy's often thought of that as one of the more perfect moments of his life. He doesn't like to talk about it – he likes to keep it to himself. It *had* been romantic.

'Does Phil have a crush on Mum?' Freya asks, carefully picking her words, as she stares over the water. Guy feels a knot of alarm, inside, like he might only partially understand his situation. He decides to be straight with Freya. Her perceptiveness deserves it.

'He's always fancied your mother, even before she was your mother.'

'Don't you mind?'

That amuses him. 'Yes, of course I mind,' he starts, wondering whether that's the truth. 'Judy has a presence about her – she attracts people – I've always known that. I mean I feel it, so why shouldn't I know it? Every now and then someone has a crush on her, but that's all it is, it happens. He's a popinjay.'

'What's that?'

'A special kind of fool.'

'But doesn't Phil have other girlfriends?' Freya asks, getting a little upset. Children are so moral.

'Yes. But he really admires your mother, I think that's the difference.' He thinks of some of the girls he's seen hanging on Phil's arm over the years. They're a ragtag bunch, and they didn't last.

'But, Dad, he only *has one* leg!' Freya blurts out.

'Yep, I've noticed.'

Freya stares at the water. Her profile looks sad. Her lips stick forward in a relaxed, unaware fashion, and they naturally look too full and upset.

'Heh,' he says softly, thinking she might be getting lost in an adult world which is refusing to make sense. He's a little lost himself. She has a lifetime of her own rejections, attractions and disappointments ahead of her.

'You know what we're going to do when we get to Texas? We're going to go to a rodeo,' he says.

She brightens at that, but says nothing.

'That's something to look forward to,' he says.

'I don't know.'

'You don't know what?'

'Mum won't like it.'

'Yes she will,' Guy says, but also thinking Freya's probably right, imagining Judy gazing at the rodeo through the smoked barrier of her sunglasses.

He puts his arm round Freya and strokes the smooth skin of her upper arm. All that arm's done, he thinks, he remembers seeing that same right shoulder in the second prenatal scan, ten years earlier, grey and illuminated, on a monitor. All that arm will do, he had thought at the time, a first secret glimpse of a body, a potential, a future. It had made him cry at the time, at the sheer sense of newness and unknowability – his sense of being a creator and guardian of such a small life in all its beginnings. Judy had hugged him, but not cried herself. She hardly ever cried, in fact, when he thought about it.

'Let's go,' he says.

Judy stands centre-stage, in the heart of the song, hardly moving. A middle to this sound which is pure and full, like a well. Still waters run deep, he thinks, marvelling at her posture, at her balance on stage, neither leaning in to the space before her, nor afraid of it. She is held there, in a kind tension between audience and band, a soft light falling on her, making her glow. The spot changes colour every eight bars or so, from orange to blue to crimson. She has a scarf in her hair as a headband, a bright red one he's never seen before. It exposes more of her face than he's used to seeing, giving her an innocent, slightly naïve look. It's nice.

The song has such a quiet opening, he's always liked how it asserted its own calmness, whatever the occasion. It's a brave song too; one which can leave the voice above the music, adrift for a cruel second or two, before surrounding it once more. The guitar is Judy's closet ally here. Of all the instruments it's the only one which seems likely to follow her, the one most reluctant to leave her stranded. He hates to admit it, but Phil plays his new instrument well. His notes follow hers, a loving echo of her melody, occasionally they push forward, taking a lead, suggesting a new path. Phil watches her, then glances at his fingering on the fret board he adores. He appears honest in this light, a buffoon in so many others, but here on stage he is at last part of something he truly believes in.

Judy looks at the new guitar, anticipating the chord changes on it. Guy reluctantly notices how his wife and Phil understand each other, as they explore the breaks – the tiny rhythmical stresses that stretch between them. That's where the music lies all right, that's where heart and soul come from, and Guy knows it, knows that this is a language which has developed between them over ten years.

For a second Judy looks up from the mic and gazes at Guy. He sees a friendly look in her eyes, a recognition, but beyond that a confusion, as if she's slightly intoxicated. It makes him feel kind towards her. It's a courageous thing she's doing, laying out her soul up there, so far from home, and he wants to offer his support. But her eyes close as she rises up through the melody, and he feels shut out, again. It's like she's coming in and out of consciousness – little moments of intimacy and familiarity surrounded by a situation which doesn't belong to either of them. It was like that at Freya's birth. He remembers holding Judy as the waves of her labour hit, the look in her eyes as something dark and impenetrable hardened within her, in expectation, in preparation, holding her while the pain struck, making her wince, then draining away and she was returning, bewildered but returning, looking into his eyes again. That small glimpse of Judy, disorientated, he's never quite managed to forget that experience in all its vividness, and as a result he's a little haunted by it, as if he's been allowed to see a truth he shouldn't have witnessed. She had seemed mysterious and full of an inner sense of strength and survival which had left him frightened, and a little bit in awe, always. Frightened even now, because he knows that's in her, below the surface, an immeasurable well.

When she's on stage he sees remnants of this independence, and is reminded that Judy is only part of him because their lives have coincided over the last fifteen years, and part of him because they have shared Freya. Freya is where they have met – the space between them which was given life – but they are still as separate as they ever were.

Freya's sitting awkwardly on a barstool, holding a glass of Coke with both hands, drinking it with two straws. He looks at the hair bands tied round her wrist. They must comfort her. She's in a pair of jeans with a pink trim running down the length of the leg, a touch of flamboyance, but here she looks shy and nervous, reluctant to move, not wanting to draw attention to herself. Guy moves to her and puts his arm round her – he's still a bit unnerved by their conversation on the riverbank.

'That's your mother on stage,' he says.

'I know,' she says, the straws still in her mouth. She can't take her eyes off Judy. 'Do you think she'll be famous?'

'Don't know,' Guy replies, automatically. He's never really considered it, never really considered how it would affect them all. 'Probably not,' he adds, wishing not, and thinking about the track she recorded today, already held in some digital memory across town, waiting to be heard by people who might offer her more, take her away, like it's a letter which is dropped in a post-box, and nothing can stop it being delivered now.

Judy waits while the guitar plays out the sweet remains of the song, nodding her head in calm rhythm, and about twenty or thirty people in the bar start to clap. They're an appreciative bunch, used to the hundreds of bands doing brief sets up and down these streets each year. There are a few tourists, just listening to whatever turns up, but Guy's most impressed by the bar staff, who seem genuinely touched by Judy and her song. Maybe it's her Englishness they like – her blend of folk and more familiar sounds like the pedal steel guitar she has in the group tonight. Or maybe it's that new B-bender Tele they like. One of the barmaids is beaming at Judy – it's not quite country, and she's loving it.

He feels in love with her all over again. Judy looks back at him, and he gives her an enormous grin – she's made it – she's come all this way over the ocean and has actually performed her best. She's magnificent.

Judy starts a new song – this is one of Phil's tunes. It's an upbeat sound full of borrowed country references, with a lot of guitar. Too interested in himself, that Phil. Guy watches Phil step forward on his artificial leg which is still covered up in his jeans and new boot, swinging that new sunburst Nashville Tele, grinning wide-mouthed at the bar, and Judy bends to take a sip of water. At his cue she joins in with a melody which simply follows the guitar up and down. Phil's going for it with his expensive new toy – he's pushing down on the strap to bend the notes and going behind the nut to do some country licks. Quite impressive in its own way, but a monkey that can do tricks is still a monkey, after all. And the song's nothing like the last one. Still, it has a beat, and a couple of people in the bar step forward and start to dance in front of the stage. Phil loves that. Stupid Cupid.

Guy doesn't dance, certainly not to another man's tune, and has a slight fear that Freya might ask to dance with him, but luckily she's dug into her barstool now and seems to be there for the evening – a touch of her father in that kind of solidity. Around them, the talk in the bar increases – it confirms Guy's suspicions – that the last song had captivated them, and that this song is louder, more showy, but is just a background. He must tell Judy this – well, tell her without being too critical of Phil – he's made that kind of mistake before.

Guy closes the diary and leaves the saloon to stand on deck. It's gone dark. The water shines up at him, flattened with a mirror-calm sheen. The fisherman's still at the back of his cuddy, looking at the tip of his rod. Across the river he looks at the Rushcutter's Arms, a view of golden light shining through its windows like photographs in an album, a fond time remembered. Either side of it the shore is a blank depth of trees and, as he looks towards the sea, there is nothing, just a velvety black void. The scent of the brine rises up in soft warm lumpy air. Maybe another thunderstorm will come.

There are sounds, of cables stretching along aluminium masts, of boats settling in the high tide and, closer by, the rhythmic stroke of oars being rowed through the dark. Someone returning to their boat no doubt, and he searches for it, sees a glimmer of light briefly curl along a rail of polished wood, then the beads of water shining in the ripples of a wake, emerging in a smooth pattern from a point which heads towards his boat, coming right at him now and he sees a figure lifting out from the darkness and turning to steer the dinghy alongside the *Flood*.

He kneels down at the gunwale and reaches out to take Marta's hand.

Position: In the saloon. 10pm

She's wearing a dark Icelandic sweater with a bright yoke design across the shoulders, a long skirt, and is drinking her second glass of amaretto, sitting in the same easy chair he used this morning when he wrote about the recording studio.

'Ro has a headache – a really terrible one,' Marta explains, in a whisper, as if even here she has to be quiet. 'She gets them, you know. Migraines.'

Drinking the syrupy liquid has brought out a subdued calmness in her. She wants to talk about last night. She tells Guy that she can't believe Rhona could fall in like that, she wants to know exactly what Guy saw.

'It was dark, Marta. I've been over it several times – I just saw her slip, I suppose.'

'Yes. She slipped.' But she keeps looking down at her hands, holding the thin-glassed tumbler of soft brown liquid, and occasionally she swirls the glass.

'She drinks too much. I don't know what to do.'

'I'm sure you're doing everything you can.'

'Yes, I am, aren't I? But I wasn't there to save her, was I? When it came down to it, I wasn't there.' She looks at him. 'You were,' she says. 'I want to thank you.'

'You don't need to.'

'You were a hero,' she says, trying to lighten her tone.

'Let's not talk about it,' he says.

'OK. But thanks, again. Really.' She pauses. 'We've given up now. We're going to go back to Cambridge.'

Guy sits in a chair near her. Again he is struck by how sad she looks, when she's not trying to smile.

'Do you know what you'll do, when you get home?' she asks.

'Not really.'

'I mean, the very first thing. I've been trying to work out what I'll do, and I can't picture it. I can only think that I'll stand by the stove and make a pot of tea.'

'That sounds perfect.'

'I'm not sure.'

'I think I'll collect my dog.'

'That's nice.'

'Yeah. His name's Banjo. He's scruffy.'

'Even better.'

'I left him with the woman who runs the B&B at the pub – it wasn't fair to take him out to sea, just in case. If you want to know what I'll do – I'll take him on this walk of ours, up into the woods. Yeah. It's beautiful – it reminds me of my mother – we used to go walking in the woods when I was a kid.'

'What are you doing here?' she asks, in the same quiet manner. 'You didn't come here to see the estuary, did you?'

'No,' he says.

'It's a miserable place. It's like an open wound.'

'It can be.'

'You're just as stuck as we are, I expect?'

Guy feels he can hide little from this woman, with that direct pale-eyed gaze of hers. 'I wasn't going to come here at all.'

'Really?'

'I was going to go out into the North Sea. Like, a long way.'

'Why?'

'I don't quite know, yet.'

'Well, that's enigmatic.' Marta looks up at him, shyly. She's caught the sun, and her face seems a little raw, it gives her a vulnerable look. 'You don't have to be enigmatic, you know.'

'The North Sea's a big place. It made me think, being out there.'

'Yes,' she says, sucking her breath in as she says the word. It's a foreign intonation. 'I've been doing some of that myself.' She looks at him with a watchful expression. 'The sea meant something special to my husband.'

'Right.'

'He loved sailing – actually, he was quite boring about it. We were always going to sail round Britain – we never had a honeymoon because Ro came along, so we were always going to do that one day.' She takes a breath. 'My husband died three-and-a-half months ago. His name was Howard and he had a stroke, and he was a very lovely man.'

Marta gathers herself. 'See my hair,' she says, 'where the henna's grown out? That's how long he's been gone. They thought they could save him but they couldn't. He was fifty-three.'

She looks at Guy, resolutely. 'They thought it might have been a stroke, right from the outset. Howard was sailing in the Solent and they had to winch him from the boat. I've imagined him in that harness, with his eyes screwed shut and his hair being blown crazy. You see, Guy, all that drama, all that noise and action and urgency – at the precise moment when he was being hoisted up in the winch and flown to the hospital, I was at the supermarket, looking for the cheese he liked. It's Caerphilly. I was looking after him, but I wasn't there for him either, when it came down to it.'

'You can't blame yourself. That's not right.'

'But you see I do. Sailing was *his* thing, and I always disappointed him about that, because I like to stay at home. I probably disappointed him for years – he was full of such spirit. I've only become a worrier.'

Marta pauses, troubled. 'Ro's like him – she has his restless energy. I won't be able to hold on to her. Everybody leaves, Guy – sometimes, they leave in the middle of the night and sometimes, like Howard, they get hoisted up by paramedics into a Sea King, like an angel has come to take them to heaven. When they took Howard it was like he was being lifted out of this world. And behind there's this little space that's left that you have to fill.'

Guy looks down into his drink. There's never been an answer in there. He strokes Marta's arm.

'And now Rhona's dropped out of art school and she's drinking every night and that stunt she pulled last night – I just don't know . . . I don't know whether I can continue. It's all messed up. That's why I'm with a strange man late at night miles from anywhere at all.' She glances at him, anxiously. 'Please don't take that the wrong way.'

'Marta,' Guy says, 'cry as much as you want to.'

'Cheers,' she says, brightly, then begins to cry more.

'Three days ago, Marta – my first morning out at sea – it was that amazing dead calm we had. I looked at where I was on the maritime map over there, and it had nothing written on it, just a blank space – it should have said "wilderness", you know, like they used to put on the maps. It was that really fantastically sunny morning. I went for a swim – as soon as I went in the water it kind of took my breath away. You mind me telling you this?'

'No.'

'I swam away from the boat, till I really didn't know whether I'd be able to get back. I think I was trying to get lost. The sky was so high and blue and I don't know how long I swam for, and I'm not pretending I wasn't scared being in there, being so disorientated and cold and thirsty, but I just didn't want to do anything else. I just swam.'

Marta looks down at her hands, silently.

'And eventually I came back. I was trying to find something out there, something I'd missed. You know, it's like looking over the edge of a cliff – it makes you face up to things. And I think I did find something. I think I found my daughter, Freya.'

'I didn't know you had a child.'

'Marta, I don't have a child. My child died – Freya died.'

Effortlessly, without moving, new tears begin to fall down

her cheeks. 'I'm so sorry, I had no idea,' she says. He holds her hand.

'It's OK,' he tells her.

'Except, it's far from OK.'

He agrees. They smile at each other.

'I shouldn't have asked.'

'You didn't know, and I'm glad you did ask. I'm glad you know now. Freya died five years ago. It was an accident – a one in a million accident.'

'Oh, Guy.'

'So you see, I *am* here for a reason. I'm here because of her.'

Guy looks around at the saloon of the *Flood*. So much empty space on this boat, surrounding him always, like a numbing insulation he can't break through. When he was younger, space meant nothing to him – it was a neutral thing, just a separation between one thing and another. But all that has changed since the people he loved left his life. Now, he looks around and sees a different kind of emptiness. It's an emptiness where there should be someone, or an emptiness where there once was someone. When he looks at a chair now, he imagines the person it should be supporting; when he sits at a table, the other side of the table is a blank wall to him, as powerful as a mirror, reflecting the half a life that he now lives. He tells all this to Marta. He tells her about the times he has reached out into that emptiness to try and recover what it once held. And he tells her that he's never known a space more absent than the space where a child was.

They sit quietly after he's finished talking. He feels closer to this woman than he has to almost anyone over the last five years.

'I understand.' She smiles, bravely. 'Guy,' she says, cautiously, 'when you say you found your daughter, what do you mean?'

'Being at sea?'

'Yes.'

'She came to me. She came to be with me.'

'Thanks. Thanks for telling me that.'

'I don't often get the chance to tell anyone how I'm really feeling.'

'I understand.'

'So thanks for listening.' He's light-headed, literally light-headed after removing this burden. He can't remember the last time he told someone about Freya. Even saying her name out loud seemed strange.

'But, Guy. That was a stupid thing to do, swimming away from the boat like that.'

'I know. But somehow, a life without getting to the answers doesn't seem real enough.'

'Funny isn't it?' she says. 'We're both here to get away from the ghosts, aren't we? Or maybe we're bringing them with us.'

'Yeah,' he says, quietly. 'I have this way of dealing with it. It's something I've been doing pretty much every evening since my life changed.' Marta looks at him, expectant. He remembers giving that look himself, just after Freya's accident, how he searched everything and everyone for an answer. 'It's nothing miraculous, but it helps in the quietest way – I write a diary.'

If anything, Marta looks a touch disappointed.

'It's not an ordinary diary,' he says, not convinced he'll be able to explain it at all. He begins badly: 'When Freya was born, and she was that little warm squashy body all covered in vernix, with an ancient screwed-up face, she, she became everything – instantly. I loved that. I loved handing my life over like that, being less important, and then learning about her – this thing that's arrived in your life, complete with her own character. You know, seeing parts of her mind emerge, how she viewed the world. But when that was taken away, I just didn't want my old life back at all – the one where I was the end of the line – it felt like becoming a kid again, after being a dad. I didn't want to give up on that really beautiful, really simple thing of watching a life grow – so I – this sounds so hopeless, Marta – I have tried to carry it on, tried to write a future for her.'

'By making up a diary.'

'Yeah. She's grown up in it. She's nearly ten now.'

'And you do this every day?'

'Every night. And I'm still with my wife in the diary. We split up three months after the accident, but in the diary, she never left me. I wanted to see how it might have turned out, you know, if things had been different.'

'But how can you possibly find that out?'

'Well, you make it as real as you can. It's not like moving chess pieces over a board, you have to use everything you knew about your family, all those moods and moments of stupid laughter and the times when you're all strangers to each other, and you bring in all the random things that can happen too, you give each other colds in winter, you lose your keys, you forget to buy things at the supermarket, the boiler breaks down. I wasn't very good at it in the early days. It just seemed made up. But I've got better. It's as if I'm no longer writing it at all.'

Marta listens kindly to his enthusiasm.

'If you want to know what we're up to, right now, we're travelling, the three of us, across America from Florida to California. I made this promise once, that we'd cross America, listening to its music. I made that promise right here, in fact, at the Rushcutter's Arms.'

'How far have you got?'

'We drove to Nashville last night. You see, Judy, that's my wife – she was the singer in our band. She had a really great voice. In the diary she's actually had some success, I gave her that. She's got some backing-vocal work at a studio. The next entry I write will be about the place where we're staying, in Nashville.'

'But you've never been.'

'No. Marta – I know it's all made up, I'm under no illusions about that, but it helps, really. It helps to have these things alive, whenever you want them.'

'But you *have* to believe in your own life, too, surely.'

144

'I do. I really do. Like swimming the other day, just being out there on the North Sea, in the nothingness – it's made me think how glorious the world really is. Just swimming and looking up at that high blue sky, feeling the water – there's even this sound of the gulls I've been listening to – have you heard it? I've never actually seen the birds that are making it, but it's the most amazing sound.'

'So what happens when you finish the diary?'

It halts him. He's never considered that before. He's always felt the diary might ease itself away from him, like an illness receding, till he wrote less of it and one day didn't need to write any more.

'I'm not sure,' he says, full of ambiguity. 'I'll only know what to do when I get there.'

'If,' she says.

'Yeah. If.'

'Does it have a title, this diary with no end?'

He laughs. He's talked too much about it – he can't tell whether it's done any good. But the thought of giving his writing a title feels surprisingly attractive to him – giving it a name would be the first step in parcelling it up, defining it, possibly separating it from spreading into all parts of his life.

'Maybe you could give it a title,' he says.

Marta smiles warmly at him, perhaps a little drunkenly. 'I'm going to go now, Guy,' she says, in that quiet flat voice of hers. 'You're a good man, you've been lovely to me. You should be happy, Guy.'

'Both of us should,' he says.

'You know, in Icelandic we would say *Ég segi allt ljómandi*.' She laughs. 'It's sweet. It means everything's shining.'

She stands, putting out her hand to stop him getting up. 'Please, don't come out on deck. I'll see myself off.'

He hears the brass rollers of his wheelhouse door sliding open, her sandalled footsteps on the planks, and the knock of the dinghy as she climbs down into it. He thinks he hears her oars, moving

145

calmly and rhythmically in the night for a long time, the only sound worth listening to.

The space she leaves behind feels unresolved. He pours himself another drink – he's quite light-headed now, but it's not numbing him, not giving him the anaesthetizing quality he wants from it.

The diary is a vast unanswerable object, filling his room. He takes it from the desk and sits with it in Marta's chair, reading the passages he wrote about their night in Nashville.

He turns to a new page and poises the pen above the paper. There's a reason paper's white, he thinks, it has the colourless look of a cloud, it's a fog, dense and impenetrable and easily misleading as you head into it.

Very consciously, he looks at his pen, poised there – at the dark vein of ink in its centre. Since he started this sea journey, the level of ink has shrunk by half an inch as it's unravelled into the long inflected line of his writing. He wonders about the ink left in that pen. What it will reveal to him.

It's late at night and they've all come back from the bar where Judy and Phil did their set. They're in the rented house Phil has organized – it's a small clapboard bungalow about ten miles from downtown Nashville, in a rundown district that looks threadbare. Guy's in the front room, it's around three-thirty, he thinks. He's been drinking Jack Daniel's. Soon the night will tip towards morning, he can already feel that heaviness across his forehead which means he's deeply, deeply tired.

In the other corner of the room is a strange object: Phil's artificial leg. It leans casually against another chair, as if that's all that remains of the man. Could they make the shade of that pink plastic any more lifeless, he wonders? It gets painful, that leg, after a long day. Phil has the habit of sitting down, rolling up his trouser, unstrapping the apparatus and massaging the loose stump of flesh he has below the knee.

So Guy's been sitting getting quietly drunk in this chair, just him and the leg, while from another room he hears the occasional

146

sound of a guitar. A guitar and two voices, trying out new chords. Phil's demonstrating techniques on his new instrument, anticipating key changes and going half-a-step higher a beat before he should. That kind of thing. Judy's voice has deepened, it sounds lazy, a little breathy, whereas Phil's, if anything, seems to be a touch lighter. Both of them are speaking in hushed tones. They think he's asleep. It's affected them, being in Nashville, it's making them act rashly.

After the club Guy had driven them across town in the rental car. For as far as he could see, the lights at the interchanges were winking amber, a road without impediment, urging him on, giving him the glimpse of escape. Yet there was Phil in the backseat and now, the car is parked on the front yard of the bungalow. He can see it through the window, its familiar shape reminding him of the days already spent in it driving from Florida. They become friends, these hire cars, they carry you and they carry the whole journey with them.

Guy tries to concentrate. He can't allow his thoughts to get unfocused. He has to keep on guard here. It's gone silent in the other room. He glances at the floor – it's an old wooden one, and it will creak if he tries to move, he knows that and they probably know it too, so he sits there, staring at the grim plastic leg with the fittings Phil must know so well, wondering why it's gone so quiet where the others are sitting. You're a damn fool, he thinks, indulging in such a fantasy, a damned fool. And even while he's thinking this chastizing thought he sees, along the length of the corridor, a polished brass coal scuttle by the fireplace. How could he have missed it earlier? It has a shallow convex surface, and in it he can clearly see a reflection of his wife and Phil, sitting side by side on a small red corner sofa. The guitar is lying on the floor by their feet, alongside a flash of bright red, which must be Judy's new headscarf. Guy squints in the effort to see it clearly. The two people have been given a distorted metalled appearance in the reflection, a sepia glimpse of them, as if caught in another time, but it's a potent tableau nonetheless.

Phil's hand appears to be moving forwards and backwards, possibly on the sofa, but just as possibly on Judy's leg, which remains unmoving. Then a slight bend to the image, and Judy appears to sink in towards Phil. Guy watches this, entranced, but with a growing anxiety that this is something very important, something he must try and remember in all its detail. Every single part of it he will look back on and try to recollect. But even while he is watching it he's not entirely trusting of what he sees. Just a twisted reflection. How can that have any kind of surety? It's nothing. It's the drink. It's the middle of the night. But an angry curl of doubt is growing in him, hardening like wire, a tightness which is stretching through his body. He's come a long way to see this. Drunk, in a chair, incapacitated, while something startling emerges in the next room, something which has been forming for however long, on the fringes, across the phone calls, in the glances. He is struck by a sudden rising of panic, almost a sickness, that now he has to act.

He thinks, naturally, powerfully, about Freya asleep in the other room, and on an impulse he moves. The floor creaks immediately, and as if the sound sent a ripple of alarm through the house, he sees Phil and Judy change posture in the reflection. A new distance created between them, and it's in *that* gesture – in *that* single gesture – that he knows.

He does a strange thing then. He picks up Phil's artificial leg, and walks with it like it's a baguette he's just bought at the bakery, feeling the rigid plastic weight and shine in his grip, into the other room.

'Here,' he says to Phil, holding the leg out.

Judy is curled into the other corner of the sofa, nursing her own drink. Her red scarf is on the floor. Innocence discarded.

'Let's go to bed, Judy,' he says. 'It's late. We've got a long drive tomorrow and you must be exhausted.' It's like a line from a film.

'I'm a bit beyond tiredness,' she says, conceding, but not quite looking him in the eye. And then she does, uncompromisingly, a level look of her calm green-brown eyes. 'You're right,' she says, 'I think it's time we all went to bed.'

Phil holds out his arm and for a second this confuses Guy. Does the man want to shake his hand for some reason? And then he realizes: Phil wants his leg.

'Oh. Yeah,' Guy says, handing the leg over. An interesting transaction, that, to give a man his leg back. Phil doesn't strap it on. Instead he rises unsteadily on his other leg, and Judy and Guy help him from either side, Guy thinking how ludicrous all this actually is, to be helping the man.

It's not a long way to Phil's bed, and Guy's thankful for that. At the doorway Judy peels off to go to the bathroom. Phil reaches for a crutch in his room and starts to move about in there, putting some sidelights on, and Guy is left awkward and large in the doorway.

Guy goes to his room and sits on the end of the bed, the spot for thoughts his whole life long. That's where he sits when he and Judy have any kind of discussion, and in this way he feels he's preparing for it, right now, however late it might be.

But by the time Judy is out of the bathroom, Guy has gone back to the lounge. It's quiet and very empty. He looks at the red sofa as if it's a guilty thing. An object tinged with shame, part of the betrayal it encouraged, how dare it sit there in the corner as if nothing ever happened.

Phil's door is closed. It would be easy to go to bed now, Guy thinks, but he knows just as well what would happen – he'd just lie in turmoil, until the morning, while Judy no doubt slept. Instinctively – and getting a perverse pleasure from it – he gives Phil's door a quiet knock. Too late now, Guy thinks, wondering whether Phil might, in fact, think this knock is coming from Judy. He hears the rubbered foot of the metal crutch take two steps across the room, then Phil opens the door.

Before the door is even fully widened, Guy has thrown his punch, putting every ounce of his weight behind it, straight into the side of Phil's face, where he sees a fantastic moment of sheer alarm registering the split second before his fist strikes, followed by the enormous wide-eyed shock of Phil's expression as he falls to the floor.

Phil stays on the floor, crumpled like a heap of clothes to be washed, fully accepting it. Guy says nothing, and doesn't bother to close the door as he walks back to his room.

Position: Anchorage in Deben estuary. 11pm

Guy stands at the wheel and starts the *Flood*. Immediately the engine growls heavily beneath him, vibrating the floor and rattling the windows in the frames. He steps out on deck, preparing to cast off from the mooring buoy, and feels the whole boat is shivering with expectant life, with possibility and direction.

But it's getting on for midnight. Where, realistically, can he go? The estuary is two directions of the blank nothingness this side of England is famous for: go upriver, and you end at a collapsing notch of thick mud where the *Flood* would be grounded; or go the other way, to the open sea, with its sandbanks and endless water, its gathering storms and lethal swells, a wilderness out there waiting for him. In this darkness it would be ludicrous, even if he knew the river.

Writing tonight's entry in the diary has shocked him. He knows now why he's been dreading the trip to Nashville so much. An affair, after all this time. He should have listened to Freya – she has instinct in bucketfuls. And he wonders, really, why he's doing all this to himself. You make it as real as you can, that's what he told Marta. You give the diary every chance to surprise you, and as a result, you have to take what comes.

But Judy choosing Phil? It doesn't make sense. After all these years of his support and love. This is how he's to be repaid?

He cuts the engine, defeated. To calm himself he tries to remember Judy as she was. His Judy, not the one she has become, full of secrets and unpredictability, but the one he remembers. And the image he has of her is beautiful. She's surrounded by a soft blue light. But this time she's not on stage. They're in a bluebell wood. It's early spring, and they're entering the hazel copse – a gentle place full of birdsong and a smell of earth and dust but in this moment, transformed, as it was every year, by the flowers. Together, they walk in the shadows under the slender trees, spellbound by the emerging haze of eerie deep blue that surrounds them, under their feet, rising like a tide.

They stand, in awe.

'We mustn't tread on them,' Judy whispers, her voice already affected by this special place.

'There are more than last year, I think,' he replies, and he squats on his haunches, to maximize the sight of pure blue above the stems of the flowers. 'Wow,' he says, simply, then prefers not to say anything more.

'Guy,' she whispers, 'I'm going to write you a song about this place, so we can remember coming here.' She wanders off, into the maze of flowers, and he sees their colour saturating the air around her. He sees her as a soft object herself, in a suede jacket, with high boots made out of some synthetic fur, a small brown shape moving among the blue. She appears as if she's weightless, in a dry watery glow that seems to lift her.

'How can this come out of the soil?' she asks, inspired and amazed. And he remembers it now – the song she wrote:

> I'll remember you in a soft blue light
> Each year,
> A softened air, arriving
> Never fear
>
> Blue-bell
>
> I'll hold you in a soft blue light
> A petal's clasp,
> With the birdsong, rising
> Heartbeats last.
>
> Blue-bell

That's his image of her. His perfect image. His life had been without anchor really, till he'd met Judy. Judy who'd stood outside that cabin in Norway letting the drips from the icicles splash on her face, who'd put her whole head into that ridiculous fountain at the Rushcutter's after their first gig. 'Promise me we'll go, Guy,' she'd said. Across America. 'OK, I promise,' he'd replied, and he'd kept that promise to her, in the diary. But now she's looked back at him in the stolen reflection of a brass coal scuttle, and she's broken all her promises to him in return.

There'd be nothing in the bluebell wood now, no sign of the flowers or the plants, the coppice would have an extra absence to it, like looking at a meadow after the fairground has packed up and left. You'd think all that blue would stain the ground, but it never does. Vivid colours never last.

It's after midnight when Marta returns, tying her boat to the side, climbing quietly on deck and letting herself into the wheelhouse. Guy's in his bunk, just about to turn in, when he sees her shadow, long and undecided, being cast across his cabin floor.

For a moment, Marta stays like that, her shadow coming into his cabin, but not herself. Then she gives a polite knock to the side of the hatch frame and begins to climb down the ladder, afraid to look him in the eye, but unafraid to be entering his room, which seems suddenly very small for them both. She's holding her plimsolls in one hand, by their laces. Her feet look cold and muddy and have red marks where the shoes have rubbed.

'I've come back.'

'Yes.'

'I'm sorry.'

He looks calmly at her, trying to gauge the situation. 'Where did you go?'

'Just rowed.' She smiles, embarrassed. 'Sorry for being upset before.'

'You don't need to be.'

'I feel I need to explain. Rhona thinks these migraines, they might be the same thing, that her father had.'

Marta sits down at the foot of his bunk, suddenly full of purpose. She puts her shoes on the floor and rests her hands on her lap. 'And I've been thinking about what you told me. I think you should probably stop writing that diary. Please don't take this the wrong way, but this fiction of yours, because that's all it really is, it sounds like it's more important than the rest of your life, and probably will be until you move on from it.' She pauses. 'Am I speaking out of turn?'

'No.'

'The first few days after Howard died I felt like that. I felt like I'd died too, but somehow they'd forgotten to bury me – like in that film with David Niven when he's an airman. I just couldn't contemplate carrying on. I really expected to fall asleep one night and not wake up the next morning. Well, I felt like that, but it never happened. I think I'm too healthy, really. And then I began to wonder whether it was Rhona who was keeping me going. Having a daughter meant I couldn't give up. But you know what – I was wrong – it was me who wanted to keep on going.'

Guy listens to her – the effort of saying all this is taking its toll – and he thinks about Freya, her small limp body as he ran with her from the field, even the stallion knowing that something unnatural had occurred – it had walked away, defeated; he thinks about this Howard man, in a hospital bed, covered in wires and tubes and hooked up to colourful monitors. The dead seem to be with them, always. And if it's not the dead themselves, it's the closeness to death that's with them, too. His swim into a North Sea wilderness, Marta's quiet wondering whether her heart will give up, even Rhona, afraid of a darkness within her, afraid there might be a path between regular migraines and the stealthy wound which grew and grew in her father's brain until it killed him.

He looks at Marta's subdued profile, and realizes she is now nearer to him on the bed. The intimacy of the moment has brought them closer, quietly, they've been working together, taking the obstructions away in a calm order, so that Marta leans towards him, softly, and kisses his neck. A warmth from her touch spreads through him, he smells the scent of her hair, and feels her lips kissing his cheek, her hand holding his shoulder, and then she guides him towards her and kisses him again, more fully. He feels his glasses being nudged aside by her cheek. He kisses her, like that, for a few seconds it seems, before he pulls away, and looks at her, so close, so changed with the arrival of what they have just done. Her expression looks dreamy, a little drugged even, with the slackness of her mouth, still opened, still shadowed within. A tiny glimpse of that quirky tooth, between her lips. And when her eyes open he sees them change shape a little as she focuses. A moment later, and a small frown appears between her eyebrows, the hint of fear and embarrassment he knows might come if he doesn't kiss her again.

For some reason he is paralysed, by indecision, or by a fear of consequences. He doesn't know. But he doesn't move, and gradually he sees Marta drifting back a little. She looks down, away from him.

'I'm sorry,' she says, quietly. 'That was a mistake.'

He feels terrible then. Terrible to have seemed to have rejected her. Maybe he had, he's not quite sure.

'Don't,' he says, then doesn't know what else to say.

She looks up at him, braver now. 'I shouldn't have come back,' she says, 'it was bound to have ended like this, and now I feel stupid.'

'You're not. I'm the stupid one.'

'You don't have to make me feel better.'

'I know.'

'So don't.'

'I'm, confused I suppose.' He anticipates the conversation

tripping down familiar alleyways of explanation and excuse, all of them inadequate and all of them utterly predictable. He doesn't want to spoil things like this, not with her.

'I'll leave now,' she says, firmly.

'You don't have to,' he says, unsure what he might be promising. She's no fool, she's not going to make herself vulnerable again.

She stands and pulls her skirt straight – curious how our clothes take it upon themselves to go ahead of the situation. That skirt, it's trying to be taken off already. He smiles.

A hardness seems to come over her expression. 'Is it Rhona?' she asks. 'It's Rhona you want isn't it? I've seen you look at her. Oh Christ, what a mess I've made of this.'

'No,' he says, confused, 'that's not it.'

'You're what, thirty-seven, thirty-eight? I'm ten years older than you, and Rhona's fifteen years younger than you. I mean, I'm too old and she's too young – is that it?'

'Marta – you're getting hysterical. It's nothing like that.'

'But I can see it's quite a dilemma for you.'

He realizes, quite suddenly, that he's been a fool. All he has is nothing compared to the love of someone else. Company. Friendship. All the world can offer a man in the prime of his life – it means nothing if there is no one to share it with. Otherwise, his days are like an endless collection of events and experiences, to be housed in cabinets that are never opened, display cases that have no visitors. This might just be a moment that could change his life. Marta is a wonderful warm-hearted woman and he's made her feel hurt and rejected and he had no intention of that at all. Not at all. He stands, always so big under the cabin's low wooden ceiling, and he moves towards her, wanting to wrap her in his arms and hold her, all night, regardless of what it may or may not lead to, he'll take whatever comes. All he knows is that he wants to share with this woman, at this moment he wants to share everything with her. He's been such a fool. But as he approaches her she is retreating, steadily, misreading him as a man who's trying to let her down gently, not wanting to put herself on the line again.

He stops, clumsily, midway between her and his bed. All he needs to do is go to her, hold her, but he can't. He just can't move.

She looks at him from the hatchway ladder. 'You know, she says, 'I meant everything I said to you.' She smiles at him, and climbs out of his sight.

Guy looks at his abysmally empty cabin, which still has the gentle fragrance of the woman who has just left. His space, again, but he's not enough to fill it. He should go after her. *Go after her*. But he doesn't, he stays in his cabin, feeling wretched, yes, that's it, wretched, no other word for it.

And while he's thinking this way, he imagines he hears a tiny tap on the wheelhouse glass, but he knows it's not a tap on the glass at all, it's a vibration coming from the engine, that's all, a sound coming from the car or the road – Judy hasn't heard it yet, and Freya might already be asleep in the back of the car, he's not sure.

He sits down to write, looking ahead of him, at the relentlessly straight American road with its central yellow ribbon in his headlights, as it stretches through the night into Mississippi.

They have driven all day and much of the night, too far and too long. He can feel the ache of the journey throughout his body and he knows that Freya and Judy are feeling it too. It's been the biggest distance yet, and he'll probably have to suffer the consequences of that, he thinks. A sense of argument is already there, in the car, without anything having been said. Right now, it's just a looming worry, shapeless and vague, but it's there nonetheless.

'I need to stop soon,' Judy says, rather suddenly, from the passenger seat. She's been quiet for some time, and the voicing of her tiredness is a real alarm bell. He knows she's right. He's been driving this straight road all day, and now, in the dead of night, it's still not letting him feel he's getting closer. At every sign that slides forward out of the dark he expects to see the name of the town he's aiming for, but it never arrives. Other place names, more lengths of straight road, it has the feeling of a dream he can't escape from.

Even America seems to have vanished. The hills and rolling countryside of much of their journey has been replaced by a sudden and frightening flatness. Pitch black. Featureless. It's the Mississippi Delta, and there's no end to it, there's nothing he can grasp out there.

'Where *is* this place?' Judy says impatiently. He wants to snap at her, tell her to shut up because he's trying his best, he's doing the driving, but he's learned over the years to hold his tongue – she can elevate an argument effortlessly, citing a whole bagful of resentments he never knew she was carrying and, right now, he's not really in a state to defend himself. Yes, he's driven them as far away from Nashville as he can today, but why the hell not, given what he left behind?

'OK, I think this is it . . .' he says, calmly, offering her some hope and taking a sheer gamble that he's close now. Sometimes, you just have to stick your neck out. There are some dotted lights out there, in the cotton fields. This must be right. But there again he's been looking at the same patterns of lights in the fields for about forty minutes now. He's been driving fast, too, trying to eat up those miles while the others have been unaware.

'I thought you might be asleep,' he says, taking a glance at her. The dim light of the dashboard picks out her profile, giving her a mournful, overly absorbed look. He wants to chase up his comment with a question about how she is, how she *really* is, but he knows he has to wait for that. No point breaking down walls when the roof might fall on you.

'This is like the fens,' she says. It is, he thinks, it's as flat and as agricultural. Replace the sugar beet with cotton, that's all.

'We've come a long way just to be driving through Lincoln-shire,' she adds. He smiles at that, hopeful that her joke might buy them some time. Then he wonders at her, how she can flip from acerbic comment to gentle humour so easily. She's a puzzle to him.

Suddenly the sign he's been looking for flies by like a ghost, dirty and half-forgotten. God, if he'd have missed it! He slows the car and a second sign confirms he wasn't just seeing things. Not quite the lights he'd been looking at, but another vague collection of lights and windows not far off in the field to the right. He slows more, and turns the car off the road on to a rough farm track, and they bounce their way carefully along that until they reach the buildings.

It's an old plantation house, with guest rooms out the back, but to Judy and Guy it seems like a film set, with wide wooden verandas wrapping round it, old clapboard facades, and bales of cotton tied up on the back of flat-bed trucks parked in front. They drive round the building, watching it pass like a slowly tracking shot in an old movie, till they find a space that looks fine to leave the car.

When he opens the door he's struck by how warm the air is. Again, they seem to have driven into a different climate. It's exciting. Judy is gently waking Freya up, and Guy steps away from the car in order to get a glimpse of how it looks, from the outside, with the thin shine of its courtesy light glowing from inside. He sees Judy, her face shadowed, bending over Freya, adjusting the seatbelt, and Freya waking up disoriented, surfacing from wherever she was.

'Hi, Dad,' Freya says, through the glass, and Guy raises his hand back in greeting. This is like when she was young, he thinks, he and Judy driving through the night with Freya bent double in a child seat in the back, her tiny head lolling with the motion of the car, so painful it looked, although no manner of clever cushioning could keep it from doing so. They'd arrive and Freya would gradually come round, bleary and tearful, with hot cheeks and red crease marks from the fabric on her skin. It felt so cruel, always.

The girls close their doors and join him on his side of the car. There's a soft wide sound of insects, filling the night air – a distant enveloping hum of crickets and cicadas, and every so often a thin reed of that hum slides forward in the air, separating from the background noise and rising in pitch as something indecipherable flies though the air before them.

'Are we staying here, Dad?' Freya asks, confused.

'I hope so,' he replies, noticing how undecided Judy looks. She's not going to back him up until she sees what kind of place it is.

The main building is long and grey and unlit, with no clear entrance and no apparent sign of life. But then he sees it, a glimmer round the windows at the far end of the building – there must be heavy curtains hanging inside.

'This way,' he says, hopefully.

He opens a screen and knocks on the door, then opens that too.

Inside he's amazed to see a warm golden-lit room, full of books and shelves and several chairs and tables. Oddly, there's the sound of a blues guitar playing, though he can't see anyone, and as he leads his family in he realizes there are three men seated at the far end of the room. One of them says hi, then continues to watch the guitar being played.

Guy and the others walk right up to them while the song plays out. The guitarist is fairly old, black, in denim dungarees, and he's bent right over the fret board. He has long dry fingers, curling round the chords like crab claws, but when he stops his hand hangs down, his fingers relaxed and loose.

'Sweet tune, P,' one of the men says. He's a greying man with a wide waxed moustache and a pleasant smile. 'I real lyak that,' he adds, drawing his words out in a Southern drawl.

The black guy, P, shakes his head and laughs deeply, then

looks at Guy. He has small glistening eyes and grey stubble, and he wipes his forehead with a bright red neckerchief. ''s hot tonight,' he says, his arm hanging over the guitar.

The third man decides to stand up. He walks languidly across the room to a shelf, goes to a second shelf and finds some specs there, then goes to a desk and switches on a small lamp, as if he's finding his way around. He introduces himself as the owner, and welcomes them. It's so wooden everywhere. The floor, shelves, walls and ceiling are all planked or clapboarded, and the smell of dryness and wood dust is overwhelming. The lights have the glow of a subdued fire. Still, Guy can see Judy's mood is immediately lifted – these kinds of strange little worlds really inspire her. Freya's less sure. She stands shyly behind Judy while the moustached man smiles at her, probably hoping she won't be asked anything.

'You come far?' the owner says, looking over his glasses.

'England,' Guy says, as Judy says 'Nashville'.

'Right,' the man says, humorously.

'I mean we came from Nashville today,' Judy explains.

'I gathered that, mam,' the man says, sliding a ledger to Guy. 'You put your paw-print there,' he says. 'We got some rooms out back we done up.'

Guy walks with the others over the grass with a key in his hand, following a vague direction towards some outbuildings.

'This is amazing,' Judy says, conspiratorially. 'I can't believe this place – did you see the moustache on that man?' Guy's heartened by this, heartened that it's probably going to be a good place to stay after all.

They pass a collection of old farm trucks, some gleaming silver Airstreams, and find their key fits a small wooden shack with a back porch and two rooms inside.

It doesn't take long to get Freya to sleep – she's half gone already, but Guy's become oddly energized by this strange shack, with its dense wooden sound, its creaking floor, gingham curtains against the windows and thin single beds. Places like this make travel worth the effort. But he's also secretly glad to know he'll be in his own bed tonight, while Judy sleeps on the other side of the room. He's been awkward in her company, has felt it all day, as if their silent argument has been forming relentlessly, to the point where now it seems impossible that he might share a bed with her.

His plan is to open a bottle of Jack Daniel's and pour her a glass on the back porch – the moon is up and the cotton field beyond the yard glints silver. They can sit and drink like teenagers, hearing the insects and getting through the bottle. There's a rocker on the porch too, painted white – he'll let her have that. They can drink till some sort of balance is restored. An old fellowship between them.

Judy is sitting half on, half off a chair, with her overnight bag opened by her feet, while Guy finds the bottle. Her long hair hangs over the bag and he gets a glimpse of the things inside – the familiar objects that make her who she is. A comforting sight. He can see how tired she is in the way she leans. She has her sandals off, and her feet have a tragic look of dust and dryness – the toes look stubby and without direction, and the skin on her heels is almost cracked. Parts of our bodies age at different rates. But as he goes to place a hand on her back she straightens, looks him in the eye, and says, 'You damn near broke Phil's jaw.'

Guy stops, caught mid-room by her.

She stares at him, expectant, though he knows it's not the moment to say anything. He needs to sit down, needs to find some sort of room for manoeuvre. It was the cheek in any case, he thinks, he didn't even hit the jaw.

The possibility of any number of questions Judy might ask at this point fills him with horror – all of them naturally bend towards a complete exposé of their failing marriage, and yet this silence, this complete disregard for his feelings – it's the first blow, and he has a real sense that he's now involved in some-thing way too advanced. He had made the assumption that he'd caught this thing early, but maybe he's very wrong. Maybe she doesn't have any feelings for him at this point. That would be terrible.

'Honey,' he begins, already knowing how weak and pathetic his voice sounds.

'You don't have to explain,' she interrupts. 'Phil's already done that.' She sits motionless, in a red-patterned dress which hangs limply to her body, draped in a sad fold between her legs. He remembers that dress the day she bought it – how she wore it in an orchard. He has a photo of that.

'I'm not going to deny it,' he says. This gives him the moment to sit down, but as soon as he's done that he suspects it might be a mistake, to face her, sitting. He wants to drink that bottle – he wants to drink with her – offer her the chance to go back on what she's said and never mention it again. But there is another force, too, the one which tells him that to live a lie like that would be nonsense, and no alternative at all.

'Are you having an affair with him?' he asks, sickened to say the line so many thousands have said before him, a line he never imagined he would ever say.

'Yes,' she says.

He takes that calmly, always so bloody good in a crisis, but he feels the heat of it and the utter awfulness, the utter finality. He doesn't quite know what he says next. He doesn't know if he says *oh* or nods his head – he's thinking he must ask those formal questions, like when you're told bad news from a doctor, questions like how long have I got and is there anything I can do and have you told anyone else, and all these questions seem to be way too considerate, way too understanding. He realizes he wants to help her, even now, when she's telling him this awful thing, because she's in a tricky spot and he's always the one for her in situations like this – but he knows that he truly *doesn't* understand, and the only question that really should be asked, the only question worth asking is *why*. Why with a man like Phil?

Her mouth tightens and she says, 'I'm surprised at you, Guy, that a grown man should punch a man like he's in a street fight. That's no way to be, whatever the provocation.'

Guy listens, scalded. It's amazing, the effortlessness by which she can turn things. What provocation indeed! But again she steals the moment. She gets up and touches him on the shoulder, and says, 'I'm sorry, really,' very quietly. He cannot move. Doesn't know what to say or do. She may have rehearsed this moment a thousand times, and she's played it magnificently, not letting him in at all. They are strangers.

She squats down by her open holdall and pulls out a small bag of make-up. He looks at her from behind, at the tiny ridge of her knicker elastic sticking through the dress, girdling her bum in a complimentary contour. At the tiny blonde hairs along the edge of her shin, the sandals with the flower buckle she bought in Florida, the tiny scar on her ankle she got on that barbed wire fence on the marshes. He wonders whether he's already barred from that dress, from touching her, from all that she is? Is she a foreign land now?

She puts on a little make-up – a gloss, she used to call it, and he sees her take a sly glimpse at him with her compact mirror. He thinks of the night before, at the stolen reflection in the brass coal scuttle by the fireplace. And he knows that that glimpse of her in the compact mirror, distrustful and wary, is another one he will remember all his life.

She snaps the compact shut and stands.

'I think it's best I go out for a while. I'm going to listen to the guy playing guitar.'

And with that, she leaves him, leaves him in the middle of this strange little shack, the room as wooden as a coffin, somewhere at the end of a very long road and a very long day, but feeling entirely without a sense of time or place. So bewildering, that his entire friendship, relationship and marriage to Judy should arrive at this haphazard place, so completely unfamiliar to them both, and that it's here a moment of such enormous significance should happen. When it comes down to it, there's no sense, no plan, no shape to things. They just occur. They occur and then you carry on, because time carries on, you change, you adapt, you just have to.

He imagines how she must have walked across that warm patch of grass to the back of the plantation building, the world changed for her too, irreversibly, but still a resoluteness in her which was alarming. Both of them, dealing with the same crisis, which ironically should bring them together. But is she alarmed too, or does she already have a warped sense of relief? He imagines her going back into the room where the man is playing blues guitar, how they'd welcome her and make space for her at the table, honoured by her interest, discovering that she is a singer, that she can add to the evening. It's sickening, that he's left here in the shack, with Freya asleep and so vulnerable, so innocent in all this, while Judy eases herself into a social world of strangers playing music into the night. She's a coward.

Guy doesn't know what to do. There's no sense in drinking that bottle now, he knows that much, and he can't concentrate on anything else but what he has to do now, how he has to act, the things he has to fill his head with. It's terrible.

He sits at a table and opens the road atlas of America. It's so important, suddenly, that he knows exactly where this place is, this little damned spot of the earth which will change his life. He finds it by following the orange latticework of roads he drove down an hour or so ago, passing through the junctions with his finger, remembering how he had felt, driving the car, so late at night, so responsible for dragging them further than they'd wanted to travel today. He remembers views over dark fields, a casino complex lit up with neon and flashing lights, all gaudy and inviting, a couple of large wooden crucifixes set by the road in front of a floodlit church. All of those things, he'd seen in his previous life, though he'd not known it then, his life which had been one thing, and now it was another.

He finds where they are staying, after a while, between two

anonymous crossroads. That's all it looks like on the map. A few miles to the west is the looping thick blue swirl of the Mississippi, flowing north to south. They are close to it tonight, perhaps a ten-minute drive, nothing more. It dissects the continent as an unavoidably clear divide between east and west. He looks down at it, sadly, feeling very lost, thinking they didn't even make it half-way, they didn't even get that far.

Guy realizes he might have been crying. Writing tears the life out of him, it makes him a husk, he thinks. He lies on top of his bed, full of doubt. Family grows, it strengthens, it ripens, then sometimes it splits – the result of some forgotten weakness in its make-up. Couples get together, they blossom, then they destroy each other. It feels almost natural, but it never is. Judy will always leave him, he knows it, and Freya, she will go too.

Lying on the bunk in the dark he tries to conjure their faces, tries to colour the room with remembered scenes where they were all together and happy, and he sees fragments of East Anglian sunshine, the glint of an estuary between trees, the feel of long wet grass in a water-meadow. The past seems shifting and unreliable, it's shadowed, but memories arrive with unexpected intensity, of colours, of specific touches. They seem more vivid now than ever before. Damp bricks on a farmhouse wall, separated by a powdery mortar, Freya's multicoloured dresses – their hems brushing through the bending stalks of long summer reeds, her legs in woollen tights, pulling them up at the knees, Judy squatting down and pinching Freya on the nose, to make her laugh. That crease of a worry line, between Freya's brow, though she was too young to worry about anything.

Yet mixing with the airy East Anglian blend of salt and water and sunshine, is now a huge presence, the murderous call of the sea, promising a new sobriety in his life, a seriousness he never thought he would be cut out for. Solitude, unwanted. And then there is Marta's face, appearing curiously alongside the other visions, worried for herself and for her daughter, seeking companionship everywhere because that's what she's lost. You know, he says to her, I can't do it, I don't want to fill the space of your dead husband. Did he say that? Did he tell her that before she left? He can't remember properly – it's too recent to feel reliable about what happened.

She had looked so lovingly at him. All he had to do was to accept it. But he hadn't. And he wonders why not. He wonders why we can't take the choices in life that could make us happy.

Out of simple exhaustion, Guy falls asleep, and immediately he is dreaming about Freya. Something about her, yes, uncovering, Freya's face, happily walking towards the horseradish plant. The touch of her hand in his, now, just there, he can feel it again, how cool it is, how small, tightly fitting within his own. He holds her and walks forward, calmly, away from where they are. He walks, listening to her happily chatter away, her voice the sound that sunlight makes.

And suddenly he's awake again. It's the early hours of the morning. Something very real is bothering him, something there in the room – the shape of something nameless, a change in the air. He lies in his bunk motionless, wondering what it might be, listening to the sounds of the estuary outside, the trickle of water never ceasing its movement, the sound of air stirring in the trees on the river shore, and then he listens to his own breathing, which still has the sound of sleep to him.

Gradually, softly, he hears another person breathing a few feet away. He strains to hear it, makes sure it's there, yes, there is someone in the cabin with him. The breathing is calm and steady, but more shallow than his own, and with a quicker rhythm. He holds his breath, hoping to hear more, and is surprised to hear the other person holding their breath too. When he breathes out, the second breath comes a second later, like it's an echo of his own, and for the first time he's certain who's in the room with him.

'Freya?' he says, in the dark, 'You're there, aren't you.'

There's no response. Guy reaches up for the wall light and switches it on. He looks across the cabin and sees he's totally alone.

Position: The wheelhouse. Deben estuary. 5am

Quickly, without fuss, within ten minutes, he has readied the *Flood* for leaving. It's dawn, and the tide has risen with a soft shine that's brighter than the sky. The water seems like a new element, like mercury, unnaturally flat and shimmering. It's flooding into the creeks and saltmarsh holes and cracks as if the sea is surrounded here by a giant porous verge. This giant rip in the texture of the soft East Anglian soil, gathering in and expelling out, the way all things appear in this part of England.

A thin breeze has arrived with the tide, lifting up from the water with the smell of wet salt and, gazing down the length of the channel, he watches the brightness of the sky, above the beckoning sea, filling with wisps of salmon-pink clouds.

He tunes in to the shipping forecast at 5:20am. A comforting voice, the voice he's listened to all his life, even when he was a child.

Good morning and now the shipping forecast issued by the Met Office on behalf of the Maritime and Coastguard Agency, at 05:05 on the fourteenth of September . . .

. . . he remembers being ten years old, a dark winter's morning, tuning his first radio into the BBC long-wave. A child eavesdropping on the world of men. Hearing a man's voice, so calm and authoritative, but speaking about storms and waves, of winds veering and backing, of spray crashing over the bows of a trawler, chains and cables straining in the pitch of a violent sea, somewhere in Malin or Hebrides, blocks of the ocean with no fence to them, but overseen by this gentle English man, who faced the wrath of the ocean, the plummeting gauges, the rising seas, with complete assurance . . .

. . . *there are warnings of gales in Viking, North Utsire, South Utsire, Forties, Humber, Thames, Dover . . . the general synopsis at 01:00. Low, Hebrides, 992, losing its identity. Atlantic low moving rapidly east, expected Fastnet 990 by 01:00, tomorrow . . .*

. . . he'd imagined that voice, speaking from the calm soundproof cube of a London studio, the meteorological report squared precisely on the desk, the steam from a coffee rising on the side and, the furthest point where the voice reached out to, a wave-drenched trawler man, in dirty yellow oilskins in a wild ocean gale, grabbing the radio and holding a wet ear to its crackling, God-like message.

. . . *Forties, south or south east, becoming cyclonic in Viking and Forties, 5 or 6 increasing 6 to gale 8, perhaps severe gale 9 later. Showers and rain, good becoming moderate or poor . . .*

A long way north, Guy thinks, looking at the *Flood*'s barometer. Those warnings are coming from the trackless parts beyond Scotland, but his area, Thames, is mixed, too. He watches those clouds again, losing their pinkish bloodstain, turning in squally vapour several miles away. But he's decided, the light is growing, the estuary is losing its meditative shroud of darkness, and it holds nothing for him now. He must leave.

Just to start the engine, to hear its sturdy old revolution beneath him, imagining its thickly greased piston-heads rising in obedient order, then the gushing sounds of the propeller screw, deep at first then rising as it bites the water, makes him feel restored. Motion is the answer to most things. He rings the ship's bell, just once, and sits down at the wheel, reads the inscription of *Voorhaven, 1926* on its nave-plate, and touches its brass-ended central king spoke for luck. Then he brings the revs up and the *Flood* turns into the current of the tide, a long, heavily blunt shape building up pressure against the flow.

. . . inshore waters for Great Britain and Northern Ireland, valid for the following twenty-four hours issued by the Met Office at 06:00 on the fourteenth of September. General situation low, just north of Scotland, losing its identity. Atlantic low will move into the Irish Sea and extend into the North Sea. Strong to gale force winds will affect many coastal areas.

Enough of the bad news. The *Flood* pushes forward through the calm water, the shores inching by, the nearby moorings passing much quicker, his boat sending a measured wake that rocks the other boats, a single wave of it pressing up against the *Falls of Lora* now, the merest of touches, the only sign of his departure in a patch of water which will hold no memory of him. Even the damp shape of the Rushcutter's, with its brawny man still grasping the reeds on its sign – a final glimpse of it – being swallowed into a gap between the trees as the estuary bends and removes it from view.

His last sight of the anchorage is of the fisherman at the back of the cuddy, still watching his rod. Guy tries to see the man's face, but the rain peak of his oilskins is pulled too low. So long, old chap, nice to have seen you, in fragments.

The deep channel twists like an eel, but is well marked, and in less than an hour he has come alongside the diesel barge that's tied to a pontoon near the mouth of the estuary. It's a strange sight – two fuel pumps on a floating platform, with a modern kiosk between them, lit by a harsh fluorescent light. An attendant has just opened it. It's a young lad, coming out briskly to take the mooring ropes and tie them to the cleats.

'Hi,' the lad says, brightly. 'You're the first. Shouldn't really open till half-six, but that's just a shit rule.'

'Cheers,' Guy says. The boy has a strong Suffolk accent. 'Fill it will you? And I'll need water. What else is there?'

'Kiosk ent got nothing. There's stuff in that shed.'

While the boy fills the *Flood*'s tank, Guy takes the greenfinch to a spot on the bank where he can release it. There, he squats in the rough grasses and the mats of reeds washed up by the high tides. It smells of fish and oil and hay and, as he opens the flaps of the cardboard box, he looks along the stretch of shore at the gulls standing on the stones and mud, hunched in the early morning coolness. The greenfinch startles itself, flapping to a corner and staying there. It won't last the morning on this bank, with those gulls.

Guy closes the box again. 'Looks like you're off to sea again,' he whispers. 'Till you're better.'

On the way back he visits the shed and picks a bag of green-gages, some plums, a dozen eggs and a jar of marmalade, dropping the money for them into a wooden chest with a padlock on it. He looks out through the doorway at the long clog-shaped profile of his boat, tied to the platform. It's like a whale, he thinks, unbelievably big compared to the rest of the boats in the estuary. It's a fine sight, tied up by its ropes, in the fresh morning air.

'Nice food,' Guy says, walking back to the *Flood*. The pontoon has a slightly swinging motion to it. The diesel hose pulses like a dark vein as it fills the tank, and the pump registers the litres in a series of soft clicks.

'You goin' up the coast?' the boy asks.

'I'm going out to sea.'

'Yeah? What for?'

Guy looks calmly back at the lad. He shrugs, and the boy smiles.

'My gran would call them swimmer's clouds,' the lad says, giving a single nod at the sky.

'Meaning what?'

'Meaning go out in a boat, you come back swimming.'

'You serious?'

'Half.'

The lad finishes filling the tank and goes to the kiosk to print out the bill. Guy follows him. Inside, there's a CD playing and a smell of instant coffee. 'See that village,' the boy says, as he takes Guy's card, 'that's the absolute worst village in the whole world.'

'You sure?'

'For the fifth year running,' the lad says, grinning.

Guy laughs, and offers some greengages.

'No thanks, sir. Sick to death of them.'

Guy climbs back on the *Flood*, puts the produce and the box with the greenfinch on the bench seat of the wheelhouse, and is cast off. He waves to the lad as he leaves, and the lad waves back, watching the *Flood* go for a long time.

Soon after, the mouth of the estuary widens on both sides, a gaping sandy jaw, fringed with mud, opening like lock gates it seems, to let him pass, both shores curving away into the wide emptiness of the North Sea, then vanishing from view.

From his seat he looks down at the passing water. It quickly loses its river character, its muddy sullen quality – here the water is churned with a new deeper energy, and he sees the point where the river finally gives way to the sea in a long curved line of tea-stained clouds of sediment, rolling below the surface. There's a fresh smell of salt and air and increasingly an absence of land, of its smell. No more scents of agriculture and woodland and vegetation here, just the smell of the wind that arrives without obstacle from as far as it wants to, from Denmark, from Norway, from the Arctic Ocean. Empty places with little on their breath.

Guy's elated to be in this wildness once more – facing a horizon that has no mark in the sea other than the line the planet gives it, but the wind is stiffer and the waves more choppy and streaming than he'd imagined. Through the binoculars he checks the horizon and sees it's a dark land of waves, peaking, foreshortened by the perspective, as rough as oak bark. Even here, so close to the coast, the bow rises in soft arcs as the waves pass by his window with gushing noises, making the boat dip in uncomfortable rhythm with the troughs. He hears objects shifting below in the saloon and cabin, a result of his river laziness, of being in calm water – the longer these boats are in the estuary the more cluttered they get – but soon all that clutter will settle into new positions, the way things tend to at sea. The *Flood* is strong, he thinks, it's been afloat for years. It's iron strong.

Ahead in the east the sun has risen in a pale dazzling blaze. The wheelhouse is illuminated by its brilliant whiteness, coming at him on a level, a vivid sea light that cauterizes the air, unlike the estuary light that had seemed heavy with a green stain. He steers towards it, symbolically, allowing its flood of clarity to cleanse the boat, cleanse him, shine its light against the dark scenes the diary has brought: glimpses of betrayal in a brass coal scuttle, the oddly clammy skin of the artificial leg, held on his lap, late night drives through Mississippi with wooden crucifixes in front of floodlit churches, plantation shacks where relationships fall apart surrounded by cicadas.

The cabin in Mississippi had resembled the interior of the *Flood*. And though he'd added embellishments, such as the gingham curtains and the rear porch with its flaky-painted rocker, essentially there was too much similarity for him to deny what's really happening: his imagined journey and his real journey have been growing together, in a kind of reproduction.

Even the American hire car has changed, adopting the shed-like air of the wheelhouse, along with the broken-backed feel it gives him after a day of driving. Sometimes, writing about it, when he imagines a glance into the rear-view mirror, he doesn't see America with all its lushness and roadside signage, but he sees the North Sea instead, scraped bare and lifeless, stretching away endlessly.

And he remembers the way Judy had sat across the cabin room, just at the point when he was going to invite her out to the porch to share the Jack Daniel's, the way she'd levelled her gaze and told him about her affair. That wasn't meant to happen, Guy thinks now. What was meant to happen was they drive across the States as a family, not bog themselves down in the soft underbelly of Mississippi and casually, effortlessly, destroy themselves.

'Are you having an affair?' he'd written.

'Yes,' she'd said back.

He cuts the engine about ten miles offshore, the last point where he can see England, nearly gone, it's as fragile as an eyelash on the curve of the sea. The waves seem to collect round the hull of the boat, toying with it. Guy wants to feel how strong they are. It's OK, he thinks.

He goes down to the galley and makes a breakfast of warm rolls and coffee and chocolate, and follows this with some of the greengages he bought at the fuel platform.

He looks through the windows at the sun, where a wide bleaching light is shining in the air – it's still fairly early. The taps of his sink glisten like they've been varnished – they have the appearance of being intensely real and entirely false at the same time. Marta and Rhona will be having their own breakfast now. He wonders whether Rhona's migraine has lifted during the night, whether Marta has noticed his boat has left. It was rude what he did, to her, and to leave like this. He's behaved like a child.

The thought of her in his cabin last night, how calm it had seemed, how the space had closed between them in effortless intimacy – how could he have acted as bluntly as he did? That frown of worry on her forehead after she kissed him, her mouth still slackened with anticipation.

Something very strange had occurred: for the first time in five years Guy had not wanted to be alone any more. Just a little move to one side and she could be there, with him, both of their absences with new life to fill them. The thought had arrived with such a force he had been shocked by it. Shocked by how easy it could be.

He'll see Marta again, he's sure of it.

Sitting in the bright bathe of the North Sea sunlight, he feels as though he has steadied something, albeit briefly.

He thinks about America, and he thinks it's time they all woke up to face the new day.

He wakes groggily in the morning to hear Freya laughing outside. She's on the back porch, going wild on the flaky-painted rocker. He can hear Judy too, laughing with her. When he walks out there he enters, briefly, a picture of domestic bliss. Freya's straddling the rocker, laughing at her own pantomime, while Judy takes photos with her old Olympus. Freya's grinning so widely her gums are showing pink and clean above her teeth. Judy says hi, still framing Freya in the viewfinder, and tells him there's a jug of fresh orange juice on the side. Automatically he sits at the table, seeing the juice next to a small basket of rolls with a linen cloth over them.

'Where are these from?' he asks, bewildered.

'George,' she says. 'The owner.'

'Oh.'

'I had an egg,' Freya chips in, leaping from the rocker and walking over to a plastic child's tricycle which has been left in the grass.

'She's loving it,' Judy says, smiling at Freya. Guy hasn't the words to join in. He can't just go along with this pretence. But maybe that's all there *is* to do now? A mean vine twists above him along the woodwork, and a green lizard flits along the boards, near his feet, full of eyes and fast energy.

'You sleep?' he says.

'Badly,' she says, with a hint of acknowledgement.

'Me too,' he says. They really are in the same boat, he thinks, they're both having to deal with this, but it won't bring them closer. It's like an illness which will kill them in separate ways.

The thought of asking her what has or hasn't gone on with Phil, or what her plans are, fills him with horror. He should probably say nothing. You have to wait for the pain and recrimination to emerge – you can't just expect it to be fully formed. And Judy seems to be in the same mood. She clearly doesn't want to go into it now, and then there's Freya, a few yards away on the grass – nothing can be discussed here. They will all just have to pretend this is like any other day.

During the night Guy had watched Judy asleep on the other bed. She had drawn her body up into the shape of a question mark, and her hair was spread in a wound knot across the pillow. He'd resented her peacefulness, she didn't deserve it, and he resented other things too, like how she must have lived a double life. Whole scenes and experiences that have been kept private from him. She must have had worries too, no doubt, about getting involved with another man – it's plain ridiculous, that he and Judy talk about so many things, all the food and shopping decisions, the mundane running of their lives, the meaningless chatter that makes up a relationship, and yet this enormous event, this utter betrayal, has never even been hinted at.

He imagines the times when she's returned home after seeing Phil, from sleeping with him even, only to chat about day-to-day issues. Guy has a sudden image of her sitting outside their house in her car. A moment as she turns the engine off and just waits, thinking about being with Phil, the memory of his arms round her, the discovery of his body perhaps, where the hairs are, where the skin is paler, the smell of his neck. Intimacies she is exploring. And she sits out there, thinking about the trouble she's in and the excitement too, and how in a second she will have to walk into her family home, put the keys in the bowl on the table, and kiss Guy chastely on the cheek. A Judas kiss.

Sensing a day filled with mistakes arriving, Guy decides to eat. Appetite never leaves him, whatever happens. He tucks into the rolls, cutting thick slices of butter on to them and spreading honey on top of that, pouring it on. A condemned man, enjoying his right. He downs the orange juice and fills the glass again, and discovers a metal pot of hot black coffee. Judy looks slyly at him scoffing the food, a little amazed – she might be denying what's really going on, refusing to talk about it either last night or this morning, but Guy's sheer hunger is unfathomable to her. He knows she won't have had a thing for breakfast. It amuses him, grimly, that she is more bothered by his ability to eat than anything else.

Freya sits on the tricycle and tries to push it through the grass. A wheel is missing, and the grass has grown long and tangled through the rest of the toy, but she still tries to steer it. An endearing sight, Guy thinks, when a child plays with a toy they're already too old for, glimpsing Freya's own sense of nostalgia.

The coffee perks him up. He puts in an extra spoonful of sugar, and dunks his last roll. A thin sheen of honey spreads across the surface of the drink. He's eaten the whole basketful of bread, and he has the curious pleasure of knowing that Judy can't tell him off for it. Strange, that she's so quickly lost the right to be critical about his behaviour. Ordinarily she would have made a comment, that's for sure. It's a surprise to them both.

A second surprise is that sitting there, looking out over the grassy back yard, the strange farm machinery and broken down trucks, and the wide flat expanse of the cotton field beyond – with the smell of the coffee mingling with the warm sunny air, he feels the sense of holiday returning. He's travelling, he feels alive, he feels oddly free. It gives him a strange sense of inner strength, yet to emerge, but preparing, a thing he can rely upon. Yes, Phil's a prat and he's a few hundred miles away now, heading to an airport for a long and troubling flight home – and he only has one leg – let's not forget that – while Guy is here, the man of his own family, still. Maybe it's Judy who's worried. After all, it's one thing to rehearse your grand gesture – how to tell your husband that you've been cheating on him – but really that's just a tiny moment, a few seconds perhaps. The real struggle comes after. Sit back, Guy, and enjoy the ride.

Position: About ten miles offshore, say, 51° 59'N 1° 38'E. 11:50am.

Know your place in the world, Guy says ironically, as he studies his maritime map. The North Sea is an odd shape – like a dissected rat pinned out over Europe. Blue, on the chart, but grey in reality. He looks at the countries round its edge, all of them changing the world at some point as the shoals of herring have swum past their coasts, awakening their hunger and industry. And to the north of the map, there's nothing. Just the empty terrifying wastes of the Arctic Ocean, where the world's latitude lines seem to converge in fear, as the distances of the sea expand.

He starts the *Flood*'s engine, hears the axle revolve like a spade turning in gravel, the taps of the piston heads like far-away typewriter keys, and the thick spin of the propeller below him. So comforting, the droning chug of an engine that's neither irritating nor relaxing, just a persistent sound of work never done. He listens to all this, and heads further out to sea.

When he dozes off, he dreams about what keeps him awake: Freya. He feels her presence sitting by his side. They're next to a river, in East Anglia, at the neck of the estuary. The tide has turned, and the bulrushes are moving eerily among themselves as the water wells up from below. Freya is four again, marvelling at the sights of nature she knows her father loves. Wanting to learn, wanting to be part of the moment her father is creating. Her wellies are muddy and he wonders if her feet might be cold in there, she refuses to put on thick socks because she doesn't like the feel of them. Too itchy. Her hair-clips sparkle at him as she edges down the bank and tries to throw bits of broken reed into the water, but the water is too far even for that, and her throws are pathetically mistimed. But still she's trying, she wants to hit the water, and he's worried now because the water seems too near, too menacing, his fatherly apprehension once more so strong, keeping her close, keeping her away from danger. Steady love. And he can't remember, he can't even remember whether this moment actually happened, or whether it's just like the rest, just another dream he's making up.

Guy wakes, blearily, slumped against the felloe of the ship's wheel. He's been holding the spokes but the boat's been turning in a large wide curve. Behind him, his wake has encircled an area of sea like it's his own personal claim. An island of small waves. He checks the compass and steers once more.

He plays some music, loudly, on the stereo in the saloon. He tries to match it to where he last imagined himself in America – that dirty blues area of the Mississippi Delta. He has the blues all right! *Ma baby's juss left me*, he shouts, over the track he's playing, enjoying the abandon of it, enjoying the motion of the *Flood* as it takes the waves on. They seem to be a little stronger here. *Yaar!* he shouts as the bow rises a touch too high, every so often, opening the windows of the wheelhouse so the sea air rushes in to drown him, the water passing noisily below, bubbling up in cresting foam, and in the distance the growing darkness of storm clouds and rain. A rough black voice on the stereo now, complaining about his own wife. Relationships are such a *mess*, Guy thinks: they shift so slowly, almost too slow to see the changes emerging, yet every so often they have to be realigned completely, like an osteopath cracking the vertebrae to set the spine straight – it's grown out of true while you were asleep. And he thinks of that wonderful realignment he performed himself, that wonderful cracking punch he sent into the side of Phil's face. Forget being liberal, when it comes down to it, striking a man with all your might is an *immensely* satisfying act. What a tremendously pleasing thing to be able to replay in your memories! That look of total surprise. Yes, that look, of defeat.

Guy thinks back on it now, how politely he'd knocked on the door, with the same fist that was already clenching, and that little wait while Phil found his crutch and hobbled over, legless. Legless! The look of intrigue mixed with a hint of confrontation in Phil's expression, a man who has always reacted badly, petulantly, as if he's never quite grown up. Despite his pursuit of Judy, he's always taken his lead from Guy, who was a man before Phil was, who had a child first, who's seen more of life. And when Guy looks back on that great punch he threw, it now has a cartoon image in his head – a wonderful *THWACK!* reeling across the room over Phil's startled face as the man falls down. Phil, shattered on the floor and crawling off towards his bed, while Guy stands enormous in the doorway – his animated shadow flung far across the carpet in front of him.

Learning how to punch someone properly had been a lesson from Guy's father. In great detail he'd been told a punch is not really a product of the arm, but begins further away than that, in the swinging of your body, near your waist in fact, till the shoulders are already rolling with a momentum which naturally carries all that force and weight, the arm continuing and adding to it with explosive energy, the fist instinctively tightening into a little block of wood, into a terrific blow.

'If you've ever got to punch a man,' his father had said, 'for God's sake do it *right*. 'Cause there's only one thing worse than punching someone, and that's punching them badly. You hit someone, you're trying to break bones in them. Got it?'

After the lessons in pugilism, his dad would want a wrestle. They'd be on the bed or occasionally in the back garden, and Guy would get his dad in a weak-limbed headlock and listen as his father huffed and groaned and pretended to suffer like a bad actor. He always knew, even in his earliest memories, that his dad was putting it on, could easily get out of the headlock, and was over-emphasizing Guy's physical prowess.

'Good one, lad, now try and pull me down,' he'd say, and Guy would look at his father's face, just a few inches from his own, in the curious pocket of their interlocked bodies, look at that spiky moustache and the furtively untrustworthy eyes trying to carry this whole act off – the act of a father proud of his son – and Guy would dig his fingers into some soft part of his father's flesh and he'd see his dad react, surprised, irritated even, irritated that he could fool so many people in his life as a salesman, but he couldn't fool his own son. And Guy would feel a force rising somewhere and realize he was being flung. The world would spin over, his father's face free now and passing like they were on some kind of fairground ride, and Guy would land on his back, winded. 'Maybe next time,' Conrad would say, or something like that, the residue of a fatherly tone still ringing false in his voice.

And Guy wonders about his father, possibly still on the road even now, a new car and an updated suit, with smaller lapels, but still keeping the wheels moving because he can't face being still. Are you still selling cameras? Or did your clients see through that game a long time ago – who exactly do you think you are, to be selling them these intricate Japanese machines, who are *you* to tell *them* how to frame their family memories, when your own album is blank?

He hits the mackerel shoal in the early afternoon. He'd seen it a few hundred yards off on one side, and had steered the *Flood* to cross its path: a rising, pitted boil of the sea as the fish darted and breached and dived in a frenzy. The gulls had spotted them also, folding their wings and falling into the sea in dirty ragged shapes, paddling clumsily in the water and lifting off with bits of silver fish held in their beaks.

As the *Flood* reaches the same point, he drops the revs and lowers in his mackerel line, pulling it with a soft long-armed motion through the wheelhouse window. The fish have dived again, but the lures – brilliantly gleaming strips of feather and foil – are irresistible. He feels the stabs on the line in quick succession, of the hooks being taken, of the line itself being wrapped around the flashing tails, and he cuts the engine and pulls the gear up, stepping out on deck to do it. In the moss green light of the water he sees tiny particles of light suspended around his line, which is pulled taut into the deep shadow at the side of the barge, and then the first glimmering shapes of the fish, compliant, confused, lifting through the shades of the water like treasure from a well, their backs a camouflaged grid of dark blue bands.

There are seven on the line, full, fit, muscular fish with strong glistening backs and bright terrified eyes. He lifts them clear and admires them, hanging, metalled and varnished by the light, stunned by the air, before lowering them on to the deck where they flap and bounce and dance with panic across the boards, too many of them, too wild a sight, as if they've fallen from the sky. Unprepared, and with one already freeing itself from the lure and flipping over the side, he pulls them off the hooks and flings them into the wheelhouse where they arc their backs and hump their way into the corners. He drops the rig in again, and even as the line is falling there are more hits on it, interruptions in the descent as the fish grab the lures and run.

He pulls up five more and throws them, again, on to the floor of the wheelhouse. This time he follows them in, sitting above them in his chair and looking down at their wild shapes flooded with exhaustion and fear, the blood-red fringing of their gills panting in vain as they think about dying. He has a surprising and overwhelming feeling that he's being watched, that this moment of the dancing fish flapping in each corner of the wheelhouse is not just his experience and his experience alone. He looks about him, unnerved. The fish settle slightly in their death throes, then start up again as he gets off his seat to put the music back on. He plays it loud, very loud, accompanying him as he sets about clubbing the mackerel on the jamb of the door. Occasionally they even jump in time with the beat of the music, all eleven of them, leaping in strong twists of their backs, one flies out of his hand, slippery and full of energy, straight out of the door and into the sea. He doesn't care.

He guts and cleans them in a bucket of seawater and then he fries two, with butter, in a large pan he's set on deck on a Calor gas ring. He cooks them quickly and eats them hot, just the oily flesh above their medial lines, ignoring the tails and the belly meat. It's a richly oiled taste of salt, sea air and fried juices, and he throws the remains over the side, and it's only at that point that he realizes the weather is deteriorating.

In line with the shipping forecast, the barometer is losing pressure as the low deepens. How had they phrased it – the low was *losing its identity*. That's a strange way to say it. Such a magnificent force as an Atlantic pressure system, all wrapped up in godly ocean vapours, swinging round the top of Scotland's bare rocky coast, only to lose its identity. Into what?

He tidies up as flurries of the storm begin reaching the *Flood*. Rain comes in thin bands out of the dreary air, stinging the glass of the wheelhouse in uncertain bursts. There are no birds in the sky now, and the sea has lost all its reflective quality. It streams past in flat pewter grey, in meanly curved waves that are low but fast, belonging to a weather system which is somewhere else still, far away, beyond the horizon.

Guy gets into his wet-weather gear and makes sure the hatches and skylights of the barge are fastened shut. He makes more food and ties it to the handle of the saloon, along with a flask of fresh coffee and the bottle of *Gammel Dansk* the trawler skipper gave him. He's going to need a proper ocean drink, he suspects. On the bottle's label he reads a curious Danish inscription: *Gør godt om morgenen, efter dagens dont, under jagten, på fisketuren*. He wonders what it means. Drink in the morning, at lunch, all day if you have to, when you're out fishing, with God's blessing, something like that. The language has the feel of a warning.

He lifts the bench seat behind him and looks at the inventory of his safety gear – flares, a raft, ropes, lights, first-aid box and lastly, the life-jacket itself, lifeless in there, he can't imagine the dire circumstances of having to put that round his neck, water sloshing around his legs perhaps, he doesn't want to think these things. He closes the bench and faces the sea.

He notices gas rigs in the gloom, several miles off, their girders and platforms and accommodation quarters looking half-constructed and fragile against the darkening sky. How they manage to stay rigid in all this seething movement seems impossible; welded steel and fastened cables surrounded by supply vessels, warning buoys and guard ships, all rising up and down in the swell. And as he gets closer he sees how dark it is becoming, by the lights that shine on the platforms themselves, and the ragged flames of gas flares burning at the top of the derricks. Clear white light, like the light on a film set, burning on to the production platform, with warning signs and gangways illuminated in shining precision. He thinks he can see men up there, in bright rubber coats, performing inspections, although he's not close enough to be sure. But he imagines the living quarters, brashly lit and cheaply equipped – TVs and DVDs and fixed plastic chairs, a smell of chips and sugar, a world of men, surrounded by porn and machinery and high-pressured gas, coaxing this prehistoric vapour into pipes and tanks, containing it, but only just.

Through the binoculars he studies the rigs, standing on the seabed with jointed legs and a mosquito's poise, the thin needle of their drills merely pricking the rocks below. He steers the *Flood* well clear of their exclusion area and, with a touch of alarm, notices how high the swell is rising up and down each of the platforms' legs in turn.

Have they seen him? Has anyone noticed the old Dutch coaster that's lumbering through the sea, its engine grinding in the water and its wheelhouse rocking as the waves tip it playfully from side to side? He doubts it. The sea hides everything in its constant movement.

Soon the rigs are passed and Guy's aware of the breadth of the North Sea again, in every direction a heaped sense of water that rises and dips in unpredictable patterns. It feels shifting, illusionary; several times the *Flood* rises and he can look across the surface of the swells for miles, and then he is taken down, lower it seems, than the level around him, where the sound rumbles in at the boat, caught in a dish of the waves. There, he hears a sound of creaking and deep groans which he can't believe are coming from the boat and can't be coming from the sea.

Guy looks to the north, where he's still heading, and sees lightning flashes illuminating the horizon with a ghostly pallor. Each time they ignite, he tries to make out the cliff edges of cloud above them. If the storm comes at him, he hopes it will be tomorrow. Facing the waves at night would be terrible, if not impossible. And as if in heavenly answer, the swell does seem to subside as the light begins to fall. The waves lose their bite – the sound of the wind blowing round the corners of the wheelhouse lessens, and again he is struck by how quickly the sea lets go of the daylight – within half an hour it's almost completely dark – and he remembers the light falling near the Inner Gabbard bank while he watched the trawler, before he headed for the shipping lanes off Harwich. Less than a week but another world away, already. A different sea.

He lowers the revs of the *Flood* to just above an idle. This way he can keep the bow pointed at the weather, but nothing more than that, he doesn't want to push the engine – he might need to run it all night and all tomorrow too. Maybe more. Tomorrow's a daunting prospect. Even now, he has the sense that the sea to the north is coming for him, the waves overriding each other. It's so alive, out there, beyond where he can see.

He locks the steering and, when the *Flood* is balanced, he opens the inspection hatch in the corner of the wheelhouse and slides down the metal ladder to perform checks on the ancient Kromhaut engine, noting its pressures and levels and the general sound of the piston heads as they tap and rise in a chattering rhythm.

Enclosed in the engine compartment, the noise of its hotly turning insides is an alarming sound. It reverberates unpleasantly in the cramped space, bound in by damp thwarts and brackish iron plate. A sheen of dark oil grime covers everything, smelling hot and wet and slightly salty. *How can this engine work?* he wonders, not for the first time. Hosing and valves and pipes snake away from this beating heart, each one capable of a multitude of possible breakdowns. Its metal is as hot as a stove, yet curiously still too, welded into itself in a thickened patina of iron and paint and grease. It's more like a rock, really, sitting there in the hold of the boat, a dark block of granite.

The *Flood* is already tipping more than he expected, it must have slid from the direction he set and is hitting the swells at an angle. He quickly scrambles back up the ladder into the wheelhouse and trims the heading. So he's learned one thing – he can only be away from the wheel for a matter of minutes.

Looking out beyond the bow he can see the restless patterns of the waves in the gloom. Every few minutes the motion of the swell changes as the waves cancel each other out – the *Flood* at these moments feels calmed and steady, giving him just enough time to go forward this time, through the saloon, to a store room he rarely ventures into.

Built right beneath the bow, it's a small space, lit by the greasy light of a battery lamp, with curved iron walls where the welds and bolts of the *Flood*'s hull are exposed. In five years he's shoved a lot of things in here, and the sea has tumbled them further into a horrid pile of wood and metal and cardboard and fabric. He tries his best to gather the tarpaulins, push a deckchair away from him, and drag out a length of cable with his foot that seems to have bound everything together. What he's looking for is a strange object, a thing he only kept because he liked its curious name, something he never thought might have to be used one day. The *Flood* is beginning to roll again – he can feel the pressure of the waves building, and from inside the store he hears them slamming the bow on one side, each one reverberating like he's inside a tin drum.

After he's trimmed the direction again he runs back to the store and, miraculously, finds what he's looking for almost immediately. That's great, he thinks, knowing it's really only the start of his worries. On the way back to the wheelhouse, dragging the canvas sacking and iron hoops and chain through the saloon, he takes a heavy weather manual from the bookshelf. Back in his chair, at last, with one hand on the wheel, he finds the chapter he'll need: *Assembly and Deployment of a Sea Anchor*.

When the waves die down again he makes the last series of checks, out on deck, walking the length of the barge with a heavy-duty torch to look for damage. Luckily, the waves haven't breached the bow yet, but he still checks the fastenings and ropes and anchor housing and bow thruster in case the wind and roll of the boat has moved anything. He also checks the inflatable dinghy, making sure there's plenty of fuel in the outboard and the chains to the davit are secure. Satisfied, he climbs on to the roof of the wheelhouse and looks out at the sea. The wind has dropped, and he hears the water more clearly – it seems to gather round the boat as if it has noticed him, in a choppy motion that feels welcome. The waves are smaller now, busily sweeping past with their own individual characters, some rising briefly and nervously, being swept aside by larger, more robust rolls of water. The *Flood* has been magnificent, he thinks. He's miles and miles from shore, there are no lights on the horizon, no sign that man has ever lived or is alive at any place; the sea and the sky are alone as having no lasting touch of man upon them. His world is this boat. There is nothing else.

Position: Eighty or so miles offshore? Guess about 53° 56'N 1° 42'E. 9:30pm

Although they'd travelled half a continent to reach it, crossing the Mississippi had been disappointing. The bridge had appeared too suddenly, and then a high safety barrier and a heavy lattice of girders virtually obscured any view of the river. What they saw were the briefest of glimpses of a wide, impossibly long stretch of water, way beneath them. That was all.

They had entered another state, Arkansas, relentlessly flat, and their journey had suddenly seemed to lose its sense of purpose. Guy had been wrong about the morning. Those feelings of optimism hadn't lasted. A trick of the coffee, he reflects as he drives, making everything so unbelievably positive. His mood had sunk soon after leaving the plantation, whereas Judy's mood – if he had any gauge on it – had brightened. It really did seem that admitting the affair the previous night had been cathartic. In her view she's no longer betraying me, he thinks, because she has said as much.

The sheer recording his mind is doing is exhausting, and has given the day an epic, stretched dimension that is in itself disconcerting. Just this morning, he'd been eating those rolls on the back porch of the shack, and yet that feels like it happened a few weeks ago, a scene from a play even, strangely lit and full of improbability. A lunch, too, where they'd stopped off at a family-run restaurant, specializing in home-fried chicken. Guy had walked in to discover the two men who ran it, a father and son, were both disfigured by burns on their faces, tending to the serving dishes of vegetables, corn, chicken and coleslaw in a dimly lit part of the room. Judy and Freya had noticed, and become quiet about it, and Guy had gone to pay for the food and stared right into the man's eyes – they peered back at him as though through a mask.

He'd taken the food to the table and they'd all eaten in comparative silence, worn out by the travel and unnerved by the restaurant, and Guy had looked at the elderly man shuffling back to the kitchen, as if he was a ghost. It's all unreal, he'd thought, and was thinking it again right now, sitting behind the wheel while the road rolled endlessly by. Louisiana, passing without event. A westerly direction. Scenes from the day, recurring to him now, while the daylight faded. The heat at noon as he'd climbed out of the car to stretch his back. A slight click of his vertebra as he leant from side to side, a comforting feeling. Relieving himself at the corner of a cotton field, his warm urine falling on to dry stalks and dry dusty red earth. Freya collecting cotton buds from the plants a few rows away. How she'd held the cotton tufts to her face like a beard. Judy, biting her nails in an unguarded moment, then tying her hair back in a swift professional motion, the hair twisting obediently to her fast-working fingers. Her reliance on wearing sunglasses, her three cups of coffee at lunch time. His entire family – that unit he so easily took for granted – had felt threadbare.

At times he'd looked to America itself, passing left and right, to give him a shot of inspiration. But America was flat here. Just another hundred or two miles of the same. And as a result he'd driven them hard today, driven and driven with few stops and no plan in his head. Driving west, that's the plan, as it always was, the family might be falling apart but the journey continues, stubbornly, towards a bright and fantastical California which waits like an advertising hoarding. Pacific surf, rolling in, dazzling light, a living dream.

When it's properly dark, about nine o'clock, Freya begins to complain. 'I don't really want to go much further,' she says, politely, wary of a growing atmosphere she doesn't grasp. The air in the car is getting brittle and charged.

'OK,' he says quietly, knowing he's pushing them all too far. 'I'll stop when we see a place. I'm sorry it's been such a long day.'

'Me too,' she says. 'Thanks for doing all the driving.'

He smiles weakly at her. An unexpectedly huge rush of emotion hits him, a welling of feeling which has been mounting all day – it floods him, but he can only understand it in fragments, it's so consuming. His responsibility, his care, his deep love of Freya. All this hits sharply, and he thinks he might cry, just pull over on to the shoulder there and cry, while Judy sits silently in the back, so close and yet so distant.

The lights of a motel approach, and he turns in without asking the others. He will make the decisions now. He's damned if he's going to listen to Judy on this.

He parks right by the office and gets out immediately, but it's only once he's in there under its punishing fluorescent light that his tiredness overtakes him. He catches a reflection of himself in the darkened windows and he's shocked at how worn out he looks. Bleary, impatient and old – this is the cost, he thinks, this is how it's going to be from now on.

He pays for two rooms, next to each other, and drives the car over the lot to park in front. He opens both doors, but says nothing about who will sleep where, knowing that Judy will be trying to work it out, trying to second guess him on this. It's rattled her. Guy sits on the edge of one of the beds and then lies flat across the mattress. He can hear the others bringing in some of the luggage. He looks up at the ceiling and says one thing to them – a thing that he only learned himself about five minutes ago:

'We're in Texas.'

Freya's asleep within minutes, in the first room they went into. Judy's moving around, trying to keep quiet, and Guy just stands, grabs her wrist, and takes her to the room next door. She immediately sits on a chair, by a small table. He sits on the bed facing her.

'I won't let you ruin things for Freya,' she begins.

'If there's someone who's ruining things I think we both know who it is,' he replies, instantly. He's not going to stand for her trying to turn things on him. She did that last night and it's not going to happen again.

'I don't want to talk tonight,' she says, wearily.

'Then you'll listen,' he says.

His abruptness is working. She sits there quietly, drawn in, mouth firm and chin set. He feels a pang of guilt for being harsh, but pushes it aside. He doesn't know where to start.

'Where do I start?' he says. He gets no response from Judy, she's not there to help him. 'Why are you doing this terrible thing to us? To all of us?' She remains quiet, retaining the air of being scolded. 'I can't just accept it, you know. You can't just tell me outright that you are having an affair and expect me to . . .'

'. . . I expect nothing.'

'Right.'

She looks at him, her eyes a little watery, but filled with a defiance that's easily a match for anything he might say.

He stumbles. 'Why are you . . . why are you talking to me like this?'

He looks away from her, and notices the room for the first time. It's small with ochre walls and brown carpet, designed for softness, comfort and could be anywhere in the world. A television faces the bed – its dumb lead-grey eye looks watchfully back at him, he can see his reflection in its lifeless blank screen – how tense he looks in the arms and shoulders – and sees how he's become curiously distorted by a subtle curve. They should provide curtains to hang over these things – TVs have become bigger, and so have their dead reflections.

'Jude – this is crazy. I can't believe this craziness.' He's already sounding inarticulate. Worse, defeated. 'I never thought we would be in this situation. Did you? I mean, we are in a situation, aren't we?'

She nods, rather than say anything. But even that gesture seems guarded. There's just no way in. This kind of quietness in her, it's dangerous, because it draws him into saying too much.

'Are you going to speak?' he asks, regaining his anger.

The anonymous motel room seems designed for this kind of night they're having. Characterless, presiding over them with complete indifference. It unsettles him.

'I thought I was here to listen,' she says.

'Don't be smart.'

She shrugs, dismissively.

'You need to listen all right, you need to listen to yourself,' he says, trying to be smart himself, but feeling foolish, feeling he's losing so easily.

'We'll find a way, Guy,' she says with surprising tenderness, or at least the hint of it. He brushes it off with an impatient *pah* sound. He won't be so quickly dealt with. He looks around, exasperated. Now the room seems laid out for an argument, scene for a fight. It strikes him poignantly, and he yields towards it, wanting to share how he's feeling with Judy – he wants to tell her how alone this is making him feel – she's been his sounding-board for so long. But he knows confidences like this just can't exist any more.

They look at each other. Stalemate. It's like they're playing some kind of game – as though someone's told them to wait in here and not talk.

'Why the two rooms?' she asks.

'You tell me.'

'We're not going to get anywhere if we fight.'

'Believe it or not, I don't want to fight. But you've stung me and the poison's still there, in the system.' He's being too flowery. He mustn't lose her here. He tries another tack. 'Why Phil?'

She looks away and lets out a quiet sigh through the little slot her mouth has become. 'Let's not talk about him here.'

193

'Isn't he exactly who we should be talking about?' Guy's on the attack again – he must keep the heat down – she'll shut him down the moment he goes too far.

'He's kind to me,' she says, quietly, conceding, damning Guy with the implication of his own possible failings. What exactly *are* his failings? She is all dead ends and dark secrets, and he's a fool to be groping his way forward – even his right to be asking these questions appears to be in doubt. And Phil – his presence seems to be there in the room with them, skulking, cowardly, yet strangely arrogant, offering a hand to be on Judy's shoulder, and her accepting it, it's like she's possessed. This is Judy sitting here, he has to remind himself, the woman whom he knows most about in all the world. He knows every inch of her skin, he knows the precise shape and weight of her arms, the tiny rough patches of her elbows where she applies the moisturizer, the back of her neck where the hairline grows – where it occasionally has to be shaved by the hairdresser – the widened shape just high of her hips, the memory of childbirth there, forever. The shortness of her shinbone, the shapeliness of her calf muscle, which hangs like a breast when her knee is raised. Her thin tapering fingers, the skin in that place slightly darker than the rest of her, and her childlike toes, slightly clenched in, always. These are *his* details, just as he is a familiar landscape to her, mapped over the years till it's indelibly part of both of them.

'How long?' he asks her, unimaginatively. She replies with a slight shake of her head, a cool liquid glaze over this moment which gives nothing away.

'We need to talk about Freya,' she says.

That shuts him up. Its cold assertion of widening this situation out into a public field, its suggestion of finality, of practicality – this is an advanced conversation they are having. Here's Guy wanting to discuss the whys and wherefores, the moral dimension to the betrayal he's unearthing, and Judy's just not interested at all. It's a *fait accompli*. She wants to talk about who Freya will live with.

'We will need to sit down with her and explain what's happening,' Judy says, a little recklessly, implying Guy will sign up to the situation without question. She sees her mistake, and makes half a plea. 'Let's not make this messy.'

This time it's Guy who plays the silent card. Judy waits, in no hurry, her father's bank-management skills showing through – she's a businesswoman, after all this, it's a new revelation to Guy and, predictably, it's he who backs down first.

'Judy,' he says, 'I'm still in love with you.'

The start of so many cherished moments between them, a word that usually unlocks her, but here, it's the end. She gets up, stretching her back as if she's been in there for hours, and walks calmly towards the door.

'I'm not sleeping in here,' she says, flatly.

'Is that it? Our discussion's over?'

'Yes.'

'So what am I meant to do?'

'You paid for the room. You may as well use it.'

'Well, I'm not going to.'

'No? Where do you think you're going to sleep then?'

'In there. In the same room as Freya.'

Judy's had enough of this. 'Suit yourself,' she says.

She goes, leaving the door open, a politeness in that gesture about not wanting to shut the door entirely on him, not quite. It gives him the slightest glimmer of hope, but he knows it's no consolation. She doesn't want to be followed.

After a few hours on the motel couch he knows sleep won't come to him tonight. It's just not possible, given the nature of their talk and the feeling that something so ugly and of enormous proportion is growing between them. Once such allies. Its presence is there in the room, like the smell of death, something that can't be disguised. God, he's tired. Already this business is demanding a new stamina, a kind of constant attention within him to be wary, to be on guard, to prepare for all discussions, all eventualities, all hurtful. He was stubborn to insist on sleeping in here, given the perfectly good bed that's unused next door, but he's determined not to be seen as the one who has to leave the family room. Yet it's odd to try and sleep while Judy's there on the bed. If anything, *he* should be on the bed – he is the wronged party here – surely he deserves the bed. He paid for the room, he did all the driving, he's long and the couch is small, but it's his for the night, and for some reason it seems fitting. The men always take the couches.

Judy's impenetrable shadow on the bed is a troubling one. He imagines she is full of potential actions now – of zipping up cases and writing him aggressive notes and new ways of standing, too – stances where she will have a rigidity to her posture, waiting for him to back down, the kind of thing that up to now he's only seen her do when she faces someone they both have issues with. Well, he's the enemy now, of sorts. She's a dark reservoir in that bed, of private thoughts and agendas, and he just doesn't know the depth of it, or the depths of her.

And his mind turns to the thing that he's been trying to ignore, unsuccessfully, all day. Freya.

Asleep, unaware, still so much the child, though she's on the cusp of adulthood. This will damage her – will bring out in her a seriousness he knows will not suit her – will not make her attractive among friends. She takes trouble badly, seems to accept it like a punch and wears it like a bruise, she's like him in that respect.

Freya is still with them, but this night, she's on the far side of the room and she can't be seen among the shadows, and he feels his daughter's absence with a sense of panic. Freya, alone, beyond his reach – it's something he's never before considered happening. His daily protection of her, his daily right to be with her, it's so natural – yet here, he's on the verge of losing it, or more precisely having it taken away. Where will she live? Who will she choose? Judy and the ridiculous one-legged guitar man, or her father, tinged with a hint of tragedy even now? Whatever the outcome, a compromise, a splitting of her identity before it's properly formed.

The couch is bloody uncomfortable. It begins to break his body quietly and efficiently in the night, starting with his neck and spreading down one side. He ends up moving the cushions on to the floor and trying to lie on them there. He gets a moment of relief, but then discovers a draught, and a mushroomy smell from the carpet which is old and unclean and inescapable.

The morning arrives with a grey stealth which begins to illuminate the room. He looks at the chart of fire precautions pinned to the back of the door, which he reads from top to bottom – he's wild with his lack of sleep. A song, a trashy song from the eighties, playing out in his mind over and over again while the room gradually gets lighter. Still a calm place, still time for an hour or two's sleep, but sleep is not coming. He sees a picture of cacti in a false desert sunset materializing on the wall near the bathroom. It shines at him like an omen, a call to the desert, to endlessness.

Guy slides open the door of the wheelhouse and looks out into the night. The clouds have mostly cleared, surprisingly, and the bone-coloured glow of a moon he can't yet see shines across the sky. The stars look silent and icy above him, more like a winter sky than anything he's seen all summer. Perhaps the seasons advance quicker out here? It's much cooler now outside than it was before. He walks along the deck and looks out at the sea, passing in front of him in terrible blackness. Full of a coiled movement, rocklike in its depth and sheer presence. A single wave breaks menacingly alongside, bursting with a seething sound which rushes away into the night, leaving behind its ocean breath of salt and air.

When he turns back to face the wheelhouse, he sees the silhouette of someone sitting in there. He knows it's Freya, on his seat, but the shock of seeing her, like this, so unannounced, strikes him with amazement. It's very dark – the whole deck is only palely illuminated by the starlight, and before he left the wheelhouse he'd turned the lights out inside, so the shape of his daughter is hard to separate from the rest of the shadows around her. But it's undeniable. It's true. It's Freya.

He cautiously walks back along the deck, keeping hold of her shape among the glint of reflections of the sea that shine on the windows. There seem to be layers in there, of water and movement, and among them he keeps losing her, and by the time he's at the doorway, she has vanished.

He puts the lights on and the honey colour of the wood springs forward at him with real intensity. His wheelhouse, empty, with the padded benches and the loose cushion with its faded river scene embroidered by someone he's never met. His own friendly space, so familiar after these five years of living on the *Flood*. It's been a good home. Controls and gauges – for weather, knots, depth, direction, all you need to navigate, where there is essentially no map to follow. The gauges, set in their brass mountings, recording oil and wind and water and magnetism and pressure both inside and out – they seem at once idle and watchful, forever busy but here right now, neglected. He sees a dark patch of wood above the hatch handle made by the grease of hundreds of hands, all of them naturally pushing in the same place. And he sees the sight of his impending emergency – the bag of food hanging from the door, the fastened hatches, the untidy and possibly incomplete apparatus of the sea anchor, the imagined scenes of an approaching catastrophe.

He calls her name but all he hears is the thin sound of his voice in the emptiness of the boat. He checks the saloon, the cabin, the toilet and shower-room, the cupboards, thinking he's losing his mind and feeling a presence, everywhere, that he didn't feel before. Eventually he goes back to the wheelhouse. Deliberately, he tries to absorb his mind with the complicated business of assembling the sea anchor. It turns out to be very frustrating and intricate, and he never quite manages to dispel the feeling that she's there, with him, as he's putting the anchor together.

'Maybe you're here? Are you?' he says, stopping to listen to the silence around him.

He attaches two iron hoops, either end of a tapering canvas bag about ten feet long, like an airfield windsock, then fixes that to a float and chain. It's fiddly. The book has complicated diagrams of trough lengths and wave height and cable spans for ideal deployment of the anchor ahead of the bow. There seems to be a whole science to this thing, but the purpose has a simplicity: if the engine's not up to keeping a direction against the waves, the *Flood* can be held on the right course by this cumbersome dragging anchor, like a horse has its rein. At least, that's the theory.

When it's finished he sits back to admire the contraption. It resembles a giant squid, curled round on the wheelhouse floor. He feels calmer, and no longer feels haunted by a presence he can't explain. He's preparing for the storm, and he's thinking clearly. Impulsively, he gets his mobile from the cupboard and switches it on. It bursts into life in his hand with a series of chattering beeps – the screen glows back at him in a precise glare, full of battery and life and ridiculous can-do optimism. Any number in the world, its childlike belief, each number on the keypad fringed with a halo of perfect blue light. I'm ready, it's saying to him with shameless self-belief, with no awareness at all that out here it's lost, without signal, beyond communication.

Guy climbs down the ladder into his cabin to lie on the bunk in the dark. He must rest. He'll need his strength. He listens to the busy sounds of the *Flood*, of the metal creaking in distant corners, of the joints in the woodwork stretching and relaxing, the wheelhouse glass as it trembles in the frames, then the sounds of water passing outside – a smooth flow brushing the outside of the steel. He listens to all this and knows there will be no chance for sleep tonight. Instead, he concentrates on his breathing, taking long inhales and letting them out gradually, and as he's doing this he becomes aware of that second set of breaths again. From the other side of the cabin. The shallow calm breaths of a child, following his, keeping time with him. He listens, by holding his breath, but hears nothing. Then softly, from a few feet away, Freya whispers to him.

'Why are you upset?'

Guy feels enveloped by an instant cold sweat. He's immediately, intensely awake. He strains to listen to the room, but can only hear the other noises of the boat.

'Daddy?' she says.

'*Freya?*'

'I liked you catching those fish,' she whispers, mischievously.

Guy smiles, full of an unbounded elation, despite the turbulence of his thoughts. 'You saw that?' he says.

'I was watching you.' Her voice is calm, older than he remembers, coming out to him from the dark like a soft curve of air. She's carefully picking her words. 'But you shouldn't have killed so many of them.'

'I know,' he says, spellbound by what's happening. 'I got carried away. You forgive me?' He feels the need to ask questions, to keep hold of this voice, not let it drift away.

'Daddy,' she says, 'you know there's going to be a storm tomorrow?'

'Yes.'

'Do you think that clumsy parachute's going to help?'

'I don't know. What do you think?'

He hears a faint giggle, then Freya's voice coming to him as one of her characters: 'Ain't no playground you know,' she says, impersonating the skipper of the trawler he met.

Guy blurts out a laugh then bites his fist like a madman. He can't believe this. It's his turn for an impression – he says, 'We're going to need a bigger boat,' like Roy Scheider in *Jaws*.

'You're funny,' Freya says. It sounds like her voice is slightly further away this time.

'Freya?' he asks.

'Yes?'

'You're still there?'

'I'm always here.'

'It was you in the sea, wasn't it – when I went swimming, I felt your dress in the water.'

'Yes. It was cold. Your hand was cold.'

'Darling, it's so lovely to hear you. Do you know how much I've wanted this?'

'Why are you upset, Daddy?' she asks again.

He stares into the darkness of the room, trying to make out her face against the velvet blackness of the opposite wall. A tiny glimmer of light is coming down the ladder from the wheel-house, but with each rung it seems to half, and down here in his cabin there's no clue – it's like being in a well. He so wants to see her.

'I'm upset because of writing that diary. And I don't think I can do it much longer. Since I lost you I wanted to believe in something – I wanted to believe that all three of us would have been happy. But I can't honestly say that's true any more. I was trying to keep everything together, see, but it's all falling apart. All over again. I can't control it.'

She doesn't say anything. He has the feeling that she's no longer with him in the cabin.

'I'm scared, Freya.'

'What of, Daddy?' she says.

'I'm scared that when I turn on the light, you're not going to be here.'

'Oh.'

'Shall I turn on the light?'

'I don't know. Don't be scared.'

'OK. Thanks, love – you're good to me. God, I so want to see you. I'm going to turn the light on.'

He reaches for the pull-cord of the wall lamp to the side of his bed. He feels the small metal bead at the end of the cord and hesitates, anticipating the flood of cold light that will illuminate his cabin. He's scared, right now, after all this time, to see her.

Guy pulls the cord and the cabin fills with light and he looks at the emptiness of the room. Empty square space reaching into each corner.

Position: Not sure. The North Sea.

As the new day arrives – its light spreading in a greasy unremarkable stain across the sea – Guy is buttoned up in his warmest coat, sitting in the pilot's chair. He hasn't slept. He switches off the light in the wheelhouse and his surroundings change from a cosy orangey glow to a grey and shadowed room – all the life drained from it. The windows feel cold and brittle, and the deck of the boat stretches in a horribly damp shape into the sea, covered in a salty dew. The sky promises something awful. A fatigue presses him across his forehead, but he knows he won't sleep. He knows the storm is imminent. He escaped it yesterday, but he can't escape it now.

With a sense of trepidation, he takes the assembled sea anchor to the bow of the boat, fixes its cable, and secures it with rope. Then as a final measure, he attaches a can of engine oil to the anchor's float, and pierces its lid with several stabs of a screwdriver. He's hoping an oil slick might calm the water – the manual said it was worth a try. And he's willing to try anything.

Below, the water rushes by with a swift noise, like the sea has become a river, sweeping its weather towards him.

He has a shower in the tiny cubicle forward of the saloon, sliding the roof light open to let the steam out. And as he stands there, looking up at the thin stream of iron-smelling water coming from the showerhead, and the pale grey square of the sky beyond, it is like a surreal rain is falling on him, and he wonders whether he might faint. Sleeplessness has done that.

He goes back to the pilot's chair and sits at the wheel, looking at the map of the North Sea. There's nowhere to go, no direction any more, except back, he supposes – but there's no chance the *Flood* could outrun the storm now. This is the end of the line for him. With every minute the weather is worsening.

'Where was I?' he says out loud, finding his last entry in the diary.

'Oh yeah,' he answers.

In the morning he goes into the en suite and stands under the rigid force of water gushing from the showerhead for as long as he can take it. Hot Texan water, full of its own right to be vital and strong, rushing on to the back of his neck and down his arms, wrapping him in a false vigour.

Judy is sullen, carrying an injured air, as though she is the one who hasn't slept. She avoids Guy, spends a long time in the bathroom, and seems to have taken a sudden interest in the map, where they are, how far they still have to go perhaps. In contrast, Freya is bright, and keen on finding out breakfast possibilities and discussing routes.

'Ah'm gonna go out an' shoot me a ra-coon,' she says, as Calamity Jane, 'and you can have its foot for a key-ring, coz I already got me my gator claw,' which she produces from behind her back. An alligator's claw as a lucky charm, but bringing them no luck when it came down to it. She knows something's wrong with her dad. She'll make a natural partner for a man one day, Guy thinks.

Judy doesn't ask how he feels or how he slept, but she does ask if he's all right to drive, the suffering of the night must be as clear as day. He's unsure himself, but gets into the driving seat regardless, resigned to this westerly direction which he doggedly wants to protect. And then they drive, once more leaving a place on the earth which has the feel of a scarred spot, a lightning strike of pain and discord between them, occurring there, vanishing in the rear-view mirror. They drive, west as always, through a Texas which seems as wide as a continent. He knows their route across America should begin to rise up here, becoming a lovely positive arc into New Mexico, Arizona, Nevada and California. Drawn across the map it would have the shape of a smile, a warm smile of well-being. They should be crossing America with the naturally curving grace of a line strung between the two points of arrival and departure. But instead the curve seems to be turning downward, as if running out of energy as it falls. Flying on one engine, he thinks, almost deliriously, they're bound to crash. But where? Where can they go?

Guy has no idea where the *Flood* is now. It's in the centre, heading east, but the waves are growing, and as their direction veers he has to turn into them. He's in the approaching grip of the storm, that's all he knows. He opens the window – Spin me round, my darling, he shouts to the rising wind, then wonders whether he's above the Dogger Bank yet, that wonderful trackless part of the North Sea, so curious in the shipping forecast. They dredge mammoth skulls from the seabed here, covered in thick black peat.

On the charts Dogger is a simple square shape, the first of the areas not to have a coast to call its own. It belongs to the sea, but with its oddly comic name it seems friendly, unlike the areas going north like Forties or Viking, names that in themselves seem full of waves and danger.

Faced with such a dismal view of the mounting sea, he has a pang of homesickness for the damp calm of East Anglia. He misses the wet prismatic light of England. The clouding scent of wet woodland. The feel of a sodden tree trunk, the cloggy odour of fallen leaves, the smells of his own estuary at low tide, of its wrecks and repairs, its stink of mud and rust and oil.

Closing his eyes, Guy imagines the woods along the shore at the Tide Mill anchorage. He gets fleeting images of his dog, Banjo, rummaging through the pinecones, gathering several into his mouth and trotting busily beneath the trees. He remembers the feel of his shoes slipping on the mats of fallen pine-needles, and a breeze stirring – splitting into a thousand threads of sound as it's combed by the trees before settling, without substance, around him.

It's a special place. Woods *are* special. Guy's mother used to love them – used to love touching the trees and looking up at the wide span of branches, her mouth slightly ajar with open-eyed awe. Looking for permanence, always. He remembers how she would take a detour in the car, stopping it when the road passed through a wood, just to hear the sound of it, how she'd wind down the window and theatrically breathe it in.

Guy remembers his mother in a flowery jacket and cheap wellingtons, a smell of old rubber about her, while he wore a bright orange anorak and hunted for any tree he could climb, his hands and knees already dirt-green and scratched by the bark. He'd be seven or eight, the golden age of childhood, but already then without a father, running in quick darts between the trees, occupied by the desire to climb, while his mother walked dreamily behind him.

Other times they'd sit on grassy banks by the side of the road, blowing dandelion heads or trying to find a four-leaf clover. We'll find one today, she'd always say that, it was a kind of mantra for her, and Guy would pretend to be casual about looking for it, but really he was determined to be the first, determined to be the man of the occasion, solving all, the one who'd bless them with the luck she so often wished for. What exactly this luck was, Guy hadn't been sure, but he remembers the sight of the clover, its springy bright green parting with his fingers, so often a clover with four leaves, until he moved the plant and the heads would seamlessly separate. *Got one*, he'd cry, every so often, to raise his mother's spirits, but the look of instant unbridled pleasure on her face – taking ten years off her for a glowing second – upset him, even though it fascinated him to see her younger like that, glimpsing the woman she had been.

He realizes now, too late, how lonely she probably was during those times, walking in the woods or sitting on the verge by the car, how aware she would have been that a man wasn't there with them.

Strangely, Guy smells a faint whiff of cigarettes, and he opens his eyes mistrustfully. It must be a trick of his breathing, like tasting a bonfire in the back of your throat long after the fire has gone. But its eerie evocation of his father's secretive habit unsettles him, briefly. A father's presence is a shifting, long-lasting one, taking many forms. It lingers, like an anxious stink that remains in a shirt, however many times you wash it.

There's a marshy area he remembers, too, where the path has been partially boardwalked as it passes a mire of rushes and pools of thick oily water. In spring it's a busy place, full of damselflies and dry-cased beetles crawling up the stems. The bright young spikes of the bulrushes burst out of the mud, but at this time of the year, things would be dying back. The reeds and grasses would be bleached by the sun and spent by such over-reaching growth. The bulrush heads would be burned brown and crumbling, they'd have the soft gripped look of church bell ropes.

Daffodils grew here, emerging each spring out of nowhere, in wide banks of brilliant yellow, so many of them the ground seemed to have an extra sunshine to it, emanating in a haze above the flowers. They were so plentiful he was always constantly corralled into dead ends in their labyrinth of flower walls when he tried to get through. He remembers how he'd snapped one of the heads off to put in his pocket, it had made a hollow tugging sound, and the cut stem had had the peppery green smell of a salad.

He'd been there with Judy. They hadn't been married long, and Guy had been enjoying the sight of her, lying there on the fallen trunk of a beech tree, in dappled sunshine. His wife, peaceful, but already with a closed-eyed look of her own secret world.

Beyond her, a small woodland pond was filled with lily pads. *Guy*, Judy whispered, *look*. When he turned he saw her entire body had become rigid with an effort not to move. A tiny patch of light flickered by her eye, seemed to bend, or fold, and he realized a butterfly had landed on her cheek. Judy stared skyward, unblinking, the only thing that moved in all this world had been the rhythmic folding of the butterfly's wings, each time, its lampshade pattern of orange and gold vanished into a thin black velvety line, a second closing eye it seemed, momentarily, next to hers. Guy and Judy had been transfixed. The butterfly had possibly mistaken the brown of Judy's iris, almost green in that light, for the centre of a flower. The ribbon of its thin uncurling tongue was touching her eye, in the corner, where a glisten of moisture shone like glass.

'I can't believe this,' Judy said, 'can you see it?'

Guy nodded, mesmerized by the sight.

The butterfly continued to dab the eye, unravelling that impossible tongue, uncurling its tip in the moisture, and as it did this, the tongue brushed an eyelash. With an unavoidable reflex, Judy blinked and the butterfly lifted upwards, without weight, into a slow papery dreamlike flight.

They watched it leaving, dappled by the woodland patterns, till it was just another fleck of the sunshine, a falling leaf, a trick of the light.

'Did you get a good look at it? I want to know what it was.'

'A Marsh Fritillary,' Guy had said, later that evening, sitting in his armchair at their house, after looking through one of his wildlife books. 'It's rare.'

'How rare?'

'To have been licking your eye – I'd say it was pretty much unique.'

'It was amazing, wasn't it? I mean, really amazing. I could have stayed like that forever. All I could see were those soft wings, closing like that.'

'Could you feel it?'

'No. It did touch my eye, didn't it?'

'Yes.'

Judy falls silent, satisfied that the moment was perfect and needed nothing more. And Guy had realized it had become *her* moment, already, part of the myth she felt she needed to create about her own life, that her life traded in beauty.

'Mind if I do some practice?' Judy had said.

'Go ahead. Need me on the piano?'

'No.'

'You looked lovely, you know, with that butterfly on you.'

'Thanks. I felt like an angel.'

Guy had been left in the living-room, by the fireplace, looking at the ugly helmeted heads of garden beetles, listening to the sound of his wife doing singing practice in the room upstairs, the room where he hoped, one day, they might have a child.

Guy wakes, startled, realizing he must have finally nodded off, his feelings of calm immediately interrupted by the very real sight of the grey sea advancing at him, parting either side of the bow. It seems like something has vanished from the world. Life and the clutter of living things, just where have they gone?

He looks at the time, still early, then checks the barometer's continuing fall and, momentarily, feels the day itself might be reversing, the light is fading so rapidly.

It never had a chance to shine, not today.

The road becomes full of traffic going his direction. Cars and trucks of all sorts, covered with a dizzying array of religious, Texan, confederate and cowboy bumper stickers, all of them heading west in a crowded stream. He slows down, becomes familiar with the rear of the car in front, while Freya asks what's going on. Guy doesn't know, but he soon finds out. It's a rodeo, he says, as they approach a wide banner fringed with bunting strung across the road. It's big, he adds. Freya gets excited, winding down her window and watching the country roll by. Cattle glance back at her, from the other side of a ranch fence, with a knowing look.

'Will we go?' she asks.

'Yes,' Guy replies, automatically, seizing the occasion, any occasion to make this journey intentional. From outside he smells a warm dry smell of earth and grass.

'You want to go?' he adds, looking at her.

'Is it cruel to horses?' Freya asks.

'I don't know. I don't think so.'

'I don't want it to be cruel to the horses.'

'No. Neither do I.'

It takes them a while to find somewhere to stay – most places are full – but a shabbily painted motel on the edge of town still has a room. Just the one room. He's not interested to know the name of this place or just how far across Texas they have driven. That can be Judy's concern, as they drive further and further, away from airports, towards a dead end which is Mexico.

Guy goes into the motel room. It's the same as all the others they've stayed in. My spot on the earth, he thinks: vacant, pending. He lies on the bed and puts the TV on and watches a programme about the building of a railroad.

They eat Mexican food that night, in a small restaurant next to the motel. Guy's feeling very strange with the lack of sleep, and the restaurant is oppressively crowded with trinkets, strings of multicoloured tasselled fabric, pottery watermelon slices and model donkeys. Painted faces on coconut shells peer down at him with peasant grins. Sunny, brown faces. It makes him shudder, to think of Mexico so close out there, filled with a wide sun-drenched life and, pocketed here, in such gaudy colours.

The tables are small and the food, when it arrives, is huge. Guy digs in to every dish, meeting his tiredness head on with the decision to overeat, embarking on a pointless game to uncover the patterned design of the plates. He thinks there are pictures of rural scenes, under the beans and the tortillas. He eats a pork stew, deliberately chewing the chillies, though they burn his mouth badly. A guitarist comes to play at the table, in a sombrero and charro suit, and a waiter gathers them together roughly, then takes a picture. Somehow, the photo is printed off and presented to them midway through the meal. He looks at himself in the photo, grinning next to a grinning mariachi player, all of them grinning, it's grotesque.

The motel is full of guests, and as Guy lies on the bed, alongside Judy, he can hear the mixed noise of family life through the walls, like the sound of water in the pipes, energy constrained, channelled. Some children are up late, they're going wild a few doors down, and Guy imagines each square space of motel room between himself and them, each block filled with its own addition of sound, its own scene of men and women lying on beds, while the clamour of the children increases. At least it sounds lively – he's been afraid of silence for the last two days, but the excitement of overheard family life contrasting with his own sombre room hardly needs drawing attention to.

Judy lies close to him in the bed, but there's been no touch between them. She's on her side, resting her head on an arm, looking towards him with eyes as dark as charcoal.

She's just asked how easy it might be to change the flights. He has no idea, and out of stubbornness he's insisting they go on, all the way to the Pacific.

'Clearly that can't happen, now,' she says, whispering so that Freya won't hear. Guy looks up at yet another blank ceiling in his latest motel room.

'What if I want to go on?' he says, obstinately.

'Then you're going alone. Look, I don't expect you to find this easy, but at least treat this with maturity. I don't want unpleasantness, and I think there's a way forward for us all.'

He doesn't like her planning for him – it clearly won't be in his interest.

'You sound like it's all worked out.'

'To some extent, I think it is.'

'So?'

'We separate.'

Guy accepts that, the waves of tiredness finally hitting him to the extent that he feels nauseous. She's a chameleon, adapting her argument to his mood, outwitting him at every turn. He thinks she's been waiting for this moment, this insomniac weakness where there is no fight left in him, where the events of the last couple of days cease to have any logic.

Judy lies back. Pathetically, he goes to hold her, to remind himself that her body, its intimate collections of shapes and smells, its history of their relationship which is remembered in every last part of her, is still somewhere he can go to. But she pushes him away, gently.

'Do I even get to know the reason,' he asks, 'for all this?'

'Let's not rush to put labels on what's happening,' she says. 'The past was good, but there can't be a future. You know that.'

'Actually, I didn't,' he says. 'I thought we'd done all the changing. I thought we were just going to grow old together.'

She doesn't answer, carefully sidestepping his route into sentimentality. He waits for her to talk again, but she doesn't, and his mind seems to dim and lurch forward to that inviting realm of sleep that he so craves, so needs, without it there's no clarity in all this, and that's all he gets, because his thoughts spring back at him, newly positioned with alarming proximity, and he knows he's awake, really awake.

For the second night he doesn't sleep. He stares at the ceiling, which is featureless, then at the soft gauzy shadows of the motel room. Leaning against the TV is the photo from the restaurant. How ironic, that the picture captures a moment when a man who plays guitar has come between them. Judy's breathing comes at him regularly, relaxed, and Freya mutters something incoherent from her dream. Gradually the other pockets of noise in the motel complex fade out, and he is left with a wide empty silence, the sound of Judy's shallow breathing, and of Freya shifting uncomfortably in her sleep. An hour or two passes. He moves over to Judy and strokes her back – feeling the gentle curve of her where the knuckles of her spine dip below the surface, becoming a crease where they join her pelvis. He holds her briefly, burying his nose in the warm towelled smell of her T-shirt, and then in the peppery curls of her hair, the scent of her he's known so long. Her head generates a heat, always, which radiates while she sleeps. Her bum is like a hot polished dinner plate, round and large because she is curled up – her skin feels as smooth as glazed porcelain there. And she stirs in her sleep, straightening and moving away from him.

He has a fantasy of tapping Freya on the shoulder, waking her up with a finger over her lips to stop her speaking, coaxing her into the car, then driving, bleary-eyed, towards Mexico, his conscience clear but his heart muddled with disaster. He worries the fantasy, till he begins to see them racing the old hire car down some dusty desert track, while Judy points them out to a state trooper from high up on a cliff. A tell-tale glint from the trooper's Lone Star badge, then two more as he raises his mirror-shades, puts the rifle to his eye, a shot rings out and the film of Guy's great escape is over, as he slumps, bloodied, across the wheel.

Other fantasies jostle for space, of Phil, sitting on a trans-Atlantic flight, his artificial leg resting on his lap because his stump is beginning to swell, the poor sod, how he massages it, full of self-pity; of the wet black bears of Georgia sniffing outside the door, getting hungry; and all the mariachi players in all the world in all the badly fitted charro suits and still, still, he doesn't sleep.

At about four in the morning, he gets up and quietly leaves the room to stand on the porch. His hire car sits patiently, as dumb as a horse tied to the rail. The air is cool and empty, the distance beyond the lot looks liquid black and pure to him. Inviting. He walks there, passing the cars and over a small wire fence till he's standing in an area of barren scrub. Looking into the blankness, he can't see any signs of habitation. No houses, no lights, but the land is full of a thick sound of insects. It smells different to him, too, it smells of dry stones and woody plants with small leaves. It's magical. He gives in to it, fascinated by the night's soft contour of undefined, limitless space. Dogs bark distantly, their calls answering each other in plaintive avenues of sound, and a lonely voice mixes with them, from far away, the long drawn call of a coyote.

On one side of this nothingness a ridge of bare rocky cliffs stretches away, as smooth as dough, bone grey in the night. Ink-black crevices and holes puncture the rock, like the buttons on a leather armchair. A warm dry scent of dust and cooling sand rolls down towards him, and he senses, for the first time since they started this journey, that here is a smell of endlessness, a frontier, the intoxicating smell of the desert.

As Guy looks out there, into this fragrant empty night, he sees a kind of freedom. He sees a place where he might be, alone, his life stripped down bare, an empty page. And he imagines a time when he might someday disappear, journeying to find escape, into a wilderness.

Position: Storm

Guy hurriedly gathers the diaries for the last five years, seals them in a watertight bag and ties the package to the polyurethane life-ring under the bench seat. With more string he ties the arms of his glasses together round the back of his neck so they won't blow off. He tries to clear his head by having a large gulp of the *Gammel Dansk*. It really does taste like ear-wax. Then he faces the storm, trying not to panic, dressed in his zipped-up wet gear, staring through the wheelhouse glass at a sea the likes of which he's never seen before, a surging of waves that by the minute seem to be rising and breaching in utterly unpredictable patterns, as the wind begins to howl, begins to batter the windows, making the puddles already collecting on deck shiver with anticipation.

He touches the brass-ended central king spoke of the wheel for luck.

Then he increases the *Flood*'s speed to full, and turns the wheel toward each wave that arrives, trying to hit it in the middle, head on, the bow sinking and cutting into the wave at the last minute to give a brief moment, a solid groove of the sea where the boat feels level and stable. The sheer weight of the barge, as it cuts into the waves, sends a bright foamy spray over the bow which seems to hang suspended in the air, before it travels quickly across the deck at a constant speed to hit the wheelhouse in a wide slap of cold water. The wipers are on full, but hardly able to keep the view clear.

Above him, the clouds are dark grey and low and seem to be much calmer than the sea. Despite being part of the same storm, their true force is elsewhere. There is no rain. No lightning. But no escape either, just a narrowing gap between the rising sea and the lowering clouds where the *Flood* must find some room to manoeuvre. *It's too much*, Guy says, his mind focused on every rising ridge of water that appears in front of him, spinning the wheel as best as he can to meet the unpredictable edge that snakes in ominous approach. Each wave, as dead in colour as grey flint, but glowing with a strange green translucence near their tops where the water is thinnest. *You get a forty-yard swell it'll roll that*, the skipper of the trawler had said, and Guy tries to gauge the length of these waves as the crests sweep by the side of the *Flood*, hugely fast now, with marbled patterns of foam stretching back across their receding slopes. Each one passing a wave he will never have to face again, but a ceaseless flow of new ones arriving, sometimes head-on, sometimes coming sideways at the boat. And a new disturbing noise adding to the rushing noise of the storm – the sound of the ship's bell, beginning to ring of its own accord.

As the *Flood* breaches each crest, the wheelhouse is lifted high into the air and he sees, briefly, a rugged unknowable landscape in the gloom. He looks in awe, then the wave passes underneath, and he hears the iron of the boat groan as it tips forward and the engine over-revving as the propeller momentarily lifts clear of the water. When this happens he feels the loose-jointed swing of the wheel when the rudders turn in the air, before the *Flood* sinks back, the bell ringing with alarm as the propeller bites into the back of the wave.

And when the boat slides into one of the calm dishes of the troughs, he hears sudden intimate sounds, of bubbling, the sounds of a frightened sea in the middle of the storm.

It's during one of these lulls, when several waves had collided to wipe each other out, that he runs out along the deck towards the bow. The wind springs at his face as wet as the sea, and on either side of the boat he's aware of grey sloping waves rising almost as high as the deck, marbled with streaming white foam like streaks of fat. The lenses of his glasses are immediately covered in water. The deck's never seemed so long, so perilously tipping and rolling from side to side, and just as he reaches the prow a surge of water hammers the front, knocking him and the boat still, almost pitching him straight off his feet, then a wall of spray rises magnificently in front of the bow, as if off a harbour wall, and slaps him hard with its cold rain.

He grabs the windlass and for a second everything is blurred and drenched, he knows the *Flood* is turning, a few more like that and the waves will hit from the side and roll him – he must act quickly. He tears the securing line off the sea anchor and tips the contraption in, punting eighty-feet of cable off the side too, with his foot, into a wave that rises up like it's come to seize him, unawares.

'Not yet!' he shouts, and the wind takes the shout away and he loses its sound entirely.

He runs and half slides back to the wheelhouse as the wave streams by with a deafening gush, the same speed as him, and he throws himself at the wheel, turning it hard to counteract the pitching of the boat, while things fall from shelves downstairs, the bell rings, and the inflatable dinghy bangs against the davit behind him, and he sees the sea rising almost up to the scuppers on one side, it can't hold, he can't hold this for much longer.

The engine is too slow, the waves are now too fast, each time he aims towards the crest of one he knows the engine can't climb it, and he's been relying on luck that the wave will pass and the one behind it will be something he can turn at. So far, luck has been with him, but luck is not enough, and he imagines that sea anchor cable paying out, even now, to eighty feet, the canvas sock inflating underneath the water, then straightening in front of the boat and through the smeared windscreen he sees the cable suddenly spring tight at its cleat, and he knows the anchor is out there, skewered through the tops of two waves each time, like a giant needle and thread that might just hold, might just keep him pointed at the waves that are coming for him, one, several, maybe thousands out there that have the power to drown him.

Guy waits, intent on that cable at the far end of his boat. He tries to lower the revs, but fears that might make things worse, the engine has been his only ally so far – so he brings the speed up again. The cable seems to slacken, twist and spring to one side, then pull taut again.

'Come on, come on,' he mutters, his teeth clenched like a drowned man's, already, he has no idea what to do. Maybe that anchor will pull him under, he's only just thought that, it seems odd to put something into the sea that will attach the boat to anything, when suddenly he senses a new motion to the barge, something he hadn't really expected, an extra aid to his effort to keep straight.

It must be working, it must be, and he slaps the wheel and wipes the steamed-up windscreen glass and stares out to sea and all he can imagine is that the anchor is down there, eighty feet in front of the boat, holding him with godly strength.

Every so often an unearthly wall of water rises impossibly in front of the bow, forming in the gloom like a world tipped on its side, gathering, then rolling upwards and towards him and he feels the old barge lifting without weight, dreamily, then rushing forward into the sinking sea and he's pitched almost out of his chair and on one occasion he shouts 'HOLD ON!' and instantly he remembers saying the same two words to Freya, years ago, at the beginning of a fairground ride as the long metal safety bar was lowered in front of them.

The ride was a giant octopus shape, covered in multicoloured flashing bulbs, that would turn and spin and send each seat towards the edge before bringing it back at great speed. Freya was four, only just old enough to be let on, and as the ride began – a slow gliding motion – she was already giggling with anticipation.

'I'm not scared, I'm not scared,' she said, and then said 'Faster, faster,' as the seats began a gentle acceleration towards the edges, for a moment hanging above the onlookers, then being sucked back in reverse, spinning, making a complicated pattern among the other riders. It was balletic at this speed, but Guy remembered hearing a new gear engaging, almost a surge in electricity which flickered the lights, and a flat male voice overhead saying *Come on now, that's right, let's fly,'* and the speed had picked up, powerfully, sending them lurching to the sides, spinning them – he heard Freya yelling with delight, then the forces of the ride pushing her voice back into her as he felt her gripping his hand, her small thin body sliding from side to side on the slippery plastic seat, the centrifuge pressing him against her at certain points so strongly it was everything he could manage not to crush her. His small child, in the arms of that metal monster, he had wanted it to stop, return them to how they were. The crowd had been a blur to him, whizzing past, then every so often he'd been suspended above them for the hold of a second, enough to look at a face below, and it was during one of these hiatuses when he had seen Judy, beneath him, almost close enough to touch. Her face was illuminated by the unnatural shine of the light bulbs that encrusted his seat – she had seen him in the timeless eddy where they shared the same concern, that the ride was too fast – like a look shared in the eye of the hurricane. Then the forces had risen again and he'd felt the mechanical pressure building up to lurch him away and Freya had screamed unpleasantly in his ear and a strand of saliva was flung from her mouth, the saliva transcribing the same looping movement of the ride, and she laughed again and screamed *'FASTER!'* one more time, and he had become happy, he was with her in the blur of lights and smells of diesel and candyfloss and he screams back *'HOLD ON!'*

A wave strikes the *Flood* with venomous power, rolling on to the barge as high as the wheelhouse and the boat reacts in a stunned fashion, floundering for a moment, gathering itself against a series of punches and pressures it's unable to deal with. The spokes of the wheel strike Guy's hands as the rudders are caught. Curves of the sea lift up at his side, coiled like cobras, watching him, before striking the wheelhouse glass. The glass must hold, Guy knows, or he'll be blinded. And for the first time he notices water around his feet, a few inches deep, sliding from side to side on the boards and running across the inspection hatch to the engine compartment. There's no time to bail it, but its presence makes him fear there's more water in the boat, in its dark corners, sloshing around near that steaming machinery below the floor. If the engine goes he will have no chance.

For the rest of the day the rolling sea comes at him ceaselessly, wave after wave, the *Flood* pitching head on as best as it can into the direction of the swells, but each time, just the merest imbalance in the water sending it sliding one way or the other. Sometimes as the boat tips he sees the water almost lapping into the wheelhouse door, pooling against the scuppers as calm and unmenacing as a duck pond, then, miraculously, absurdly, the *Flood* keeps returning to a righted keel.

When the rain eventually comes it lashes down straight, turning the view of the sea into a misty haze of steam and water. It's as if Guy can only look at the waves through a gauze now, as they come without warning, lurking there in front of the bow, waiting their turn. And he sees little silver flashes coming down in the rain and he realizes fish are falling on to the boat too: tiny sprats and sand eels, like drops of molten lead hitting the deck, being stunned, then swept, mad-eyed, back into the sea when the boat tips.

Guy knows that both he and the *Flood* are now way beyond their limit. The sea has been too mountainous, too fast, he's been acting out of sheer exhausted adrenaline all day, aiming for the cresting water like some diabolical game. The waves have breached across the bow, their weight pressing the old barge deeper into the sea as they land, yet somehow the boat carries on, and so does he. The thought of that ocean beneath him, all round him, indifferent and murderous, it's too much.

It would be so easy to turn broadside to the storm and let it roll him under, down to where the mammoth skulls are. A home for the fish, they love a good wreck, eels sliding in and out of the cabins, he's thinking this way, deliriously, without two nights' sleep, fighting the waves in a dream, it's as if someone else is now turning the ship's wheel. He feels disembodied, protected by something, or someone, like the ghostly presence of the old Dutch bargeman has returned, finally declaring himself to take the wheel with his blunt-jawed determination.

Godverdomme! Krijg nou de pokke! he would growl, damning Guy with disapproval, but saving his beloved boat and his precious cod-liver cargo, and gradually Guy becomes aware that the storm is beginning to blow itself out. The night is arriving, and the waves are losing their power, they're falling into a more rhythmic pattern. Less foam bursting from beneath, less sound, less wind.

The spoke of the storm must have revolved somewhere else, for other boats to fight, and in its wake is this smaller sea, almost apologetic.

He can't quite believe it. Can't quite believe many things in fact, that he's survived, that the *Flood* can cope with all this, that her old rock of an engine has kept going, that he used a sea anchor against the odds.

As nightfall finally comes, he is at last able to drop the speed and go out on deck, where he sees it has been swept clean of all the things he'd left out there. He pulls off the string that's been tying his glasses on all day.

The water glints up at him in a soft waxy light, the waves no more than long gentle swells now. He stares out at the black void of the North Sea, in awe of it. Humbled by it. The ebbs and flows of the sea have given his life its rhythm – its salt is in his bones and its presence, so enormous and malign, has been a natural filling of the empty spaces his father left, his wife left, his daughter left.

Above him, the sky is filled with stars, glittering icily in a distance which seems to have no atmosphere. He sees Orion,

Cassiopeia, the Pleiades – stars he's recognized all his life, but here, given a new context, a renewed vividness. There seems to be no barrier between where he is and what's up there.

The small figure sitting at the prow of the boat is Freya. She's huddled up against the cold, but is looking dreamily out to sea. Guy walks calmly towards her, rounding the bulkhead fastenings till he is a couple of feet away. She looks up at him and smiles. He sits down next to her on the cold steel plate of the foredeck.

'That was quite a storm, Daddy,' she says.

'Yeah, yeah it was. I can't quite believe we got through it.'

'That dumb sea anchor worked, didn't it? I couldn't believe it when you ran out to kick it off the side. You looked so panicky.'

'Cheers.'

'You nearly went in yourself.'

'I know. Did you see what I did with my glasses?'

She nods, smiling. He looks at her face, how it's changed over the years, and so shadowed in this light, but he can still see the girl she once was, the four-year-old he loved so much. He can see that face, submerged in this one, still guiding its expressions, even after all this time.

'I've missed you more than I thought was possible,' he tells her, and he hears his voice cracking with a rush of feeling. 'I've been writing this diary about you for five years and . . . I just can't do it any more. It's gone wrong. I can't keep you alive like that. Do you understand?'

'I think so.'

'What do we do now, Freya?'

'I don't know. I don't know,' she says, sadly.

'I'm going mad,' he says.

'You've always been mad, you silly man,' she says, her eyes glinting up at him.

'Yeah,' he says, smiling. 'But you know, properly mad?'

She looks at him, kindly, proprietarily, the way that only a daughter can. 'You need to go to bed, Dad. I'll look after you and the *Flood* while you're asleep. Don't worry.'

'But I want to stay out here, with you.'

'It's too cold out here for you. The sea's too cold.'

He looks about him, at the curves of anonymous water sweeping past each other – he's never seen such a huge emptiness as this moment, ever in his life.

'You'll be here?' he asks.

'Always,' she replies.

When he goes in he collapses on to his bunk, still in his wet gear. Instantly sleep is there for him, and he is dreaming of sunlight, blazing down. He's walking along a dusty track through the desert scrub of Texas. About a mile away he can hear the thin metallic sound of a man's voice, spilt up and then amplified out of synch on several tannoys, drifting across on the morning air. Freya and Judy are with him. Freya's excited, full of life, but it's a life which feels beyond his grasp, as if he's not quite there. Inevitable, Guy thinks, all this is inevitable, as he is ushered onwards.

He's holding Freya's hand tightly, too tightly, he feels her wriggling free of him and walking on ahead. A path too narrow for them all to walk side by side, so they continue, single file, in funereal fashion, towards the rising clamour of the rodeo. The combined smells of hotdogs and candy and sweet straw and fresh dung begin to wash over them, in waves. The sun is hot and startlingly bright – it springs off the tops of parked cars and pick-up trucks like camera flashes. He reaches again for Freya's hand, finds it in the crowd, and won't let go, even though he feels Judy's presence – like an electric current – holding Freya's other hand and pulling her away from him.

He listens to his family in fragments: Freya's fascination with horses, Judy's half-hearted answers, but also Judy's silence towards him, Freya's instinctive unease that her father's not seeming to be there, among them. He holds out money, is given some tickets, then more money, a paper plate of deep-fried doughnuts is handed to him, then a coffee in a Styrofoam cup. It does no good, the doughnuts make him nauseous, he drops his on the dirt and sees a snakeskin cowboy boot step round it. He sees ropes slung over galvanized steel fences. Trailers, hat stalls, flags hanging limply in the sunshine, crowded with strings of bunting. Every surface washed by a desert wind that has left them dirtied.

Judy glares at him, telling him to shake himself out of it, whatever mood he's in, whatever state he can't shift, and the tannoy shouts down at him from the top of a bleacher and he looks up towards it like it's an annoying voice from God and he sees row upon row of people, in hats, in sunglasses, chewing, talking, taking their seats, eating their way through the morning, grinning and laughing and sucking drinks through straws and he feels utterly sick, sick of the people, everywhere, and so alone among them.

That's when he hears the cough-like whinny of a stallion from beyond the fences, from the back of a truck it seems, or buried in some deep cave, and he reacts with a wave of startling fright, a wave of horror, and he thinks precisely about loss, about how he can't imagine a life without Freya. The rodeo swamping him now with its nightmarish reality of garish bunting, announcements, its confusing array of fences, paddocks, rules, corralling him and his family.

He panics, reaches for Freya, needs to hold her, finds she's gone. An empty seat next to him, always, now, for the rest of his life, that empty seat to look at, and he can't see her anywhere, not in all the faces of these people he doesn't know. Then suddenly he glimpses her, walking into the dirt arena, although it's not her, it's her as he remembers, Freya as a four-year-old, in that faded lilac dress she wore. The small trippy walk of hers as she heads across the little patch of dry dirt, the confusion of fear and delight on her face. Horseradish leaves growing through the grit and sawdust. And a dark disturbance enters his vision, the shape of malignity, arriving in the ring, thundering, agitated, a lone stallion which snorts wild-eyed, noticing her. The animal in all its brutish posture and anger. Startled, rushing towards her, its muscles shaking down its flanks, the overbearing weight on its brittle hard hooves. And Freya starts to do her death run – that moment when she chooses not to be with them any more – that moment when she decides once again that they will be a family of two now, not three. That awkward little pathetic run and stumble of hers right into the path of the stallion which bridles, but is unstoppable, arriving at the same point as his daughter, their shapes becoming one unnatural form for the merest of moments and Freya is knocked, twisted, in the way he has seen so many times over the years, during the sleepless nights, the image of her falling, projecting indelibly every time he needs to see it and all those times he doesn't need to see it too.

Like the first morning he spent at sea, Guy is woken by the sound of birds, perhaps hundreds of them, flying somewhere above the boat. But again he is unable to see them. The *Flood* is surrounded by a total fog, grey in the early morning light, which has lowered on to the sea in an impenetrable bank. He goes out on deck, remembering fragments of yesterday's epic fight with the waves, and the surreal glimpses of a desert light that has filled his dreams. The North Sea is calm, with a thick glassy quality to the water, as if the storm has left it exhausted.

He sits on the wheelhouse roof and peers into the fog. Shapes slide about in it in indecipherable distances, ghostly textures of waves, emphasized by the trickle and lap of the water that gathers round the *Flood*. 'I forgive you,' he says out loud, to the sea, and the sea makes a startling sound back, like a sigh, he strains to listen to it, somewhere out in the fog, he hears it again, the unmistakable sound of water breaking along a shore.

A few minutes later he is sitting in the inflatable dinghy, motoring towards the sound that comes stronger now by the minute. The beach emerges from the mist like a phantom ship, long and low and impossible. Until the moment the inflatable bumps on to its foreshore, he can't quite believe it's truly there. Where is he? Denmark? It looks and feels like East Anglia, it has the same smell of wet shingle and salt, but it must be Denmark, or one of the low countries, Germany, even Holland, the storm span him round all day. But he thinks it's Denmark.

He climbs out on to the beach and drags the boat up, then

stares in both directions to the point where the beach disappears into the mist. The air is clearer here than on the water, but he still can't see further than a few hundred feet. There's no one around, no sign of anyone, no footprints or tracks that lead off through the dunes. He sits in the shingle and examines a handful of stones, sees how the carnelian has been rounded over the centuries and, noticing a piece of jasper, he licks it, tasting its cold salt, making it bright red as if he's dabbed it with varnish.

Along the shore he sees the skeletal shape of some abandoned machinery. As he walks towards it he sees it's an old winch, buckled and blackened by age and salt, standing above a length of iron cable. It's connected to nothing, and sits half sunk in the ground.

He leans against it and closes his eyes, wondering where he is and thinking about all that has brought him to this place. He remembers floating on his back in the sea, watching that gull flying in circles way up in the sky, heading away from the coast; then the greenfinch, like a crushed flower on the water, how it had made that single oar flap of its wings to try and get away from him, from being saved, how it was still with him – amazingly, it has survived the sea a second time. It nearly died in the water and those mackerel he caught died dancing in the air – we don't do well out of our element.

All the waves he's faced. What was he doing? Where has he been going in this shallow tongue of an ocean that is as lawless and as ancient as any place on earth? If it's the frontier he wanted, he found it. He found emptiness and, at times he found Freya too. He survived the swim, the shipping lanes and the storm – an angel has been looking after him, no doubt about it. Could it be her?

The journey and the storm have purged him. Quite literally, he feels on the other side, swept clean, a new blank state. And for the first time in years he feels able to view his life with unparalleled clarity. He thinks of the month that followed Freya's accident. No one called them, because it was unspeakable, consolation was impossible, it was a mortal wound for the parents, and everyone knew it. They had been marked out by this tragedy. People had kept a distance from them, almost superstitiously. He remembered the fear of going into Freya's room, every object in there a simple and incisive ambush on him, every poster and toy, a clear sign of a life that was led and a life that was lost. A pair of her socks, drying on the radiator, no need to be put away; a tiny woven handbag hanging off the end of the bed; a crudely drawn outline of an animal in her scrapbook, how she'd rubbed the neck out and redrawn it, the tiny bits of the eraser still there on the paper. Each one of these things was now frozen, belonging to a chapter of his life which was past, and each one of these things would have to be dealt with, somehow. It had seemed insurmountable, either by himself, or with Judy. You just don't have the facility to cope, there just isn't an answer, there is no right or wrong way, there is just the unassailable truth that life has stopped but time has not.

After a month they had reached the same conclusion. That they would put their own end to it. They hadn't come to this decision hysterically, or out of a series of discussions – it just seemed to be the inevitable and right thing to do. The only talk he remembered having with Judy was about how to do it and where to do it, guided by the practical issues of having to let someone know, after the event. They had discussed this in a kind of emotional shorthand, as if the decision whether to do it or not no longer needed to be mentioned. It was liberating, in a way, to be thinking of such an escape, that they could after all do something about all this untenable pain, that there was an option of a numbing darkness that they could manufacture. It had almost made them giddy.

Guy had wanted to do it at their house, with a recorded delivery letter sent to their GP, but Judy had felt uneasy about the plan. She hadn't liked the thought of sending that letter, committing themselves before they absolutely needed to, a decision like this couldn't be taken in two parts. She didn't want the immediate transferral to be dealt with by the authorities, either. *How do you mean?* he had asked her; *Our bodies*, she had replied, chillingly.

'Fergus and Cindy's,' Judy had said, with finality.

So their plan had been to invite themselves over for a night with their friends. In the early hours they would take sleeping pills, and leave an apology by means of a letter on the table next to the bed, alongside all their instructions. Fergus and Cindy would take a long time to accept it, but they wouldn't, ultimately, hold this against them. They'd understand.

On a Saturday evening they had driven to Fergus's house on the island in the estuary. They had had to wait for the tide to clear from the Hard – the stone and seaweed causeway that connected it to the mainland. They'd sat in the car, waiting for the water to drain off. The seabed emerged across the estuary, and the road began to lift through the water, bordered by blackened seaweed. The sense of finality was immense, that they were leaving the land behind them on the first step of their plan. It was an awful moment, but oddly calming, too, because it was so resolved between them. Judy had been driving, and her hands looked small and pale on the steering wheel.

'I feel all right about this,' she had said.

'Me too,' Guy had replied. And they hadn't said much else. Usually they would have talked about their Sunday plans, but Sunday was a nothingness – it was a blank footstep into a void, arriving by the minute.

There had been strange pleasures that night. Fergus had made a bonfire, and after dinner he and Guy had sat by it, watching the logs burn down to a softly crumbling glow of embers. Guy was drinking a vintage wine, which he'd brought for the occasion, and was enjoying the hint of luxury it was giving him. A glow, from the fire, from the wine, a feeling of rightness, and a sense that life in that moment was a very vivid thing. All evening he'd had this feeling. Fergus had cooked tiger prawns in chilli and garlic, and their taste had been exquisite. Guy had savoured every last morsel, knowing they were some of the last things he'd ever eat, save for the bitter-tasting pills which Judy had somewhere in her handbag.

Fergus had unearthed some Smithsonian Folkways recordings, and in particular played an Appalachian vocal piece – a plaintive ballad of three men singing to each other, with the sounds of cicadas in the background and the occasional crack of a fire. They'd all listened to it before dinner, but for Guy and, he supposes, Judy, it must have had the feeling of a lachrymosa. God have sympathy on us.

Guy had brightened after the meal, and he'd entered that exclusively male world that Fergus was so good at creating. They'd sat by the fire, looking at the stars swimming eerily in the rising thermals, and listening to the oystercatchers calling to each other in the creeks, just beyond the garden. It was a magical place. Behind them was the garage where they'd all met, so often, to play their music, Fergus on fiddle, Guy on the piano, Phil on guitar and Cindy on drums, with Judy sitting cross-legged on a tabletop, singing her heart out.

'Good times,' Guy had said, to Fergus, nodding towards the open door of the garage.

'Yeah, the best of times,' Fergus had replied. Fergus was drinking beer, and the can nestled comfortably into his full beard every time he took a swig. 'I go in there sometimes, to listen. It's like the music's still in there, in the walls.'

'That's nice,' Guy said. Fergus was a lovely friend, big and soft and bearded. What a fantastic person.

'You know, Guy, we'll have good times again. You do know that, don't you? I can't tell you how desperate I've felt for you and Jude this month, but all I do know is I'm certain, you know, that we'll get through.'

Guy listened, accepting Fergus's gentle assertion, and feeling slightly ashamed for what was hidden, what was really unfolding that night. He'd thought of Judy, up in the bedroom already at the top of the house, under the watchtower platform, in her own private world of thoughts.

'Cindy says you'll have another child,' Fergus said, 'and I've been telling her to shut the hell up.'

Guy smiled. 'Thanks, Fergus.'

'She's annoying at times like this.'

'You don't have to tell her off.'

'Oh, you know, I enjoy it. There's not much else to do out here.'

Guy had looked deeply into the fire, admiring its timeless beauty. The realization of what would be transpiring a few hours later had suddenly hit, an awful twist of panic in him, filling him with doubt.

'Thanks for everything, Fergus, you're a great friend.'

'I'm your only friend. Phil's a jerk.'

'Yep. Phil is a jerk.'

Was this to be the last conversation he'd ever have, before going to his wife's bedroom?

'Jude looked tired tonight,' Fergus said.

'Yes. She is.'

'You have each other, Guy. That's important. And women are marvellous, you know. They really are life's best thing. It's no secret, that.'

'Yes, Ferg. You're always right. I should grow a beard like you.'

'It would help.'

'That was a great recording you played tonight,' Guy said. 'There was something very special about it.'

'I've been kicking myself for putting it on. It sounded sad to me, and that's the last thing you need.'

Guy drank more of the wine, aware that he was finishing the bottle, that at the end he'd have to go up to the bedroom. The level of the drink was his clock, now, and it was draining. He could drink slower, but finishing the bottle was inevitable. The

231

wine had given him a stealthy optimism that was disconcerting.

'I'm nicely pissed,' Fergus said. 'Everything seems all right.'

And with that Guy snapped out of his emerging feelings of contentedness. No, everything was not all right. Everything was far from bloody all right, and Guy had seized the opportunity, before his resolve could weaken any further, retreating from that glimpse of a possible future, to think about that room at the top of the house, about Judy lying on the bed, waiting for him like an angel of death.

'I'm going to turn in now,' he'd said to Fergus, forcing himself not to hug his friend, or say anything that might arouse suspicion. At times like this, everyone is watchful, and Guy felt he reeked of his plan. He reeked of death already.

He had gone into the house and given Cindy a kiss on the cheek, while she was wiping down the work surfaces in the kitchen. She looked at him with her gentle browned-apple eyes, respecting him in every move he made. Grief had given him an amazing authority.

'Has Judy gone up?' he said, his voice cracking a little.

She nodded. 'Tell me if you need anything.'

He left her quickly. She had instinct, Cindy, he'd always felt it, and the house was becoming something else now, a place of ritual order.

Judy was waiting for him in the room, not on the bed, as he'd expected, but sitting in a chair by the window. There was a darkness to her eyes, and a glint of something almost venal there too, something that felt untrustworthy and shifting. Understand-able, he'd thought, before sighing, and lying down on the bed. Should he take his shoes off? Who knows the rules in this situation?

'Well, this is it,' she'd said.

'Yeah,' he sighed, again, thinking of the weariness with which he'd climbed up the narrow staircase, with all its eccentric twists and turns to get up to the bedroom.

'I liked that music Fergus played,' she'd said, surprisingly, stopping herself short of saying we should get him to do us a copy. It would have been an absurd thing to say, given their plan, but the essence of her liking the record, with its assumption of wanting to listen to it again, had remained in the room, stubbornly.

She lay on the bed and kissed him, once, on the mouth. He looked into her eyes and again feared what he saw there, some foreshadowing of a madness that he knew could come, or might not.

They had talked, about the meal, the bonfire, Fergus and Cindy's friendship. It was a usual routine for them. Guy began to think about Freya, but couldn't mention it to Judy. He'd felt his daughter's presence in the room, between them, in a place where they might follow her to. There was so much to think about, so much to set right in his head, but at that moment, it had all felt unnecessary. He was beyond caring. He felt tired and wanted to sleep, and was unsure why Judy was dragging the moment out. It was odd, how unbothered he had felt.

She had cried, silently, and he had looked about him at the room. It really was special, with windows on three sides and a high dark view over the salt marshes outside. They'd stayed here several times before. In fact, Judy had written some of her song lyrics in here, at the desk in the alcove. It was an inspiring place.

'Guy,' she had whispered, and he'd known this was the moment the whole night had been leading up to. 'Guy, I love you.' She lay back on the bed and stared up at the ceiling. 'I've flushed the pills down the toilet.'

Guy waited, listening to the oystercatchers in the creeks outside, at the wind that was beginning to pick up in the chimney.

'Right,' he had said.

Soon, both of them had fallen asleep.

And two months after that night, they split up.

He doesn't know much about what has happened in Judy's life in the five years since that night. He knows she's having a relationship with Phil and that they've recently moved in to-gether. Their lives, and his diary, have followed a similar route. He also knows she no longer sings. But he's only been to her new house once, and that was nine days ago. It was the night before he began this journey of his into the North Sea.

It had been so strange, after all those years passing, for him to be standing on the damp brick path in a little pocket of East Anglian calm between a forsythia and japonica, looking at his former wife, haloed by the light of the living-room behind her.

She hadn't registered much surprise when she'd answered the door. But she'd taken a step forward, just the one, as though she was naturally moving towards something she recognized. Then she'd crossed her arms and leaned against the jamb. The threshold of her house seemed to run through the line of her shoulders.

'You're more predictable than you think,' was what she'd said, the first thing she'd said to him, in fact, for several years.

'Since when?' he'd said, willingly falling into their old roles of him playing catch-up with her.

'I've always known you'd turn up here one day,'

'Really? It's more than I've known.'

That had been their opening exchange. Probing their territorial positions, with claims coming from both of them about how much they knew about each other. But Guy hadn't driven all that way, after all these years, to find out things he already had the answers for.

'You're pregnant, aren't you?' Guy had stated, trying to stay calm.

She'd taken a breath before nodding, shyly, just the once.

'Why couldn't you tell me? Why did I have to guess?'

'Because I'm a coward, Guy. You know me better than anyone, don't you?'

She gazed back with a level, dark expression. She had no apology for him. She couldn't even give him that.

'How long?'

'Five months.'

'I'm glad, for you. For Phil, too. Tell him I'm glad, will you?'

'Do you want to tell him yourself?'

'Not particularly.'

Judy acknowledged that with a smile, having brought it out in Guy, but accepting him, too, it seemed. Perhaps she had been curious to see him like this, unannounced and unprepared. 'Life moves on, you know,' she'd said.

'Yeah. Well, thanks for telling me that.'

Judy had given him a quick questioning look, sensing the brittle charge of argument that always seemed to spark so naturally between them. 'Let's not have a scene,' she'd said.

'Oh, Judy, I – I just wanted to see you, that's all.'

She seemed satisfied by his honesty, or satisfied that he was at least no match for her. 'I know.'

'To know that you're all right.'

'I am. I am all right. Are you?'

He hadn't been sure how much of his espression was visible to Judy – his part of the brick path had been a shadowy place. In fact, he wasn't sure how much Judy had *ever* seen in his expression.

As always, she had backed away from the essential. 'How is life on the boat?' she'd said. 'I think of you sometimes, on cold days. It can't be nice.'

Guy hadn't replied. He didn't want to be led into an offhand conversation so easily. Judy's good at that, at avoiding. He'd remained quiet, hoping it would draw her out. Her house, it wasn't so dissimilar to the one they used to own. And she'd planted things in the garden that he had once planted, in theirs. It was revealing.

'Do you want to come in?' she'd said.

'Me? No – I'm OK out here, on the path.'

'Sure?'

He had tried not to stare at her. But she was fascinating. This was Judy, with shorter hair, curls less springy than he remembered, with a slightly thickened shape already, although he didn't want to look. Still the same sharp angle between shoulder and neck, the same small earlobes that were so soft to touch, the same sunken dip at the base of her throat. But a new necklace there, something he didn't recognize, and not her taste, either. New clothes also; colours she always chose but now she was dressed for comfort and warmth, not for style.

His silence seemed to disconcert her. She'd known you can't truly hide from someone, once you've shared all with them, however long ago.

'Guy. Are you going now?' she'd said.

Guy didn't know. A few hours later he would be heading out to sea in the *Flood*. Everything was packed and ready. 'I think so,' he'd replied. What, actually, had he expected from her? For her to acknowledge her mistakes? It wasn't her way.

'Well, I'm glad you came here. I really am,' she'd said.

'Me too,' he'd lied.

'We should be in touch.'

'Yeah,' he'd lied again, blandly, his voice sounding disembodied to him, from his actual presence there at her doorstep. It's as if he and Judy were now talking on the phone to each other, with the feeling of distance as a given, between them.

He realized he'd been stripping the forsythia of its leaves. 'Sorry about the plant,' he'd said, lightly.

'Guy. I want to tell you something,' Judy had said, suddenly cautious. 'It's going to be a girl.'

There'd been the hint of an apology in her voice. A significant moment for them both, and Guy had felt the closeness, suddenly enveloping them, as if there'd been some strangely physical tie, after all these years, which still bound them in a way he'd never quite understood before. The presence of their child, it must be.

'I'll go now,' he'd said, simply.

'OK,' Judy had replied, suddenly sounding a little less sure of herself.

'Judy? Should we have a hug?'

She'd considered it.

'Yes.'

He'd held her, the small shape of the wife he once knew, so

236

well, touching the thinness of her bones in her shoulders and the shallow curve of her back and the unmistakable shape of the new life that was growing in her. Her hair was thicker. He remembered how that had happened last time.

'For Freya,' he'd whispered. She'd hesitated. Then he'd felt her arms reaching round his sides.

'Yes. For Freya,' she'd whispered back.

Guy stares into the patterned shades of shingle spread along the shore, remembering how he'd walked back down the path from Judy's house as the door shut behind him. A chapter closing. He had driven without looking back, away from her house, he knew, for the last time. Ready now, to head into the sea. Having seen her, pregnant, the centre of her own life now, it had made him realize what he had to do. Maybe she's happy, maybe not yet, but she's on her way to it. That's enough for any of us.

He thinks about the journey that's arrived at this point. Of all the water that's passed, the waves he's seen, the tides that have come and gone, and the nightly reinvention of a life he lost and has wanted to recreate. Unpacking the daily miracle of ordinary life, albeit a remembered or an imaginary one. He thinks about the wake of the *Flood*, erasing all that time. All you leave behind is a path that can't be followed.

And as the beach begins to lighten, incrementally, beginning to stretch in distance away from him, he has an uneasy sense of something being in the gloom, a presence he's been unaware of.

Ghosts, he thinks, of the lives he's led or might have led, and the people who are no longer with him, always in his mind, urging him forward. They're out there and they're in him, he carries all these scenes and imaginings and can never be truly alone, even in the most empty of the world's places. The sun will grow stronger in the next hour, and it might break through this mist, making the shore glow with renewed vigour, whether it's for him or for no one at all, it will shine and dazzle with its own sense of creation.

But the feeling of being watched persists, unnervingly, and he stares into the murky half-light and sees, about half a mile away, the thinnest of smudges separating itself from the background of sand and shingle. A second later it is gone, the stones slide their patterns among themselves in the gloom, and then it is there again, stronger, lengthening, the way things do in a wide flat landscape, coming his way. He stands to watch it, this strange whip of the mist, this weird trick of the sea-light, and in a few seconds he realizes it's an animal. A low thin animal trotting along the shoreline in a direct path towards him. He feels naturally wary, thinks he should scuff his feet in the shingle to announce his presence, but is also transfixed by the jaunty way the animal is jogging towards him, each foot rhythmically picking up and dropping in a precise line, it has a dancer's lightness, he doesn't want to scare it. But then he realizes the animal is fully aware of him, and is approaching with a poised determination. As it closes down the distance between the two of them, he sees that it is a wild dog.

The dog is terribly thin, with long sinewy legs of bone and loose muscle and a tattered, gaunt face. It comes at him straight, without fear, with a cold flash in its eyes, furtively looking side to side, increasing its pace, and he sees the neck hang lower and its wary glance at the banks of stones around them, suspicion in every gesture. Just a few steps away it suddenly stops, dropping to the ground.

It arrives like that, in a manner of straightforward malice, as if it's reacting to some act of territorial transgression. Its hind legs rise, bending its spine as it prepares to spring at him. Guy feels a hotness of panic, like a rash across his skin, and he stands completely motionless, entirely without defence. The dog makes a sudden growl, raising its upper lip in a snarl, revealing the yellowed enamel of the wilderness, tapering to bright sharp points in the shadows of the mouth, a thin pool of saliva caught behind the lower edged rim, and a livid tongue, quivering with energy. The dog stops growling, checking either side in sharp quick glances, then continues again, a low wild snarl interrupted with tiny yips and half-whimpers. Its eyes turn fractionally towards him, and a retinal flash of pale green light reflects from both of them.

Guy sees how desperate the animal is. A shore scavenger. Maybe it hasn't eaten for days, its sides cave with each quick breath to show a line of ribs, and he knows he is no match for this thing, and as he's thinking this he realizes he hadn't even noticed the second dog's approach, following the line of the first, in its very footsteps perhaps, till at the last minute the second animal has almost magically emerged from the body of the first, the matted pelt dividing diabolically, till the second dog is its own thing too, a few steps back and to the side.

Both dogs, ignoring each other but following some timeless instinctive strategy, begin to inch forward, their eyes filling with a sparkling murderousness. He knows that they are going to attack, and he will be unable to defend himself.

Guy faces them, stoically. He imagines the moment the first one will leap – the unnatural sight of its body extending, showing just how thin and empty it is – hitting him with a terrible force of wild hair and eyes, of hardness, too, of pointed pain from the teeth. Going for his arm, perhaps, pulling him down, while the second one arrives a split second later, shaking him with a body-weight of tense sinew, rolling and pawing to try and expose his neck. He assumes it will be over quite suddenly, like a terrible crash, the slamming energy of the animals almost not registering on his body, the pain arriving in a rush of so many other things, with his life obediently giving way without fuss in the manner it will have to.

But a new sensation begins to rise – an imperfection – an imbalance between himself and the wildness that has come to challenge him. Is it the fragment of a memory perhaps – the thought that something is not quite finished, not quite able to be put down? Look at the things you missed, he thinks, retrieve the things you lost. All is not lost, it's in there somewhere, you just have to find it.

He wants to stop them, wants to raise his hand to halt the senseless inevitability of the attack, and as the feeling grows he realizes what it is – that small nub of doubt, that tiniest hint of a current running against the overwhelming force of the flow, it's his will to survive, to go on regardless, to take all that can be given, because not to take it, to give up, is no way at all. That simple, all along, *you must continue*.

He feels his heart finally begin to race with the arrival of fear, that these two wild animals might take something from him he doesn't want to give, and an echo of another time strikes him too, a remembrance of being in that field again, with the stallion running at him, and the surprising dawning of his own strength, as if the greater the force of the assault, the greater the defence. Life has that pattern, now, a perfect equation: what doesn't kill you makes you stronger. Guy feels decided and invulnerable and glad that his instinct has come, at last, to survive. He owes it to her. All that you left behind is more than I was before. This has been the answer that has eluded him, the answer he sought, the purpose of all these countless miles of North Sea and storm, and he smiles at the crouching dogs, at the coiled muscles of their back legs, the claws gripping the gritty beach, the look of sheer evil in their ungodly eyes. He takes a step towards the first dog, sees confusion in its eyes and, as if he is pushing some invisible force in front of him, his own protective bubble of certainty, of resolution, he sees the dog move to one side. Its head lowers, its eyes no longer maintain contact. Guy walks closer, convinced that the threat is transferring with each step, his own strength growing as these shore dogs give way, and he sees the second dog adopting the same weakened attitude as the first, both of them, lying down in the sand as he passes.

When he looks back along the beach he sees them half-turned, half-facing him. They look windblown and abandoned and untrustworthy. The first dog is shivering with the attack it nearly made, a twisted strain in its eye that Guy still can't trust, can't quite turn his back on. And knowing the danger has not truly passed, he carries on walking, steadily, one step at a time, destroying their wildness with his own simple desire to continue, returning now, needing to return, his journey over.

III

It's late at night, later than she intended, and Judy is still sitting at the small desk in Guy's cabin on the *Flood*. She's been here for several hours. When she arrived, the barge had been at an angle on the mud, but in the past hour or two it has lifted with the tide. She doesn't like the new motion the boat has, the way the shadows move inch by inch every so often in the room, the way the barge makes quiet noises as the water drifts outside. The boat feels alive to her – the empty spaces of its cabins feel expectant and eerie.

On the desk are his diaries. All of them, from the past five years. She's spent the evening reading them, and a few seconds ago a single tear had welled in the corner of her eye and then tipped on to the page, instantly smudging the ink. Judy had looked at the mark the tear made. She hasn't cried for such a long time.

She looks around her at his cabin, his possessions, his photograph of starlings flying over the estuary that hangs above the desk. She knows so little about the years he has spent on this boat, day in, day out, making his life here, in this space. She thought she knew Guy – completely knew him – but she doesn't. He has had a life since them, and she's been no part of it.

Judy moves the diaries to one side. She composes herself, then dials a number on her phone.

'Hello, is that Marta Sheridan?'

'Yes.'

'Hi. I'm sorry to call you like this. Can you talk?'

'Who is this?'

'My name's Judy. I think you might know my ex-husband.'

Judy waits, but there is no response.

'Guy? From the *Flood*.'

It takes a moment before she hears a reply. 'Oh – oh yes.'

'Sorry to be direct, but I assume you haven't heard from him?'

'No. I haven't.'

'I see.'

'Should I have done?'

'I don't know.'

She hears Marta give a quick, confused laugh. 'I'm a bit lost. Could you tell me what this is all about?'

'Of course. Look – is there any chance we could meet? It's just I'd rather we didn't do this on the phone. It's – delicate. Where do you live?'

'In Cambridge.'

'Would it be possible for you to drive here, to his boat? It's moored on the Blackwater estuary, at the Tide Mill, really not very far from you. Maybe an hour's drive? Do you know it?'

'Why?'

'I'm absolutely swamped here – there's so much to do. Please come and we can talk this through – I'm sorry to be so mysterious, but I think it's best. We should meet in person. You'll understand. Would that be OK?'

Marta is a long time considering this. 'Well – I'm not sure. It seems very strange.'

'I know, but I'd rather. I have something for you.'

Judy's insistence is hard to refuse.

'OK then.'

'Thank you.'

'Judy – just one thing – how did you get this number?'

'Oh. It was on his mobile.'

It's a bright sunny morning when Marta parks her car at the Tide Mill Arms and walks along the quay to the *Flood*. For the last half an hour she's been getting increasingly nervous. From what she remembers, she didn't think Guy was even on speaking terms with his ex-wife.

Several of the barges are beyond repair, and have been left in this place to rot in their own pools of leaking engine oil and snapped cables. Water shines darkly within some of the hulls. But among the general dereliction, his boat stands out as being stronger, more cared for. She sees how precisely Guy has painted *The Flood, Blackwater* in glossy green letters on a white signboard below the stern, and the neatness with which the varnish has been seasonally applied to the wheelhouse mullions.

At the end of its gangway she sees a dog, lying patiently in the sun, his head resting on his front two paws. He starts wagging his tail as she approaches, so she bends down to him and makes a big fuss of rubbing his belly and stroking his hair.

'That's his dog,' a voice says. 'He's called Banjo.'

Marta glances up to see a small woman with dark hair looking down at her from the wheelhouse. She looks older than her voice had been on the phone, with a serious expression Marta hadn't imagined. She's wearing jeans and a man's shirt covered in splatters of paint, and has her hair tied back away from her face. Everything about her gives the impression she's busy. 'I'm Judy,' she says, quickly.

'Marta Sheridan.'

'Thanks for coming here. There's so much to do,' Judy says, moving a box full of papers from one side of the wheelhouse to the other.

Climbing the gangplank Marta feels suddenly overwhelmed – there are things that are demanding her attention, all round her, differences to this boat that she should be noticing: someone has recently fixed a heavy padlock across the sliding wheelhouse door, and a glued paper notice has been stuck to one of the windows. Enquiries, and information, care of the Harbour Master, it says, followed by a phone number and an email address.

The deck is scoured clean with the signs of a considerable storm. And the greatest difference on the *Flood* is now a specific absence: the winch above the stern, where she's sure the inflatable had hung from two chains. There's nothing there now.

'Sorry it's such a mess,' Judy says as Marta enters. 'And thanks so much for agreeing to this.'

Marta sits on one of the bench seats in the wheelhouse, thinking it might be best not to speak. Tread carefully. She's instantly wary of the way Judy is avoiding looking at her.

'I feel stupid asking you to come all this way. It was dumb of me,' Judy says, sounding hesitant. 'I'm a bit all over the place – and I was curious I guess, curious to meet you.'

'Is Guy here?' Marta says.

Judy reacts, taken aback, giving Marta a quick dark look.

'Guy's been missing for two months,' Judy says. She seems suddenly calm and watchful of Marta's reaction. 'I wanted to tell you in person.'

Marta looks away. She hadn't expected this. She looks at the grooved planking of the wheelhouse and is struck by the smell of polished wood and enclosed space in here, of oil and salt-water and somewhere, she thinks, the smell of the man, in the trapped air. She leans towards the door and slides it shut, not wanting this fleeting presence of him to escape. She feels entirely unprepared for this.

'What do you mean, *missing*?'

'I'm sorry, I guess that was a shock?'

'Yes.'

'The *Flood* was found off the coast of Germany – we've just had it brought back, so his stuff can be sorted out.' Judy softens slightly, having said what needed to be said. 'Sorry to surprise you like that. There's no easy way to say these things.'

There *are* easier ways, Marta thinks, but she doesn't want to be antagonistic. She nods, in acknowledgement. She doesn't know what to say.

'I should've told you on the phone. I'm sorry.' Judy seems full of doubt, on his boat, surrounded by his things, talking about him. 'Are you all right? Would you like a glass of water?'

'I'm OK,' Marta says.

'How did you know him?' Judy asks.

'Well – I'm not really sure how much I did know him. We met on the water, at the Deben Estuary in Suffolk.'

'At the Rushcutter's?' Judy says.

'Yes.'

'We did our first gig there.'

'He told me.' Marta looks out of the wheelhouse window at the length of the barge. His boat. It's so full of his presence. 'I don't understand.'

Judy reaches down for a map she's clearly had prepared, by her side. She passes it to Marta. 'Look,' she says, 'I've marked the place.'

Marta sees it's Guy's map of the North Sea. On the right hand side, near the German / Danish border, a small collection of islands has been circled with a pencil. While she looks, Judy tells her that a couple of months ago, on a Sunday morning, she'd had a phone call. She tells Marta how odd it had been, to suddenly hear the thickly accented German coastguard. And his professional politeness as he explained where he was calling from, how he had to spell out *North Friesland* twice, how, after telling her that the *Flood* had been found adrift off the island called Sylt, he'd hesitated, had said the inflatable was missing, but there were no signs of foul play. And how he'd added, as an afterthought, that in the saloon they'd found a bird in a box, which they'd released on the dunes. They had been happy to see it fly, he'd said. He didn't know the English name for it, but had said *Grünfink*, and spelt that out, too.

'After I put the phone down, I had to look it up on an atlas. You see them? Just down from Denmark. *Sylt, Nordfriesische Inseln*,' she says, with a flourish. 'See – that weird shape at the top – it's a spit called *der Ellenbogen* – which means elbow. It's like an arm, isn't it – like it's stretched out to sea to catch his boat. It was found near there.'

'This is quite a lot to take in,' Marta says.

'Sorry. Am I rushing you? I often rush.'

'When you say it was drifting . . .' Marta asks. She can feel how reddened her cheeks must be. She's always blushed like this. Especially with unexpected news.

'I don't know much about boats. I think that just means it wasn't sinking.'

Marta feels totally empty. Emptied. '*Grünfink* means green-finch,' she says.

'Oh. Does it?'

She explains. 'He had it in a cardboard box in the cabin. He said he'd found it floating in the sea – it must have blown offshore.'

Judy looks back at Marta, nonplussed. 'I have to ask you, when you were with him, did he say anything that might give us some kind of . . .'

'. . . hope?' Marta guesses.

'Clue, I was going to say.'

'I don't think so. I didn't really get to say goodbye.'

'He was a very private man, don't you think? Very private. Do you know about his diaries?' Judy asks.

'A little.'

'Did he talk about them?'

'No. Not much.'

'But you do know what they're about?'

'He told me they're about you and him. And your daughter.'

'Freya,' Judy says.

'Yes.'

'What exactly was going on between you and Guy?' Judy asks quickly. 'It's just I don't really know who you are, or why you meant so much to him.'

'*Me?*'

'I'm sorry about all this, Marta – I really am.' Judy seems suddenly without her energy. Marta waits, wrong-footed again, and when she's sure Judy's being sincere, she nods.

'Was there any kind of note?'

'Nothing. Nothing for two months.'

'It's unbelievable,' she says. Marta looks out of the window at Banjo, still sitting at the end of the gangway. 'What's going to happen to his dog?' she asks.

'He'll be looked after here. You know, he sits there every day, apparently, looking out over the water. It's sad.'

'He's waiting.'

'Yes.'

Marta looks at the dog. Sensing he's being talked about, Banjo begins a slow sweeping wag of his tail.

'Why are you looking at me like that?' Marta asks, aware that in the corner of her eye Judy is studying her.

'Well – don't you think it's strange, you and me meeting like this?'

'Yes. It's very strange.'

'I'm like his past, you see. And you – well, you might've been his future.' Judy gives Marta a smile. It's not convincing. 'Wait here a second,' she says, standing in order to go down to the saloon. She's a small woman, and as she passes, Marta realizes Judy's pregnant. She hadn't drawn any attention to it. But now, going down the ladder, she holds the guide rail as carefully as she can.

Marta sits still, confused by their meeting. Judy seems impenetrable. Marta thinks she's seeing her in minor details, like a wall built too close, which she can't see beyond to find out why it was put up in the first place.

The wheelhouse is just as she remembers, apart from the signs of a search the German coastguards must have made. Maybe they went through the emergency gear to see what may have been used and what may be missing. The postcard of the Norwegian fjord is still there, next to the magazine picture of the basking shark, stuck behind the wheel, like clues in a mystery; and the embroidered cushion she'd noticed before – a curiously sweet image of a river scene, is still there on the side. She puts her glasses on and looks at the Norwegian postcard. Strangely, she sees it's addressed to the skipper of a fishing trawler, the *Indomitable*, care of Yarmouth Harbour.

Judy takes a long time. Marta sees the steps leading down into Guy's cabin behind her and remembers the night she'd rowed over to visit him. She imagines descending the steps now, half-expecting that he would be in there, lying on his bed, like she'd last seen him. She had wanted to offer herself that night, to share herself, except she'd been clumsy and rash and had driven him away. She's sure of it.

She wishes she could go down those steps once more. But what would be down there? What remains of the man after he's gone? She would sit at the same spot she'd chosen before, at the foot of his bunk, looking at his empty pillow. Maybe she would smell the pillow, or maybe she'd stop herself short of doing this.

'I've come back,' she would say, out loud. The same words she said to him before, sitting in that place. But this time she imagines their conversation would have to swap round, with each of them speaking the other's lines:

'I'm sorry,' he would say.

'Where did you go?' she would reply.

'Just rowed.'

She would smile at him.

'Sorry for being upset before,' he would say.

'You don't need to be.'

Judy returns to the wheelhouse, carrying several hardbound books. Marta recognizes them for the diaries Guy had been writing.

'They were found tied to the life-ring,' Judy says, with a smile. 'Quite symbolic, don't you think?' Judy reaches out and touches Marta on the shoulder, surprisingly. 'I've been rude to you.' she says. 'I'm sorry. It's hard to know that a man you once loved could ever choose anyone else.'

With that, Judy looks frankly at Marta. 'You're different to how I imagined you,' she adds, and Marta looks back, knowing, in this instant, in the slight readjusting of Judy's gaze, that she is seeing an unguarded truth. An understanding that passes between them: that their lives have intersected and will part almost immediately, but that they share a connection.

'You're different, too,' Marta acknowledges. 'I wondered about you.'

'I never knew about Guy writing all this,' Judy explains, her voice softer and deeper. 'I've read them all now. Maybe I'll regret that – I'm not sure. This other life he had – I guess it was his way of dealing with – with what happened. He really *tried*, you know, to believe in it. I never thought I'd say this, but until I read these, I don't think I ever knew him. Isn't that strange? It's made me change my view of the last five years. I wish I could tell him that.'

'And why are you telling *me*?' Marta asks.

'Because at some point out there' – Judy points towards the sea – 'he stopped writing about me and Freya. Maybe he found out all he needed to know. We might never get the answer to that. He began to write something else. I have it here. He wrote about coming back to England in this boat, imagining what he would do, and how his life might turn out. It's all about you, Marta. I want you to read it.'

With that, Judy hands a small black notebook to Marta.

'This is it,' she says. 'You see, he was imagining a new start.'

'Have you read it?' Marta asks.

'Would you, if you were me?' Judy replies.

Marta looks down at the notebook. All that remains of him. She looks up at Judy.

'Did Guy know you're pregnant?' Marta asks.

Judy gives out a sigh. 'Before he went, he came to see me. He guessed.' She smiles, bravely. 'I'm going to go now – I've spent too long on this boat already, it's upsetting. Could you close the padlock when you leave?'

'I'm glad we've met,' Judy adds. 'We won't see each other again.'

Marta nods. She watches Judy leave the wheelhouse and walk thoughtfully down the gangplank, taking the rest of his diaries with her.

'Judy?' she calls. 'I need to tell you. Guy saved my daughter's life. I'm pretty sure of it. She fell off the boat. He saved her.'

Judy looks down at the water, calmly, working this out.

'Good,' she says. 'That's good.'

Yes, Marta thinks, it was.

'Judy,' she asks, 'what do you think happened?'

Judy waits a moment before she answers. 'I have an image of him in a European city square, sitting at a café table, in the sunshine, eating a pastry.'

'Really?'

'No, not really. I think he's drowned. The dinghy was missing.'

'But there's a chance?'

'There's always a chance.'

Almost immediately after Judy's car has reversed away from the quay, Banjo leaps on to the deck of the boat and wanders into the wheelhouse. He jumps on to the padded bench seat and lies down next to Marta, looking up at her expectantly. She roughs his hair up.

'Don't worry, boy,' she says, affectionately. '*Vertu sterkur*,' she adds, in Icelandic.

Across the water, a flock of starlings is beginning to collect in the sky. She watches them for a while as the flock thickens and stretches and pulls apart. This boat. His boat. It's all she can think.

She opens Guy's notebook and sees page after page of his handwriting, knowing that this must be a new diary, a new life that he had imagined in the days before he disappeared. Writing gave him a future, that's what he'd told her.

She thinks about Guy, how he went to sea to search for his daughter. She hopes he found her. She hopes that he realized, in the end, that Freya was with him all along. Then she reads:

Although it's dark, there is the familiar scent of mud and river, of saltmarsh plants, of the sea, then the sounds of oystercatchers and redshanks calling in the beds, in the creeks, the sounds too, close by, of the other boats settling in their moorings, of the nudge the wooden gangway always gives as the engine is finally cut, then the smooth cast-iron bollards where the mooring ropes have worn their own groove in the metal, the hollow sound of the timber planking of the jetty, the slight bend to the wood as each knot is checked, the sheer familiarity of it all, the curve of the gunwale and deck, back home, the patiently empty quayside, the dampness, the smell of wood smoke, he returns to all this, all that he knows, and it seems he's returning to another man's life.

In the mirror he sees a changed face – more rugged, tanned from a sea wind, a look in the eyes he doesn't recognize as belonging here. Back in the berth where the *Flood* has been for the last five years, but *he* doesn't feel the same man's returned. Away from the sounds of his engine and the ceaseless movement of the waves, all is too still, too fixed.

Going on to the deck, he looks out over the cold dark width of the Blackwater estuary, in a breeze which is airy and fresh and ever so slightly fishy as it mixes with the unmistakable smell of wet ropes and diesel, of fuel oil, grease and turps, of seaweed and mud.

On the far bank is the dull fringe where the trees come down to the shore, and the orangey smudges of the villages, a brighter white light on the yacht marina over there, which shines across the water in a spear shape, touching the backs of the ripples to show which way the tide is flowing.

The estuary is full – its banks are flooded with a mile of inky flat water, and he loves the feeling, he loves the proximity of all this bulging mass of sea and river, lying there.

It literally makes him feel brimful.

It's past eleven. Rude to call so late. But he finds her number on his mobile and before he has a chance to reconsider, he dials. Sometimes, you must grasp that nettle.

'Hello?' a voice says.

'Marta?'

'Yes?'

'It's Guy here – I'm sorry I'm calling so late.'

'Oh.'

'You remember me?'

'Of course. Hi.' She sounds cautious. 'How are you?'

There's a coolness in her voice he must get beyond.

'Marta, I've been wanting to call, you know – I feel bad for leaving like I did, without saying goodbye. I behaved like a fool, I suppose.'

'Is that why you're calling?'

'Because I was rude?'

'To tell me you're a fool.'

Was that half a joke? He can't tell. It's his turn to consider. Just why is he calling? 'Not really,' he says, flatly.

'I've been thinking about you, too,' she says.

'You have?'

'Yes. It's quite late. I don't really want to talk.'

'Right – I understand.'

But he has the feeling that she's glad to hear his voice.

'I've thought about you, Guy,' she continues, 'not because you left like you did, but because I spent three weeks travelling with Rhona and when I look back, I don't think of her, I think of you. That upsets me.'

'I'm sorry, really.'

'And because I messed things up.'

'You didn't.'

'Nice of you to say, but I did.' She waits. 'I guess you touched a nerve.'

'Yeah,' he says, not really in reply, but because he's agreeing with her. This woman touched a nerve in him, too. That's why he's calling. He listens to the static on the length of the line – he still thinks in terms of telephone wires stretching across dark fields, that for a brief moment he and this other woman actually own a line, and its tension, as it reaches between them. 'May I come and see you?' he says.

'I live in Cambridge,' she says, humorously.

He tries a joke. 'I like driving.'

'I thought you might.'

'I could be there tomorrow?'

She laughs. 'You're very persistent.'

Does he need to convince her? He's not sure. It's difficult to read the silence. Eventually she speaks:

'OK, what the hell.'

Guy mouths a silent *thanks* into the phone.

'You're quite something,' Marta says.

He laughs. 'There's one thing – do you mind if I bring my dog?'

'Your dog?'

'A scruffy one.'

'Then yes, yes you can bring your dog too.'

'Thanks, Marta.' He really means it. It's beginning to hit him, quite simply, how long overdue it was to make this call, how important it is not to miss the chances in life.

'I'll prepare the way with Ro,' she says, 'I'm afraid her opinion of you since you left is not so bright.'

'I understand.'

'In fact she thinks you're a rat.'

'OK.'

'But you're not a rat, are you, Guy? I'm not inviting a rat to come and see me, am I?'

'No. No, you're not. Not this time.'

In the rear-view mirror, Guy watches the sea recede as he drives away from the estuary. In the morning sunlight, all he can see is a thin strip of water between the trees, a glint of shining light in the corner of the mirror, and then it is gone, behind him. The smells of dry soil and farmland take over from the salt, and he thinks of his father, all those years before, driving away from the life he never wanted to be part of, driving into one he could believe in. One eye on the mirror, the other on the open road. Departure and destination in the same view.

Banjo has been over-excited about Guy's return. He's jumping over the seats and sticking his head out of the passenger window. He's had a muddy few weeks, and as the car drives along he's letting the wind blow his hair and his eyes are weeping with pleasure. Guy tells his dog about the sea, about the waves that came out of the dark, about the storm and the ridiculous sea anchor, and Banjo wags his tail with delight.

Marta lives in a large brick Victorian house with overhanging eaves and tall windows, on a leafy street which smells of wet autumn trees. There are conkers on the pavement and across the drive as Guy turns in, the wheels of his car crunching on the gravel. He notices the clean shine of the windows, the curtains inside held back with broad velvet ties, the ordered pruning of the summer's flowers and shrubs, organized in formal beds according to height, English respectability in every detail.

It still has the plaque of the dead husband by the front door. *Dr Howard Sheridan, Osteopath.* It halts Guy, right at the moment where he feels most convinced to be there. He doesn't ring the bell. Someone is already walking towards the door on the other side of the frosted glass – her silhouette growing more definite, more real, as she approaches. A hand goes up to brush hair to one side, there's a pause – perhaps an expression is being checked in a wall mirror – perhaps she's looking at how long it's been since the henna started growing out.

Marta's wearing the complicated green cardigan he remembers from before. She smiles warmly, her mouth pulling to one side in a slightly coy fashion.

'I should've let you ring the bell.'

'Why?'

'To prove I wasn't waiting.'

He smiles. 'I could ring it now?'

'Come in,' she says. They go down a thickly carpeted hall to a large kitchen built at the back. He sits at a solid oak dining table, in a farmhouse chair; immediately he wonders whether he should have sat at a different place – it's clearly a man's seat. But she doesn't seem to notice. She stands by the range, leaning against the worktop. The floor beneath her feet looks like it's marked from many years of someone standing in the same place. She puts a kettle on the ring, asks him about the journey, and both of them are grateful for the dog's presence in the room, trotting round and sniffing the corners, a natural disturbance to counter the oddness, the sheer unfamiliarity of their meeting. It gives them something to look at. She gazes at the dog, rather than him, and Guy notices the way she stoops slightly when she asks a question, the way she only looks at him after she's spoken, the way she's conscious of her hands, not knowing quite what to do with them, how she clasps a mug, even though she's not made the tea yet.

'I'm glad you're here,' she says, directly. 'But it's a big house full of big spaces and I'm not used to guests – so forgive me if I'm nervous.'

'I'm nervous too,' he says, helpfully, 'I feel like a teenager, meeting a girlfriend, and out of depth and tongue-tied and not at all sure why I'm here. Except that I'd rather not be anywhere else.' It's developed into a clumsy speech, but he doesn't mind. She encourages this emptying of his thoughts – he noticed that before. 'I'm afraid of breaking your crockery or saying something out of turn or the dog making a mess.'

'Well then, in advance, I forgive you. And I forgive you sailing off in your Dutch boat without saying goodbye, too.'

'Thanks.'

'Anyway, I like dogs.'

She's made him a casserole, which they eat at the kitchen table – her place is surrounded by various letters and notes and lists of jobs to do. He sees his own name, half-way down one of the lists, next to a note which he thinks says 'buy flowers'. She has larger handwriting than his own – his handwriting turned out curiously neat from an early age. He notices a bunch of fresh lilies in a vase on the side.

She tells him the *Falls of Lora* is up for auction, and that the library of books it contained are boxed up in the next room. She refers to it as the consultation room. He doesn't pursue it. There are clearly areas of the house sealed off, and maybe areas in her, too, equally hard to intrude upon. They steer clear of mentioning her husband directly, colluding subtly with each other not to spoil the fragility of the evening, there are too many ghosts surrounding them always and, as a result, they grow liberated, free to talk at will about other things, they grow friendly and content and this lasts until the moment Rhona turns her key in the front door, coming down the hall like a rush of autumn leaves, her jacket smelling of smoke and leather and coldness.

'Ro?' Marta says, sounding confused. 'I thought you were at Mark's tonight.'

'I was.'

'Meaning you've been there, or you're meant to be there?'

'Both. Hello, Guy.'

'Hi.'

'Is everything all right?' Marta asks.

'No. Actually, far from,' she says, theatrically. 'It's a mess.' With that she abruptly leaves the kitchen, scuffing a chair loudly on the tiles as she does so, making Banjo spring up.

'I'm sorry,' Marta says. 'They have a tempestuous relationship.'

'I can see.'

'I thought it was all ironed out, but . . .'

'. . . Maybe you should go up and be with her.'

Marta looks at him kindly. 'Would you mind?'

'I'm fine.'

She kisses him, on the cheek, gratefully, and goes upstairs. Guy looks at Banjo, who comes over to lean against his leg. What is it about this woman? Why does he feel he's known her for years and years? The way the strands of hair fall to the right of her face, the line of her chin which again has a sadness to it regardless of her expression, the softness of her pale eyes, one eye a little quicker in expression than the other – these things seem overly familiar.

He looks at the rows of ornaments and objects on the shelves, postcards tucked between mugs and champagne corks and fresh

260

conkers from this year mixing with dried ones from last year, pictures of the *Lora*, a plan of the back garden, more drawings that must have been done by Rhona, a picture of Marta he recognizes from the sketchbook Rhona showed to him. It takes years to build up shelves like that.

Marta is with her daughter for over an hour. He hears partial sounds of their conversation coming down the stairs and along the hall. Long murmurings as whatever is being talked about is brought into a more reasonable light. Guy drinks the rest of the wine he brought and realizes it's making him tired.

'You're not the rat any more,' Marta says, returning at last. 'Mark is. Mark's the new rat.'

'Oh, well, I'm glad, I suppose.'

'Has it spoiled the evening?'

'No.'

'Will you stay?'

'Should I?'

They're talking in whispers. Allies, it seems, brought closer by Rhona's distress – oddly, it's the best thing that could have happened.

'You're in the spare room on the first floor,' she says, quite flatly, then immediately follows it with a rash promise. 'Guy, do you want to do something crazy with me? Do you want to go away for a few days?'

'When?'

'Tomorrow. Shall we? We can go to the bothy.'

'What's that?'

'Howard was Scottish, we had to have a cottage in Scotland – we've had it for years, it's in Argyll. It's so lovely up there, Guy, let's go. What do you think? Let's go in the morning.'

'Well, it does sound crazy. Just you and me?'

'Plus your smelly dog.'

His bedroom is on the landing at the back of the house. It has a small single bunk in it and a computer set up on a desk and an exercise bike in the corner. He believes Marta's room is one flight up, under those big eaves of the house, but he's on the first floor, where, two doors along, Rhona is too. Coming back from the bathroom he looks in on her – she'd left the door open, seemingly as an invitation.

Inside, he sees a room that's clearly a mix of Rhona's recent years. Candles set into wine bottles, a tasselled lampshade that gives the room a red boudoir glow, a poster on the wall of a chiselled-jawed man, emerging from the surf, he has an impossibly toned body with dark small nipples and an expression of sheer delight to be who he is, out of all leagues. There are souvenirs from foreign holidays on the shelves, a Mexican tile he can't imagine is her taste. And prominently on the bedside table, the mobile phone – hot, it seems, from the last few hours. She's very aware of the phone's presence, as he comes into the room, as if it's saying they're not alone in there.

'You OK?' Guy asks.

'Yeah.'

'Sorry you've had a tough evening.'

'Me too,' she says, a touch hostile. 'I'll see it coming next time, yeah?'

'Maybe.' He sits at the foot of the bed. She's sitting up on top of her pillows, leaning against the wall. She has her arms wrapped round her legs and is looking at him with her chin resting on her knees. The red glow of the room gives her a sultry, poised expression. Her pupils are drawn wide, giving her a dark-eyed look, directed at him.

He thinks he should leave. 'If you can't sleep, I don't mind you moaning to me, if you need to offload.'

She lightens. 'Cheers.' Her mouth curls up into the slightest of smiles, at one side. Mark's a bloody fool, he thinks.

'I'm in the guest room.'

'I know.'

Guy gets up, hoping he wasn't sounding too suggestive saying that. The man on the poster looks at him smugly, a man who's never known awkwardness in front of women. He's the rat, if ever there was one.

'Guy,' Rhona says, 'Mum might seem the most level-headed

person in the world right now, but she's only just holding it together, right?' There's an accusation in her voice – a remnant no doubt of all the bitter rancour she's spilled out this evening.

'I'm aware of that,' he replies.

'Are you? Are you, really?'

'Yes.'

'It's just, she can do without you, you know.'

'I know. But maybe she can do with me, as well.'

She looks at him, trying to outstare him with her intimidating looks and clumsy pout.

'Night, Rhona. I hope you sleep.'

He leaves, shutting the door quietly behind him, the click it gives suddenly taking him back to shutting Freya's door, each night, after a kiss to her warm forehead. A smell of cotton and books and the taste of her skin still on his lips, forever. Is this room, with its boudoir glow and its ridiculous poster – is this how her room, too, would have become?

He goes to his single bunk in the characterless spare room. Banjo is lying on the duvet, wagging his tail. Guy sits down and strokes his dog for a long time.

They drive all day, a crisp autumn day, crossing the Pennines and skirting the Lake District and driving into the forest and the rolling lowlands of Scotland, then further, to Glasgow, to Loch Lomond, to Oban, then down the Argyll coast, the road getting smaller, more narrowed, each mile more enveloped by a wildness of moor and rock as the night eventually falls.

The Scottish darkness grows increasingly around them, pricked only now and again by the small precise glow of windows in isolated houses. The weather becomes dreary, then foul, the road bends unexpectedly, flurries of rain hit the windscreen, there are drifts of fog on the moor, the eyes of cattle shine back at them at each unexpected corner, bewildered.

'The times I've driven this road,' Marta says, her face lit unsympathetically by the reflected light of the headlamps. She looks so tired, or possibly it's a growing preparedness too, that she's bringing a new man to a special place. 'We're nearly there, though,' she says, kindly.

'I'm OK,' Guy replies, 'don't worry about me.' I've been travelling a long time now, he thinks to himself, it's the journey that looks after me.

'We had a picnic here, once,' Marta says, as they pass a small parking area surrounded by trees. It looks a pretty inhospitable place, tonight. 'There's a small tarn through those bushes, with stepping stones that go out to an island. There were highland cattle standing in the water. It's a cute spot, except the midges spoiled it.' Guy smiles at Marta. The memory is relaxing her. 'We cracked boiled eggs on the rocks and dipped them in salt I'd wrapped in tin foil.'

The valley descends into an area of tall dense conifers with long mossy threads hanging from the branches. Guy winds the window down, and smells the wet forest and dark peaty earth. He hears the sounds of dripping, everywhere, and the further sound of fast water rushing through the rocks.

'Hear that?' he says to Marta.

'Shall I stop?' she replies.

He shakes his head. 'Let's get there, we're both tired,' he says, thinking of his mother, always stopping the car to listen to the sounds of a wood or forest.

A few minutes later he sees the lights of buildings scattered through the trees, and the valley opens into a small bay between the hills. For the first time he spots the sea, cloudy grey, with the lighter bands of surf rolling in smooth curves to the shore.

'Ah,' Marta sighs, 'this is it.'

They turn into a village of small stone houses, most of them unlit, and turn again into an alleyway. Marta switches the engine off, and leans exhausted over the wheel, gathering herself, before facing Guy and smiling happily. 'We made it,' she says, sounding a little nervous.

'Thanks,' he says. On the back seat, Banjo wakes, blearily, looking back at him with glossy dark eyes.

They get out and carry their bags to a small terraced cottage, while Banjo scampers up and down the street. It's a tiny place, built of granite, with two windows and a door to the front, opening directly on to the street.

'Look,' Marta says, pointing to the bone vertebrae set into the stone, below the gutter. 'Several houses round here have that. It reminds me of home – in Reykjavik they found a Viking ironing board made from a whalebone plank.'

She turns the key and gives the door a hefty shove to open it. Inside, the house smells damp and is extremely cold. Guy stands in the front room, unsure where to go, while Marta moves about swiftly, flicking the switches on the fusebox and wall heaters. He watches her hold her hand above the metal vents, making sure the warmth will come, then sees how she looks quickly round the room, taking in its details. It suddenly hits him that she's not been here since her husband died – how could he not have thought of that before? It's awful for her. But Marta is waiting for the warmth to rise and she's busying herself with the jobs to do. It's as good a way to cope as any. Guy takes his shoes off – a habit from living on a houseboat surrounded by mud – and puts his bag down near the door, the natural place of a visitor, while Marta disappears into a back room.

The front room is full of shadows, with a dark fireplace and, like the *Flood*, has too many chairs. Shelves either side of the chimney brace are rammed with books. He reads some of the spines: highland geology, coarse fishing, archaeology, local history. Howard must have been a man of ideas, then, of placing himself only after he knew the knowledge of the area. Some people are like that – they seek connection. There's a man's presence throughout this room – fishing rods leaning in the corner, some sticks of driftwood that seem to have been carved by a penknife, and he sees with a touch of panic a whole wall devoted to a photo gallery. He hadn't anticipated that. That's the fellow, the dead man, standing on the rocks near the sea, with a fishing rod. He was large and stocky, quite fat really, with a beard. Guy decides he'll look more closely at that at some point.

Nearby he sees more photos, of Marta and Howard raising dark pints of oatmeal stout, a picture of a big dinner laid out on a small table – roast goose by the look of it, a sunset over the bay, a highland cow standing in the shallows of a tarn. And there's Rhona – it's odd to see her here, she doesn't seem a natural fit in this place. She's younger in the picture, with punky hair, standing with her arm round a slim young man in jeans with a trendy haircut. That man, whoever he is, is also in the other picture, sitting at the dinner table with his eye on the roast goose. He looks a type, Guy thinks. Posh. Maybe it's the fool, Mark. He wants to study more, but realizes Marta has returned, leaning in the doorframe, watching him.

'It has a lot of memories, this place,' she states.

'Are you all right?' Guy asks.

'I'm OK. A bit spooked.'

'Yeah.' Guy expects her mood will flatten now, her arms are hanging limply, like the breath's gone out of her. He should probably give her a hug, but he wants to be polite, he wants her to get used to him physically being in this place.

'Can I do anything?' he asks.

She seems undecided. 'Maybe. Maybe get some firewood in?' she says. 'There's a little store in the yard.'

He's pleased to help. Passing her in the doorway, he holds her elbow.

'Thanks,' he says, 'for bringing me here.' She nods, obediently, and looks down. 'This must be hard for you,' he adds, 'I'm grateful.'

She nods again, unable to speak, and gives him a little smile. 'Go and get that wood,' she whispers.

The second room turns out to be a kitchen, very small, very cluttered, with a worn brown Formica table in the centre. Cookbooks overcrowd the shelves and mugs hang loosely from a Welsh dresser. He sees the back door is already ajar and, outside, there's a small cobbled yard.

He's about to step out when Marta says helpfully, 'There's a pair of shoes, by the door. Don't get your feet wet.' He looks down and sees a pair of ancient leather brogues, without their laces, clearly used for the purpose of bringing in firewood. Howard's. Slipping his feet in, in the dead man's shoes, his heels hang out over the back. He doesn't turn to see if Marta is looking, or not. He thinks she is.

An hour later, sitting by a small fire in the hearth, the front room looks more cosy. Banjo's stretched out in front of the fire, snoring like an old man. Marta has put on several sidelamps, and there are little orangey pools of light in the corners. She's drained a couple of glasses of wine, too quickly, and is curled into one of the chairs, with a rug over her lap. She has a shadowed look beneath her eyes that the wine hasn't managed to shift.

They've not spoken for a few minutes now, both of them have been listening to the fire hissing in the logs.

'I think it's time to turn in,' she says, quietly. 'I can't keep my eyes open.'

Guy's a little shy to look at her – it's not entirely established where each of them will sleep. He realizes he hasn't even been upstairs. It must be a tiny place, just how many bedrooms are there? Rhona and the posh boy, they must have slept somewhere which wasn't Howard and Marta's room.

'I want you to sleep with me, in my bed,' Marta says, quietly.

Guy was unprepared for that, but relieved by her frankness. That's typical of her, to be so clear.

'You know,' he begins, 'I can stay down here, if you want, I'm fine about . . .'

'. . . I'll take that as a rejection, shall I?' she says, coyly.

'No.'

'We're not kids.'

'No. We're not kids.'

'Then – that's agreed?'

'Yes. You and I, we're going to sleep in the same bed.'

'All night.'

'All night long.'

She looks at him, with a level, decided gaze. Her eyes have darkened as the night's grown late, like Judy's used to. Then she looks at the fire. Her profile, with that high foreheaded shape that Rhona has so strongly. A woman in profile is amazing, he thinks, especially at a moment like this, which is full of awareness, about what has gone before, what might be to come.

'Come here then,' she says.

Guy's up early in the morning. Spending the night with Marta has earned him the right to Howard's dressing-gown, which he wears without discomfort as he goes into the kitchen. Banjo's been up hours, it seems. He's full of a naturally overflowing excitement that's reminiscent of how he himself must have been, as a child on holiday. Get out, explore, Banjo wants many things right now. Guy bends to rough the dog up, push him down on to the rug and pull his ears affectionately, then he opens the front door and Banjo skids off the rug and charges into the street, slowing down into a confident trot to sniff along the walls of the other houses. He stops for a long thunderous slash against a post, shakes his back leg out, and trots off happily. What great characters they are in our lives. A man's not complete without one, Guy really believes that.

The air is cool and sunny and there's a lightness to it which is synonymous with Scotland. Ingredients of moss and water and cold chiselled rock, mixing with the sea's fluid abundance of ions and ozone. Intoxicating. He breathes deeply, filling those parts of his lungs that rarely get used, the lazy wedge around the sides, where the stale air is no doubt trapped, part suffocating us always.

He leaves the door open and goes to the kitchen, finds the kettle, finds a pan, begins to break eggs into a bowl and whisk them with a fork. Get some of this magical air into the mix, he thinks, fill us with it. There are jars of pebbles and shells on the windowsill, and in the yard outside he sees a palm tree – which he hadn't noticed last night – growing in the corner. It's a strangely incongruous sight. On the shelves there are pens and damp matches and candles half-burned and bending in the sunlight. He loves it all. Loves to be here, alone with Marta, cooking her a simple breakfast of eggs. The butter sizzles, releasing its odours of the dairy, then he slides it round the pan, watching the foam beginning to bubble. He pours in the rich yellow eggs, still fluffed up with the air, and grinds in black pepper and adds some damp salt he found on a little dish. He licks his finger to taste the raw egg and the salt, then folds the mix over, lifting the pan above the ring which is now glowing too hot.

Nothing better in the world than cooking eggs. Banjo trots in from the street and he hears Marta making her way to the bathroom upstairs, the ceiling bending slightly above him.

He tips out the scrambled eggs on to a warm plate and puts two rolls next to it. He cuts a slab of butter and puts that on a cold plate. He pours the coffee he's been brewing in the cafetière, and realizes he doesn't know whether Marta takes sugar or not. Probably, he thinks, women usually do.

He sets all this on a wooden tray and takes it upstairs to the bedroom, where he finds Marta back in bed, sitting up against the headboard. He wants them to eat in here, to bless this space where they spent the night.

She looks up at him, coy and glad and ever-so-slightly amazed at herself. It's the first time he's truly seen her, he thinks. Everything he's known of her, before, up to this point, can be forgotten. It begins here, he thinks, with this.

'How are you?' he asks.

'Very well.'

'Me too.'

'*Ég segi allt ljómandi*,' she says, smiling.

'Everything's shining,' he replies.

He sets the tray down. The room still has the smell of the night before, of their breathing, of their journey, of their slight uncertainty, and their growing comfort, too, their sheer relief of having chosen to be with each other, with no one else around, no one else knowing. The room seems quietened, as a result.

'I've made you eggs,' he says.

'You're a marvel.'

'And I put one sugar in your coffee.'

'Perfect.'

And what he doesn't tell her should really be the only thing he needs to tell her, now: that the love he thought had left his life – it can be found again.

He has a simple realization – that he doesn't have to face things entirely by himself. There are people who are willing to share your burden, share it with all their heart, for every breath, every day, for as long as they live. If you are lucky enough to find someone like that, then you are blessed, and right now, Guy feels blessed.

It's a brilliantly sunny morning. He walks through the village, passing its weathered stone houses and small front lawns bordered with white picket fences, out along the single road that skirts the bay, through the rising outcrops of rock, all lying at the angle of their bedding planes as they point out to sea in long grey slabs. He looks back, at the huddled village, surrounded by the low treeless braes of limestone, and he sees Marta standing where he left her in a small cove of the bay. She's taken her shoes and socks off, and is about to paddle when she sees him, looking at her. They wave at each other.

Banjo runs up to Guy and leans, panting and friendly, against his leg. Banjo's mouth hangs open and his teeth are wet with spit and black with soil, while the long candy-strip of his tongue hangs out, quivering. There's a wild-eyed look of exertion that makes Guy laugh, the dog wags his tail in response, and swallows several times in gratitude.

He disappears among the rocks, crawling and scrambling along them till he reaches their furthermost point where they slope at an angle into the sea. Not his sea this time, but an ocean: the Atlantic.

The sea floods on to shelves of the rock, then drains off, leaving behind glistening mats of gold and green seaweed. He realizes this is the same rocky ledge where the photo of Howard was taken. Guy stands in the same spot, looking out across the vastness of the ocean and at the mountains on the islands in the distance, wearing another man's trunks and swimming goggles. A dead man at that. It's a fine way to end up, he thinks, but he isn't unduly bothered by the thought. Accept all, he thinks. We slip in and out of each other's lives constantly. We hold on to things, we should let things pass, because all things must pass.

Long tubular sections of kelp stick out of the water, steaming softly in the morning light. When each wave sweeps in, he watches its motion suddenly braking and dispersing, the wave slowing to half its speed, and lifting the necks of the plant in long wide rafts, as if the seawater is suddenly as thick as oil. He can see the kelp swaying eerily beneath the surface in long bronze horsetails. There are deep clear pools in it, and avenues where the seaweed closes and opens as the water pours through.

Guy fixes Howard's goggles over his eyes and slips into the water, immediately feeling the greasy stroke of kelp around his legs. He pushes his way through it and slides into one of the open pools, sinking beneath the surface into a silently fanning world of weed blowing in the currents. The kelp surrounds him in waving fronds. It feels dangerous and mysterious, the distances opening up and separating and then closing in front of his eyes.

Above him, suddenly, is a sparkle of light, and he sees a cascade of bubbles spearing down towards him as Banjo's feathery paws paddle the water, the dog's long belly hair streaming as he swims. Guy surfaces and comes face to face with his dog, huffing away with his chin out of the water, a useless piece of driftwood in his mouth.

'You OK?' Guy asks, as Banjo paddles in circles round him.

Guy dives again. The water is cool and light and about as refreshing a substance as he can imagine. He kicks and reaches forward into the kelp, which parts effortlessly into a glimpse of open water, and he swims towards it, as the fronds of weed caress his legs and arms. Below him, he notices the seabed is now not so rocky – it's dusted with a finely crumbled white of coral. There are starfish down there, rubbery and bright orange, with the tips of their legs curling upwards. He sees a crab, scuttling one way, then the other, a rusty pincer raised at his shadow. Nature in all its wonderful abundance, in sparkling glory.

Guy swims through the last ribbons of the kelp, and he notices the seabed lowering steeply. Then he watches how Banjo's paws, fanned out wide, dig fast at the water, as the dog moves from left to right in uncertain little changes of direction, suspended above the deepness like a puppet.

He treads water, next to his dog, who still has the piece of wood in his mouth. Banjo swims towards him with a newfound urgency, then turns quickly and heads back towards the kelp and the rocks. Guy watches him clamber out, drop the wood, shake and bark. He looks skinny.

Now Guy swims faster, remembering the time he swam in the North Sea, the coldness and the feeling of being cleansed, of being anointed. Around him the water seems so crystal clear, so sparkling, but as it reaches away into the open ocean that same water begins to lose something, its own sense of lightness, its own sense of clarity, but gains something too – a shadow, a wide deep shadow which has that same soft blue light he has sought so many times before. The glow that rises, haze-like, in the bluebell woods. The blueness at the edge of things, where the world seems to reveal a hint of its own true nature. Mysterious. Beyond reach.

He thinks he is on the verge of a great understanding. That the true nature of all things is that of calmness, that the true spirit of all he's been searching for is here, so close to him, emerging all around. This soft blue light which surrounds us at times, so gentle, so essential. He goes towards it, welcoming it like a pleasant memory, a sense of himself which is balanced and full of well being.

But while he looks there, far away where the water seems to thicken with shadow, he sees something entirely strange and confusing. A stubborn shape, darker and more impenetrable than the water that surrounds it, moving slowly towards him. He looks hard in the attempt to define it and as he does so it vanishes, or fades, into the wider gloom of the ocean. He stays, trying not to move, looking all around. There is nothing. But a sense remains that he's no longer entirely alone.

The basking shark takes shape again, solid among the shadows, swimming with an effortless side-to-side motion towards him. Its mouth hangs open, enormously, as it filters the plankton, and as he looks into the jaw he can see how the giant fish is ridged from within, like a Zeppelin model, with a structure that seems to be both inflated and solid, its mouth suggesting an open tent-like interior, but a darkness inside which is nothing but flesh, so dark in fact, that it appears to come from a tunnel longer than the length of the shark would allow.

It swims closer now, mottled like a gherkin, coming at him with an easy rhythm, and he makes out its eyes, set either side of the nose like a pince-nez, but as unreflective as a cut of black flint, and when it passes, close by, he sees the rows of gills that strangely turn the shark into a watery soft shape at the front, as if it's rippling – giving it a sense of illusion, that it's not really there.

The basking shark has passed a few feet away from Guy, never once deviating from its route, although it must have seen the man looking so closely, so full of amazement. He turns to watch it leave, its long asymmetrical tail waving effortlessly, its tip feathering the surface of the sea like the tip of an oar. Nothing to steer it, no direction for it to go, except on, into the ocean, into the blue distance that seems to collect round it and remove it from view, in parts, in totality.

He lies on his back to stare up at the sky, once more feeling that he's on that taut line of nothingness, above nothing, below nothing, then he begins to swim back, rounding the rocks, towards Marta. He sees her standing in the cove, knee-deep in the water, the colourful sarong tied round her waist, such a small object in all this hugeness.

To reach her he wades through the water for the last few steps. She holds out her hand and he takes it and he doesn't let it go. They embrace each other, an intimacy in all this space. Home at last. And he sees, on the ridge of her shoulder, a perfectly formed bead of water on her skin. It trembles and glistens with the sun caught inside. He smiles affectionately at it, at the memories it brings back to him, not of pain and loss, but of love. The whole world in there, if you look close enough. And he brings his hand up towards it, choosing a finger, choosing a different finger, watching the sparkle of light go out as the shadow of his hand approaches. Then he touches it, marvelling at the fragility of the curving strand between his finger and the drop of water and, a moment later, it has vanished.

In loving memory of Kate Jones

Acknowledgements

Thanks to Kate Barker and the editorial team at Viking, and to Karolina Sutton, for all her hard work. Thanks also to Kathryn Court, Alexis Washam and Sloan Harris. I am indebted to my family, especially to my mother, for her ceaseless energy and spirit, my father, and to Andrew, for his guidance. Thanks also to Juliette Howell, James Clatworthy, Barley Norton, Laura Sampson and Cormac McCarthy. For the boat, thanks to Dominique Rivoal, the *Corlea*, the *Vriendschap*, and all the boats of the Fresh Wharf Creek. Also to Neil Trevithick, the *Flood*, the *Anna-Gale* and the *Albatross*. Apologies to the *Janet*, for crashing you into the bridge, and bless the *Misty*, which was lost in the North Sea.

Thanks to the shed, where this book was written.

Thank you Liz, for your love and wisdom, as always, and for driving across America with me.

And to my children, Jacob and Barley, for bringing such happiness.

JEREMY PAGE

SALT

'Striking, funny, terrifying. I admired and loved it' Margaret Forster

'Stunningly good. Captures the landscapes with a truly deft, water-colourist's touch' Rose Tremain

In the watery half-land of north Norfolk's satlmarshes, Pip attempts to piece together the fragments of his mysterious family history. What happened to the man who was found buried in the mud, after he fell from the sky one early morning in 1944? How did the marsh fever that claimed his mother and, increasingly, the rest of his family, begin? And where will his life-long infatuation with Elsie lead? In a land flavoured with smoke, fish and fire, where omens are read in the clouds, will Pip untangle this past or lose himself between the creeks and samphire?

'A powerful new voice. Funny, flavoursome. Page brilliantly evokes Norfolk's bleakness, the harsh round of the seasons' *Independent*

'With mesmerizing attention to detail … *Salt* will transport and transfix' *Good Housekeeping*

'Unforgettable' *Guardian*

'Remarkably haunting, an atmosphere you can taste on the tongue' *Time Out*

He just wanted a decent book to read ...

Not too much to ask, is it? It was in 1935 when Allen Lane, Managing Director of Bodley Head Publishers, stood on a platform at Exeter railway station looking for something good to read on his journey back to London. His choice was limited to popular magazines and poor-quality paperbacks – the same choice faced every day by the vast majority of readers, few of whom could afford hardbacks. Lane's disappointment and subsequent anger at the range of books generally available led him to found a company – and change the world.

'We believed in the existence in this country of a vast reading public for intelligent books at a low price, and staked everything on it'
Sir Allen Lane, 1902–1970, founder of Penguin Books

The quality paperback had arrived – and not just in bookshops. Lane was adamant that his Penguins should appear in chain stores and tobacconists, and should cost no more than a packet of cigarettes.

Reading habits (and cigarette prices) have changed since 1935, but Penguin still believes in publishing the best books for everybody to enjoy. We still believe that good design costs no more than bad design, and we still believe that quality books published passionately and responsibly make the world a better place.

So wherever you see the little bird – whether it's on a piece of prize-winning literary fiction or a celebrity autobiography, political tour de force or historical masterpiece, a serial-killer thriller, reference book, world classic or a piece of pure escapism – you can bet that it represents the very best that the genre has to offer.

Whatever you like to read – trust Penguin.